IN THE SHADOW OF
MR. LINCOLN

Melissa Zabower

ISBN 978-1-64003-909-4 (Paperback)
ISBN 978-1-64003-910-0 (Digital)

Copyright © 2018 Melissa Zabower
All rights reserved
First Edition

All rights reserved. No part of this publication may be reproduced, distributed, or transmitted in any form or by any means, including photocopying, recording, or other electronic or mechanical methods without the prior written permission of the publisher. For permission requests, solicit the publisher via the address below.

Covenant Books, Inc.
11661 Hwy 707
Murrells Inlet, SC 29576
www.covenantbooks.com

This book is dedicated to
Ruth Wuchter, the first one to read it.
The book you hold in your hands is not what she read.
It's better because of her.

Chapter 1

ABBY

Abby straightened, stretched her back, arms akimbo. The sun beat down on the harvesters as they shocked the corn. Her father, Frederick Weimer, worked at the speed of two men. The hired men, Joe, Paul, and Harold, tried valiantly to keep up. Brian O'Bern, Abby's uncle, stood to the side, trying his best not to participate.

Abby walked purposefully toward him. "Are you going to work at all?" She wiped her brow on her sleeve. Unlike the men, she worked without a hat, the slight breeze wafting her brown hair from its bun to annoy her about the face, sticking to the dirt and sweat. Unlike most women, she was working in the field to bring in the harvest.

Brian looked away toward the west, where the sun had not yet begun to sink. "Oh, blast it all!" Brian was a head taller than Abby but only two years older, sixteen to her fourteen. He had arrived on the farm when Abby was just two; he was as much a brother to her as eleven-year-old Ben was. He had the same brown hair and straight jawline as Abby and her siblings, but his eyes were different, deep blue instead of brown, snapping fire with every look.

"I'll take that as a no." And she walked away.

Abby stood next to Joe, held the corn shock buck while he loaded it with fifty stalks and tied the bundle with number 51, then helped him stand it up. The buck was a plank of wood with another piece of wood where the sheaf rested. The corn shock buck was a tool that allowed the workers to tie the stalks together, and afterward, the shocks were placed on their ends, with a roof made of more stalks protecting the whole thing from the rain, waiting for the next step in the harvesting process.

The crew had covered nearly half of the sixty acres of corn. This was the third year that Joe and Paul had worked with Frederick, so they worked quickly and well. They were bachelors without their own farms who went where they could find work. Harold was from Massachusetts; he groaned at the immense openness of the fields of Lower Macungie Township, but he worked to Frederick's rhythm. Abby had worked in the field for as long as she could remember, enjoying the labor and the teamwork, and for as long as she could remember, Brian had stood by and watched.

A figure approached from the direction of the house. Abby continued to shock corn until her sister Sarah was close enough to be heard. The younger girl called to them, and everyone trotted over to meet her. It was just after ten in the morning; breakfast had been so long ago that Mary Weimer, wife, mother, and food magician, had sent Sarah with a basket of food. A hearty snack would keep them working until the full meal at one.

Sarah was twelve, a pretty girl still in knee-length dresses, this one of lightweight cotton. Her brown hair was covered by her bonnet, which shaded her eyes and prevented the pernicious freckles from appearing across the bridge of her nose. Her sleeves were rolled up and damp, and Abby was quite glad that she was in the sun and wind instead of elbow deep in suds.

Frederick unpacked the basket: apples, bread and a crock of cheese, strips of jerked venison, and a jug of water from the springhouse. Mary took care of her men and Abby. Abby chomped a slice of bread and cheese. They ate in a loose circle, breathing deeply of the humid air, which pressed on their lungs. They did not bother to sit but finished quickly and returned to their work.

The rest of the morning passed as the group methodically worked their way to the far corner of the field. The shocks would be left to dry in the fields for three or four weeks. They'd harvest other crops in the meantime. Then, at the end of September, all of the neighbors would gather at a local farm with their wagons full of corn for the husking bee. It would be the highlight of the season.

Also in the interim, Frederick and his crew would prepare one hundred acres for wheat. It needed to be planted in September; the winter wheat grown near Millerstown rested in the ground during the cold months, covering the cool spring earth with a blanket of green, and ripening to gold in July.

When they entered the stone farmhouse for the midday meal, they were greeted by welcome aromas. Before they could become completely enveloped, however, they had to stomp their feet in the mudroom. Mary insisted on it. She kept a clean house, working incessantly to keep dust and dirt from her furniture and floors. Somewhere in between, she found the time to cook meals like the one on the table: a meat pie filled with vegetables and gravy surrounded on top and bottom by thick, flaky crust; summer squash; corn on the cob; warm bread and melting butter; coffee and water; and for dessert, the first peach pie of the year.

Abby loved this time of day. The table was filled with food and family. One nourished her body, and the other her spirit. Father joked and talked with the men, Mother smiled and hummed in-between mouthfuls, and her siblings chatted or simply ate. Abby quietly enjoyed her private thoughts and the simple joy of the meal. Glasses clinked, silverware scraped on plates, and before long, the table was empty of both food and family.

Abby began walking out with the rest, but Mary stopped her. "Abby, I need you this afternoon."

Abby closed her eyes and sighed. Much as she disliked the dull responsibilities of womenfolk, she knew better than to argue with her mother's largesse. Mary allowed Abby much more autonomy than other mothers would have: Abby often did not do the daily cooking or weekly washing, the two chores she detested more than all the others. She helped with sewing, canning, baking, and some cleaning, which was no doubt the chore her mother had in mind today. Arguing with the little her mother asked her to do was the perfect way to be asked to do a whole lot more and lose all freedom to do what she wanted.

Abby and Sarah cleared the table. Sarah bumped into Abby at the kitchen doorway time and time again. Abby knew it was on purpose, but she let it go.

"Abby, let Sarah do the dishes. I want you to go to town for me," Mary said.

Abby smirked. Sarah reacted as Abby knew she would. "Ma, she's filthy! Look at her! I'm surprised the flies aren't buzzing about." Sarah added agreeably, "Let Abby wash the dishes, and I'll go to town for you." She smoothed her skirt with carefully cleaned hands, tossed a braid off her shoulder.

Mary shook her head. Ben stood near the counter, snitching bites of what was left of the pie until Mary rebuked him with a look. "Abby, take Ben with you. Go to Meyer's store, please." She handed a list to Abby and reached to the top shelf in the pantry to the jar filled with the family's ready cash.

A few minutes later, Abby and Ben were walking the two miles to Millerstown. They followed the railroad tracks to the still-growing borough of a few homes, a few taverns, a few mills, a few churches, surrounded by rolling miles of hills. The German settlers had recognized land similar to the old country and had worked for years and generations to rid the land of trees, prepare it for planting, and ready it to raise crops and families.

"Abby, Ben," a voice called as they started up Main Street, leaving the tracks. Peg Kelly stood outside the stone tavern, Kelly's Tavern, with a bucket in one hand and a rag in the other. No doubt, she had been washing windows or would soon start. Almost every day, the plump older woman completed the task with vigor and a song.

Ben hurried up to her, barely looking as he crossed the busy street. Abby followed more carefully. Mrs. Kelly set down her bucket and rag, stood with plump hands on ample hips, a welcoming and wonderful smile on her pale face. Wisps of red hair danced about in the breeze. Her green eyes sparkled. Not a beautiful woman—she was too buxom and her clothes were tight and her skin a bit too pale and pasty—but she was lovely to all who knew her.

Abby smiled at her. "Good afternoon, Mrs. Kelly. How are you today?"

"I'm well, child, well, indeed," Mrs. Kelly said in her musical brogue. "Brian just took Daniel off somewhere. I expected you'd be with them." Daniel Kelly was Abby's very best friend. He was taller than Brian, seventeen years old, and built like a farmer. He had red hair that grazed his collar, green eyes that were often somber and pensive in a freckled face, and shoulders that filled a doorway. He had calloused hands, like her father, although Daniel's manual labor consisted of feeding the horses or carrying a keg of beer. He spent most of his time with books, she knew, but he wasn't a slouch like Brian. Yet, the boys were best friends.

Wishing she could have run off with the boys, Abby shook her head. "I don't shirk work the way Brian does," she teased good-naturedly, but the frustration showed in her voice, nonetheless. She did wish sometimes that her conscience was a bit more lenient, just once in a while. Today would be a perfect day to walk in the creek or climb a tree.

"But sometimes you wish you could." Mrs. Kelly laughed, and Abby laughed too.

"Is William around?" Ben interrupted.

At that exact moment, as if he had heard his name—and perhaps he had—William Kelly came galloping around the shaded side of the tavern, George close behind. Ben fell in behind George, and the three boys disappeared down the road.

Abby's eyes followed them up the street, came to rest on the store which was her destination. "I must be going, Mrs. Kelly. Perhaps there will be news sometime soon, and I'll come to hear it."

With a wave, Abby continued up the street. The town was dynamic with wagons, horses, and people. No one stood lounging against a building or gossiping in the shade. Farmers were always busy, true enough, but in late summer especially. People would catch up on gossip on Sunday after church or in little snatches here and there.

Mr. Meyer stood behind the counter of his shop. Abby waited while Mrs. Lauer paid for her purchases. Ma wanted coffee, white sugar and brown, a packet of pins, and an earthenware pitcher. Abby also wanted to look at fabric and patterns.

She had her chance while Mr. Meyer was filling the order. She left her basket and list with him while she walked to the far counter. Various colors, patterns, and weights of fabric were crammed onto the shelves. Cotton was the most common, but there were a few flannel and one or two wool choices. Abby's eye was drawn to a brick red wool. She could almost feel the weight of it on her back as she held it in her hand, and in the summer heat, she began to sweat. Too heavy for summer, obviously, but Pennsylvania winters were cold, and the fabric was beautiful.

Mr. Meyer walked up softly behind her. "That's a mite too expensive for you, I think." A lean, white-haired man, Mr. Meyer was slightly bent and walked slowly, spoke slowly, and worked slowly. Abby had always felt it was part of his charm, along with his densely wrinkled face that had once upon a time been very handsome. He told her the price of the wool, and she blanched. Pa would never consent. Mr. Meyer's store carried the best fabric in the township, and this wool was lovely. She'd come up with something.

"Doppich!" she muttered as she paid for the goods and walked out of the store into the glaring sunlight. Her father used to affectionately call her "doppich": *awkward* in the Pennsylvania German dialect, and as a child, she had been. Now, though, it was an oath that she uttered whenever things didn't go just right. It sounded good and made her feel better.

Abby walked back toward the tavern, crossed the street, and followed the tracks back toward the road on which her family lived. First, she passed the Lichtenwalner's expansive fields on either side. Then the Lichtenwalners's stone farmhouse, quite close to the road. More fields, both the Weimers's and their neighbors', passed on either side, and then she approached her own stone farmhouse.

Her grandfather Weimer had built it a quarter mile from the road. It was a two-story building made of local limestone, covered on the outside with plaster and lime to keep out the damp. It had a front parlor for company, a living room, a storage room off the hallway, a dining room, and a kitchen where the family spent most of their time. One set of stairs led up to one large bedroom and three smaller ones, and one set of stairs led down to the cellar where canned goods were stored. The attic was also used for storing dried foods. All the walls were plastered on the inside. The front parlor had a fireplace, as did the kitchen, and the chimneys heated the upstairs rooms in the winter. Well, in the summer, too, in all honesty, but the natural quality of the stone kept it cool most of the time.

Abby walked around to the back of the house and met her mother in the kitchen. She could see Sarah out past the springhouse taking down the wash. Abby grinned at Sarah's struggle with the wash while the oak trees that shaded the house swayed in the hot wind that picked up to a stiff breeze rather than a gentle one. Mary wiped her hands on her apron as Abby entered.

"Thank you, Abby." Mary's red face showed her exertion as she strained to knead an obscenely large pile of dough, but she appeared as groomed as she had at dawn. Somehow, her curly brown hair never came undone; Abby could not recall ever seeing her mother with soft wisps about her face. Even hair did not dare go against Mary Weimer.

Once upon a time, she had been Mary O'Bern. She was a farmer's daughter, but unlike her husband, her Irish father had not owned his land. The Irish tenant farmers never did. The oldest of five, Mary had left home at age sixteen to travel to America as a cook for the daughter of the landlord, who was set to marry a wealthy Philadelphian. Mary had worked for them for two years, until Frederick came and swept her off her feet when he had been in the city to sell his crop. They married, she moved to the rolling hills eight miles west of Allentown, and that was just about all the story Abby could ever extract from her mother. About her family, all Mary would share was that one sibling had died in childhood, and two others, Sean and Bridget, had come to America at the start of the famine years; they settled near Gettysburg. Finally, in 1848, Patty O'Bern had had enough; he packed what he could and set out for the coast with his wife, also Bridget, and four-year-old Brian, intending to join his children in America.

The rest of the story was usually lost in tears, and Abby only knew it from Peggy Kelly. Patty and Bridget, with broken spirits, stopped in Galway to rest before getting on the ship. They stayed at Patrick Kelly's original tavern, and over a pint, Patty O'Bern laid his heart bare, a true shanachie. He told a story while his wife died of hunger upstairs. At Bridget's quiet passing, he followed her soon after, leaving young Brian all alone. Patrick and Peggy talked long into the night, sold up, and brought the young boy to his sister in Millerstown. Then they, too, decided to stay. Their son Daniel, aged six at the time, and daughter Kathleen, aged two, had come along, the only two of the five siblings born in Ireland. But you'd never know it to hear them; they almost sounded Dutchy most of the time!

Abby watched her mother knead dough for a moment. Mary made excellent bread, and she made it often. The aroma of yeast and flour often filled the farmhouse. Finally, Abby decided to mention the fabric to her mother.

"Ma." Mary indicated she was listening with a short sound, not looking or pausing in her work. "Ma, Mr. Meyer had a beautiful piece of cloth. I would love to have it for a winter dress. I'm going to need a proper woman's dress for winter," she added. This spring had been the first time she had worn long skirts. Next year would be her first winter in long skirts; perhaps logic was her best bet.

"What kind of fabric?"

"Wool."

"Did you ask the price?" Abby told her, and Mary stopped working, hands stretching and clenching in folds of dough.

She was a bit out of breath when she said, "Ach, Abby. Too much, dear, too much. You've grown. You'd need seven yards at least. We can't, dear, we just can't." She looked truly sorry, and Abby knew she was.

"I thought so," Abby admitted, "but I had to ask."

"Of course, you did. Go dig some potatoes, please," Mary said, and the conversation was over. When Abby returned from the kitchen garden with the vegetables, Mary dismissed her. Abby took the opportunity to run off.

Abby found Brian and Daniel at Swabia Creek, sitting in the deep shade of the willow trees. Brian lounged on his back, chewing a straw, for all the world, a carefree boy. Daniel sat tailor-fashion, plucking at the grass, tossing clover blossoms into the meandering water. Wordlessly, Abby sat next to Daniel, stretching her legs, crossing her ankles, and leaning back on her hands. Three inches of stockings peeked between her skirt and boot tops. Daniel glanced at her and quickly averted his eyes.

"How are you today, Daniel?"

"Fine, fine." He looked out through the undulating branches at the brilliance on the other side of the creek. "Newspaper came today. Someone brought it from Allentown."

Abby sat up a bit straighter. "What news?"

"More of the same. Lincoln, threats of secession. Some news about the railroads going through . . ."

"What about secession?"

"Senators from the Southern States are saying that if Mr. Lincoln is elected, they will secede."

"Why?" Brian asked in a lazy voice.

The other two gawked. All summer long, the country had been anticipating the next scene in the interminable drama of slavery and states' rights. More than once, war had been avoided by compromise, compromise usually suggested and written by one Mr. Henry Clay, a Southerner who seemed to love the Union as much as any Northerner. But Mr. Clay was gone to eternity, and people—politicians and farmers and tavern owners and newspapermen—were saying that this time, war could not be sidestepped like a pile of horse dung. Last year, Mr. John Brown, infamous to some and celebrated by others for his bloody work in keeping Kansas free of slaves, had plotted a revolt in Harper's Ferry, Virginia, and he had hanged for it. Now abolitionists wanted blood as badly as the Southern slaveholders wanted to keep the status quo. How could Brian not know that?

Patiently, as to a child, Daniel explained. He gave more details than Abby would have; she could see Brian's eyes glaze over before Daniel had gotten halfway through the report. Abby respected Daniel, for he diligently followed every news article and every piece of tavern gossip, and most of what she knew came from him, for he loved to discuss what he knew.

"I thought it was all about slavery," Brian interrupted. "Isn't the real issue slavery?"

"No," Abby replied. "That's just the excuse."

"I wouldn't call it an excuse," Brian muttered. "People in chains for another person's greed or convenience. Remember that man—"

Abby pursed her lips and shook her head only slightly, but Brian got the message. He had almost mentioned the escaped slave who had arrived at the Weimer farm in the middle of the night a few years ago. It was the only time either Brian or Abby had seen evidence of the Railroad—or even the fact that Frederick and Mary were conductors—but they had suspected. That cold October night, after dinner, Brian had overheard Mary mention freight coming through, and he had stayed up all night, watching. He had dragged Abby with him to the springhouse, following Frederick in the shadows. But even if they had walked upright and confidently, no one would have seen them. It was a moonless night, and Frederick did not carry a lantern. There was a scraggly hunched-form walking with Frederick, and after the form was shut into the windowless outbuilding, and Frederick had walked away, Brian had led the way to the hiding place.

The two children—they had truly been children then—had never spoken of it, not the brisk air and the crisp autumn smells, not the man who hunkered behind the barrels of sauerkraut when they opened the door, not the wounds that still bled through his shirt or the wounds so visible in his eyes, not his name or his predicament. They had not spoken of it to Frederick, and as far as Abby knew, Brian had never again spied. Without discussing it, they both knew that they could not talk about it with anyone.

But the fact remained: they knew. Frederick was a conductor on the Underground Railroad. He was breaking the law for the sake of his conscience. Talking about it with others, even their best friend, could mean—would mean—trouble for the family. But until now, Abby had not realized how much Brian was affected by what they had seen.

Brian began again. "Well, I'll tell ya, if Mr. Lincoln wins, and the South does secede, and if Mr. Lincoln declares war—"

"Congress declares war," Abby interjected, but Brian went right past her like a freight train.

"I'll join the fight!"

"I've heard said that it will be quick," Daniel said, looking from Brian to Abby and back again.

"Not too quick, I hope," Brian said. "I want some action. Adventure. Get me out of here." And with a rough push off the ground, he struggled with the willow branches and stalked off.

Daniel looked fully at Abby. "Did he fight with your pa again?" She shrugged noncommittally. She could just as easily ask Daniel the same thing; he and his father fought almost daily about Daniel's desire to write for a newspaper instead of run the tavern.

"We were harvesting corn this morning, and he just stood there, but I don't know that Papa said anything to him about it."

"But you did, right?"

Abby shrugged again, but she was smiling. She enjoyed Daniel's company. The three of them were often together, but Brian never accepted her the way Daniel did. It had been different when they were children, when Brian and Abby and Daniel and Kathleen and even Sarah and Meg Kelly had played together. Then they had separated into roles, and things had never been the same. Truth be told, though, she didn't really want to spend time with her uncle any more than he wanted to spend time with her.

"What about you and your pa?" she asked.

"Ach."

That was as much as he'd say, but he again beheaded the innocent clover, and that was eloquent in its own way. Instead of pressing the issue, Abby told him about the red wool, and she watched as his hands slowed in their destructive maneuvers and finally ceased.

Daniel put his hands on his knees and looked at her. "You'll look nice in red." He pulled his knees to his chest, wrapped his arms around them as if he were cold, and looked out into the bright distance.

"Ma says it's too expensive. She's right." Once again, she wished her mother could be a little less practical, allow a splurge, allow Abby to indulge. Abby was an excellent seamstress, even for being only fourteen, and she would love to attract attention in a red wool dress she made herself. She sighed. She could pine for it, but it just wouldn't happen.

Abby and Daniel sat quietly, listening to the twittering birds above them and the gentle rush of water in front of them. They could hear rumbling water falling over the wheel of Schmoyer's mill in the distance. The air was cool and comfortable in the shade. Abby didn't want to leave, knowing that the moment she stepped out from under the tree, the harsh sunlight would blind her, and the sweat would immediately stick her bodice to her back. But the sun was near the horizon; supper must be nearly done, and she should go home to help.

As if on cue, Daniel stood and held out a hand to help her up. As she straightened her skirt, he said carefully, "If you're going to wear women's skirts, you should wear them like a lady. Don't show your ankles."

She glared at him from under squinting eyes, her lips pursed and fists clenched. The she grinned and laughed. "*You're* telling *me* how to be a *lady*?"

"Seamstress or farmer's wife, you still want to be a lady, don't you? You won't be a proper lady if you insist on exposed ankles."

"Not with exposed ankles." She mimicked. With a good-natured shove to move him out of the way, she marched into the sunlight. She didn't stop, even though she couldn't see for a good ten seconds. When her eyes had adjusted, she trotted off, leaving Daniel to head toward town.

Work in the fields progressed without Abby. Mary and her daughters began the canning season, three weeks of hot aching work. Beets were pulled up from the garden, scrubbed free of dirt, sliced, boiled, and pickled. Cabbage was chopped, put in crocks of brine, put in the springhouse, and checked every few days until the sauerkraut was ready. An assortment of vegetables was cooked and mixed with a liquid consisting of mostly vinegar and sugar, and the resulting "chowchow" was canned just like the rest, a tangy Pennsylvania Dutch side dish that brought color to a winter table. Other root vegetables were not canned but put in baskets to be stored in the cool dark of the root cellar.

Abby soon stopped talking to Sarah altogether to avoid more fighting, and Sarah, on her part, honored the truce. Still, by the third week, tempers were short, hands were blistered, and backs were sore. Abby wanted sleep but often did not get a good night's rest, her muscles screaming in the darkness.

They finished canning on a Saturday, and Sunday morning, Abby groaned as she rolled over. The straw mattress crackled under her. Abby opened her eyes and saw that Sarah was not next to her, but the sun shone brightly.

Sarah's voice broke through her fogginess. "Time to get up for church."

More sleep was a futile hope, and Abby knew it. Still, she grabbed her sister's pillow, hugged it to her chest, and tried to go back to sleep. A moment later, the pillow was snatched from her arms, and she was hit over the head with it. She threw up her hands. Sarah dropped the pillow and huffed. Without a word, she sat at the little table with the mirror over it and began to brush her hair.

Abby groaned again. Beating her sister wasn't worth it. She was still tired and more than a little sore. The result was a cantankerous spirit that wanted anything but to get ready for church.

"It's seven-fifteen, you know," Sarah finally said. "Brian did the milking, and he's not happy about it. Ma and me made breakfast, and she saved you some." Her tone implied she wouldn't have been so generous.

"How can it be seven-fifteen? The sun is barely up."

"The sun has been up for more than an hour, like the rest of us," Sarah answered. "Are you ill or just lazy this morning?"

Abby threw a pillow at her sister's face in the mirror. The mirror wobbled and fell off the nail; Sarah caught it with a gasp before it crashed into pieces. Abby got up and began to dress. As she finished buttoning her blue Sunday calico, a knock announced Mary as she opened the door.

"Oh, good, you're up. There's a bite of breakfast for you downstairs. Hurry up, dear." And she was gently gone.

Sarah stood up, stared at Abby with slight amusement and even slighter concern. "Are you having trouble?"

Abby was having trouble. Her fingers were not cooperating as she attempted to button first her bodice and then her shoes. With a bit of struggle and a grunt, she got it done, stamped her foot, and pushed Sarah out of the way so she could sit down. Sarah left Abby alone to finish her grooming.

Abby hated the pretentious hairstyles the ladies wore, complicated chignons and sometimes curls. Oh, a bun was fine for every day, but an eligible lady wore more complicated arrangements for going out, even if only going to church. Church was just about the only place to meet an eligible bachelor, anyway.

Not that she wanted to meet an eligible bachelor. Meeting one would eventually lead to marriage. The only option open to married women was housework and motherhood, and Abby didn't want that!

"Doppich!" Her sweaty hand lost the grip on her hair, and the whole chignon fell out, cascading long brown hair down her back. She tried again, using brush and hairpins furiously.

Abby did not desire the life her mother lived. The last romantic thing that happened to Mary was meeting Frederick. Mary's life was dull, redundant, never-ending. Not unlike the life of a farmer, but at least a farmer was able to be out in the world. For both farmer and wife, it was a cycle that started at one season, progressing through the year until it started all over again. Mary was good at what she did, Abby had to admit, but Abby wanted to be a seamstress in the city, at least for a while. She took in some sewing from bachelors around Millerstown, but it wasn't enough to make a living. More than anything, she wanted to be on her own, free to go where she wanted and when. Not likely to happen, she knew. And eventually, she wanted land of her own.

She patted her hair, turned this way and that. It looked fine, she decided, and she left her room. Breakfast was waiting, and then the family would walk three miles to the Baptist church at the top of the hill. On beautiful days like this one, Papa liked to give the animals a rest too.

The day was warm and smelled of autumn. The leaves had not yet begun to change colors, but the air smelled tangy, like apple cider and cut hay. They passed fields that had given up their corn harvest, passed Swabia Creek, the shallow water running serenely over smooth rocks, and passed Mr. Lichtenwalner's cows grazing near the road. The fluffy clouds passed by overhead, beckoned by a windful tune only they could hear.

Mary was from an Irish minority—the Protestant minority. When she married Frederick, there was no threat of excommunication for living in an area devoid of Catholic churches. It was not hard for her to leave the Anglican Church for the Reformed one. The family had attended the Reformed Church on Church Street, near the top of the hill, until the Baptists broke off and began their own church only a few hundred feet higher up the hill. When members of the Lutheran and Reformed churches disagreed with the leaders on the right form of baptism, a landowner just up the hill from the Reformed Church had donated the use of his pond for immersing new believers. With that, the Baptist Church of Millerstown had begun. The members built the simple wooden structure some years later.

The Baptist church service began at ten, and the churchyard was filled with wagons and horses hitched to posts. People chattered and gossiped until the meeting started. Families sat together, and Abby noticed Frederick held Mary's hand as they sat to listen and stood to sing.

Abby did not notice the preacher's message, although she sat without fidgeting. Once or twice, she reached across Sarah to touch Ben's knee lightly without turning her head; he was often restless. She would have done the same to Brian, on the other side of Ben, if she could have reached. Sarah, as always, sat prim and straight, eyes ahead, every hair in place beneath her straw hat, trying to catch some boy's eye without him realizing she was trying.

Somehow, Abby had caught the eye of Thomas Lauer. He waited at the door for her. He removed his hat, revealed disheveled blond hair, and bowed to Mary and Abby. He spoke with Frederick and Brian, but it was obvious to everyone that his eyes were on Abby.

She stood next to Mary, her hands clasped in front of her, her dark blue reticule cutting off the circulation in her wrist.

Just as Abby thought he wasn't going to speak to her at all, Mary did the unthinkable. "Mr. Lauer, if you don't have plans for dinner, would you like to join us?" Mary asked, putting her arm through her husband's and looking up at Thomas Lauer. Abby almost groaned audibly when he agreed, too readily it seemed.

He spoke softly to Abby then, "I did not bring the buggy, but I would be pleased to walk with you." Abby was about to deny the request, but again Mary stepped in. Abby smiled and fell in silently next to the young man.

Frederick and Mary walked arm in arm, Frederick's head bent in conversation with his wife. Brian and Ben barely managed a dignified pace; only a reprimanding word from Mary to keep their clothes clean prevented them from running ahead. Sarah walked a step behind the boys. She glanced over her shoulder every so often to look at Abby and Thomas, who walked some distance behind at a much slower pace.

Thomas was not a talker. He was a tall man with tan skin and brown eyes that crinkled almost perpetually. He worked the mill up on the hill with his cousin. He had not been in the township long, but he had made friends of varying ages and professions. Although only twenty-five or so, the older men of town accepted him as a careful thinker and man of conservative action. The younger men esteemed him and enjoyed his quiet friendship. Abby had not yet learned what he wanted to do or where he wanted to settle permanently; perhaps farming was not in his nature.

"You are looking well, Miss Weimer," he said finally. He glanced at her quickly and then away.

"I am well, thank you. And yourself?" Abby looked straight ahead, matching his slow, measured pace.

"Yes, I am well." A pause. "I have noticed you in town recently. Do you come to town often?"

"Not every day, but often enough, I guess."

"Mrs. Weimer sends you to town for things at the store?"

"Sometimes, but I also spend time at Kelly's Tavern."

"Oh, you spend time with Mrs. Kelly?"

Abby knew what he was hinting at, and she knew her answer would shock him. He probably already had an intimation of the truth, otherwise he would not have asked. With some small measure of perversity, she said, "I listen to the men's conversations. I even put my two cents in when I have something to say."

Thomas's step faltered for just a second, but then he was walking rhythmically once again. "What would you have to say exactly?" he asked, and she could tell he was striving desperately to be polite.

Abby took a deep breath. If they made it through dinner, she knew it would be a miracle. If he was still talking to her when they reached the house, it would be astonishing. Her pretty face had not prepared him for her independent nature, and she knew he would probably not join them for dinner a second time. Evenly she said, "I read the papers when I get a chance. I can discuss politics and finances and such. I was discussing with the men at home the other day the price of wheat this year."

Thomas did not speak for a moment. "I had no idea." He looked up to where the family walked, quite a distance ahead now. "We should catch up," he said, and Abby knew that was the end of the discussion as well as the courtship.

Sure enough, when they caught up with the family, Thomas engaged Brian and Frederick in conversation, still walking next to Abby, but obviously not thinking of her anymore. As they reached the farm, Frederick turned to look at his daughter. He noticed the gritted teeth and unhappy expression. It wasn't that Abby wanted Thomas's undivided attention; she wanted his respect. She knew in her heart the only man she could marry was the one—and there might be only one on all the earth—who would respect her independence.

"Abby, what do you think about the election?" Frederick said.

Brian groaned. "Don't get her started."

"I think it is a very important election. Perhaps the most important in the history of the United States. The senators from the South are threatening to secede if Lincoln is elected."

Brian cut her off with a swing of his hand, as if he were swatting a fly. "I say let them!"

"It would destroy the Union! Everything our Founding Fathers stood for! If the South is allowed to continue in slavery or to secede from the Union, then liberty and freedom are null and void."

"But don't you think the North could continue on its own as it is?" Thomas asked. They were approaching the house now, and Sarah hurried ahead.

"Not on the same continent with slaveholders and traitors," Abby answered.

"That's some strong language, Daughter." Frederick's thick beard barely hid his smile as they entered the yard.

"Of course, it is!" Abby began, but this time, Mary cut her off.

"Abby, will you please help me in the kitchen? Frederick, take our guest into the parlor."

Frederick led the way through the front door and into the parlor. Mary and Abby continued down the gloomy hallway to the bright kitchen. Abby was seething, and so was Sarah.

Sarah slapped her straw hat on the table and brushed her hair back with her hands. "How could you be so stupid? You ruin everything!"

"What are you talking about?" Abby demanded, hands on hips, her own hat askew on her head.

"A nice young man coming to call, and you've ruined it! You'll never get married at this rate. Talking about the election as if you know what you're talking about! No man wants a wife who has strong opinions on politics!"

"What if I don't want to get married at all? And what do you know anyway? You're twelve, for pity's sake!"

"Not get married? Mother, do you hear what she's saying?"

"I hear her just fine, and Mr. Lauer may be hearing you just fine, too, with your voice loud as a locomotive." Mary calmly tied on her apron. "Sarah, go check the chicken."

Sarah huffed and stomped out the door to check the chicken cooking in the summer kitchen. The summer kitchen was meant to keep the main kitchen bearable throughout the summer heat whenever possible, but when Abby and Sarah argued, it wasn't possible.

"Abby, sit."

Abby sat. Mary produced potatoes, knife, and slop pail. Abby set to work.

"Abby," Mary said softly after a moment, "do you not like Mr. Lauer?"

"I don't know him. And until now, he didn't know me. He liked the way I look, and he liked my family, but he didn't know me." She put down a potato and picked up another. Mary took the finished potatoes and cut them into chunks before dropping them into a pot of water.

Sarah returned, sweating and red in the face. "Not done yet," she said.

"I didn't expect it to be," Mary returned. "Sarah, tea."

Sarah began the task, and they worked in silence. Finally, Sarah said the tea was ready, and Mary told her to take it to the parlor and entertain Mr. Lauer. "Shouldn't Abby do that? He came to see her, after all." Sarah sneered behind her sister's back.

"Sarah, I will not put up with impudence."

"Yes, Ma." The girl meekly carried the tray out of the room. Abby knew that by the time Sarah reached the parlor, a sweet smile would be firmly in place, and she would bubble with polite and pointless conversation.

Abby slammed her fist on the dark wooden table, clattering the tin slop bowl and almost spilling the peels. A tear dropped from her eye onto her hand, and the lump in her throat was choking her. She peeled another potato, almost taking all the flesh off with the peel.

Muttering more to herself than to her mother, she said, "I have the caller, and I'm the one doing the potatoes. Why can't Sarah help? Delicate, ladylike Sarah. Brat."

"Abby," Mary said softly, placing a light, cooling touch on her daughter's head. "Marriage is what most women are content to have."

"I'm not content with that!"

"I know, dear. You are a fine seamstress, and if you decide to live here forever and do your own work, your father and I will be overjoyed to have you," Mary whispered.

For a moment, Abby wanted to shout that she didn't want to stay here at all, let alone forever. Then she realized what her mother had said. She turned in her chair to look up at Mary. "Wouldn't you rather have a teacher for a daughter?"

Mary shook her head with a smile. "I want you for a daughter, and that's all." Without another word, she walked out the back door with the pot of potatoes. Abby began shelling peas. Her mind was reeling, but she didn't settle on any one thought or feeling.

The dinner was wonderful: the chicken was tender and lightly flavored with thyme and basil, the potatoes were mashed, and the melted butter formed pools in the white mound in the serving bowl. The peas were perfect and fresh, the bread was soft and warm, and the apple pie was heavy, the idyllic ending. Mr. Lauer exclaimed over everything and even smiled at Abby. Somehow, she managed to smile in return.

Mrs. Meyer came to call a few weeks later. "Mrs. Weimer, how are you?" They sat in the kitchen and waited for the tea to brew.

"I am well, Mrs. Meyer. What brings you all the way out here?"

"Oh, 'tis not such a walk." Mrs. Meyer was red, breathing heavily, and she was wind-whipped. October had arrived as windy as March; the white-haired lady had probably been tossed to and fro on her trek to the farm.

Mary sat down, bringing the teapot and a plate of bread and butter. Mrs. Meyer helped herself as Mary poured the tea. They chatted about small nothings as they nibbled and sipped. Finally, Mrs. Meyer revealed her reason for coming.

"Is Abby about?"

"Abby went with Frederick to Harris's horse farm up in Fogelsville."

"Ah, then I've come for naught," Mrs. Meyer said sadly. "Perhaps you can have her come to town tomorrow, if she does not have other chores."

"Gladly, Mrs. Meyer, but what is this about?"

"I haven't taken in sewing for years. My eyes aren't what they once were." Mary nodded compassionately. "Yesterday, a man came to the store. From up near Allentown way. Seems his daughter is marrying some rich Philadelphian, and he wanted to order a trousseau. We have the finest fabric in the township, you know." Again, Mary nodded. "I can't do it, but I thought of Abby. He will return tomorrow with the exact measurements and other details."

Mary nodded, a sparkle in her eye. She was sure Abby would agree. "I will definitely tell Abby, and she might even come to town this evening if they return before late. I can't imagine why she wouldn't agree."

Mrs. Meyer stood. "Good. I will pay her well. Tomorrow, the gentleman and Abby and I can work out the terms." The old woman pushed herself stiffly from her chair. "I must get back to town. Thank you for the tea." Mary escorted her to the edge of the yard then returned to the kitchen.

Mary sat for a few minutes, sipping a second cup. Abby would be excited. Depending on the order, Abby's time might be too taken up to help around the house and farm. Sarah would have to help more, and Ben could help with the eggs and milking. That boy ran too free, anyway; a few more chores would do him good. The harvest was in, so Frederick and his hired help could manage without Abby.

Mary thought of the red wool, which she had examined herself on a trip to town. It was beautiful, and expensive, and worth every penny. If Abby earned enough, she could afford to buy it for herself, and the resulting dress would be that much more precious. Mary smiled into her cup of tea. If Abby worked late at the store, perhaps Daniel could walk her home.

Abby hurried to Millerstown. Mrs. Meyer had not told her mother when the gentleman from Allentown would be arriving, but she wanted to be there when he came.

Mrs. Meyer welcomed Abby into the parlor that abutted the store. It was plush, pink, and ornate. The pillows were delicately embroidered. The rug was clean. The windows were recently washed. Mrs. Meyer's dressmaker's dummy still stood in the corner by the window, but it had stood idle for at least eighteen months when she had begun to hire Abby to help occasionally.

Mrs. Meyer offered Abby tea and cookies, although breakfast had barely been cleared. Millerstown had not yet begun its bustling day, but Mrs. Meyer was ever the perfect hostess. They sat and chatted about the farm, sewing, friends, and the like.

Mr. Meyer ushered a gangly gentleman into the parlor at about nine-thirty. The man was dressed in clean but wrinkled gray slacks and a black coat and cravat. He held a top hat in his hands, hands that were weak-looking, pale, and shaky. His face was pleasant, with a receding gray hairline and lackluster blue eyes. Mrs. Meyer introduced him as Mr. Wallington.

"This is Miss Weimer," she said, and they shook hands. He bowed over her hand, and Abby felt distinctly uncomfortable. Standing next to him was a rail thin brunette with the same eyes. He introduced his daughter, Emma, in a voice with a light British accent.

"Miss Weimer will be doing the sewing, Mr. Wallington," Mrs. Meyer stated resolutely. "I am unable to see delicate work, but I can vouch for her, and I guarantee that I would have no one else sew for me." Abby felt even more uncomfortable with the compliments. Mr. Wallington smiled pleasantly.

Abby realized the girl was staring. Emma Wallington could not have been much older than Abby, perhaps sixteen or seventeen, but she held herself with poise. Her hair was beautifully done, her fingernails were clean, and there was just a hint of rouge on her pale cheeks. Abby would not have called her beautiful, but she was, well, not unpleasant looking.

Miss Wallington spoke. Her voice was light and airy, like springtime. "I am marrying the heir to a fortune, Miss Weimer. Can you create for me a trousseau that will put me in the society pages?"

Abby didn't care a fig if the girl got on the society pages, but she nodded. She was confident in her abilities. The four of them discussed terms—well, Mr. Wallington and Mrs. Meyer did; Miss Wallington looked distressed with the conversation, as if discussing money was akin to getting one's hands dirty. Abby listened with veiled anticipation, and by the end of it, she was going to end up with more money than she had ever had in her life!

And the seventeen dresses, not to mention the unmentionables, needed to be finished by the first week of March. That allowed less than six months.

The sky was clear blue as she walked home. The clouds scuttled overhead, and the variegated leaves of the trees rustled in the wind. A formation of geese flew past, communicating their banks and turns and changes of the guard through obnoxious honking.

Abby laughed out loud, running, then spinning in circles with arms outstretched, then panting in contented fatigue. Every day she would spend some satisfied hours in Mrs. Meyer's parlor, preparing dresses for a snobbish Brit who was marrying an heir. The patterns and fabrics of the first three dresses were chosen, and she and Mrs. Meyer had measured Miss Wallington. Tomorrow, she would begin her self-sufficient life as a seamstress.

Upon arriving home, Abby gushed with excitement, increasing Mary's joy and Sarah's jealousy. Abby raved about the beautiful fabrics, disparaged Miss Wallington, and exclaimed over the payment she would receive. Both her mother and sister, at that moment, looked at her with shared excitement and complete respect.

As Abby was about to bounce her way to the barn to spread her excitement even further, she remembered the letter in her pocket. Mary had requested she stop at the post office, and in her excitement, she had almost forgotten to do so. Now she handed the letter to her mother. Then she was gone.

Mary set Sarah to work chopping vegetables for the midday meal, then she settled herself at the table with a cup of tea to read the letter. It was postmarked Gettysburg, and the handwriting was her sister's.

Bridget Pummer was twenty-eight, married to a seminary student, the mother of three boys. Bridget had come to America in 1846 with their brother Sean, and after spending a few months at the farm with the newly married Mary, they had traveled to Gettysburg, Pennsylvania. Sean had heard of the cheap land, good for farming, near a new but growing town, where he could begin a new life. Sean had worked on a farm until he could purchase his own. Having proved himself to his employer, the bank took a chance on giving a new immigrant a loan, and Bridget kept house until they both married. Sean had married a pretty German girl, Anna, and Bridget had married John Pummer, at a double ceremony, so Mary could attend both.

The day of the weddings in the year 1852 had been the last time the siblings has seen each other. Sean and Anna, no doubt, spent some evenings in the company of the Pummers, but Mary had not seen either of them, and neither Sean nor Bridget had seen Brian since he was two years old. Their only communication was carefully crafted letters that the sisters mailed as often as life allowed.

As Mary carefully tore open the envelope, the joy Abby had so recently shared was greatly multiplied. She smiled even before she started to read.

Bridget shared the usual affairs of life—new clothes, friends' weddings and births, John's schooling and work as a clerk. Sean and Anna were well. Anna was again expecting. As always, Bridget expressed the desire to visit her sister.

Bridget had a beautiful hand, even though she had only learned to read and write through the love and devotion of John. Her handwriting was as beautiful as art. Mary read, reread, then folded the two sheets covered in small script. She, too, wanted to see her sister again.

Abby looked around the Gehmans's barnyard. The sun was heading toward its orange-and-yellow-and-red autumn blanket to sleep away the night. The moon was nearly full, already suspended well above the eastern horizon. The barnyard was crowded with people, corn, benches, and tables laden with food. The husking bee was attended by all: married, unmarried, families. It was mostly a courtship dance, this bee, but everyone enjoyed the time to commiserate over a job that needed to be done and would be very boring otherwise.

Abby took a seat next to Kathleen and Meg Kelly. Kathleen was fourteen, Abby's age, and Meg was one year younger. Each girl had a pile of corn in front of her, and some helpful soul appeared from nowhere to overturn a bushel basket of corn at Abby's feet. The sisters were chatting amiably, and they included Abby in the conversation.

"Are your eyes on anyone, Abby?" Kathleen whispered, Meg leaning over her lap in order to hear the answer.

Abby shook her head.

"His eyes are on you, though!" Kathleen said with a giggle.

Abby followed Kathleen's look. In the corner, sitting on a long bench between other young men, Daniel was talking with Thomas Lauer as they pulled unyielding husks off yellow corn.

"No, I think I've ended that quite nicely," Abby said without bitterness.

She could remember a time when she and Kathleen had shared secrets. Those were years of games and tree climbing and getting dirty. Years ago, before long skirts and piled hair and even the thought of romance. But since the end of those years, their closeness had become less so. They were still cordial toward each other, but their goals were different. With a shake of her head, Abby admitted her purposes were probably contrary to those of every unmarried woman in the yard.

Abby wanted to be a seamstress, preferably in a city. But that was not her ultimate goal, only a means to an end. The city beckoned loudly, not for its own sake, but because it was where she could make the most money. If she could find a position in Allentown, or even Philadelphia, she would save her pennies and dollars so that she could return to the valley and buy her own farm. She enjoyed the sun on her head, the strength she felt in her back muscles as she worked with others in the field, the smell of the earth, the satisfaction of seeing things grow. It was a dream, a deep dream, so deep that no one had ever heard her voice it. She wasn't sure she would ever share it, unless her plans came to fruition.

Someone played a tune on a fiddle. Some people sang along. Young children ran in and out of the circle. Men took finished piles of corn and replaced them with new ones. Someone kept track of how much each farmer was due, so that he left with that which he had brought. Young people casually got up to get food, then returned to sit back down next to whomever "they had their eyes on".

"May I sit?"

Abby looked up, saw Thomas standing next to her with two plates. He offered her one, and she was obligated to let him sit. Kathleen and Meg moved down the bench, bending their heads together, no doubt to comment on the situation.

"Thank you, Mr. Lauer," Abby said kindly, managing a smile. She paused in her husking to eat the roasted pork and cranberry sauce. It was good.

"Are you having a good time?" he asked.

"Yes, I suppose. It makes a boring job easier to husk together."

"I wanted to tell you how much I enjoyed dinner at your house." That had been weeks ago, and Abby had not thought much about it.

"Well, thank you for taking notice of me, sir." The usual niceties did not come easily for her, but she felt Mary would be proud of her for trying.

"I would like permission to call. May I?"

Abby met his eyes. He was handsome, young, and kind. She could do worse. But the fact remained that what she wanted did not match what most men wanted. Quite honestly, she was surprised that she hadn't already scared him away; she had been sure he would never talk to her again.

"I've been away," he added, "otherwise I would have been by sooner. I was talking with an investor in Catasauqua. I've been thinking about investing in the anthracite iron furnace that will be coming to Alburtis soon."

"I don't know much about that," Abby admitted.

"I think I could do well, maybe expand later on." He stopped eating and looked her in the face. "I could provide for a family quite nicely."

Abby swallowed hard. She had finished her cup of cider and held her cup out to him, though she wasn't really all that thirsty. "Husking is such dusty work. Might I have some more cider, please?"

Mr. Lauer jumped up, eager to please. He left his plate on the bench, hurried away.

Abby turned to Kathleen and Meg. "He's a nice man."

"Yes?" Kathleen prompted.

"I don't know that I want to marry him, though."

Kathleen's eyes edged passed Abby's shoulder, watching the topic of conversation on his way back. "You don't need to know that yet."

"But is it wrong to let him call without knowing? What if he wants to marry me and I don't want to?"

Kathleen only shrugged, but Meg whispered, for he was almost upon them. "Then when he asks, you say 'no.'" But Abby couldn't think of a woman of her acquaintance, her mother's friends, ever mentioning a woman who had turned down a proposal once it was offered. Perhaps it just wasn't done.

"Miss Weimer," Mr. Lauer said with a smile, handing her the full cup. She smiled in thanks, and he sat. And she was no better off for sending him on an unnecessary errand.

Abby straightened her back, placed her plate on her lap, met his eyes. "I want independence, sir, not marriage and family." She said it as bluntly as she could. And immediately regretted it. She did this all of the time—ruined relationships for no purpose. She wanted her independence, it was true, but seeing the disbelief on their faces replaced by a mixture of disgust and distaste always left her with a pain in her heart. She wished she could have her independence and their respect too. Even her own sister looked at her as Thomas Lauer was looking at her now, as if a two-headed monster was eating a toad. His plate was empty, and with a perfunctory bow, he got up and left.

Kathleen tried unsuccessfully to again engage Abby in conversation. But Abby's night was ruined, and she husked in silence.

Chapter 2

DANIEL

As late as it was, Daniel could still hear the shouting outside in the street. Earlier that evening, men had been firing guns into the air, drinking heavily, and in every way celebrating the election of Mr. Abraham Lincoln. Kelly's Tavern had been filled with men spending lots of money, so of course, his father was in high spirits. Daniel had to admit he was happy, too, wishing he could be on hand to interview the new president-elect.

If everything men had been predicting was right, war might break out any day. The newspapers had been filled with predictions and promises before the election; he could only imagine what they would contain in the coming weeks. Although he did not relish the idea of war, as a newspaperman, he was eager for the chance to write about it, and about the man who would be leading the nation if war happened.

Daniel sat at a table in his room, the lamp low. He was still dressed, and the bed's quilt was wrapped around his shoulders, making it difficult to write. But the alternative was sitting in front of the drafty window defenseless against the cold. November had fully arrived, and winter was not far behind. On nights like this, he wished he remembered Ireland as his mother did, for she remembered wet but mild winters and constant green.

In Ireland, though, the only thing to write about was the oppression of one people by another. The British controlled Ireland, not satisfied to simply rule their own island, and the Irish were beaten down, physically and in every other way, if you listened to Da. When in his cups, Patrick Kelly was a loud proponent of taking Ireland by storm and drowning the British in the sea.

Daniel had grown up hearing the stories. Peggy told pretty stories: leprechauns and fairies, kings at Tara, lush green land as far as the eye could see, raucous-colored dresses and stockings, and warm barmbrack and tea. She entertained with tales of St. Bridget and St. Patrick. She painted word pictures about the people and the land.

Patrick, on the other hand, painted horror-filled pictures about the Battle of the Boyne and William of Orange. He wove tapestries with yarns of the O'Connells and Young Irelanders, but even they ended in sorrow and ugliness. He told the truth about the potato famine that indirectly had led them to America: coercion bills, evictions, burnings, death ships, and absentee landlords. Enough sadness to embitter even the luckiest and most joyful of Irishmen.

Daniel sighed and dipped his pen. With some measure of disgust, he realized the inkwell was frozen. Enough for tonight, then. He had nowhere to publish it, but he still enjoyed the act and art of writing. He picked up his half-finished article and began to read.

> Kelly's Tavern was filled with men this evening. As election results came in, men toasted the new president-elect, Abraham Lincoln.
>
> Men discussed the possibility of war and the likelihood that volunteers might be needed.
>
> Brian O'Bern, a nearby farmer, spoke loudly for the cause when he said, "Lead the way, Mr. Lincoln, and I'll follow!" Shouts of "Hear! Hear!" and "That a boy!" followed.
>
> Some men took a more conservative stance. Mr. Frederick Weimer cautioned the folk of Millerstown to not rush hastily into war. A few men nodded in agreement, but Mr. Weimer was

rather loudly shouted down by the younger set in the tavern.

Mrs. Peggy Kelly, wife of the tavern's owner, agreed with Mr. Weimer. "I do not desire to see blood shed," she said. "I do not desire to see the sons of this town killed for something that does not concern us."

Some would not agree with Mrs. Kelly. Some would say that it certainly does concern us.

And that was where he had stopped, at a loss for words. He did not know how to write with conviction his thoughts on the disagreement between the northern states and the southern. Disagreement! Hell, this was worse than sibling rivalry! The topic of slavery and states' rights was so hot that it just might burn down a town or two.

Daniel turned down the wick. With the utmost speed, he unbuttoned his boots, stripped, and leaped into bed wearing his long underwear and socks. The pan of hot coals in the foot of his bed had long since grown cold, and even with the quilt up to his chin, it took a long while before he fell asleep.

A pounding on the door woke him with a jolt. He had just gotten to sleep, it seemed. He rolled over and grunted. Kathleen poked her head in the door. In her unassertive voice, she said, "Breakfast is on the table, and Da is feeling the whiskey from last night. You had better come down quick!"

What a way to start the morning, he thought. Da in a bad mood, and he had to go and oversleep.

Daniel stretched, dressed quickly, ran a hand through his hair, and walked out the door. He was instantly bombarded with the aroma of eggs, bacon, and flapjacks. He hurried down the narrow steps, making a lot of noise with his clomping feet, and not really caring if it gave Da a worse headache.

He was welcomed with five surprised stares and one growl as he entered the kitchen. Peggy stood next to George, serving flapjacks. Next to George was William, and then Daniel's empty chair. Kathleen and Meg sat on the other side of the table. All of them were staring with different versions of distress on their faces. Patrick was turned almost completely around in his chair, eyes bleary and red, a scowl of considerable fury on his face.

With barely concealed resentment and a little fear, Daniel sat at his spot. He reached for the flapjacks that his mother had set in front of him. No one spoke. Ma sat at the foot of the table between Daniel and Kathleen. She stole glances at her son, looked at her husband, slowly put a bit of eggs in her mouth.

Daniel began to eat, but he knew it was just a matter of time.

"Do you have no respect for the other members of this house that you would sleep the day away and make such a racket joining us for breakfast." It was not meant as a question; at least not one Da wanted an answer to.

Angry thoughts raced through Daniel's mind. *I hate this. I hate Da after he's been drinking. And I hate my weakness. Why don't I stand up* to him?

"I'm sorry, Da. I was up late writing."

The moment the words left his mouth, he knew it was the wrong thing to say. Patrick pounded his fist on the table. The tin cups quaked. Daniel saw Kathleen lower her head but still looking at him covertly. She was afraid for him but knew from enough experience that it was best to stay invisible.

"You waste time with that writing. You're a tavern owner's son. You don't need those silly stories."

"They are not silly stories!"

"I will not have you wasting my time!"

His time!

"I forbid you to write any more stories!"

Daniel was about to answer when Peggy put a comforting hand on his. The fight left him like beer left the tavern on St. Pat's. He took a few flapjacks and left the table.

Daniel had a bucket of water and a rag. He had worked his way through half of the sticky tables in the tavern when Patrick pushed through the door that connected the bar with the family's space.

It was always this way. Daniel did something to anger Patrick. Patrick reacted with loud words and fury, sometimes with a fist. Then Daniel slinked out of the room and did something he thought would ease the situation.

They worked in silence. Patrick wiped glasses while Daniel wiped tables and chairs. The rowdy celebrations from the night before had left a wake of upturned chairs, tables, and spilled beverages. It had been late when the last customers finally left, and Patrick had told Daniel to go to bed. Nice, a welcome rest last night, but it made for a harder cleanup the morning after. As Daniel set a chair on its legs, he noticed a gouge in the table. And the chair now wobbled. He carried it over to the doorway. He'd have to fix it later.

Kelly's was a fine tavern, Daniel had to admit. Patrick had inherited his Galway tavern from his father, and he expected to pass this one on to Daniel. Daniel would be quite content to allow one of his brothers to take it, but he was the oldest son, so that was the end of the argument.

Except it never was.

Daniel and Patrick were startled by a loud knock on the door. Patrick opened it and admitted John Peter. John was an Allentown merchant that often traveled to Reading and took a side trip to deliver a copy of the Allentown newspaper to Kelly's Tavern. Patrick ushered him in and called for Peggy to bring coffee. They sat at one of the clean tables.

Allentown had four newspapers. Three were published in German and one in English. One was politically neutral, but that was a rarity for most newspapers. Two were democratic, and one was Whig. *The Lehigh Bulletin* was democratic and English, and that was the paper John Peter flopped onto the table in front of Patrick. He took it and glanced quickly at the front page, then leaned over and handed it to Daniel, who only pretended to wipe another table.

While the two men chatted about the election, Daniel sat down to read the paper. The paper was last week's edition, but Daniel read it eagerly. The *Bulletin* was published once a week, and usually Mr. Peter delivered it the day after, but he must have been busy earlier in the week. This week's edition would be published in a few days.

Even last week, the main news was of the election. The presidential race took precedence, of course, but there was also mention of Andrew Curtin, the prospect for governor of Pennsylvania. He, too, was a Republican, so the *Bulletin* did not portray him in a good light. Andrew Curtin desired to see an end to slavery. More importantly, Andrew Curtin desired to uphold the Union if the South decided to secede. The *Bulletin*, then, desired to show him as a despicable nigger-lover and did a pretty good job of it.

Daniel didn't agree with the paper most of the time, and this was no exception. He wanted more than anything to read a Republican paper and get the real scoop. Most of the Lehigh Valley, except for the cities, was democratic territory. Even Millerstown was mostly democratic, but most of Kelly's customers were of a like mind, and that mind followed Lincoln. Most nights, a gathering of Democrats at another tavern in town rivaled the comrades of Kelly's. Patrick was an odd Irishman, a Republican, and his tavern was open to the small Republican contingent in the area.

The *Bulletin* also published Philadelphia news. Philadelphia was only a day's journey south. It was a conglomeration of immigrants and Quakers, businessmen and society folk, wharfs and factories. Irish immigrants had been pouring into the city for a decade at least, and they held more sway than most immigrant communities, although even in America the Irish were not treated as equals. Daniel read the news of important businessmen and their businesses and the crimes committed by the Irish, knowing both stories were likely inflated.

Daniel had never been to visit Philadelphia because shipments of beer and whiskey came up the Delaware River and to the tavern by way of Allentown. As a six-year-old, he had passed through Philadelphia on his way to Millerstown, and he vaguely remembered streets crowded with people and carts, like Galway on Market Day, and different languages being spoken by people of all shapes and sizes. He remembered brick buildings and cobbled streets. But he wished to see it again—experience it—and make his own determinations.

Eventually, John Peter left. After that, Patrick kept Daniel busy past noon and through the afternoon, through opening time and supper, on into evening. Daniel could sense that Da wanted to prove that being a tavern owner was a worthwhile occupation, and for Da, Daniel could not disagree. But for himself, he certainly did. He didn't want a repeat of the argument at breakfast though, so he held his tongue and bided his time.

Talk of war had faded by the beginning of December. Farmers did not see war as glorious or necessary. They needed their sons' help more than they needed a reason to pick up arms. The Lehigh Valley had always opposed a strong government that could force unwanted decisions on the people; many men were proslavery or at least antiwar. The farmers had more things to worry about than a war that might be nothing more than an idle threat, and so tavern talk turned to other things.

Men talked of the economy most nights, laughing and shouting over their drinks. Kelly's sold more beer than whiskey, and most men had a pint when they came in. Some had several before they left. The room was always loud but usually good-natured. Even those men who had more than several were usually upbeat and friendly as they faltered home. Da had said with a laugh more than once, "I don't care how long they talk of the economy as long as they help improve mine."

The Lehigh Valley was almost immune to boom-and-bust. Drought years hurt, of course, but Germans were by nature conservative, not risk-takers, and the early settlers had passed that on to their descendants. Allentown had become a hub for the movement of iron ore from the mines to the furnaces, the hub of a wheel that had moved more quickly since the East Pennsylvania Railroad had been completed last year. The men had lately been discussing the local mine. It hadn't produced much yet, and the conservative thinkers in the tavern squabbled about the likelihood that it would produce more of a profit than farming could.

Talk of the East PA Railroad led to talk of the Catasauqua and Fogelsville Railroad that had gone through Alburtis in 1855. Some had heard rumors from the town of Catasauqua, farther north in the valley, that the Welshman who had founded the first American anthracite iron furnace in that town was looking at land in Alburtis, the next town over from Millerstown, to build another. Men discussed the likelihood, the profit, and the damage such a venture would cause to the township.

"It would create jobs," Thomas Lauer stated matter-of-factly. "It would bring more families into the township."

"Is that a benefit or a drawback?" Someone laughed. Others joined in.

Thomas said, "I think it is a benefit. More families mean more business for those of us with services or merchandise to sell, and even you farmers can do more business with nonfarming families in the area."

"We farmers," someone said dryly, "can do just fine by shipping our wheat and corn through Allentown to Philadelphia. That city gobbles up more wheat than we can produce."

Thomas's cousin, owner of the mill on top of the hill, joined the discussion. "Not too long ago, there were men in this tavern discussing the advantages and disadvantages of the railroad coming through. There will always be benefits and drawbacks for any enterprise." His mill was halfway between Millerstown and Alburtis; he would gain business from both sides of the mountain.

"Wise man," Frederick Weimer said. He had just arrived and sat down with a pint of beer at a table with an empty chair. The beer wouldn't be half-empty by the time he left, but Patrick never complained that he purchased so little. Frederick's wise, quiet counsel kept more brisk voices in check. He was always welcome.

"So you think an iron furnace in Alburtis would be a good thing?" Carl Meyer asked. He supported such a venture for the exact reasons Thomas had supplied, but he was a bit surprised to hear Frederick say so. Frederick was one of the most conservative men in the room.

"I think I don't know enough yet to form an opinion," Frederick stated, sipping his beer. "I try to give everything a good thinking-through before I debate an issue." He winked at Thomas.

As the wink and a smile were exchanged, someone recalled the visit Thomas had made to Weimer's farm some weeks ago. Someone said, "Mr. Lauer, have you talked to Mr. Weimer yet about calling on his daughter?"

There was a chuckle from somewhere in the back, a call to Patrick for another pint, but the room fell oddly quiet. Patrick and Daniel had discussed more than once the propensity of men to be as much a group of gossips as their womenfolk at a quilting bee. Tonight, it looked like Thomas would be the center of the discussion and backslapping.

Abby had told Daniel about Thomas's visit and about the husking bee. Brian had also talked about Thomas's visit. They were two different accounts. Abby had said Thomas was unkind and unthinking in his dealing with her that day. Brian believed Abby made a fool out of herself and her family by talking politics. Daniel knew the truth lay somewhere in between. He was unsure, though, how he felt about her actions at the bee. Still, he kept his own counsel.

Before Thomas started to speak to the eager crowd, Daniel recalled the rest of the story, the story that had taken the past two months to complete. As much as Abby said she had tried to be open and polite, the truth of her nature had finally won out, and Thomas has ceased his courtship.

Thomas looked uncertainly at Frederick. Frederick nodded slightly, giving Thomas permission to speak truthfully. Frederick would handle the backlash.

"I did visit Mr. Weimer's farm with the intention of calling upon Miss Weimer," the young man began carefully. More chuckles and hoots of encouragement.

One brave or inebriated soul spoke loudly enough for all to hear. "Buck up, son, that girl could take on John C. Calhoun and South Carolina single-handedly. And win!" The tone indicated the statement was less than a compliment. Daniel held his breath, as did a few others.

"I have no doubt that Miss Weimer—" Thomas began.

Frederick interrupted, "If my daughter can take on South Carolina, then perhaps I should send her after some of the troublesome men of this town."

Lots of laughter, some hearty and some embarrassed. A bit more drinking. Thomas was clearly glad to be off the hook so quickly and so completely.

"Frederick, why do you let that girl run wild?" someone demanded, this time not unkindly.

"My daughter is not wild. She is independent and intelligent, and if that makes some men uncomfortable, then I will have to look elsewhere for a suitable husband for her." Silence. Thomas stared into his pint. "I will not have a man turn my daughter's brilliant nature against her. A true man will have her as she is or not at all." Frederick leaned across the table, raised Thomas's empty mug, and called, "Patrick, another pint for young Lauer."

The exchange was smoothed over and soon forgotten. Well, they at least stopped talking about it. Daniel knew the truth: Frederick was right that Abby was independent and brilliant, and he was correct in his assessment of the men of Millerstown, and he ignored the constant conversation Abby stirred up. Millerstown was as full of gossips as anywhere else on earth, and Abby provided a clear and easy target because she refused to hold her opinion to herself, and the fact that she even had an opinion about politics and money and education was enough of a reason to talk. Abby refused to be associated with any woman who seemed flighty and stupid. Abby's words, not the townspeople's. No, the town unhappily observed Abby's tendency to avoid "honest, upstanding womenfolk." But if Abby ever left town to make her own way—it wouldn't be to marry, he was sure—the town would soon lose interest and find another reason to gossip.

As the men began filing out one by one and in groups as the evening drew to a close, Frederick spoke softly to Thomas. Daniel could not hear what they said, but he saw Frederick slap the young man on the back, and Thomas had a slight smile on his face. The young man nodded and left, and Frederick came over to the bar where Daniel was wiping down glasses.

"You look distressed, young Daniel." Daniel shrugged noncommittally. "Don't be distressed on Abby's account. I meant what I said. Men who don't appreciate my daughter for who she is will never have my permission to marry her. I hold no ill feelings toward Mr. Lauer, and neither does Abby."

Daniel was not so sure about that. "She was hurt, sir," he said softly, not looking up at the kind bearded face on the other side of the counter.

Frederick eased himself onto a barstool, glanced over his shoulder to where Patrick was shaking hands with the last of the patrons. "Why do you think so? Did Brian tell you that?"

Daniel raised an eyebrow. "How would Brian know? No, Abby told me, though not in those words."

"I didn't realize she would share such a thing with you."

Daniel put down the glass and braced his hands on the counter, finally looking at Frederick. "Is it inappropriate, sir, for one friend to speak to another? Abby and I have been friends since we were both in dresses, practically."

"Daniel, I did not intend to insult you. I just did not realize that you and she talked of such things."

"We talk about everything. There are no women around here who will let her state her thoughts and feelings and opinions, and you can only imagine what would happen if she tried it here. What *has* happened," he corrected. "And I don't mind listening. Like you said, she's brilliant."

As if feeling his way through a riverbank lined with traps, Frederick asked, "So what did she say exactly?"

"That she tried to be what everyone thought she should be, and as long as she watched her tongue and talked about nothing important, he liked her just fine. But when she started looking into the railroad and anthracite coal so that she could talk with him intelligently about it, that was when he stopped calling."

As Patrick approached the far end of the bar, Frederick stood up with a look of having just figured out a mystery. Without another word to Daniel, he waved to Patrick and left the tavern. Daniel stood for a moment, the wet dishrag still in his hand, wondering what had just transpired.

"Finish up here, then go to bed," Patrick said, the last word a command which left no alternative. Daniel nodded, glad his father was going up without him, glad that he would have time and quiet to think, if nothing else. Patrick locked the front door and then was gone.

Tonight, the men had talked war and secession, railroads and iron furnaces, conservatism versus freethinking, Abby and the way a woman should be, and a bunch of nothingness before the end of the night. There had been no raised voices, no hurt feelings, and even the exchange about Abby had not put a damper on the evening. Why could men in a tavern with a pint in front of them figure things out, and the men in Washington couldn't?

What was the solution? Did the men of Millerstown not have all the facts that the men in Washington had, and so missed the big picture? Or was it the other way around? Were the men of Washington too involved in the minutia to successfully conduct the business of running a country?

After a half hour of wiping glasses and contemplating the questions, he still didn't have an answer. He turned down the last lamp, threw the dishrag in the basin, and walked quietly up to his room.

Brian came to the tavern late one morning several days later, covered with sweat and dirt and looking quite angry. His jaw was clenched, as were the fists at his sides. His breathing was coming in quick gasps, but Daniel didn't believe it was from running to town. Without asking questions, Daniel ushered his friend into the front parlor, which was actually at the back of the house, the tavern being in the front. Peggy was baking with Kathleen's help, and Meg was helping Patrick take inventory. The two younger boys were nowhere to be found, but they would show up before dinner, no doubt.

After he had closed the door, Daniel stood facing his friend, who paced back and forth across the new carpet. After a moment, Daniel asked what had happened.

Brian almost shrieked in frustration, but he caught himself in time and simply flopped onto the settee. "Frederick! Brother Frederick!"

Daniel waited. He knew Brian and Frederick clashed, much as he and his father did, but he had never seen Brian so violently angry.

The other boy looked ready to tear apart the pillow in his hands or tear a head from a neck with as much ease.

"We were logging on the new field," Brian finally said. "We tossed a log onto the pile in the wagon, and the axle broke, and he blamed me!"

Daniel was sure there was more to the story because Frederick was not as intense or impossible as Patrick. He must have had good reason to blame his young brother-in-law. Sure enough, the whole truth came out after a few tense moments. Brian had neglected the chore of greasing the axle and wheel of the large box wagon. The wagon was built for hauling, and the weight of the load was not the problem. At least not directly. The axle snapped when the animals attempted to pull it out of the frozen field, a result of a heavy box on a wheel and axle that could not move. Frederick was on the seat and fell off as a result of the jolt.

Frederick had been indignant, as he had every right to be in Daniel's opinion. Brian often disregarded chores he didn't like. No doubt, Brian knew in his heart that it was his fault, but the indignity of being scolded like a child overrode the truth.

"Was he hurt?"

Brian looked at him, the anger still loud in his eyes. "Yes, he hurt his wrist," he snapped.

"How long will it take to heal?"

"Mary doesn't think very long. It is a bit swollen but not broken." He seemed to be calming a bit, or perhaps he was just seething quietly. It was hard to tell with Brian.

"What about the wagon? Fixable?"

"Yes." Brian was definitely seething. He breathed the one-word answer with undisguised challenge.

Daniel took up the challenge. "Perhaps you should see about getting it fixed."

"Perhaps you should shut up! I come to my friend to tell him about the horrible injustice that was committed against me, and you act like it's my fault!"

"What horrible injustice? Seems to me it *is* your fault." Both boys were standing now.

"He hit me! My brother-in-law *hit* me! I don't care how much older he is! He is *not* my father!"

"Why did he hit you?" Daniel asked softly.

"Because he was mad, why else. 'A week's work lost,' he said. 'You never think of anyone but yourself,' he said. 'I'll teach you to think of others,' he said, and took a switch and swatted my backside with it. Twice! And then I hightailed it outta there." He was pacing again.

"I am not a child," Brian said. His voice was low and controlled, and it worried Daniel. "I will not stay and be treated like one." He faced his friend. "I'm leaving. I'm going to Philadelphia, and no one is going to stop me. Are you with me?"

This was one challenge Daniel did not want to take up. It didn't matter because tomorrow Frederick and Brian would have reconciled, on the surface at least, and there would be no more talk of running away. Just like Daniel's spats with his brothers, this argument between brothers-in-law, although more serious than any other they ever had before, would blow over in a day or two. Daniel tried his best to calm Brian, and the two talked of other things for a while. Brian left before dinner, but Daniel doubted he went home.

Daniel was right and Daniel was wrong, and he was very sorry to discover it. Brian had not gone home. Brian had also not stopped thinking and planning his adventure.

After church that week, Mary invited the entire Kelly clan to the farm for dinner. The Kellys attended early mass at a Catholic church in Bally, and they were often home again before the Baptist church had gotten through the first hymn. The Weimers stopped by that morning, and the Kellys walked with them to the farm. Daniel thought a moment about waiting for Abby, but she was in her Sunday best, hoopskirt and all, so she walked serenely with Peggy, Kathleen, and Mary. Daniel and Brian raced ahead. When they reached the farm, Daniel and Brian climbed into the barn loft.

The German settlers had been building barns into hills, or banks, for generations, and the size of each one corresponded directly to the size and wealth of the farm. Frederick's was larger than most, but not as large as some. It was sixty feet by one hundred feet, the lower level for animals, and the upper level, entered by stairs from the animals' level or through the sliding door at the top of the bank, was the threshing floor for the wheat. One end of the barn held hay and one straw, the first for feed and the second for bedding. The bank allowed a full wagon to be driven into the barn and unloaded into one of the two areas, or into the third area reserved for the wheat harvest. In a few weeks, Frederick would begin threshing the wheat, and the chaff spit out by the hand-turned machine would fly out an open door overhanging the stable doors below.

Brian and Daniel climbed over the chest high wall into the straw. It was scratchy and warm; and scratchy or not, the pile made a nice bed. They stretched out and were simply quiet for a while.

"Wheat threshing starts soon," Brian said. Daniel "um-hmm'ed." "Frederick takes the wheat to Danner's mill, and then Danner takes the flour to Allentown. Mr. Kagen in Allentown ships it to Philadelphia on the river. Well, first to Easton, and then down the river."

Daniel wondered at this queer lesson on the life of threshed wheat, but he stayed quiet.

"I've talked to Mr. Danner. He's willing to take us to Allentown and pay us, to help transport the flour. He said that the riverboats can always use help, so it shouldn't be difficult to get a job on one. A one-way ticket to Philadelphia, and a little money in our pockets."

Daniel sat up and looked at his friend. "We? Our? What are you talking about?"

"I told you I'm getting out of here. Are you coming with me, or are you going to stay here and let your da treat you like he does? You're a man now! Act like one! Don't be such a coward!"

"Are you crazy? What makes you think they'll let us go? My ma won't, and I'm sure your sister won't let you go, either."

"Who said I'm gonna ask?"

"You have to! You can't just leave!"

"Watch me." Brian's voice was too calm, too self-assured.

"Brian, be serious."

"I am serious." He sat up and gestured out toward the yard and house. The two families had arrived. "They don't really want me here. Maybe they never did. I was supposed to live with Ma and Da somewhere nearby, not in the same house and on the same farm. Frederick doesn't need me. He has help. He can afford to hire more if he needs it. And Abby would certainly fill in when it comes to that."

"I'm not going."

"Come on, Daniel. Think of the adventure! Think of the fun!"

Daniel didn't need or want adventure or fun, unless it was with a pen in his hand. Brian's next argument proved he knew it too.

"You could finally be a newspaperman, Daniel. Do you think you'd ever work for a paper in this town? Or Allentown? No, not unless you learn German because I don't see you working for the *Bulletin*. Reading it is one thing, but writing for it would go against everything you believe," Brian finished, watching Daniel's face with excited anticipation.

Daniel tried to hide it, but Brian had struck home, and it showed on his face—a newspaperman in Philadelphia. Where Benjamin Franklin had published a paper so many years ago. Where news happened daily. Where he would find fame.

He nodded, just once, and Brian whooped and jumped over the wall.

Daniel followed more slowly. While Brian raced out of the barn door and down the bank, around to the front and across the yard, Daniel climbed slowly down the ladder, patting the neck of the animals as he passed. Frederick was successful: two cows, a calf and a yearling, two mares and four geldings, a coop full of chickens, and a separate pen for pigs. The animals, all except the chickens and pigs, resided in the barn, adding their warmth to the chill December air. Daniel walked down the aisle between the horses and cows and out the door.

Brian was coming back out of the house sent by the womenfolk to fetch Daniel. He motioned impatiently. His face glowed with the prospect of adventure, and Daniel wondered again what they were getting themselves into.

Them. Yes, Daniel would go along. For how long was still up in the air, as far as he was concerned. He was not yet ready to make a commitment to move to the city for the rest of his life. Much as he dreamed of being a newspaperman, he doubted he would find a job writing for a newspaper quickly, or even at all. What else could he do? Work in a tavern, obviously, but that was exactly what he was running from.

And there was the rub. Brian's accusation of cowardice was proven in the running, not in the staying. Running was easier than staying to fight the same battle day in and day out. Daniel did not want to own and run a tavern, and he was willing to leave everything he knew to avoid it, yet he knew that he might end up as a tavern keeper anyway.

The farmhouse smelled of ham, mashed potatoes, butter squash, stewed tomatoes from Mary's stockpile of jars, and warm bread. The two families, as well as the hired man, Paul, had gathered around the large table. They were already passing bowls and platters, chattering and laughing. As soon as Daniel took the empty seat between George and Abby, everyone joined hands, and Frederick said the blessing.

It was a happy time. The women talked about Abby's work on the young woman's trousseau, the children chattered about Christmas approaching and the first snowfall, and the men talked of the election and price of flour. Daniel enjoyed sitting in the middle of the table because he could join either adult conversation. He was as interested in Abby's work as he was in politics and economics.

"How do you like working with such expensive fabric, Abby?" Peggy asked.

"I'm afraid all the time. If I make a mistake, I can't afford to replace it."

"Tommy Schwartz threw a snowball and hit Hannah Diertz in the back of the head!" William said gleefully.

"Flour prices should be good this year," Paul said.

"I expect we'll top nearly $60," Frederick said happily.

"That well this year, huh?" Patrick asked.

"Danner told me you want to go with him to take the flour to Allentown," Frederick said suddenly, turning to Brian.

Daniel nearly dropped his fork. "Miss Wallington likes the color blue. She wants a dress in every shade imaginable!"

"Really?" Sarah asked. Blue was her favorite too.

"Yes, sir," Brian said, knowing he couldn't lie. He didn't meet Daniel's eyes across the table.

"Well, that will be an adventure for you," Frederick said, spearing a piece of ham. "We should start threshing soon. I know some farmers have already started."

"How's your wrist?" Paul asked.

Frederick shrugged. "No bother. I can use it just fine." He held up his left arm and rotated the wrist for all to see.

"Against my good advice," Mary called good-naturedly from across the table.

"Yes, dear." Frederick laughed, and Daniel let out a breath he didn't know he had been holding. Patrick would not have hesitated to reprimand him in front of company if he had caused an injury or lost work. Frederick was not Patrick, however, and Daniel wondered, not for the first time, if Brian knew how lucky he was.

The talk moved on to other things. Daniel met Brian's gaze across the table, and Brian winked. They all but had their parents' blessing. Well, Brian did, anyway.

Brian suddenly interrupted the conversation. "Excuse me, but I just wanted to say that I was hoping Daniel would come too."

Daniel almost threw his fork across the table. He glared. This was not the way to obtain his father's blessing! This was the way to have their whole plan razed right before their eyes.

All conversation stopped. Even the children were paying attention. Abby was looking at Daniel quizzically, then angrily, no doubt feeling hurt at being kept out of the secret. Peggy was looking concerned, eyes flitting from husband to son, and Daniel could not decipher if she was concerned about Daniel going or about Patrick's reaction to the idea. Frederick was smiling beneath his full beard. Everyone was waiting.

"Do you want to go, son?" Patrick asked, arms resting lightly next to his plate. He looked directly at Daniel, and Daniel couldn't interpret the expression in his eyes.

"I would like to go, Da," Daniel finally said. "I was going to ask permission. Brian spoke out of turn." He didn't look at his friend, but he could tell Brian was smiling.

Frederick boomed a great laugh. "Well, Patrick, it looks like we have two more men to feed! Perhaps, it's time we sent them out on their own."

Again, Daniel held his breath. This time he did look at Brian, and Brian's grin stretched to the moon and stars, it seemed. Slowly, Patrick nodded, taking a large gulp of water from his glass. When he placed the glass on the table, he nodded enthusiastically. He even smiled at Daniel.

Daniel floated through the rest of the meal. Mary always made a delicious meal, but he didn't taste a bit.

"We did it!" Brian crowed as they walked to the barn later. "We're really going! And by the time they realize we're not coming back, we'll be halfway to Philadelphia."

"Don't you feel the least bit dishonest?" Daniel asked.

Brian laughed. "Are you kidding? Frederick practically told us to go. 'Send them out on their own!' You heard him!"

Daniel nodded. He was beginning to share Brian's enthusiasm. For a while, they sat in the loft, discussing what to take, what Philadelphia would be like, who they would meet, what jobs they would find. As Brian rattled on, Daniel thought more about what they would be leaving behind.

"Hey!" The door slid open, and Abby stood against the gray sky, a dark red dress beneath a black cape billowing in the cold wind. She stepped forward and laboriously pulled the door shut behind her. She stalked across the floor, her mud-caked boots clomping an angry staccato on the floor. She stood outside the straw loft wall, hands on hips, foot tapping righteous indignation. "When were you going to tell me?" She glared first at one and then the other of them.

Brian laughed. Nothing could destroy his mood. "You're just a girl, Abby. We're men now. We have lives of our own."

"Come on, Abby, we would have told you," Daniel said. "Brian shouldn't have said it today."

"Well, when did you two decide this, huh? You could have told me then. And why didn't you ask me if I wanted to go too?"

"Abby, I just decided today after church," Daniel said. "Literally right before I came inside."

"Well, maybe I want to come too."

Brian and Daniel exchanged a wide-eyed glance. "What would you do in Allentown?" Brian hedged.

"You're not going to Allentown. You're going to Philadelphia, and there would be plenty for me to do."

"How did you know?" Daniel demanded incredulously.

Abby hooted with laughter. "I'm not stupid. There's no reason for *you* to go to Allentown, either. Allentown is a way station, and that's all. If you want to get away from backwoods nowhere land, Allentown isn't far enough."

Both young men gaped at her. Where did such a pretty girl get such a logical mind anyhow? They watched wordlessly as Abby gathered her skirts in one hand and clambered over the top of the wall, ending up head first in the straw, her hoops an upside-down bell above her.

"So your dad's reaction was a surprise, don't you think?" she asked Daniel. Her anger had fully dissipated. She righted herself and leaned against the wall.

"Yeah, kind of."

"Kind of? He said you should go. He didn't make some sort of comment about you staying to work in the tavern or what a waste of time it would be to fill your head with dreams of writing for a newspaper."

"Yeah, but they think we're coming back," Brian said matter-of-factly.

Abby stared at one, then the other, the full weight of truth finally dawning on her. They weren't coming back. Oh, how she wanted to go too!

"Well, write to me, all right?" she said, looking at Daniel.

"So you won't try to come," he said softly.

She shook her head. "I can't. I have a trousseau to create."

"And that's exactly what you want to do," Daniel said, hoping to kindle some excitement in his friend for what she had been given even here in backwoods nowhere land. Abby just nodded.

The three young people stayed in the barn until Paul came to do the evening chores. He climbed the ladder to get hay, and he was surprised to stumble upon them. Realizing how late it was, Daniel stood, brushed himself off, and reached out a hand for Abby. She stood unceremoniously, cursing her now misshapen hoops. Brian climbed over the wall and down the ladder, offering to help Paul, which stunned Paul to no end.

Daniel walked Abby to the house. "I'll definitely write to you. Maybe after things settle down a bit, you can come with my family for a visit. You couldn't come alone," he added.

"What do you mean, 'when things settle down'?"

The darkness twilight was deepening. The warm fire in the kitchen puffed smoke out the chimney. The lamps glowed happily through the windows. Daniel stomped his feet to keep the blood circulating.

"When they realize Mr. Danner came back without us, they'll be angry." He had been gazing out into the distance, but now he looked down at her. Her cheeks were red from the cold, and she shivered. His own hands were buried in his armpits. "Don't let them come after us," he pleaded. "Maybe we'll come back. Maybe the city won't be what we hope it will be."

"It will be everything you want it to be, and you won't be coming back," Abby said. "I won't let them drag you home. And I'll come to visit with or without an escort." The cold finally getting to her, she said good night and hurried to the house.

Daniel walked home in the dark. The stars were bright above him. The moon was round and full, a glowing face in the dark blanket of sky. The stars twinkled like fireflies in summer, but it was too cold for fireflies. Daniel hurried his steps toward town.

The tavern was not open for business Sunday. The family was gathered in the small sitting room, a warm fire blazing and a few lamps burning. Peggy and Kathleen were sewing in the corner, and Meg was crocheting a delicate piece of lace. William and George were lying on the floor, a checkerboard between them. George seemed to be winning, but somehow William always pulled ahead to triumph, even though he was a year younger. Patrick was reading aloud from *Pilgrim's Progress*.

Patrick looked up from the book and took off his spectacles. "Where did you disappear to?"

"Brian and I were talking in the barn."

"I'm glad you're going to Allentown. I would like you to visit a tavern there, see a friend of mine," Patrick said. As Daniel's good mood sank, Patrick simply put his glasses back on and continued to read. He had been wearing spectacles to read to the family for as long as Daniel could remember. Funny—he would miss that.

Daniel went upstairs and returned with his journal and pen and ink. He sat at the secretary near the women's corner and began to write. He did not worry about anyone reading over his shoulder. And anyway, writing down here in the warmth was worth the risk.

> I agreed to go with Brian. We told the folks we are going to Allentown with Mr. Danner. Mr. Danner actually said something to Mr. Weimer. Somehow, though, Abby figured out the truth. She was hurt that we didn't include her in our plans.
>
> It hurts me that we can't include her anymore. The three of us have grown up together. Abby has always been one of us. In dresses, of course, but still one of us. Kathleen is the same age as Abby, but she has never been one of us. She is too feminine and delicate. Abby is willing to get dirty and sore and do something that matters. Really, that's all Abby wants to do: "something that matters."
>
> If Brian and I can be considered men now, then Abby must be considered a woman. A lady. I have noticed that she has started wearing her hair up, and on special occasions, she is wearing those infernal hoopskirts that make walking next to her so difficult and that make her look like a bell. She

walks demurely when she must and sips tea and nibbles cake, instead of running and gulping and chomping. I'm not sure if I like her better this way or not.

I am sorry we will have to leave her behind. She would love Philadelphia, I think. She could be a lady and still earn her own way. She could open her own shop, and the three of us could live above it. I could read to her what I have written as she sews. I don't know what Brian would do. I'm not sure he knows or cares.

I was watching the stars as I walked home tonight. They glow and twinkle, like the morning dew on a field. They are so far away, and we never can get any closer. But Philadelphia has always seemed just as far, and now we can get closer. We are truly going!

Da will be furious when Mr. Danner returns without us. I hope it doesn't hurt Ma too much. Perhaps I should leave a letter with Abby to give to her after we go. Yes, I shall do that. And I will write to them, and to Abby, when we arrive there. The more I think about it, the more excited I get.

Chapter 3

PHILADELPHIA

Brian sat in the corner of the pub, sipping a beer and listening to the blarney being blown. In the three weeks since Michael Maloney had bought him his first drink, Brian had become accustomed to the aid of drink for camaraderie and laughter. Brian looked around at these new friends, men who left work each night tired, dirty, and poor and sat around with fellows drinking whiskey or a pint of beer and laughing as if they had never been tired a day in their lives. Brian liked these people. They were his people, Irish, not proud and stingy Germans. From the very first time he sat down in the Southwark pub, he felt like one of them, accepted and even required to join in. The stories and laughter made the dingy, dark pub seem warm and festive.

Daniel didn't like the place. He had said it was not like his pa's tavern where the lamps cast a warm and welcoming glow into the street, and the men rarely drank themselves into a stupor. Here at the Inn at Kensington, the lights were low and the laughter loud as the men drank away their cares with the last pennies they had. Daniel seldom joined Brian and Michael at the Inn.

"You started a job today, young Brian O'Bern?" The speaker was a clean-shaven redhead who wore his tweed cap at a challenging angle. He had a red nose, bloodshot eyes, and raw knuckles. Everyone called him Red O'Toole.

"Yes, sir," Brian replied.

"And how was it, young Brian?"

Brian wrinkled his nose disdainfully. "I'm working in Mr. Harding's stables. I'm the under stable, boy. I muck stalls and rub saddles and groom horses."

"And how did you come by such a *luxurious* post, my young friend?" The sarcasm was met with laughter. Someone called for another pint.

"My friend Daniel got the job the first week we got here. Mr. Harding is a newspaperman, He owns the *Philadelphia Inquirer*. When his driver was hurt last week, Daniel drove him to the office. He wants to be a newspaperman too. One thing led to another. He took a job as a typesetter, and I took his stable job."

That wasn't exactly how it happened. There was a lot of luck involved but a good bit of courage on Daniel's part to speak up and introduce himself to such a one as Mr. Harding. On one hand, Brian was grateful for the job, and the introduction Daniel had set up. But the fact remained: Brian got what Daniel didn't want.

Brian switched from beer to whiskey.

The man next to him on the bench, Mick Kelly, slapped him on the back. "Welcome to the ranks of Downstairs Irish!"

"Hear! Hear!"

"Cheers!"

Downstairs Irish. Yes, that's what he'd become. He'd joined the ranks of domestic servants not allowed into the upper floors of the fancy houses where they served. He took to the status of the oppressed as easily as he took to the drinking.

Brian laughed uproariously at the end of a yarn one of the men had been telling. These Irishmen never lost their sense of humor, their ability to tell a grand story, or their love of music and good food and drink. Their lot in life had pushed them down, first in Ireland, and now in this quickly growing metropolis, but they refused to stay down.

"You've got the gift of blarney, David O'Leary," someone shouted in a slurred brogue. "A regular shanachie!"

Brian recognized the word that had been used to describe his father, recognized it as Gaelic, but didn't know what it meant. "Michael Maloney, what's a shawn-a-key?"

Although he had spoken in what he thought was a conspiratorial whisper, the noise in the Inn was silenced. Michael and everyone else stared at him in disbelief.

"Where are you from again, boy? Northern Ireland, you say?" someone asked.

"I was born there, sure, but I've been in America since I was four," Brian answered, not sure if he was explaining or defending himself. "County Sligo." He dug the memory from somewhere deep, not really knowing he knew such a thing.

"That's not Northern Ireland."

"It is, I've seen a map," Brian insisted, again wondering where this information had come from.

"It's in the north of Ireland, sure, but Northern Ireland is where the Protestants are."

We're Protestants. But instinctively, he knew—perhaps from the clear disdain with which the words were said—to keep that bit of truth to himself.

"And your proud Irish folk never told you what a shanachie is?"

"My ma and da died before we left Ireland, and I've been living with my sister and her family. She married a German farmer," he said, and the sad and knowing looks offered sympathy and understanding.

"Shanachies, Brian O'Bern, are fantastic storytellers, the most respected men and women in the world. Given succor and good whiskey and a place to lay his head just for the price of a story, and the listeners feel like they're cheatin' the man," Michael said in his thick rolling brogue.

"Ah," Brian said. "The story goes, so they tell me, that my da was a shanachie. When he decided to come to America, we stopped at a pub in Galway. Him and Ma and me." He took a sip of whiskey, swallowed over the choking lump in his throat. "I remember sitting on his lap while he told a story in the main room downstairs. Someone came to whisper in his ear."

The listeners waited eagerly for what came next, but he couldn't get it out. "Go *on*, boy."

"Someone came to whisper in his ear. Ma was upstairs. She was dead."

"Oh, lad, I'm sorry."

"Pegeen, another whiskey for young Brian!"

"And another for me, too, pretty Pegeen!"

Brian continued slowly, quietly, pictures running through his mind. He was never sure if he actually remembered, or if he had made it up so that he would have *something* to remember. "Da left me downstairs with strangers. They took good care of me, but I never saw either of them again. He died that night too."

"And how did you get to America, my boy?"

"The pub owners. They sold up and brought me over with their kids. It was Daniel's family, actually." He looked around the circle. "Mrs. Kelly told me it was because Da was a shanachie that they did it."

Nods and raised glasses all around. Red reached over to clap him on the back. "Aye, young Brian. 'Twas just the kind of thing ye do for a shanachie's young bairn."

The moment of silence lasted barely long enough for a swallow, then the crowd demanded a tale from the son of a shanachie. The whiskey fortified him as he spun a convoluted tale of water nymphs and sprites, and the ending brought cheers and laughter, and someone bought him another.

By the end of the evening, when the gaslights along the streets had been lit and streetcars had been put away for the night, Brian and Michael walked toward home. They held each other up, but it was something like the pot calling the kettle black; any passersby would have wondered which was drunker. They walked the three blocks to the small flat Michael and his wife Katie occupied.

Michael and Katie had each come to Philadelphia with their parents, Michael and the Maloneys in 1844 and Katie with the Fitzgeralds in 1847. They had married in '53, and their small apartment was now crowded with jostling redheaded children, five of them: Alice, Ellen, Tommy, Michael Seamus, called Seamus, and baby Sean. Having bumped into the two teenage boys on their first cold morning in the city, Michael had opened his home and his heart to them, and the floor in the bedroom was even more crowded.

Daniel and Katie were sitting at the table when Michael and Brian came in. Katie was mending a frock that Ellen had torn while Daniel read to her from the Bible. Although she owned the heavy black leather-bound Bible, Katie had never read it or anything else, and having someone to read it to her was worth the two extra mouths to feed. She hummed and rocked as Daniel spoke slowly and clearly.

The door banged, and the two at the table started, staring at the bleary-eyed man and boy before them. Michael tottered over to his wife, gave her a kiss, and asked if there was any dinner left.

"Any dinner left," she repeated, not leaving her comfortable rocking chair. "I think not, Michael Maloney, and it's a wonder we have anything to eat at all with you drinkin' the money as fast as ye earn it."

"Ach," he said with a wave of his hand. He lifted the lid of the pot on the stove and grinned at what he saw, a thick stew, and the biscuits were in the oven, right where he knew they would be. Daniel and Brian had learned rather quickly that this was an almost daily squabble. Michael gave his wife a handful of change from his pocket, what was left of his daily wage.

"Did ye know, Katie darlin', that our Brian here is the son of shanachie?" The tall red-haired man handed a bowl of stew and a few biscuits to Brian, who sat sheepishly at the table, for Katie was now staring.

Michael ate and related to Katie the family history that Brian had shared at the pub. Daniel added his knowledge of what had transpired in Galway so many years ago, as well as the trip across the sea. Katie complimented Brian by calling him a true Irishman. When their overcooked meal was finished, she shuffled Daniel and Brian off to bed and motioned for Michael to stay with her for a while.

"Michael Maloney, ye should take better care of the boy," Katie whispered, her voice barely audible above the creak of the rocking chair.

"What do ye mean, Katie?"

"He's but sixteen and run away from home, no doubt. Now, now, don't interrupt me. I'm not saying ye should be sendin' him home. I'm sayin' ye should be watchin' out for him. He's too young to be comin' home drunk every night."

"Like ye said, Katie, he's sixteen. Old enough, I say."

"Your brother Sean is but seventeen, and still livin' with your ma. Would ye have him comin' home drunk?" Brian opened the door a crack and saw her shake her pretty red head. "It's not fittin', I tell ye." Brian's pallet was nearest the door between living area and bedroom. Brian forced himself to lie still and quiet, although after a few minutes, he wanted to bust out of bed yelling.

"Sean is takin' care of Ma, that's why."

"And are ye takin' care of us, then, Michael Maloney?" She shook her head again.

"I do take care of my family, woman," he growled.

She put down her mending, leaned over and kissed his cheek. "Ye do, Michael Maloney, and ye do a fine job. But young Brian is learnin' from ye a way to . . . to I don't know what. Are ye drownin' your sorrows, husband?"

"Not much to drown."

Katie smiled. "Ach, ye be filled with blarney, ye be. There's plenty of want in this house, plenty of half-empty bellies and sad faces."

"But I've got ye, Mrs. Maloney," Michael said softly. He pulled her out of her chair to sit on his lap.

"So ye have. Ye be a good man, and it's proud I am to be ye wife. But I worry about the young boy. He's as hotheaded as anyone from County Meath, and he'll get himself in trouble if he's not careful. He doesn't know how to be careful. He needs ye to show him how," she finished.

"Such a mother ye are. I'll try, Katie, but I'm not sure he'll listen to any motherin', or fatherin', either. That's probably what he's run from."

"I know you're right." She returned to her sewing, only to fold the dress and lay it on the table. "But I worry just the same."

Brian watched as the couple turned down the lamp and moved to their own bed in the front room. He gently closed the door. For a while, he lay in the dark, a bit of light from the gas street lamps pervading the small room.

Worried, was she? Michael was right. He didn't need mothering, and he wouldn't stick around if Katie insisted on treating him like a child. He had come to Philadelphia to make his own way, and he would do it!

Brian was at the carriage house just after dawn one bright cold day, with a pounding headache and a stomach full of oatmeal that might not stay there. Mr. Deary, the head driver who had completely recovered from the streetcar accident, looked at him with poorly concealed contempt, knowing that Brian was suffering a hangover. Brian set to work immediately.

As the under stable hand, Brian's duties were labor-intensive, but it wasn't too bad. He enjoyed animals, and somehow, he managed to find time to sit on the hay bales or in the shade by the door at least three or four times a day.

Before the stalls could be cleaned, the four matching white geldings had to be hitched to the grand carriage that took Mr. Harding to work. The harness jingled with small bells as the horses stomped in anticipation. The silvery manes were tightly braided, one of Mr. Deary's chores, with bright blue ribbons throughout. The tails, too, were plaited with blue ribbons, creating a regal look. Tall white plumes danced in the breeze above the majestic heads. Mr. Deary took pride in how smartly the four horses stepped out.

Brian could see his breath. His fingers fumbled with the cold harness. The horses stomped and whinnied in impatience.

"Get a move on, son," Mr. Deary said from the stable doorway where he was adjusting his driving uniform. "It's time for me to take the carriage around front."

Mr. Deary's voice was harsh and unforgiving. The man was British and took pride in his long employment history that included working in the stables of a duke or a lord; Brian never paid much attention. The old man, with a full head of silver hair that, along with the blue livery, looked like one of the horses. He was stout and reminded Brian of a blue barrel, but he was still able to do his job well, and he attempted to keep Brian from shirking his.

After Mr. Deary left, Brian sat in the warm stable on a bale of hay beneath the windows. He noticed the panes—imagine glass panes in a stable!—were dirty, and he speculated about how to get out of that inevitable chore. Soon, he had stretched out on the bales and closed his eyes. He breathed deeply of the sweetness, listened to the rustle and chomp of oats and hay, felt the warmth of the beasts inside the bright stable. His head pounded, and he wanted to vomit. For three weeks, he had been doing this. He knew it was the drink, but he didn't care enough to change his already solidified habits.

The stable door slid open; the noise startling him into wakefulness. A beautiful young woman stood silhouetted against the morning sun. She was tall, dressed in a dark green riding habit, the long skirt draped elegantly over a thin arm. Everything about her was elegant, from the blond hair tucked neatly into a chignon beneath her tall riding hat and the piercing green eyes behind the veil, down to the tips of the brown leather boots peaking from beneath the skirt, and encompassing the delightful figure in between. Brian stood up hastily and almost fell flat on his face from the wave of dizziness that swept over him.

"Boy, I'm going riding today," the elegant voice attached to the elegant figure said. "Put the side saddle on India." She tugged on her kid gloves as she spoke, never looking at Brian.

"Yes, miss," he said. He headed toward the two horses still left in their stalls. One was a tall black gelding, shiny and perfect in length of leg and arch of neck. The horse's eyes were bright as he stood placidly chewing oats, barely concealing an unbreakable nature. There was not a spot of white on him. Only clean lines and regal manner.

The other horse was a bay mare, not quite so tall, with white socks and black mane and tail. This horse appeared a bit older, a tad less fit, a smidge less elegant. Still, the back was straight, the neck beautifully arched, and the legs strong. And definitely for riding, not plowing. A plow horse would not even be allowed to set hoof inside this glass-paned horse palace. Brian took the side saddle from its hook and walked toward the bay.

"Boy," the young woman said sharply, and he stopped. "That's Duchess. India is the black." Without a word, Brian straightened his course and opened the stall of the tall black. "You're new," the woman said flatly. "I hope you'll learn quickly how things are done here."

Brian was quickly becoming disillusioned; her beauty of face did not compare with her harsh attitude. He did not answer as he cinched the girth.

"Are you Irish?" she asked, then answered her own question. "Of course, you are. Low class. Well, someone must muck out the stalls, I suppose. Might as well be the Irish. Better than the Negroes, anyway."

Brian bristled. Some unexplainable, unnerving feeling of anger welled within him when he was compared with the Negroes. To be compared to them—he brushed the thoughts out of his mind as he patted the horse on the neck.

Brian led the black out of the stall over to where the young woman still stood. Suddenly, a tall darkly clad gentleman appeared beside her, leading a black that was neither as tall nor as perfect. The young woman smiled up at the man, who was just as refined in his black riding coat and tan breeches, tall hat, and kid gloves. He held a quirt in one hand, the reins in the other.

"Miss Harding, are you ready?" he asked. He never glanced at Brian, although he did look at the horse.

"Yes, Mr. Richards. Will you give me a leg up?"

The man wrinkled his nose in disdain. "I don't want to get dirty, my dear. Let the boy do it." To Brian, "No funny business, boy. Help her mount, and that's it."

Without a word, without a second thought, Brian laced his fingers together for the young woman to step on. He gently hoisted her into the saddle, watched as she arranged one leg over the pommel, observed as she positioned her skirts over her legs. Without a word or a backward glance, the elegant young couple was out the door and gone. Brian could hear the woman's tinkling laugh as her long-legged gelding reached the cobblestoned street first.

Not soon after, Mr. Deary arrived with the carriage and found Brian on a bale of hay with his head in his hands. He removed a glove and put the hand on Brian's head. Brian looked up, a look of pain clear on his face.

"What's wrong, lad? Are you ill?"

Brian shook his head. "No, sir. I'll get right to work."

Brian worked harder that day than he had ever worked. He exercised diligence in mucking the stalls and putting down fresh straw. He conscientiously polished the tack, using small careful circles to rub saddle soap into the soft leather. He rubbed down the four white geldings, then Miss Harding's black. Mr. Deary did not mention the windows, but he got a bucket of water and a jar of vinegar from the scullery maid and washed them anyway.

Michael arrived to walk with him as Mr. Deary was locking the stable door in preparation of retiring in his abode above. Brian was standing against the wall in the darkness, trying to keep warm in the cold February night. The temperature had dropped significantly from the morning. The ring around the moon promised more snow.

"Brian O'Bern, what are ye doin' skulkin' in the shadows?" Michael demanded good-naturedly. Brian fell in step beside him. He didn't want to go to the tavern tonight, but he didn't want to go home either. Still, it was too cold to just walk around.

Michael kept up a steady stream of conversation as they walked down the street. He greeted every man and woman he passed, joking with the men and tipping his hat to the ladies. Soon enough, they arrived at the bustle and hubbub of the Inn, already filled with laughter and tales, the men already filled with joy and drink.

Michael pushed their way through the crowd, calling happily to each man. The bar maid, a short pretty lass named Pegeen, teased him as she passed with three mugs clutched in her hand. She smiled at Brian, too, but he didn't notice her.

Brian barely sipped his beer. It tasted bitter tonight, and he wondered if the proprietor had run out of the good stuff. The genial noise around him did not improve his mood. Finally, someone noticed that the young man was far from the crowd.

"Hey, son, ye all right?"

Brian barely nodded, didn't even look toward the voice, just took another sip. Someone made a joke, and they all laughed. Michael leaned closer to his companion's elbow, asked him what was vexing him.

"I'm Irish," Brian muttered bitterly.

The crowd laughed. "Of course, ye are!"

"Better to be Irish than anythin' else, I say!"

"Ye should be proud, boy!"

Brian shook his head dejectedly. As his story poured out, the crowd grew quiet and then heated. Finally, the group settled.

"Lad, 'tis a sorrowful thing, but it's the truth of it. Irishmen aren't thought much of in this town."

"Or anywhere else on earth, it seems. Not even on our own isle."

"Don't let it get ye down, lad."

The advice and goodwill cheered him a bit, and he smiled, but the deep hurt remained. When talk turned to other things, he whispered to Michael that he was going home.

The night had grown colder, or perhaps it was simply a shocking contrast to the warmth of the Inn. The stars above him twinkled so close, he could almost touch them. For a startling moment, he missed his old life. He missed the wide-open fields of Millerstown, the warm farmhouse, the family. But it wasn't home anymore, maybe never had been. He began walking toward the apartment house, hands tucked deep in his coat pockets, cap pushed down far on his head.

Brian heard the *clop-clop* of horse hooves on cobbles, and he paused to look up. A police officer sat tall in the saddle, obviously not happy with coming upon a lonely figure on this empty night. He maneuvered his tall horse in front of Brian, blocking his way and the gaslight, and Brian instinctively took a step back.

"Where are you going, boy?" the police officer demanded.

"Home, sir. Three blocks from here," Brian answered clearly and solidly. He was wary and yet not disrespectful. He had every right to be here.

"You don't sound Irish," the officer muttered almost to himself. "What are you doing in Southwark, boy?"

"I am Irish, sir," Brian said flatly. "I live three blocks from here. I stopped at the pub for a pint, and now I'm going home for dinner. May I go?"

The officer said something about getting home quickly and moved aside to let Brian pass. Brian was aware of the stare piercing through his back as he walked away. He did not look over his shoulder as he rounded the corner, and as he turned into the alley, he increased his pace.

Katie and the children were still eating when Brian arrived in the third-floor apartment. She looked up in surprise. She ladled beans and potatoes onto another plate and set it before Brian. He thanked her and began to eat.

"Mrs. Kelly brought more washing today," Alice said after a moment of industrious eating.

Brian lifted his head at the familiar name.

Katie saw his look. "You look surprised, young Brian."

He replied, "Mrs. Kelly . . . Daniel's mother?"

Katie chuckled. "There are many named Mrs. Kelly hereabout. The Mrs. Kelly that Alice was speakin' of is the landlady. She gathers wash of the single menfolk and brings it here for us to wash. It brings in a bit o' money."

Brian nodded and returned to his potatoes. They were good, lumpy and smothered in butter and sprinkled with a bit of salt. Somehow, Katie Maloney managed to take the ordinary and make it special.

"Ma, may I have some more, please?" little Seamus asked.

Katie put a red and work-roughened hand on the little boy's head. She spoke softly, with a smile in her voice, if not on her face. "No, dear one. We must save some for your da, and for Daniel."

"Where is Daniel?" Brian asked, tucking into his second helping, wondering if he should spoon some onto Seamus's plate.

"Tonight, he has to put the paper to sleep," Katie replied. Brian nodded. Once a week, Daniel stayed late to set type for the next day's edition. Brian had no idea how many typesetters there were, but they took turns.

Katie soon sent the children to bed. She noticed the handful of change that Brian had placed on the table, and she discreetly put it in her apron pocket with a nod of thanks. She sat with another bit of inexhaustible mending. She set to rocking, her soft voice humming an engaging tune.

"Did Michael send ye home?"

"No, I left. I didn't feel like drinking."

"Did something happen today?"

Brian paused before he answered. He told her about his day, from the elegant and haughty Miss Harding and her snobbish beau, to the good-hearted Irishmen in the pub to the police officer on the street. Katie nodded knowingly. "'Tis a shame that ye had to experience it, but 'twas bound to happen sooner or later, I guess. The men in the pub were right. Irish aren't looked on with kindness here, or anywhere else, and we must get used to it."

"Why? Why must we get used to it?" He pounded the table, and she shushed him, glancing to toward the bedroom. He continued more softly. "We shouldn't be treated this way."

Katie sat in silence, and Brian had no way of reading her mind. He had no way of knowing that she thought fearfully of the group within which her husband moved, a group that sought freedom for the Irish in Ireland, a group that raised funds to raise up an army to rebel against the hated English. Katie was afraid of this group. She could not see it, hear it, taste it, or smell it, but she knew it was there, and she knew it threatened the safety of her husband and her family.

Brian listened peacefully as Katie began again to hum. As she rocked and sewed, he lay on the uncomfortable, raggedy sofa, a pale green one with missing buttons and a chipped wooden armrest. The pillows under his head were examples of Alice's and Ellen's handiwork, pretty needlepoints on a black background—one a collection of red roses, and the other a Celtic knot. Before he knew it, he was asleep.

Michael entered the room and kissed Katie on the lips. She motioned for him to keep quiet. As her husband sat down to eat, she pulled her chair close to his elbow, but when he reached over for a more passionate kiss, she pushed him away.

"Young Brian had a rough day," she whispered. "His mistress, and then everthin' ye men told him in the pub, and the copper, stopped him on his way home."

"A copper, not a Patty," Michael said.

"Apparently not. The copper gave him a hard time."

"Ach," Michael said through a mouthful of potatoes. He glanced at the sleeping young man. "What did the copper want?"

"He saw a young man walking the Irish quarter after dark and alone," Katie said. "What other motive did he need?" She put a strong hand on his arm and waited until he put his fork on his plate and looked at her. "He's ripe for the pickin', that one, but don't ye be tellin' him about the Fenians," she pleaded.

"And why shouldn't I? We need young men like that."

"He's not a man, as much as he wants to think he is. He's a boy. Just a boy, and mixin' him up in that mess will ruin his life."

"How can freein' our beloved Ireland from the tramp and turmoil of the British be a means of ruinin' a life? Especially the life of a poor Irish lad who has never been told of his glorious homeland?" Michael demanded angrily. Yet, despite his heated ire, his voice was low.

Michael had pledged his life and finances to help the Fenian Brotherhood only two years ago during a rally in New York City, which he attended on a "business trip," although no business with which he had ever been associated would take him to New York. He had never revealed to Katie the truth of that trip and never would. At that October 1858 rally, at Tammany Hall, John O'Mahoney had gathered followers and fighters for the new wave of Irish liberators. O'Mahoney and "Captain" James Stevens had been part of the Young Irelanders on the Isle, but had been exiled, and so came to their American brothers for support and power.

Each week on Friday, Michael allowed himself one less drink at the pub, as did many others, for with that little bit of change. They paid their weekly 10¢ dues to the Philadelphia Circle of the Fenian Brotherhood. Michael had risen in the last two years to the rank of sergeant. After Brian had left the pub, Michael and the other sergeants had discussed making Brian a private in the organization, and Michael had even declared that he would pay the initiation fee of $1 himself.

But how to tell Katie that? As wife and mother, she worried. As a good Irishwoman, she loved her country. But she loved her family more, and she allowed Michael the space to follow the Brotherhood only as long as her security and children were not threatened. She might not even agree to that if she knew he was paying money to the group. Michael understood that. Eviction was as hard or harder on womenfolk than on the Irishmen, for the men could fight, even though it might mean death or jail, and then the women were left to fend for themselves. Some women became staunch supporters of the Fenian movement, and some vowed simply to protect their own. That was Katie's stance. And beyond the physical danger that the enemies of the Fenians might bring down on their heads, a $1 fee was more than they could afford; it would be taking food directly from the bellies of her babies, and he knew she would not agree. And unlike the 10¢ dues, he wouldn't be able to hide the initiation fee.

Michael finished his meal, then sighed and looked his beautiful wife in the face. "All right, Katie darlin', I won't mention it to him. But I think he'll pick up on some things, bein' the smart boy he is. And if he asks me, I'll tell him all."

Katie accepted the terms of peace and kissed her husband lightly. "Agreed."

As Katie and Michael lay down to sleep, Michael thought of John O'Mahoney, presently in Ireland to finalize their plans for armed insurrection. His thoughts drifted to the news on the streets, news that all Philadelphians were debating, whether they were Irish or German, Jewish or Catholic, white or free black. Another armed insurrection might be forthcoming now that South Carolina and others had seceded. Michael wondered if that would help or hinder the plans of the Brotherhood.

The cold February days passed, and Brian continued his work in the Harding stables, still mesmerized by Miss Harding's beauty and galled by her behavior. Daniel continued his work at the paper, excited about the work that he loved. Brian's loathing for his job and Daniel's passion for his own continued to drive a wedge into their friendship. They no longer spent time together. Leisure time was scarce, but Daniel talked about friends Brian didn't know, and

Daniel did not want to hear about the time Brian spent in the pub. In their separate thoughts, they each waited for the next blow of the hammer to split the block of wood completely.

One unusually warm March Saturday, Daniel found Brian walking lazily home after the workday was done. Daniel jogged to catch up. The sidewalks were crowded with women, some laughing and chattering, some dragging children who clung to their dingy skirts, and some with the haggard and worn look of life on their faces. The streets were filled with horses, buggies, and carriages, moving at a slow pace that annoyed the wealthy passengers and still-frightened pedestrians as they crossed dung-filled cobbled streets while carrying produce and packages.

When Daniel caught up, he said, "Hey."

"Hey." Brian looked bright-eyed but tired.

"Tomorrow is Sunday," Daniel said unnecessarily.

"So it is."

After a moment of quiet walking amid the heaving mass of pedestrians, Daniel said, "I was thinking of writing a letter to Ma. Have you written to your family lately?"

Brian turned on his friend, but the look of anger dissipated. He shrugged. "No. What is there to say?"

"You know, Brian, I've written three or four letters since we've been here. They have our address. They know where we are. They haven't come to drag us home yet. I don't think they will."

Brian wasn't quite sure how that made him feel: happy that they trusted him or sad that they didn't care enough to check up on him? Pleased that they were giving him his space or distressed that they might be better off without him? He didn't want to write a letter because he didn't want to know the truth.

"I'll tell them all about my job and the city and the excitement," Daniel persisted. After a moment in quiet contemplation, he said, "Planting will start soon."

"No, harrowing comes first," Brian said automatically. Strange that he would even care to correct the mistake.

"I wonder how Abby is doing with her sewing. Didn't she say that the wedding would be in March?" Daniel asked as they climbed the steps of the tenement stoop. Three small children sat playing on the stoop with wooden tops that someone inevitably had to chase, as one or the other flew off the edge.

Brian again shrugged. Abby did not figure much in his thinking.

Trying to continue a conversation that was painfully one-sided, Daniel said, "People are saying war is coming."

In the dark and fetid stairwell of the tenement, with noise emanating from closed doors, Brian stopped with one foot on a higher step and one hand on the grimy rail. "I don't care about the war. Just stop talking about it."

Daniel's hackles went up like a stray dog being teased with a stick. "I don't understand why you resist it so much."

"The liberation of Ireland means more to me than the stupid war here." And the realization of the truth of it surprised Brian as much as it surprised Daniel. Without another word or glance over his shoulder to see that Daniel was following, Brian rushed up the stairs and into the apartment.

Daniel did not see Brian much that evening. Brian went to the pub with Michael. It was just as well because his behavior was anything but agreeable. Daniel sat with the family to eat dinner, and though he enjoyed the children's chatter, he was impatient to sit down to write the letter home. The two little boys washed the dishes, while the girls sat down to work on a quilt together. Katie's lilting voice drifted through the apartment, and Daniel fetched his writing instruments.

March 16, 1861

Dear Ma,

I am well, and I hope you are well. The city is full of excitement. I enjoy my walk to the publishing house every morning, with the rumble of wheels passing in the semi-darkness and farmers coming to town to sell their wares. They don't have much to sell yet, mostly just canned food and meats.

I imagine that the farmers back home are preparing to plant. Brian and I were talking about it just today. I don't think he has written to his folks. Please tell Mr. and Mrs. Weimer that he is doing fine. He is working in the stable where I started out, and he has made lots of friends. He is with them now, as a matter of fact.

I have not yet had opportunity to write an article or story for Mr. Harding. Honestly, I have not seen him since the day I drove him to the publishing house. I work in the basement of the publishing house, setting type with four other young men, all under twenty years of age, and all of us are eager to be newspapermen.

Jack Harrison has lived in Philadelphia all of his life, and he can't imagine living anywhere else. He is more inspired than I am; I foresee him composing novels like the great Charles Dickens.

Jack has shared with me Dickens' new weekly, entitled "All the Year Round." I encourage Jack to write, but being one in a large household in a small apartment means he does not have much opportunity. I am in comparable circumstances.

Brian and I are living with an Irish family, like I told you before. Michael Maloney and his wife Katie are kind, God-fearing people, and she has taken care of us like a mother since we arrived. Right now she is singing a beautiful Irish tune that never fails to remind me of you, Ma.

Do not fret, Mother. I am exceptional in spirit and in health.

Please give Pa and the children my best and remember me always as

Your loving Son,
Daniel

Daniel reread the letter, wondering if he were doing the Weimers a disservice in covering over Brian's conduct. He tried not to, for he knew his tendency was to worry about unfixable things, but when Brian returned home from the pub drunk as a sailor more than twice a week, there was reason to worry. He couldn't tell his mother that; she would tell Mary, and that would bring the whole of the Lehigh Valley down on their heads.

Daniel sealed the envelope, addressed the letter, and put it aside. Taking out another creamy sheet of paper, an indulgence at a shop on Market Street earlier that day, Daniel sat for a moment to think. This letter was the first he would write to Abby since January, and it would be made difficult by the space of time between.

March 16, 1861

Dear Abby,

I hope and pray this letter finds you well. I have thought of you often, and I fervently hope you have not forgotten me. I am sure you have wanted to forget me, or hate me, or hurt me, for leaving you behind. I hope in time you will be able to forgive me and understand why Brian and I had to leave.

Pa and I have never gotten along; that's obvious. For the past year, affairs have been getting worse. He wants for me a life I cannot live. Abby, I have found the existence I can endure, and more than endure – here I can thrive. I have an excellent position as type-setter at the "Philadelphia Inquirer," working with other men like myself who desire to be newspapermen someday.

I have continued to write in my journal each day. Perhaps someday I will be able to share it with you. I wish I could share with you all of the excitement of the city, all of the joy in this home, which Brian and I share with an Irish family. I must tell you, in all honesty, that I was not as excited as Brian to come to the city. I would have been content to remain in Millerstown if Da would allow me to live my own life.

But now that I am here, I am dedicated to this city and these people and this life. Philadelphia was scary, at first, with all of the tall buildings and so many people! There are people here who speak every language under the sun, it seems, much like I imagine Babel might have been.

Every day I meet men and women of rank, or rather, I see them passing in their fine carriages. Every day I bump into men and women on the street who might be butlers and ladies' maids, men and women who speak with accents or very little English. Every day I see Africans, or their descendants, anyway, most of whom I imagine were born free.

At least, in the two months that I have been here, I have managed to stare a little less. I would be delighted if you could visit sometime. Perhaps your ma and mine will come with you. It is an exciting place to be!

Give my best to your family. Assure them that Brian is well. I have enclosed my address, and I hope you will find the time to write.

Perhaps, though, you are too busy sewing, and if that is the case, I thank God above that you, too, have found the life you have dreamed of.

Remember me as
Your Kind and Dearest Friend,
Daniel

That letter, too, was as truthful as he could make it, but not as truthful as it could be. The letters would have to lay on the small writing table by the door until Monday. Tomorrow was Sunday, and Daniel had been informed that tomorrow would be the biggest gala of the year, at least in the Irish quarter. Tomorrow was St. Patrick's Day.

The streets swarmed with people, like bees shaken from their hive. The churches were packed from wall to wall, and by the time the family arrived, there was no pew with enough room for all. Brian, Daniel, and young Tommy Maloney sat on a bench along the left wall, squeezed between other young men, while the rest of the family wedged into a pew near the back, with Michael and Seamus standing behind.

Daniel watched the people. Everyone was dressed in their better-than-Sunday best. This was a day for Ireland. This was a day for celebration. This was a day to revel with strangers like they were family, and even though the Mass had barely begun, the merriment had been going since dawn.

Crowds lined the streets after Mass, waiting for the parade that had been promised, a tradition ninety years in the making. The day was not as bright and warm as the day before, but no one noticed. Beer and pasties were sold by vendors walking up and down the sidewalk, hawking their produce at top volume. Michael bought four pasties, beef-and-onion-filled pasties to be shared by the group, and he bought four beers for himself and his wife and Daniel and Brian. To Daniel's surprise, as the children finished their share of the pasties, Michael bent down and gave each one a healthy sip from his mug. Katie had produced the mugs from a basket which she carried on her arm all the way to church and all the way back to where they stood in the only open spot within three blocks of the tenement. The vendor filled the people's mugs from his large pitcher.

Friends shouted greetings as they pushed and prodded their way through the crowd. Each one stopped for a moment, men, women, and children alike. Tommy and Seamus squawked as their mother forbade them to go traipsing off with some of their friends.

"I have never seen such a sight," Brian breathed. The sights, the smells, the sounds of the Irish wards were unlike anything the boys had ever experienced in the Lehigh Valley. Even on Independence Day—the loudest and rowdiest day of the year—the farmers of the Valley did not have the energy or irresistible delight that these people displayed. Oh, the German farmers would be just as drunk and therefore loud and excitable. But, somehow, and Brian could not describe it, the excitement in the Valley would be different.

As if to prove he was always better with putting thoughts into words, Daniel said, "You know, I'm not used to seeing people so carefree. People back home are more reserved on any given day than our new friends in the city. Carefree people filled with drink—unstoppable!"

"Aye, this is the life!" Michael shouted above the noise.

In addition to the screaming, plentiful masses, suddenly there was the loud, raucous, whiny sound of bagpipes, and the crowd cheered. Coming down the street was a single line of men in kilts, green sweaters, and black berets playing the awkward instrument that sent the throng into a frenzy. At first, the sound hurt Brian's ears and went right through him, like a biting wind. By the time the musicians were abreast of the family, the noise had become invigorating and filled his whole being.

Brian was in his element. He loved the noise, the crowd, the music, and the soldiers that followed. Daniel could not catch the whispered conversation Brian and Michael exchanged, but Michael put an arm around the young man's shoulders and laughed heartily. Michael pointed across the street to where a pretty strawberry blond girl was waving to Brian with aplomb, but probably only because the matron next to her wasn't looking. Brian blushed and waved his hand slightly, sending the girl into a tizzy of excitement, causing her mother to place a restraining hand on her shoulder. Daniel elbowed Brian, and Michael laughed again.

Brian slipped away from the family just about sundown. He ran through still-crowded streets, pushed passed people staggering about with laughter and pleasant jibes. After twisting and turning through various byways, Brian saw the strawberry-blond girl on a stoop up ahead, obviously waiting as she craned her neck to search the crowd.

She jumped and smiled brightly as he called her name. Shannon McKenney was a scullery maid with an ample figure and pretty features. Brian liked her ears best, cute and small when she tucked her flyaway hair behind them. Her reddish-blond hair bordered on golden. Her blue eyes were crystal clear in a round face with a straight nose and full lips. Those lips now called his name, and her lilting voice was like sweet music.

"Shannon," he said again as he climbed the steps to her stoop. Without another word, she took his hand and opened the door of the building. They climbed the stairs, hopping over sleeping drunks and hurrying past her family's apartment on their way to the roof.

The sun had gone down, and the wind had picked up; it was quite cold now. They found a sheltered corner by the chimney and sat down. Brian put his arms around her and buried his face in her hair.

They had met at the Hardings's home. She was the hardworking scullery maid who had provided him with vinegar for the carriage house windows. Lately, he had taken to walking her home, leaving the pub at nine o'clock to wait for her outside the Hardings's back door. He usually amused himself for an hour or so, talking to her and her mother and siblings, and he usually left before her father returned from the inn. As information had passed between the two of them, Brian had come to realize that he had known Mr. McKenney even before he knew Shannon.

"I've never seen such a celebration!" he said when they had made themselves comfortable on the roof. "Does this happen every year?"

"Of course, but every year, it seems to get bigger and better!"

"Shannon, do you remember Ireland?"

"No," she answered, "I only remember what Ma and Da have told me. I was a wee bairn when we came here. Even my older brother Eamon was too young to remember. Finn remembers some. He was eight."

"Do you still have family there?"

"For certain," she said emphatically. "My oldest sister, Mona, was fourteen and married when we left. There had been two babes in between her and Finn, but they died as wee ones."

"Married at fourteen!"

"No, married at thirteen," Shannon corrected. "She had been married some time before we left."

"You're fifteen now," he said. "Are you ready to get married?"

"Are ye askin' me to marry ye, Brian O'Bern?" She laughed. "Me Da won't take kindly to such a proposal, I'll warrant." They both laughed, and then she answered him seriously. "I wouldn't mind gettin' married, but with marriage comes babies, and I'm not sure I'm ready for that."

Brian nodded in the dark. He wasn't ready, either, and he was secretly glad that they could enjoy each other's company without getting muddled into anything else. He was certainly enjoying this life he had found in the great city of Philadelphia—free to go where he wanted when he wanted, and not having anyone worry about him too much.

Only half-voicing his thoughts, he said, "Such a shame, then, that war may be breaking out in America at any minute."

"Will you go?"

"I don't know. Would you miss me if I did?"

"Aye," she whispered.

Brian leaned over and kissed her. Without warning, without asking, without thinking twice. She eagerly kissed him back, but when his hand slid under her cloak, she pushed him away. She laughed.

"What kind of girl do ye take me for?" she demanded cheerfully. With that, she hurried off the roof, and he followed slowly. He paused at her door, where she was waiting, long enough to kiss her again, but he didn't stay for supper or even to say hello to the noisy bunch within. He headed for home.

Brian did not spend time and energy thinking about the man on the Underground Railroad, but every once in a while, the thought crossed his mind: *men and women are in chains.* As he interacted with his fellow Irish, he could not help but make the connection: *the Irish are treated only slightly better, in chains of poverty, if not of iron.* The connection broke through his soul when he talked to his first Negro a few days after St. Pat's.

The tall black man arrived with a cart full of brown-wrapped packages. He approached the carriage house with bowed head. "Sir," the man said to the ground, timid and quiet.

Brian was the only one in the carriage house, and he wiped his hands on a rag as he walked to the alley. "What can I do for you?"

The man told Brian his mission. Miss Harding had been shopping all morning, and these were her purchases. Brian threw the rag onto a bale of hay, pointed to the house. "You can take them up, I guess."

"Oh, no, sir," the man said with an emphatic shake of his head. "I can't go up there."

The man talked well but with a slight accent, and Brian wondered if he was from the South. He looked the man up and down: he was not tall, but he was broad across the shoulders, and his arms were strong. His legs, too, looked well-muscled inside linsey-woolsey trousers that were held together with bright patches. He did not look very old, but his light brown face seemed strained.

"Were you a slave?" he asked abruptly. If the man thought it odd, he didn't say so, but then, Brian realized, he wouldn't.

"I bought my freedom, sir." The man reached into his shirt. "My papers, sir."

Brian opened the wrinkled, folded, yellowed paper that the shaking hand held out to him. It was a deed of sale. Amos, aged thirty-eight, had purchased himself in 1853—so he was forty-six—for four hundred dollars, from Nathan Everett, of Jefferson County, Virginia.

"Where did you get four hundred dollars?" Brian asked. The sum was more than he had heard anyone pay for anything, except land.

"I earned it, sir. Took me near my whole life to do it. My master trained me as carpenter, and I earned it."

"Wow," Brian breathed, still holding the paper. "Why are you a deliveryman, and not a carpenter then?"

The man held out his right hand; there were three fingers missing. "That's how come I could buy my freedom so cheap."

Brian handed the paper to the man, took the cart, and wheeled it to the house. Shannon, the pretty maid, took the packages into the house, and he returned the cart to Amos. Brian mulled over Amos's words all afternoon: "That's how come I could buy my freedom so cheap."

On an errand for Mr. Deary, Brian walked through town. As he contemplated Amos's haunting words, he reached the edge of Southwark, Fifth Street. He walked a block farther and came upon Mother Bethel African Methodist Episcopal Church. Negroes were congregating on the steps in their best clothes. Brian watched as a bride and groom came out of the church to a rousing cheer. As he stood across the street watching the crowd, several Negroes went in and came out of a nondescript building near the church. Finally, Brian jogged across the street and entered the building, still not quite sure what he was doing. He paused to read the sign: Jacob Marle, Attorney-at-Law. It was the name he'd heard on the street, the lawyer who helped freed slaves find loved ones still in the South.

"Can I help you?" The young man who sat behind the desk, a heavy book open in front of him, was white, wearing a white shirt and black drawstring tie. He had blond hair and brown eyes that blinked too rapidly behind round spectacles. There was no one else in the small space.

"I met a man last week. A freed slave. I had a question about it," Brian said, thinking he sounded ignorant. The man blinked rapidly but didn't seem overly surprised.

The young man indicated Brian should sit in a chair. The lawyer settled himself more comfortably, folding his hands on the book, leaning closer. "What was your question, sir?"

"The man showed me his papers. I guess he thought I was accusing him of something."

"That's not surprising," the young man said. "I daresay the man was used to it."

That statement bothered Brian too. "This freed slave has to carry that paper with him everywhere?"

"Oh, yes. He has to be ready to show it at any moment. If he can't, he can be taken back into slavery."

"But he's free."

"Not if he can't prove it."

"And that's another thing," Brian said, sitting forward. "He said he bought himself for four hundred dollars. He said it was cheap because he's missing fingers, and I guess he can't do the work anymore." The blond man blinked without answering. "Is that cheap?" Brian demanded.

"Oh, yes! Most able-bodied male slaves can be sold for as much as eight or nine hundred dollars."

"How do they ever earn that much money? And as far as that goes, I didn't know slaves *could* earn money."

"Sometimes, if they're skilled workers, their master will hire them out to other plantations or people in town. The master gets most of the earnings but will sometimes allow the slaves to retain a percentage. But it's not common for slaves to buy their own freedom."

"I have seen many Negroes in Philadelphia. Where did they all come from?"

"Many are second- or third-generation freed blacks. Philadelphia has been a safe place since the Revolution. Only since the Fugitive Slave Act have freed blacks and runaways continued through the North until they reach Canada. But the ones who have been here for years have chosen to stay. It's their home." The man looked at Brian, as Brian was studying his own hands, as if they were the cause of anguish for these people. "Where are you from, sir?"

"Lehigh County. We don't have many—any—Negroes up there."

Brian thought of that moonless night so many years ago. Frederick helped slaves flee. Brian had never thought much about it. Well, he had never thought much about anything that didn't immediately and personally affect him.

"What happens if runaways get caught?" he asked quietly.

"Often they are whipped. Sometimes they are shot because the likelihood that they will try to escape again is too great a risk." The young man spoke quietly but with great authority.

"What is your involvement in all this?" Brian asked.

"I am an attorney. I help freed blacks remain in Philadelphia, and I act as go-between for freed blacks who want to buy the freedom of family members. They cannot go back to the South, so they pay me, and I go in their place to buy their relatives."

Brian sat in silence. The man sat watching him.

Finally, the man said, "We have a lecture coming up. Next Thursday night." He walked across the room, came back, and handed a flyer to Brian. It had the date, time, and location of a lecture and discussion. "Benjamin Hagerty will share his story" it read.

Brian stood. "I'll try. I'll really try." The two men shook hands, and Brian walked slowly back to the Hardings's stable.

Daniel was pleasantly surprised when, over the next few weeks, Brian spent more time at the apartment and more time talking to Daniel about the impending war.

"You still say it's about states' rights?" Brian asked.

"Well, yes, it is."

"But what about the slaves? Isn't it about them too?"

"Like Abby said, once, that's the excuse. If it wasn't slavery, it would be taxation or something. The South doesn't want lawmakers in Washington City telling them what to do."

"But *shouldn't* it be about slaves? *Shouldn't* we be trying to free them?"

Daniel looked with confusion at Brian, who sat across the table and allowed young Ellen to wind yarn from his hands. "What's this all about? Two weeks ago, all you could talk about was liberating the Irish. Now slaves? What's gotten into you?"

Brian's voice was low, almost sad, when he said, "Can't we do both?"

Daniel was surprised by the conversation, and others like it. He was also surprised to receive two letters during the week following the St. Patrick's Day celebrations. The first was from his sister, Kathleen, and the second was from Abby.

> March 14, 1861
>
> My Dearest Brother Daniel,
>
> I do not claim to know why you have chosen the road you have, but I am glad that you are happy and content. I know you have written letters to Ma, and I am writing to you now to let you know why she has not written back.
>
> When Mr. Danner told Da that you and Brian had not come back with him, Da stormed around the house. Ma was upstairs making beds.
>
> We both were. We came out into the hallway to come downstairs. Da was at the top of the stairs, and he was mad. So mad! He was swinging his arms, and I guess Ma thought he was going to hit her. She moved out of his way, and she fell down the stairs. She banged her head pretty hard. She was unconscious for three days, and when she finally woke up, she wasn't the same. She can't talk. She has trouble walking. She stays mostly upstairs. And Da is drinking all the time.
>
> Meg has been a big help to me. Meg and I have taken over the place. Meg runs the tavern most of the time, and she seems to be doing well with it,

for only being fourteen. I run the house, and it's a lot of work but not difficult, really. The biggest challenge is making George and William obey. Don't worry about us; we'll be all right.

Abby is quite the talk about town these days. She has been sewing for some rich heiress from Allentown who is going to marry a rich heir in Philadelphia. I have seen some of her work, and the beautiful cloth and patterns cannot improve her stitching, that is to say that her stitching is so delicate and exact that even the satin and taffeta pale in comparison. The girl got married three weeks ago, the first week of March, and Abby received a letter from the young woman asking her to come to Philadelphia permanently as a seamstress, I assume. Abby and I have never been good friends, maybe not friends at all, but I wish her well.

We are hearing rumors here of war coming any day, with the South out of the Union now. I try to read the papers, try to keep up with what might be happening to you in the big city, but I admit I find it dull and not commanding of my attention, when I have so much else to concern me.

Keep writing. I will keep reading your letters to Ma. I think they will break through the fog some time. Pray for her recovery, Daniel, and don't think for a minute that you should not finish what you have set out to do. We will be fine.

Always you loving sister,
Kathleen

IN THE SHADOW OF MR. LINCOLN

March 20, 1861

Dear Daniel,

You are so right about the city! It is full of life and passion!

It is filled with people and things and ideas that Millerstown has never seen and could never hope to see! I know because I am here!

Miss Wallington, the young woman I sewed for, is now Mrs. Anderson Rollins of Philadelphia. She was married nearly a month ago. She traveled to Philadelphia to see her new in-laws, and her mother-in-law was so taken with her trousseau that she asked who had done the work. Mrs. Anderson Rollins gave her my name, and Mrs. Henry Rollins sent for me to come to Philadelphia and be the house seamstress.

Women of society in town actually keep a seamstress on hand all the time. Did you know that? I have my own room for sleeping as well as sewing.

I take my meals with the servants, and I am quickly becoming friends with a young woman named Jane Clifford. I accompany Mrs. Henry and Mrs. Anderson Rollins and the Misses Rollins to all of the parties and dances to fix any tears in the hems of the skirts or do any number of things. I stay in a room during the party with all the other seamstresses, and we chat and laugh and have a great time, and sew together. And since all of them work for families who are of the same set as the Rollinses, I see the same women at all the parties. It is grand fun!

I am kept quite busy, especially since a cousin of theirs is coming to town and must have appropriate attire. But I would love to see you sometime. I have enclosed the address. Please do call if you get the chance. Come to the servants' entrance but send a note ahead of time so I can meet you. I will bring Jane, too, if I can to act as chaperone. Heaven forbid I should show my ankles, or something!

Keep well.
Abby

    Daniel sat in a corner of the apartment ignoring the cries and wails of the children. He read and reread the two letters. Kathleen's disturbed him almost to the point that he wanted to start walking home right then. Abby's made him want to stay.
    Without talking to Brian about it, he made a decision. A few months ago, Brian might have been furious. He had wanted Daniel to come with him to the city, but Brian was well-established now, and they were barely friends anymore, more like acquaintances who shared a room, their only conversations about the war, the same conversation one might have with a complete stranger on the street.
    Daniel could not help but feel he was somehow to blame for his mother's condition: if he had not angered his father, if Da had not ranted, Ma would not have fallen down the stairs. He would see Abby and then go home. Daniel sent a quick note to the address Abby had included.
    His plans were not to be. The news of the attack on Fort Sumter would change everything.

Chapter 4

FORT SUMTER

Daniel approached the large mansion, one in a long line of large mansions. The one belonging to Mr. Rollins, esquire, was three stories of brick, with wide, tall windows and expansive gardens. Daniel knew he would never see inside. He was only looking at the back of the house, and yet it was more magnificent than he'd ever dreamed a house could be, more impressive even than the Hardings's home. He couldn't imagine what the inside looked like.

Five minutes ago, his knock had been answered by a fresh-faced young woman in a cap and dirty apron. She must have been a maid or laundress. She did not seem pleased with acting as messenger for Daniel's note, scribbled hastily on a scrap of paper when he realized Abby wasn't waiting for him.

Presently, the servants' door opened. Abby and another young woman stepped through it. Abby looked lovely in a red wool dress. She must have worn it just for him; this early April Sunday morning was a bit too warm for wool.

"Daniel, this is Miss Jane Clifford. Jane, this is Mr. Daniel Kelly," Abby said. The young woman, not overly pretty but pleasant enough to look at, all but curtsied as Daniel removed his hat and nodded civilly.

The three of them set off for the hotel, Abby tucking her gloved hand in the crook of Daniel's arm. Jane walked on Abby's other side. Daniel was surprised at how much like a lady Abby looked. No exposed ankles here. Abby informed him, as if it were a secret she had managed to keep until the right moment, that both girls had Sundays off. Some domestics worked seven days a week, but Abby and Jane were fortunate, only working six days out of seven. Abby wanted to spend all day with Daniel, and she had persuaded her new friend to come along.

Abby chatted merrily as they entered a hotel dining room to eat lunch. Daniel noticed Jane could barely refrain from staring at the blatant ostentation of the hotel lobby and dining room. He, too, was awed by the décor. Daniel wondered uneasily if he would be able to afford lunch for his companions.

Abby ordered some strange-sounding chicken dish and encouraged Jane to order whatever pleased her. Daniel's eyes skimmed down the page, and the price of the chicken dish almost made him choke. Risking a breach in propriety, Daniel leaned over to whisper in Abby's ear, "Abby, I can't afford that. I'm sorry."

Abby threw back her head and laughed. Daniel's discomfort was growing rapidly. First, her ladylike appearance had unnerved him. Now her complete confidence and her unconcern for practical things, like money, reinforced the seeming distance between them. Jane, too, looked ill at ease. With more discretion than Abby had ever done anything in her life, she opened her reticule and showed Daniel a large amount of paper money in the bottom.

"I've earned my own way so far, Daniel, so I'll buy my friends lunch today." She smiled widely, and as she gazed at him, her smile changed almost imperceptibly, the lights in her eyes twinkled. She pulled out five dollars and, again with much discretion, put the money in his hand under the table. So much for a man's pride!

Daniel took the five-dollar bill. After a moment, he leaned as close to Abby's ear as propriety allowed and whispered, "I am happy for you, Abby, but it really isn't appropriate—"

Abby's smile faded. She put a gloved hand on his. "We're friends, aren't we?"

"A lady—"

Abby's smile returned. "Am I showing my ankles again?" she asked good-naturedly.

Daniel smiled, too, glad she wasn't upset. "Yes, I'm afraid you are."

"Well, too bad because it's my treat." As he watched her eyes return to the menu, he realized he didn't really want her to change. Not completely, anyway.

All three of them ordered the chicken, as well as coffee, when the waiter came for their order. Then they chatted until the food came.

"How long have you been here?" Daniel asked Abby.

Her eyes twinkled merrily. "Since St. Patrick's Day. What a day to arrive in the city! I was sore, afraid my trunks would be lost in the melee. Luckily, Mrs. Rollins sent a coach for me at the station."

"You rode the train?" Daniel asked excitedly.

"Of course," Abby said easily, as if it was nothing unusual. "I'm a valuable commodity. No self-respecting woman of worth would go to a fine party without me."

"Unlike us kitchen help," Jane said dryly, but her sweet smile softened her tone.

Daniel turned to include Jane in the conversation. "How long have you lived in Philadelphia?"

"All my life. Both my parents have worked for the Rollinses since before I was born. Mother is a maid, and Father is a gardener."

"Is that unusual that you would work for the same family?"

"Not at all. And the Rollinses are good people. They treat us well."

"Which means they ignore us, unless they need something," Abby added.

Jane smiled. "Yes, we are about the same as the fireplace or privy. We serve a purpose."

The girls laughed at their unfunny joke, and Daniel turned back to Abby. "So you're enjoying yourself, no doubt."

"Absolutely!" One or two of the hotel patrons sitting nearby looked up at the loudness of Abby's exuberance. Abby giggled at the distressed looks on Jane and Daniel's faces. Daniel shook his head ruefully.

Abby's demeanor changed as the waiter brought the food and placed it in front of them. Daniel offered a prayer, and they began to eat. Abby waited a few moments before she spoke again. "Has anyone written to you about your ma?"

The food was delicious, but it turned to paste in his mouth. "I received a letter from Kathleen the same day I received yours," he replied.

"I'm so sorry, Daniel," she said sincerely.

He took another bite of the chicken drenched in tangy sauce. "I'm going home," he said. "I never thought this would happen. I certainly never intended for this to happen."

"No one could have foreseen this, Daniel. It's not your fault."

"Of course, it is!" His voice was vehement, pained, low. "I'll take responsibility for what I've done."

"What you've done?" she repeated. "What you've done is follow your dream. You're a man, and you're entitled to your decisions. Anyway, it was your father's fault."

Daniel shook his head sadly, gave up the pretense of eating. "It was my decision, but it wasn't my idea. It was Brian's idea, and I allowed him to drag me along." He shook his head again. "A man can make his own decisions, and a man needs to stand up and take the consequences. I am deciding to go home and be the man my father wants me to be."

Abby almost groaned out loud. Why was he doing this to himself? No one was expecting him to go home. She had talked to Kathleen, one of the few times she ever really talked to Kathleen, and Abby knew that Kathleen was not expecting him to come home. Meg was not expecting him to come home and quite frankly probably didn't want him to come home.

"Did Kathleen tell you about Meg?" she asked, hoping to salvage his future for him.

"She said that Meg has helped Da in the tavern," he said, taking a deep breath. All the joy of day was gone.

"No, by the time I left, she had taken over the whole thing. How old is she? Fourteen?" Abby knew she was. "She has the tavern open every night at four and keeps it open until eleven. She has hired a man to help her. Business is good enough, I guess. His name is Carl." She was going to say more, but Daniel interrupted.

"What does Da say about it?"

"Nothing. He spends most of his time with your ma. He has forgotten everything but her, my Pa says. Anyway, Pa helped Meg hire Carl, so I met him at our house. He is twenty-something, third son of a farmer in Upper Saucon Township. Not much future for him there, I guess, so he set out, much like you did." Daniel marveled at how Abby could continue to eat while she talked. She was almost finished. Her appetite didn't waver, nor did her voice. "Carl understands the situation, but he doesn't like taking orders from Meg. Meg's quite the little businesswoman. A lot like me, I think." Abby shook her head and looked directly at him. "I don't think Meg wants you to come home, at least not to stay. She's happy, and content, and independent. Being independent myself now, I know I wouldn't want to give it up and go back to the way things were."

Daniel let the information ferment in his brain. Meg, young, pretty, quiet Meg, had taken over the family business. Meg was a regular-sized girl, neither too tall nor too short, neither too fat nor too thin. Her coloring—brown hair, brown eyes—helped her hide in the shadows. She never said much, but he had always been aware of how much she took in. The conversations, actions, and attitudes of others had always been like an open book to her. He couldn't picture her ordering a man to do this or that. She probably had to stand on a stool to reach over the bar or to get glasses off the top shelf.

"And Kathleen?" he asked. "She said that she has taken the running of the house."

"Yes, she has," Abby said. "You know, Daniel, I never liked Kathleen much. I mean, she always seemed as silly and stupid as every other woman I've ever known. But she stepped right in and took over like she had done it every day of her life and liked it! I have to admit, I've gained some respect for your sister. She doesn't know politics, but she knows her business. She has been to see my ma for help and advice and just to talk." Abby sighed.

"And how is your ma?" Daniel took advantage of the segue to change the subject. "How are you and your ma, I should say."

Abby shook her head and silently sipped her coffee. She looked like she would refuse to answer at all. Jane jumped in the conversation at that moment. Daniel had almost forgotten she was there.

"Abby, he's your friend. You should tell him."

"Yes, tell me." He encouraged.

"After you and Brian left, Ma took it hard, but she got mad. And she took it out on me." Abby shook her head. "That's not quite true. Her nerves were on edge, and everything I said or did made her mad. I probably talked too much about how lucky you and Brian were to be able to leave," she admitted.

"Did you fight?"

"Not in so many words. Sarah didn't help the situation, either. We have always been like two cats in a gunny sack. With me doing the trousseau instead of helping at the farm, it all fell to Sarah and Ben, and Sarah didn't take it kindly. Every time Sarah and I fought, Ma got a little bit tighter. You know what I mean?"

Daniel could picture Mrs. Weimer's furrowed brow and tight mouth perfectly; he nodded. "And Ben?"

"I think George and William think he has fallen off the face of the earth. Ma gave him some extra chores even before you two left to pick up the slack of me not helping, and he did it readily enough. Now, though, with Brian gone, too, he has really helped out, and I'm proud of him. Pa is pleased as punch, and he never talks about Brian being gone, but he always talks about the wonderful son he has." Abby looked at Daniel, placed a firm hand on his arm. "Don't tell Brian I said that. I don't want him to feel bad."

Daniel agreed he wouldn't say anything. He had invited Brian along today. Brian was with his girl, apparently, and had promptly declined, but there had been no meanness in it. Daniel told Abby about Shannon, and she laughed with pure joy. Daniel was quite glad their meal ended on a good note.

As they walked up and down the city streets, simply enjoying the warmth of the weather and companionship, Abby began talking politics. She had been isolated with womenfolk for so long, unable even to go out to buy a newspaper, she had no idea what was happening in the world. Daniel laughed. How ironic that Abby, who despised the associations of other ladies, was now employed in a position where the only people with whom she came in contact were women! So to get her up to date, Daniel stopped a newsie, a young boy selling the *Inquirer*, to purchase a paper. It was his last copy, and he took the penny eagerly before running down the street.

All of the sun and warmth went out of the day as the three sat on a bench in the park to read the paper. Jane wasn't much interested, but she went along anyway. Daniel unfolded the paper with a smile, and it froze on his face like a tongue on a metal pipe as he read the headline:

Major Anderson Surrenders Fort Sumter

War Imminent. Four Soldiers Wounded, One Seriously. Fleet Sits in Charleston Harbor Without Offering Aid to Anderson and his Garrison

Daniel read the article aloud. Abby was impressed by his composure. Her own heart was racing, and she doubted she could have read anything. The words continued to jump out at her from the page. She couldn't take her eyes off them: War Imminent.

Fort Sumter sat in Charleston Harbor, South Carolina. Major Robert Anderson commanded a nominal garrison of just over eighty soldiers. Confederate president Jefferson Davis had ordered United States president Abraham Lincoln to evacuate the fort, but Lincoln had refused. Lincoln's actions were quite the opposite; in fact, Lincoln ordered ships to resupply the fort, as correspondence from Anderson revealed provisions were low.

"Why did President Lincoln do that?" Jane asked.

"Send a fleet with provisions?" Daniel asked.

Jane nodded. "Why did he not call the troops out? Seems to me he was provoking a fight."

"I agree," Abby said.

"Perhaps," Daniel said slowly. "But South Carolina has been itching for a fight. Ever since they seceded in December. Lincoln said he would not fire the first shot."

Almost as soon as the newly inaugurated United States president announced his intentions to resupply the garrison, President Davis ordered the batteries of Charleston to open fire on the fort. Shelling began in the dark hour before the dawn at 4:30 a.m. of Friday the twelfth.

The eighty-odd soldiers of Fort Sumter dug in but did little else. The explosions from the fort that inhabitants of the city heard were caused by the excessive heat of the day causing the arsenal to detonate in its sealed room. Charlestonians did not think well of the fleet nearby, which did nothing to help Anderson, but they esteemed the bravery of the major so well that when the pole that flew the American flag was shot and broken, a Charlestonian rowed to the fort with a replacement, assuming Major Anderson was not yet ready to surrender.

Major Anderson finally flew a white flag of truce at five minutes to one in the afternoon of Saturday, April 13. The Stars and Stripes were hauled down, and the Palmetto of South Carolina was raised in its place. Major Anderson surrendered his sword to General P. T. Beauregard.

General Beauregard said he would not take the sword from so great a man, a man elevated in esteem by every true Carolinian by his bravery during the battle. Major Anderson and his men were permitted to recover their belongings before being sent to anywhere in the United States the Army wished them to go. As of Sunday, April 14, Anderson and his men were on their way to New York on board the *Isabel*.

Only five enlisted men were injured, one seriously. No officers were wounded. No residents of the city were injured. The city of Charleston rejoiced with loud singing and dancing in the streets.

Daniel finished reading the account, relayed to the *Inquirer* by a *New York Times* correspondent living and working in Charleston. He looked around the park. Young couples were strolling along the paths; children were chasing each other in a merry game of tag. The sun was shining warmly. There was no breeze to speak of. Philadelphia was not behaving as though the battle had any effect on them.

"Philadelphia is pro-Southern," Daniel said softly.

"What do you mean pro-Southern?" Abby demanded. "I've seen fliers and pamphlets and signs for abolitionist meetings and the like. Pennsylvania is abolitionist territory. Definitely *not* pro-Southern!"

"Abby, I read the newspaper. I don't just set the type. And I am telling you, Philadelphia supports the South. Or rather, the South supports Philadelphia. Look"—he jabbed the paper as if the answer was there—"New York and Boston have access to the Erie Canal and railroads to ship their goods west. Pennsylvania railroads don't go west because it's too hard to get over the mountains. Someday they will, but New England beat us to that market because of the Canal. So we ship our goods south to South Carolina, Mississippi, and Georgia."

"They're agricultural," Abby said.

"Exactly. They can't make their own goods, so they buy ours. Let's face it. Influence lies where the money is. Not power, necessarily, but influence. Pennsylvania, which is heavily influenced by Philadelphia, will not willingly offend the people who buy Pennsylvania products."

"That's a good point," Abby conceded.

"I wonder if Fort Sumpter will change that," Daniel muttered more to himself than to the girls.

"What happens now?" Jane asked in her quiet way.

Daniel didn't know. But by the next day, April 15, 1861, all of the United States knew. All the newspapers, including the *Inquirer*, carried the text of Abraham Lincoln's proclamation: "I appeal to all loyal citizens to favor, facilitate, and aid this effort to maintain the honor, the integrity, and the existence of our National Union and the perpetuity of popular government, and to redress wrongs already long enough endured . . ."

The Inn at Kensington buzzed with excited conversation, mostly in whispers that Brian could barely hear. He had become increasingly aware over the past two months that there was something happening under the surface. He could not see or hear what it was exactly, but he sometimes overheard a word here and there: "Fenians," "liberation," "take up arms." Except for "Fenians," the men seemed to be talking about war with the slave states. When Lincoln called for volunteers, the Irish seemed eager enough to join the fight.

Brian raised his glass. "I'll go!"

The others cheered. More men declared their intention to volunteer. Many cheers and glasses were raised those nights.

"Michael Maloney," Katie said as Michael and Brian stumbled through the door. "Where have ye been, man?"

It was late, much later than usual, for their drunken arrival. Brian was slightly less drunk and dropped Michael onto a chair. Then he weaved his way to the green sofa.

"We enlisted," he said dully, the excitement overpowered by the liquor.

"You what?" Daniel demanded.

"Shhh!" Katie said, indicating the quiet bedroom with a shake of her head. The children had been asleep for hours. Daniel had just arrived home from putting the paper to bed.

"We enlisted," Michael slurred. "In the army, ye know."

"Why did ye go and do that? I ask ye now—why?" Katie pleaded, sitting next to her husband, worry and fear written clearly on her face.

"For the Fenians, my love," Michael said.

Katie's eyes opened wide. Again, she shook her head, this time indicating Daniel and Brian.

"We'll cut our teeth on these damn rebels," Michael continued. "Then we'll take our new military might back to our green isle and kill the damn British!" With that, his head hit the table, and he was asleep.

Daniel looked from Katie to Brian. "He's asleep too," he said.

"And no wonder. They probably drank the ocean dry tonight."

"What are the Fenians?"

"Please don't ask," Katie pleaded, again the fear showing in her eyes. "If Michael was na' drunk, he would na' have spoke of it."

"A secret society?"

"Of sorts. For the liberation of Ireland, and that's all I'll say. Will ye help me get him to bed?"

Daniel and Katie moved first Michael and then Brian. They removed their boots but otherwise left them clothed.

In the morning, the two men recalled enlisting but little else. Daniel and Katie did not mention it. After careful thought though, Daniel signed his name to the paper as well, a member of the Irish Brigade of Philadelphia.

The Irish Brigade was a direct response to Governor Andrew Curtin's call for volunteers, which in itself was a direct response to Lincoln's call. The War Department in Washington City decided how many each state should send, based on each state's population, to fill the need for seventy-five thousand men that Lincoln required. Pennsylvania was allowed to create fourteen regiments, but so many men enlisted in the first weeks that by the middle of May, Curtin created reserved units of militia to be held at the ready. The Irish Brigade was trained for immediate service. The men would be released from their commitment in July. Everyone was sure the damn rebels would be whipped by Independence Day.

Chapter 5

THE IRISH BRIGADE

Entry in Daniel Kelly's journal dated May 15, 1861

It is late after midnight. That means it is really May 16, but I have not yet been to bed, so I will continue to think of it as the fifteenth. I have not gone to bed because I am on sentry duty.

The night is cool. The stars are shining and twinkling in a deep blue canopy above me. The trees are in full leaf already. The spring rains have stopped for the most part, and the days have been almost warm.

Arthur Fetterhoff and I are positioned on the southeast corner of the camp. The camp is arranged in rows and columns, very orderly. Most things about the army are orderly, I have found. Our days are very structured—drill, march, drill, drill, drill. Most of the men in the unit are Irish immigrants, which is why we are known as the Irish Brigade. These men came to America because of the famine and settled with their families in the city; most of them have never held a gun, let alone shot one. Even though I lived in "the country," I never shot a gun, either, before enlisting. So we must practice, practice, practice to make perfect.

The tents are arranged along avenues almost with campfires every hundred feet or so. The fires have burned down to embers, and most men have gone to sleep. The reveille sounds quite early! All day long, we act to the beat of the drum: wake, march, breakfast, march, and so on.

Fetterhoff and I are keeping watch on one corner, which is surrounded by trees. Our job is to stop anyone who wishes to leave or enter the camp. "Halt! Identify yourself!" That is what we are supposed to say, but so far, I have not had to say it. Every fifteen minutes, we leave the corner and walk in either direction for half the length of the camp where we meet the sentry on the next corner, and then return to our own corner. It provides us with much opportunity for discussion in an otherwise dull task.

Time to walk . . .

(Later) Fetterhoff is a private like I am. However, he is much older. He is at least thirty years old. He is average height and thin. He carries himself with an educated demeanor. I asked him about that. Well, I didn't say, "You walk with an educated demeanor." I said, "You seem different than most men in this unit. Fetterhoff isn't Irish, is it?" I was trying to draw him out. Most men in this place talk about music and food and women back home, and sometimes Ireland before the famine, but almost never about themselves.

"It's German," he said. He does not have a German accent, however. Before I could mention that observation, he continued. He told me his whole life story, it seems! He is a talkative sort, and I learned that he is also a writer. He grew up as the son of German farmers in Lancaster County and moved to Philadelphia about ten years ago when he was twenty to see if he could find work at the newspaper. He writes for the *Times*. I am talking with an actual newspaperman! Perhaps he will be able to teach me the trade.

Entry dated May 20, 1861

I have had opportunity since my last entry to speak in-depth with Fetterhoff. He has obtained permission from the captains to keep a journal of events for the entire unit. He will work quite closely with the officers. I am not sure exactly what he will record, but I am sure I will learn because I have permission to be his unofficial apprentice. This means that I am infantry above all else, but I can spend as much time as possible with Fetterhoff, and he will teach me what he knows.

I have shown him some of my writing samples, things that are in my notebook, which I am now writing with pencil rather than ink. An ink pot is not practical on marches, when a soldier must carry everything he owns on his back. So a pencil it will have to be! Fetterhoff looked at the articles I wrote in Millerstown, and he hemmed and hawed before I could get any words out of him.

"You have an eye for detail, Daniel," he said. "You write well. But it is not journalistic writing. You are too detailed in what you see and not detailed enough in what is important. You write more like an essayist or novelist."

I was disappointed, to say the least. Fetterhoff encouraged me to read other great writers. He offered to show me his own personal collection of books when the war is over; his house is on Third Street, and he has a whole room full of books, he says!

In the meantime, I will work on my journalistic skill. It is my dream and goal to write for a newspaper, but perhaps my dream should be modified a bit. Perhaps there are other types of writing that I could do successfully.

Entry dated May 23, 1861

We continue to drill. I never see Brian anymore; we are not assigned to the same tent, and his tent is in another avenue entirely. I saw him this morning, however, and he looks well. It is hard for me to believe that we grew up together, as things are so different now.

Here I sit, a soldier in Mr. Lincoln's army, ready and willing to fight for a complicated cause that I am sure I don't fully understand, but trusting my leaders enough to know that if they call, I must go. Brian is a soldier, too, but it fits him much better than it fits me, and I am not sure that he even knows what he's fighting for. He still talks about liberating Ireland and freeing the slaves. I cannot convince him that the issues go deeper than that.

He has joined a cause he knows nothing about to find glory and honor and adventure. And yet, when I see him across the way, he looks so fit and happy. I have heard that he will be trained as a sharpshooter, perhaps, because he has learned so quickly. Our officers want us to be able to load and shoot three times a minute; I can only do it twice, but I bet Brian can do three.

We talked for just a minute when we passed the sutler's this morning. He said he is well. He has made friends, it seems. I think many of the men in the unit are some of the same men he would drink in the tavern with in Philadelphia. He is excited to be fighting and restless to be sitting in camp. I encouraged him to write home, but I do not think he will. I must write home soon, or Ma will think something bad has happened to me. I hope she is better . . .

Letter from Daniel to Peggy Kelly dated May 25, 1861

> Dear Ma,
>
> Oh, how I miss you! I miss everything about you, and home, and family! I am well here in camp, but the food is nothing like yours, and the conversation is less than heartwarming, half the time. Men talk about what they miss, their wives and children and sweethearts. I miss talking about everyday things with you. I miss Kathleen's purposefulness and Meg's joy. I miss George and Will. How are they all? Are George and Will behaving as they should?
>
> Please don't worry about me, Ma. I am safe, and everyone says the war will be over by July. At the rate that we are practicing and learning, the war will be long over before we are even ready! I doubt I will see any action at all, so rest easy.
>
> I miss your soda bread. Dense and crusty and coated with strawberry jam. Hearty bread that fills your belly for days. We have nothing like that here. They are feeding us well enough, I guess. We have plenty of meat and vegetables,

and a flatbread-type substance called hardtack that is made out of flour and water. It's hard and bland, but it's food. The coffee is good, and we even have some sugar for it once in a while. All in all, I can't complain.

I have been to Mass every week since I have been in Philadelphia, and the unit even has a priest who says Mass two or three times a week. His name is Father Flannigan. He is a young man, maybe twenty-five years old. He has hair as red as flame and laughs all the time! He brings comfort and joy to us all. We are an Irish unit made up of good Catholics, and Father Flannigan will follow us wherever we go. I know you will be happy to hear that.

I keep you in my prayers daily.

Your loving Son,
Daniel

Letter from Daniel to Abby dated June 1, 1861

Dear Abby,

I find it ironic and a bit humorous that Brian and I left home to come to the city leaving you behind, then you followed, and now we have left you behind again to go off to war. I guess it really isn't all that funny. But you didn't come to Philadelphia to be with us anyway.

I am in camp. I wonder if we will ever leave this place. We hear about fighting; well, more like skirmishes, but here we sit. I can't say that I am sorry, but on the other hand, sometimes I think I would almost feel cheated in a way if we didn't at least march somewhere. What good is a soldier who sits in camp all day? Now I am starting to sound like Brian!

Are you still enjoying your work, and the city in general? Have you heard from your folks at all? I have not heard at all from mine since Kathleen's letter in March. I am hoping Da is not keeping Ma from writing. I know you said she was ill, but she must be over that by now, don't you think? And I thought Kathleen would have been good for at least a few lines.

I am working with a man named Arthur Fetterhoff, who is one of the few Germans in our unit and the only newspaperman. He has been teaching me about writing. Abby, he has a library in his own house, books by Machiavelli, Jefferson, Rousseau, Johnathan Swift and John Donne, Aristotle and Plato and Sophocles. He has promised that when the war is over, he will take me to his house on Third Street and let me borrow his books. I am sure that if I asked him, you could come too!

I miss discussing things with you. We used to talk about everything, but that is impossible now.

May God bless you!

Always your fond friend,
Daniel

Letter from Brian to Shannon McKinney dated June 2, 1861

Dearest Shannon,

Oh, how I miss you! It seems forever since I saw you last. Has it really only been a week and a half? When do you think we could meet again? I have to time the sentries just right.

I am sorry we fought the last time we were together. I am sure that if you had gone to the lecture I went to—I should have asked you to—you would know why I am so passionate about this. The Negroes are not much different than the Irish, really. They are oppressed and pushed down. I will not say that the Irish in Ireland are not treated badly, but are they whipped until their flesh hangs in strings? Are they forced to work in all weather for a bit of cornmeal? At least, the Irish of Ireland are free to leave Ireland and come to America. Slaves can run away, sure, and be brought back or killed on the spot.

And I know the Irish of Philadelphia are beaten down and oppressed too. I lived there, remember? But this is America, and anyone who wants to can better himself. That is what makes America great. There is freedom here, and I think *everyone* should have it. Negroes too.

I hope this war is over soon, my Shannon. I want to come back to you, and if your father is agreeable to it, I want to marry you. Pray for a quick end to this conflict!

All my love,
Brian

Letter from Brian to Mary Weimer dated June 10, 1861

Dear Mary,

I have found my place. I am well-fed, healthy, and eager to serve my country. I do not see Daniel much, but I know he is fine too. I have not seen Abby since April, of course, and only then because she came to tell Daniel goodbye. She looked well, but sad, that day. I am sure she is exactly where she wants to be.

Give my best to Frederick. Say hello to Sarah for me. Tell Ben that I will be writing him a letter soon!

Your loving brother,
Brian

Letter from Brian to Ben Weimer dated June 12, 1861

Ben,

Are you helping your pa on the farm? I am sure that you are working very hard, as it is past planting season. I must admit that I do not miss farming at all.

I wanted to tell you about soldiering. Of all the people I know, I think you are the one person who would care to know what it is we soldiers face. I don't know about combat yet, and I am eager to find out (don't tell your mother), but I can tell you all about camp.

We wake up before dawn every morning and drill for two hours before breakfast. After breakfast, we drill some more. During drill, we practice loading and shooting. I was one of the first men in the unit who was able to load and shoot three times a minute, which is what the army desires. I guess I have an advantage over the other men—they are all city folk, and I at least have loaded and shot a gun before, only hunting, but a rifle is a rifle. Are you looking forward to hunting with your father next fall? I bought a Winchester, one of the new rifles, because the smoothbores that the army provides are old and inaccurate. I spent nearly my full $13 a month paycheck on the rifle, but I think it was worth it. Anyway, you stand the rifle on its butt. The cartridges and powder and cap are in a bag that sits on the right hip, with a strap that crosses over the left shoulder. You reach in with the right hand, pull out the powder, put it in the muzzle. You have to tear the paper with your teeth, which is why I have seen them check the teeth of new recruits. You need the front ones intact so that you can tear the paper.

Put in the bullet, a minié ball. The man who sold me the Winchester said that the spiral grooves in the muzzle of the gun make the minié ball shoot farther and straighter than the smoothbores. After the bullet is in, you take out the rod, ram it down good, then put the rod back in its place in the bottom of the muzzle. We have to do this with the right pinky, with the thumb of the hand pointing toward the body. We do this because when the gun has been shot repeatedly, it gets hot, and if the powder gets hot and then you ram the bullet down, sometimes it will explode, so we only use our pinky and keep the rest of the hand out of the way so in case that happens, we don't lose our hand.

Last Sunday, we had parade inspection. One of the highest-ranking officers rode his white horse up and down as we stood in full dress in perfect lines for two hours. That is the part of soldiering I hate the worst, the standing at attention for long periods of time. The colonel watched us at attention, at ease, and then marching.

We had to stand in the sun with all of our clothes and equipment. Blue wool pants and jacket, fully buttoned. The army issues white shirts for underneath the jacket, but they are scratchy and uncomfortable, so we are permitted to buy or bring our own shirts. Some men have plaid shirts or white shirts or whatever. A friend of mine sent me two shirts, so I have a green plaid and a plain blue. Much better than the scratchy white ones! We also wear boots and a slouch hat, called a kepi, which I think are the stupidest-looking things. Or at least, I thought so. I have heard that some soldiers called Zouaves wear pointed hats with tassels. I saw it in the newspaper. Those are even worse! We carry our gun and bullet pouch, like I said, on the right, on the belt, and a haversack, and a saber on the left hip. Our haversack carries the bullets but also our food and what-all. On our backs, we carry fifty pounds of equipment, including clothes and cooking utensils and a bedroll.

I don't miss much about Millerstown, but I do miss fishing. Have you caught any big ones this spring?

Be good. Help your pa.

Your uncle,
Brian

Letter from Shannon McKenney to Brian O'Bern dated June 16, 1861 (The letter was dictated by Shannon to the parish priest)

Dear Brian,

I do not understand you. I cannot understand you. How can you compare Negroes to us? You speak as if they are downtrodden people. They are not people; not the same way we are. Even a dog will whimper when you beat it. That doesn't mean the dog is a person. I will not have slaves myself, but I am sure the slave owners do the best they can to keep their Negroes in line, and if that means beating them once in a while, I can't see how that is any of our business.

As far as this war is concerned, I welcome it, just as my da and his friends do. It will train the Irish, prepare them for the fight to be held elsewhere, to rid the Emerald Isle of red-coated snakes. Instead of farmers with scythes and pitchforks, we'll surprise those snakes with firearms and trained warriors. I cannot say more, especially because you are proving you cannot be trusted.

It matters little whether my da is agreeable to a marriage between you and me. I am not. You need not respond to this letter.

Sincerely,
Shannon McKenney

Letter from Abby to Daniel dated June 23, 1861

Daniel,

I received your letter. It is good to hear from you, as always. I am well. You asked if Philadelphia is everything I thought it would be. It is everything and more—more people, more noise, more traffic, more rules!

I cannot believe it. I used to think that my mother had too many rules for a sane person to follow, with how to make potatoes and plant potatoes, and sew a seam, and wash a shirtwaist. Now I understand that I had more freedom than I realized. In Philadelphia, I have the freedom to be my own woman, my own person, but there are still so many rules to follow! Society tells me who I can talk to and who I can't, who I can walk with, and the fact that I can't go anywhere by myself. I hate that! Society tells me how to wear my hair (curls every day!) and what material to make my own dresses out of. No silk for this girl. I am on the level with a lady's maid, so I must look good but not too good.

Mrs. Rollins keeps me quite busy. There is always a dress to be sewn or mended, although the Rollinses are rolling in money and would prefer to simply order a new dress than mend an old one. Depending on the style and material of the dress, sometimes I can take it for my own, so now I have more dresses than I have ever owned in my entire life!

Generally, I am not permitted to go anywhere during the daytime because I am working. I can only go to the market on my day off, which is almost never, because my day off is almost always Sunday, and no one does anything on Sunday. Once in a while, though, the young Misses Rollins and the young Mrs. Rollins ask me to accompany them downtown, but only, I have noticed, if one of the stops will be to a milliner or dress shop. But when I do accompany them, I get to hear all the gossip. Unfortunately, there is no decent conversation to be had. It seems even in the city, women are not allowed to think and have opinions of their own. Leastways, not about anything important.

Jane and I—you remember Jane, don't you?—went to a lecture last week. I cannot give you all of the details for propriety's sake, but I can tell you that I was moved in a way that I never have been before. The speaker was a Negress, a Miss Nell. She was a slave at one time in Virginia on a tobacco plantation, but someone purchased her freedom, and now she travels from city to city in the North to gain support for the Negro slaves in the South. She shared with us her life story, and I sat there thinking that it is a misconception that a person's life is written on her face because she has had a very hard life, a horrible life, but she was so beautiful! Miss Nell's face is smooth and black, and her eyes are big and brown. She has high cheekbones and an angular jaw. The lines of her face are more sharp than soft, but overall, the picture is one of determined beauty. Her voice was strong for the entire two hours that she spoke.

Daniel, she spoke of being born a slave, the oldest surviving child of her mother. She had three younger brothers who also survived infancy. When she was twelve, her mother tried their first escape. The youngest was two, and Nell carried him while her mother carried the three-year-old, and the ten-year-old followed close behind. They walked at night and slept under logs and under creek banks during the day. They made it all the way to Philadelphia, and then someone turned them in.

Their master came for them, and he killed the mother on the spot and beat the children so badly that the one child died before they returned to Virginia. As soon as they returned, Nell had to begin working again, and then she was sold farther South to a cotton plantation. I cannot relate to you the horrors she endured. No men were allowed into the lecture hall that night, with good reason. At the end of the talk, Miss Editha Pommer, the spokesman for the women's society that sponsored the lecture, helped Nell reveal her back. I cannot describe the scars, Daniel. Just believe me when I tell you that I have never been so horrified in all my life.

Why did I ever think that Negroes were less than people? You say that the issue is deeper than slavery, implying that it is about the Constitution and whether or not states have sovereignty. You are wrong. It is deeper than slavery because it is about people. People who have been destroyed in spirit and in body for no other reason than the color of their skin and the sinfulness of men.

Be well. I pray for you.

Always your fondest friend,
Abby

Letter from Abby to Mary dated July 2, 1861

Dear Mother,

Work is going well. I have continued to work for Mrs. Rollins and her daughters. I attend social events with them and work in the upstairs of their home. Mother, it is grander than I could ever imagine! They have over twenty servants in the household. I never have to cook or clean because there is someone else paid to do that. I never have to scrub floors or clothes. Unfortunately, neither am I able to work in the fields and feel the sun and wind on my face. I guess you can't have everything.

I should ask how Sarah is, I guess. Is she still angry with me for leaving? I turn sixteen in September, so she will be turning fourteen in a few weeks. Is she excited about putting her hair up and wearing hoops? I can imagine that she would be. She has been looking forward to these things for years.

How is Ben? Is he helping Pa with the farm? He must be growing into a young man. Almost twelve years old now. I do miss him!

I miss Pa too. Send him my love. And to you, Ma. I miss you too.

Your independent daughter,
Abby

Letter from Mary to Abby dated July 15, 1861

Dearest Abby,

It was so good to receive your letter! I knew you would do well for yourself in the city. I am sure Mrs. Rollins is pleased with your work. I know I am quite proud of you.

Sarah is fine. She is already wearing her hair up and hoops on Sundays. Your father gave in at the end of the spring. Sarah is rather satisfied because, unlike you, she was looking forward to using hoopskirts as a reason not to work in the fields. Unfortunately for your sister, she is only permitted to wear them on Sundays. It just isn't practical for a farmer's daughter. Your father saw through her the entire time, but it doesn't matter.

Ben is very helpful. He helped from the very beginning. He helped plow and plant. It is the waiting time now. The wheat and corn are pushing up. As long as the weather holds, it should be a good harvest, but it is too early yet to tell.

Your father is depending a great deal on Ben this year because Paul has left us. He married Hannah Schimmer, the Reverend Schimmer's daughter. I had known they were keeping company for at least a year now, but it was mostly kept a secret. At least, most people seemed shocked when the announcement came. They were married in June, like most couples. June is the beginning of the waiting time, as you know, so it is the ideal time for everyone to gather to celebrate a marriage. Paul and Hannah have moved to the farm that he has bought in Fogelsville, eighty acres, I believe your father said. He planted there in the spring, and he will be raising cattle as well.

In other gossip, Kathleen has taken over the Kelly household completely. I thought the boys were wise, in a way, although also childish in a way, when they told us they were going to Allentown and then just did not return. Although I will admit I was angry at first. I am sure they thought it was better that way, that we would all warm up to the idea. Unfortunately, Peggy Kelly has not recovered from her fall. I visit when I can, and Kathleen comes here as often as possible for advice and whatnot. Patrick, too, has changed. He is drinking heavily. Kathleen told me that Meg has assumed management of the tavern, and they hired a man named Carl to help her. Not two months later, he had stolen all of their cash and left town. Meg still needs the help, though, so your father is keeping his ears open for them when he goes to Allentown, but he advised them to not advertise. He is afraid they will not know how to choose the right person.

IN THE SHADOW OF MR. LINCOLN

I miss you, daughter, but I am happy that you are happy. You are in my prayers. Perhaps you can come to visit for the harvest festival.

With all my love,
Mother

Chapter 6

KATHLEEN

Kathleen stood at the dishpan, her arms up to the elbows in lukewarm water gray with grime. The breakfast dishes were washed, but she didn't have the energy to dump the water or dry her hands.

She didn't mind taking care of the household chores. In fact, she gained pleasure and contentment from accomplishing the daily tasks. Every morning, she woke with the rooster's crowing to dress in her modest, gently worn dress and pull her deep red curls into a stiff bun at the nape of her neck. Nothing fancy, but she wasn't a fancy girl. And fancy just got in the way.

She made breakfast each day for her family. That morning, she made eggs, bacon, and biscuits, which George and Will had slathered with strawberry jam. She had noticed the jam was almost gone. Meg often helped clear the table, but there was much to do with the tavern, and she could not be spared long.

No, the chores themselves weren't the cause of her sorrow. The sadness overcame her sometimes when she thought of her parents still alive but hardly living. Ma sat in the rocking chair hour after hour, day after day. She stared into the emptiness of the parlor, or sometimes Kathleen brought the chair into the kitchen. Seeing her mother's suddenly white hair and empty eyes was very hard, and Kathleen didn't bring Ma into the kitchen often.

Da was hardly much better. He did speak occasionally, but he had begun drinking heavily. A good, proud Irishman, he could always hold his liquor. Irishmen always drank in crowds, building each other up, holding each other up, never hanging their heads. Now, though, he sat in his chair and drank. He sat on the floor of Peggy's room with a bottle in his hand. He strode into the tavern whenever he needed a fresh bottle and refused to meet anyone's eyes. Each day was marked by his resignation and sometimes anger. He hardly ate or slept. When Kathleen or Meg could not find him, they looked to their mother, and there he would be, his weeping face in her unmoving lap.

Dr. Krommer had come when Peggy fell down the stairs. One day, Peggy had been humming and sewing in her chair, occasionally talking about Daniel and how she missed him. But then the miller returned without Daniel and Brian, saying they had gone on to Philadelphia on the barge.

Patrick stormed into the kitchen, up the stairs when he didn't fine Peggy in her chair, a wide-eyed Mr. Danner right behind. "Peggy, that boy is not my son anymore! Do you know what he has done?"

"What, Patrick, my love?" Peggy asked softly.

"He's gone to the city! That boy . . . he is no son of mine, I swear it! After all I have done for him, he repays me by running away like a child."

"Calm, my love," she said. "He will be back with the miller, and you gave him permission to go."

"No! Danner is here, and the boys are gone!" He turned to the miller, who almost visibly cowered before Patrick Kelly's anger. Patrick waved his arms, his face red, and his boots kicked a hole in the wall, and then he turned. Peggy sidestepped, lost her footing, fell down the stairs, and hit her head at the bottom with a thud that turned Kathleen's stomach. She rushed past her father and Mr. Danner, almost tripping herself and knelt by her mother.

Peggy's eyes were closed, and there was blood coming from both her temple and her nose. She was breathing, but she did not respond to Kathleen's pleas. "Meg!" she hollered. "Meg!" Kathleen looked to the top of the stairs, saw the shock on her father's face.

The younger girl, her red braids flapping behind, came running, her cleaning rag still in her hand. She had been cleaning downstairs. Meg never said, and Kathleen never asked, why she had not come when she had heard their father yelling. Perhaps she was just grateful she wasn't the brunt of it and stayed out of sight. But Kathleen's call was different.

"Get Dr. Krommer, quick!" Kathleen yelled, still cradling Peggy's head.

"What happened here?" Dr. Krommer said. It may have been minutes or hours since Meg had gone to fetch him; time passed in waves like the ripples in a pond for Kathleen, time having less influence as it passed. Kathleen explained as coherently as she could, not meeting her father's eyes as he stood as if pinned against the wall, and she was grateful that her voice was strong, and the tears did not fall. Meg was looking on with wide eyes. Dr. Krommer pushed the girls roughly out of the way, and Mr. Danner took each by the arm and led them to the parlor. Leaving for a moment, he returned with water for each of them.

Dr. Krommer was an old man with white hair that stuck out around the crown of his balding head. He was often jovial even with his patients and especially with those who were seriously ill. He was always kind, and he was no less kind when he spoke to the girls, but he was not at all cheerful. Kathleen saw him glance at Patrick. But to him, he said nothing. Mr. Danner hovered nearby while Dr. Krommer told the girls that their mother was very ill. She was breathing, and her heartbeat was weak. There was nothing to do but watch and wait. She might live, but she might not.

Kathleen sat in rigid acceptance as Meg leaned on her. Kathleen held her chin up with determination. One tear fell, and she did not give it the satisfaction of wiping it away, but rather she sat with calm dignity as she thanked Dr. Krommer. She and Meg sat on the couch as Dr. Krommer and Mr. Danner carried the inert Peggy upstairs to bed. She sat as Dr. Krommer offered to send to the Weimer farm for Mary. She sat as neighbor after neighbor came to offer help, food, and comfort, as the news spread up and down the street.

* * *

It had been so cold that morning, and Kathleen recalled that she could not get warm, no matter how many sweaters she put on. But now it was August and hot as blazes. She wiped her forehead with a wet cloth and dumped the pan of dirty water out the back door.

"Kathleen, how are you this fine morning?" Claire Hansen called. The young pregnant woman waddled over to Kathleen, leaving a line of linen flapping in the sun. Claire rubbed her big belly, proud that she was almost at her time of confinement.

Kathleen managed a smile. "I'm all right. How are you feeling today?"

"Couldn't be better!" Claire answered. She giggled again, holding up a bare foot. "Don't you think it is funny that the cobbler's wife can't wear shoes? My feet are so swollen by ten in the morning that I don't even bother putting them on anymore."

Since April, when Peggy had inexplicably taken a turn for the worse, she and Claire had become good friends. Claire was only nineteen, married to Oscar Hansen for three years, and this was her first pregnancy. Her lovely round cheeks glowed, and her lovely plump body got rounder, and Kathleen had to admit pregnancy agreed with her.

"Would you like to come into the kitchen for a cup of tea?" she offered.

"That would be lovely." Claire took Kathleen's arm through her own.

As Kathleen put water on to boil and brought two cups to the table, Claire asked, "How is Peggy today?"

"The same." Kathleen never said, "Fine." She was convinced that Peggy was never going to be fine, but she would always be the same. After the fall in January, Peggy had gradually regained mobility and speech. She tired easily, and Kathleen continued to run the Kelly home, but Peggy was not as absent as she was now. After the "attack" in April—Kathleen did not know what else to call it—Peggy had stopped communicating at all. One side of her face seemed to sag, and she could not move her left arm at all. Her beautiful auburn hair, which had been peppered with silver streaks before, was now completely white. Her green eyes were often vacant. All she did all day was rock, rock, rock in her chair. A few weeks after Fort Sumter, Daniel had written to say he had mustered into a Philadelphia unit, and when Kathleen had read it aloud, fearing the worst for her mother, there had been no effect at all. It was almost as if Peggy had not heard her.

"And how is Patrick?"

"Hmmm," Kathleen said with a shrug. Everyone knew, and no one discussed the effect Peggy's illness was having on Patrick. Who would ever have thought cold, rough, mean Mr. Kelly could have loved his wife so much? But it must be so, for after the April attack, he spent three days in a drunken stupor, crying like a baby and wailing for Peggy. As the drinking continued steadily, he lost weight, stopped eating and sleeping, and disappeared from the house for days on end. It was the first week of March that Meg had taken over the tavern, without any remarks from Patrick, and in the middle of April, they had hired a man named Carl to help her. He had worked for two months and then robbed them. Only recently had they hired another man, Will.

Kathleen and Claire continued to share the pleasant nothingnesses of life over their cups of tea. The harvest would be gathered in soon. That meant more business for Claire's husband and the tavern, although men who liked to drink didn't find many reasons not to, no matter what the season. Kathleen kept up with the war news, but only because Daniel was in it. Most of Millerstown, including Claire, did not agonize much about the battles fought so many miles south. Barely an eyebrow was raised when news of a battle at a creek called Bull Run, near the town of Manassas Junction, Virginia, were reported in the papers.

Claire eventually waddled back to her laundry, and Kathleen finished the kitchen chores. Drying her hands on her apron, she walked down the hall to the parlor. Peggy rocked contentedly in her chair, a green crocheted afghan draped over her lap. The wrinkled, frail hands fiddled with the edge absently. Kathleen knelt on the floor next to her mother.

"It is a beautiful day, Ma," she said in as normal a voice as she could. "Would you like to go for a walk today?" Peggy stared ahead.

Her face was bathed in morning sunlight. Kathleen brushed back a wisp of white hair.

On a whim, Kathleen dashed upstairs and returned with a hairbrush. She took out the hairpins holding Peggy's bun in place and began to gently brush it. At first, she talked softly, relating all of the same pleasant nothingnesses that she and Claire had just discussed. After a few moments, when all news and non-news was shared, she began to hum, and then to sing. It was a sweet Irish hymn that Peggy had sung to her daughters while brushing their hair when they were "wee bairns." As the song ended, Kathleen again pinned up the soft white hair, kissed the top of Peggy's head, and whispered, "I will be walking to Mary's house. Meg will check in on you."

Meg was in the tavern, inventorying the bottles behind the counter. Will had a chair upended on a table, tightening its legs. They both stopped when Kathleen walked in.

"Good morning, miss," Will said with a smile. He had a dimple in each cheek, very red lips and very straight teeth. His curly brown hair often hung in his eyes, and he distractedly pushed it back. His eyes were as blue as the August sky.

Kathleen smiled slightly and nodded in his direction, but she spoke to her sister. "Meg, are you very busy today?" she asked. She tried very hard not to take her sister from her work; Meg's work was as important as Kathleen's. Without Meg's tavern, there would be no food on the table. Without Kathleen, there would be no family to eat it.

"I have to finish the inventory. Will is going to Allentown tomorrow, so I need to know what he needs to buy." Meg was quite self-possessed and confident, so different from the weepy girl in January. Yet, despite the older attitude, she still looked the part of a girl: her brown hair was braided, and the two braids were tied with brown ribbons to match her dress, brown with yellow sprigs of flowers. The dress was knee-length, revealing long legs covered in wool stockings and boots. She did not wear the ruffled apron she had sewn two years ago but rather the apron Patrick always wore when he worked, a stiff white fabric that hung from her waist past her knees.

"I wanted to walk to Mary's, if that's okay," Kathleen said. "Could you keep an eye on Ma and make dinner? Don't do anything fancy. There's cold ham and a block of cheese, and I baked bread yesterday. It might be just you and Will, but if the boys come home, they can eat sandwiches too."

Meg nodded and returned to her work. "Sure, I can do that. Do you know when you'll be home?"

"Midafternoon, I guess," Kathleen said. Impulsively, she kissed her sister's cheek and bounded out the door back to the house with more energy than Meg had seen in a while.

"Well, I'm glad she is going to see her friend," Will said when she had gone. "She works really hard." He turned to Meg. "I'd say her sister works just as hard, but you just make me work!" He chuckled, and Meg scrunched up her face and stuck out her tongue at him.

"Making you work keeps you out of trouble," Meg teased, writing on her list. "And no self-respecting woman would work hard if she had a man to do it for her," she added.

"Ho, ho!" he laughed. "Now we're getting personal. And who said you're a woman, anyway? You just turned fifteen, as I recall." Will had been included in the small yet special family meal.

"That just means I have many more years to perfect my craft."

They worked quietly for a while. Then Will began to sing a loud, upbeat Irish tavern tune. Before long, Meg had joined in, and the sound reverberated off the walls. Meg enjoyed Will's company, and she knew that he knew without him, she probably could not take care of the business as well as she did. With all gentlemanly manners, he never let on that he knew.

* * *

Kathleen relished her solitary walk. The warm August wind pushed her from behind, her long black skirt dancing before her on the road. She only wore hoops for Sunday Mass or for a social event. She sighed. The last social event she had attended was a Christmas social at the community house. She had danced with a boy named Ed, and he had walked her home. Da had not liked the look of him, and she never saw him again, not even around town. There had been a quilting bee for the Schimmer girl to help her prepare for her wedding, but she had missed that women's social in April because she was simply too tired. The day after the bee, Peggy had the setback, and that was that.

Now Kathleen allowed her mind to drift as she walked the dusty two miles to the Weimer farm. Tall grass and wildflowers grew along the way. She wanted to stop and pick some; maybe on the way home, she would allow herself that indulgence.

Kathleen recalled Paul and Hannah's wedding. The young woman had been beautiful in her deep maroon dress with white lace at the collar and cuffs and intricate buttons down the front. Her hair had been laboriously curled and piled on top of her head. Her skin was perfectly white and smooth, her eyes had sparkled with joy, and the pretty smile never left her face. It was easy to see the couple's love for each other as they said "I do."

Kathleen kicked a stone. Oh, how she waited impatiently for that day! For two years since wearing long skirts and her hair up, Kathleen had waited for a man to notice her, to talk to her, to walk with her after church. Other than the disappearing Ed, no one had.

And now no one would, she was certain. She no longer mingled with the young people in town and around the county, and so no one would have the opportunity to notice. She acted and lived like a matron and mother, but really, she was on the road to old maidhood.

And anyway, she reasoned, what if someone *did* notice? Would she leave her family without someone to clean and cook and take care of everyone? Would she leave her mother, who could do no more than sit in a chair? Would she leave her father, who was absent most of the time anyway? Would she leave Meg to do it all? Poor Meg. Kathleen wouldn't—couldn't—do that to her sister.

But neither could Kathleen marry and take care of her own home and still care for her family's home. She didn't want to marry and live in her parents' home, either. No, the whole point would be to leave. But she was duty bound to stay.

By the time she walked around to Mary's kitchen door, the tears were streaming unheeded down her face. Mary met her on the back step. Without a word, Mary wrapped her arms around the young woman, and they sat in the sun. Kathleen did not see Sarah come to the screen door or Mary shoo her away. Kathleen simply cried on the older woman's shoulder.

After the tears were dried and the hiccups had stopped, Kathleen followed Mary into the tidy warm kitchen. Sarah smiled but soon left with a pot of beans for the summer kitchen. Already at eleven-fifteen in the morning, the small space was perspiration-inducing hot. Kathleen sat at the table with a cold glass of water. Mary's kitchen was delightful.

"You must be exhausted," Mary said as she sliced a crusty brown bread. "You've been working too hard."

"If I don't do it, who will?" Kathleen said matter-of-factly. With the tears dried, she was back to her old self. "Meg takes care of the tavern. The boys are nowhere to be found half the time. Da is gone or drunk . . ." She broke off in midsentence. She had not meant to bare her family troubles.

Mary kept working. "You and Meg have taken on a lot of responsibilities. How old are you, Kathleen? How old is Meg?"

"I'm sixteen. Meg just turned fifteen." She sipped the water. It tasted so good.

"Do either of you ever get a break?"

"Well, I'm here," Kathleen smiled. "But that means Meg is doing double duty. Anyway, you and every mother I know do the same thing day in and day out, and you never get a break."

Mary chuckled. "Some days I think about when I was young like you. And some days, I think I must never have been young." A pause. "It gets easier, I guess. You get into a rhythm. You move faster with practice."

"Mary?"

"Yes, dear?"

"The hardest part for me is seeing Ma the way she is. Sometimes I avoid the parlor because I don't want to see her," Kathleen whispered, ashamed even as she knew it was the heartfelt truth.

Mary set the knife on the chopping block, wiped her hands on her apron, came around to where Kathleen sat. She pulled another chair over and gazed intently at the younger woman. "Kathleen, I'm sorry. I never thought about how hard that must be. I only thought of the work."

Kathleen shrugged, determined not to cry again. Her voice broke as she spoke, but she pressed on. "Sometimes I wish she were at least talking to us, even if she had to sit in a chair every day. I want to know how to make shepherd's pie, and my soda bread never comes out right, and my pie crusts are never as flaky as hers."

"Well, now, you've come to the right place! I'll tell you what. If Meg is agreeable, if she doesn't feel that it would be too much for her, you come here every Monday. That's my baking day. We'll work together." Mary squeezed Kathleen's arm, which still gripped the glass of water, like a lifeboat in a choppy sea. "I know I can't take away . . . these feelings of . . ." Mary bogged down.

"I know what you are trying to say," Kathleen whispered. She was moved, overwhelmed. "Thank you, I would like that."

Kathleen stayed for dinner, a rich table set with chipped plates and mismatched silverware. She sat next to Ben, with her own brothers sitting across from her. They had been helping in the fields. They were tanned and growing more than she'd realized. Each of them would need new shirts before winter, and little Will's ankles were peeking out the bottom of the trousers he wore.

Sarah and Mary had prepared pork and cabbage, mashed potatoes, dark bread, and a big bowl of butter beans that steamed in the middle of the table. The men dug in heartily, and even George and Will took large helpings before Kathleen and Mary and Sarah.

"So, Kathleen, it feels like too long since we have seen you around," Frederick said. "I don't get to town much these days, but I hear your sister has help again at the tavern."

"Yes, Will is a wonderful help. I don't know how we'd get along without him. We can't pay him much, and we can't give him a place to stay. I wish we could do more."

"He lives in town somewhere?" Mary asked.

"Yes, he boards with two other bachelors up the mountain. We feed him though. We can manage that much."

"Where does he come from?" Frederick went on, chewing a mouthful of pork.

"He was in New York City for several years since coming from Ireland. He worked many jobs, he says, including managing a hotel. He came with references."

"How did he hear you needed help?" Mary asked.

"Hmmm, Mr. Granger, I guess," Kathleen said with a shrug. "He came to town in June and couldn't find work. Mr. Granger kept his letters of reference at his mill. Looked him up, I guess, sent letters of inquiry. He was going to send him away because he didn't have any work for him, but Carl had left by that time, and Mr. Granger knew Ma and Da were still sick, so Mr. Granger came to see me and recommended Will."

The day of Will's arrival had been a day when Kathleen had been at wit's end. Ma was not recovering from her attack upstairs, and Da was by her bedside, as he had been for days. He had not slept as far as Kathleen could tell, and he had not eaten during that time. He was gaunt and old. Just old.

Kathleen was in the kitchen, having swept and mopped the floor. She was boiling water for washing. She was wondering how they would survive without the missing cash, feeling ill-equipped to handle what life was tossing at her feet. Ma would know what to do. But Ma couldn't help now.

Meg came into the kitchen, carrying the tavern ledger under one arm and a bin of dirty water in both hands. The tavern had been closed since the robbery, and Meg was deciding what could and should be done. She had cleaned the place and wanted to sit with Kathleen in the kitchen to discuss the ledger. Neither knew what it would reveal.

Seven-year-old Will came tearing through the back door, dragging mud and rainwater with him, and ten-year-old George tailing close behind. It was apparent that this was not a good-natured run, for Will squealed and hid behind Meg, who carefully balanced the sloshing water to keep it in the pan. Kathleen, frustrated with her now-dirty floor, reached out a hand to grab George. His momentum sent them both sprawling at Meg's feet, and this time she could not contain the water. Kathleen and George took the brunt of the dirty water, but the floor was quite wet too.

Kathleen seethed, closing her eyes and holding her breath. Somehow, Meg shooed the boys out the door, giving George a good whack on the fanny, and began to clean up the mess. Kathleen was grateful for Meg's help, but she wondered aloud how long it would be enough.

Meg squeezed her older sister's hand. "We'll get through. It's just a little while, and then Da will be back to normal, and before you know it, Ma will . . ." Kathleen's calm, resigned face stopped her in midsentence. They sat in silence a moment.

"Well," Meg continued quietly, ever the pragmatist, "let's look at the ledger and see how things are. I wonder if Da has an account at the bank."

"I'm sure he does." Kathleen's head was beginning to hurt. The numbers on the page were small, cramped, and hard to read from this angle. She pushed the book so that it was fully in front of Meg. Kathleen didn't know what to do with the numbers anyway.

While Kathleen went upstairs to change her dress for something drier, Meg's eyes followed her finger down the columns. Income in the left marked with a plus sign. Expenses in the right marked with a minus sign. The middle column was for the addition and subtraction with a running balance.

Meg sighed. "I think we're okay," she said when Kathleen returned. "According to this, we have several hundred dollars, but I know the box only had fifty, so Da must keep it in the bank."

Kathleen did some quick mental arithmetic. She had shopped for the family for over a year because Peggy knew she enjoyed the walk through town and meeting friends. Flour, sugar, tea, lye for soap, tallow for candles, thread, cloth, buttons, needles, and corn for chicken feed, oats for horse feed, which Da had always taken care of. Meat and vegetables had to be bought because they lived in town, not on a farm. Maybe this year, she could start a garden, but they really did not have much room on their town lot. Wood for heat;

with Daniel and Da gone, they would need to pay for someone to chop and deliver it.

Kathleen shook her head sadly. "I don't know, Meg, but we have to pay Dr. Krommer and the mortgage. I don't know how much that is."

Meg nodded decisively. "That's what I thought. It won't last long enough if Ma and Da don't get better." It occurred to Kathleen that they were both speaking as if Da were ill too. "I'll have to keep the tavern open."

"You can't do it yourself. Maybe the boys—"

"No, they can't. But if I do it all myself, it means I won't be able to help you around the house. If I take over the tavern, I will have to do that full time. You need to think about that before you agree."

Kathleen quickly reviewed the pros and cons of the decision. It remained the only viable option.

Minutes later, as if in answer to prayer, a knock sounded on the back door. Meg answered, and a tall young man holding a worn cap in his hands asked to speak to the man of the house. Meg glanced at Kathleen, then said, "I guess that would be me."

The man looked startled. "I was told that the owner of the tavern might need some help. Is that true?"

"Possibly. May I ask who you are and who told you?"

"I beg pardon, miss. My name is William O'Neill," he said, sticking out a calloused hand. "Mr. Granger of the mill told me. I had inquired with him about work, and he didn't have any, but he sent me to you."

"Yes, he came to speak to me," Kathleen interjected.

"Where are you from, Mr. O'Neill?" Meg asked, motioning him into the kitchen. He walked a few steps inside, just far enough to close the door, but not far enough to be comfortable. He nodded to Kathleen, who nodded in return. She continued to sit at the table, quietly closing the ledger and drawing it nearer herself.

"Originally from County Meath, but I have been in New York City for five years. I never liked the city, so I saved my pennies and decided to move south. I see this area is a beautiful farm country. I have been in Pennsylvania since March, miss," he said. He stood a bit straighter. "My credentials, miss: I was a handyman for the landlord of the home place. Did that for, oh, six years or so before I just couldn't stand his arrogance another minute. Came to America, worked at the docks and then as a porter in a fancy hotel, and then I became the manager of a smaller place. I did that for four years. If I had not had that job, I wouldn't have saved enough to come here. But here I am!" His smile was kind and genuine.

"What about your family?" Kathleen asked.

His face hardened, like a tortoise shell protecting the soft flesh underneath. "Dead, miss. My ma and da, my sisters and brother. I have one nephew still living. He lives with his father's folks in New York City. I am as alone as a body wants to be."

Meg glanced at Kathleen, then said, "Mr. O'Neill, will you be in town for a while? We must discuss this and get back to you. Where might we send word?"

Mr. O'Neill nodded, glancing at Kathleen. "Please send word to Mr. Weland's homestead on the hill. He has been kind enough to let me stay on Mr. Granger's recommendation."

"Thank you. We will send word of our decision within two days." Meg ushered him out and turned to Kathleen. "He is godsend! He worked in a hotel, managed a hotel, even!"

"I don't think we should rush into this."

Meg sat across from Kathleen. "Mr. Granger is a good man, a good friend of the family. I trust his recommendation. I think we should hire him."

"Carl lived in the township all of our lives. We trusted him personally."

Meg sighed. "That was unfortunate."

"This whole year has been unfortunate."

"We have to do something, Kathleen," Meg insisted softly. "Someone has to take care of this family. It's you and me or no one."

"But how will we pay him? And where will he sleep? He can't sleep here."

"Maybe Mr. Weland will let him continue to stay there." Mr. Weland was an older bachelor who worked at Lauer's mill. He never spoke to the customers at the mill, unless Daniel Lauer was not available, and he came to town as little as possible. Perhaps he would enjoy the company, Meg thought.

"Perhaps. But what about pay?" Kathleen pressed.

Meg pulled the ledger from Kathleen's grasp. She grabbed a scratch piece of paper and pencil but soon realized there was more to figure out than simply how much to pay Mr. O'Neill.

They took their time that day and the next. They scratched numbers on papers, spoke with Mr. Granger, who seemed to think it was a good idea to hire him, and mentioned it to Da at dinner, but Da didn't seem to hear them. Finally, around two o'clock in the afternoon, they sent George and Will to take the short note up the hill trail.

"Mr. O'Neill, we would be pleased to hire you. Pay is two dollars a week and meals. Please arrive at 10:00 a.m., and the tavern closes at 10:00 p.m. You will be reporting to Miss Kathleen and Miss Meg Kelly. Please be prompt."

Neither young woman thought there was a chance he would not be prompt, but Kathleen felt it added importance and authority to the note.

Will—he soon became Will instead of Mr. O'Neill—worked diligently, serving the tavern and the family as if he were one of them. He sang while he worked, greeted everyone he met with respect and courtesy, and did not pry into the hidden facets of Kelly life.

Kathleen explained as much as she could to Frederick and Mary. George and Will were staring at her; she realized they probably did not know what was happening at home, beyond the change in their parents. Ben and Sarah seemed intent on the conversation as well. Kathleen suddenly realized just how long it had been since the Kellys and Weimers were together.

Frederick sat leisurely drinking his coffee. "Is there anything we can do for you?" Frederick asked as Sarah began to clear the table.

Kathleen shook her head. "I can't think of anything. Keep praying, and maybe try to talk to Da, but I don't know how much good that would do. Do you think the Weimers would like to picnic with us on Sunday? Out by Swabia Creek?"

Frederick grinned as he sat back in his chair. "Absolutely!" He stretched, stood up, and kissed the top of Kathleen's head. "Please forgive me for not getting to town to see how you've been."

Kathleen smiled up at him. "Thank you, Mr. Weimer."

"You are welcome, Miss Kelly," he said. He and the boys walked out the door, and Kathleen helped clear the table. It had been a good time, a good meal, and she had had a good cry. A good cry always made her feel better.

Later that night, Mary and Frederick were preparing for bed. "Frederick." She sat at her dressing table, brushing her long brown hair. Her husband sat in bed, reading the Bible, his spectacles perched precariously on his nose. He glanced up quickly, and the glasses fell onto the coverlet. "How long have George and Will been helping you in the fields?"

"Oh, most of the summer. And I've been grateful, let me tell you. With Paul married and Brian and Abby gone, the extra hands, little as they are, have been much appreciated."

"With not having to pay Brian and Paul's wages, or having to feed Brian and all that, do we have any extra cash money this year?"

"What are you thinking, woman?"

"Perhaps we can pay George and Will. Obviously not a full wage," she continued quickly. "They are just boys. But, perhaps, it would help the family, and it wouldn't feel like charity, and the boys would feel proud of themselves."

"Woman, I like the way you think! I think that's a marvelous idea. Even if we didn't have extra money this year." He paused, closed the Bible. "What do you think of this O'Neill fellow? Have you met him?"

"Oh, yes, I've met him. I didn't talk with him long, but he seems very polite and good-hearted. Catholic. Irish. Dotes on those girls, I think."

She crawled into bed next to him, and he blew out the lamp. "Do you think Brian is all right?" It was their typical bedtime conversation these days: to discuss Brian and Daniel and the war and Abby in the city.

"I'm sure he's fine. If not, we would have heard."

"And Abby? Abby's all right too?"

"Abby is probably better than Brian at this point. She's doing what she loves, and what else could a person ask for?"

"I'm sure if Daniel were here, the Kellys would have not needed O'Neill."

"I'm sure if Daniel were here, the only one that would be unhappy would be Daniel. He would be working in the tavern, which he hates. Peggy would be well. Patrick would be as he always was, and you're right, they would not have needed O'Neill. But God is faithful and sovereign. He did not allow these circumstances to come about for no reason, Mary. We must wait to see His purposes."

Mary sighed and snuggled into the crook of his arm. "You're right as always. What would I do without you?"

"Carry on as best you can, Mary," he whispered. They soon fell asleep.

Sunday was beautiful. They sat beneath a tree, the picnic spread out before them. Kathleen had prepared cold fried chicken, potato salad, cucumbers and onions in dressing, and soda bread with jam. Mary brought blackberry pies for dessert. Will had joined the family. It couldn't be any better, but it was.

Da and Ma had come.

Will gently helped place Ma in a bed of quilts in the back of the wagon, and Da meekly climbed up next to her. At first, Peggy sat with her head on Patrick's shoulder, not moving or speaking. Then she had begun to look around her, suddenly aware that she was not gazing at plaster-covered walls. She tilted her head to the sky, and Kathleen rejoiced to see her mother's face.

Peggy and Patrick sat by themselves on the corner of the blanket. Patrick ate a piece of chicken and a few bites of potato salad. Peggy managed to eat a slice of soda bread with thick strawberry jam; a wonder, considering she had only eaten oatmeal and soup for five months. She ate slowly and determinedly.

It really was wonderful that they had come. Kathleen couldn't take her eyes off them. Will and the Weimers talked easily and softly, as if not to disturb the others.

Kathleen was not the only one engrossed in Peggy and Patrick. Meg, too, stared openly, grinning from ear to ear most of the afternoon, and only occasionally talking with Sarah. George and little Will sat as close to their parents as they dared. As she watched them, Mary was overcome by how young the two boys were. George was almost two years younger than Ben, and Will was three years younger than that.

Frederick stood up and stretched as they finished their meal. "Mr. O'Neill, will you walk with me? Let us work off some of this delicious meal our ladies have shared with us." The young man rose, smiled his thanks at Mary, Kathleen, Sarah, and Meg and joined Frederick as he walked through the tall grass near the creek.

"How are you getting along, Mr. O'Neill?"

"Fine, sir, just fine."

"I'm sorry that this is the first we have had a chance to talk. Spring is a busy time for farmers. I've not been to town much this season."

"I realize that, sir. I have been quite busy, too, truth be told."

"Now, tell me, son, how are things at the tavern? I mean, really. Tell me honestly how the business is holding up."

Will was surprised at the question. "Sir, are you asking me to tell you their financial situation?"

Frederick paused then nodded. "Yes, son, I guess I am. I want to help in any way I can. I have not done enough for them since . . . since Mrs. Kelly got sick."

"Well, sir, I don't know the answer."

Frederick stopped walking and turned to stare at the younger man. Will stopped too. "Aren't you running the tavern then?"

"No, sir, I'm not," Will replied. "Miss Meg manages the tavern. I simply work for her."

"Who keeps the books then?"

"Miss Meg."

"Who manages the inventory?"

"Miss Meg. I go to Allentown to buy what's needed, but only what she tells me."

"Who waits on customers?"

"We both do. She's quite funny, and the regulars love to hear good Irish blarney!"

Frederick resumed walking. He didn't speak for a moment, simply thought about what Will had said. Kathleen was running the household. Meg was managing the business. Young George and Will were helping the Weimers on their farm.

"Do you spend much time with the family?" Frederick asked.

"I suppose, sir. I eat some meals with them, and I work with Miss Meg in the tavern ten hours a day at the very least. In all honesty, I wish there were more I could do for them. Without any men in the household, save Mr. Kelly, whom I don't see much at all, Miss Meg and Miss Kathleen have had to pay a handyman to do some things around the house. I have offered to help, but they insisted on paying, and that's not what I meant, so I stopped offering. No use fighting against their pride."

"You're right about that."

"Miss Meg has asked me to fetch some things at the general store for Miss Kathleen from time to time, as if that's part of what I hired on for. I gladly do it. I'll do anything to help Miss Kathleen."

"Do you talk to Kathleen much?"

"No, sir. Miss Meg keeps me right busy most of the time," he added with a smile.

The two of them had turned back toward the families still gathered around the blanket. Frederick called Kathleen's name and motioned for her to join them. As she walked toward them through the tall grass, Frederick again turned away from the group. Will did the same.

"Kathleen, join us for a moment," Frederick said. Kathleen settled into step next to Frederick, standing between her and Will. "How have you been, Kathleen?"

Kathleen felt as if she were walking through water, pushing against the current of grass as she tried to keep up. The men noticed and slowed imperceptibly. "Oh, fine, Mr. Weimer."

"How are things at home?" he continued.

"Oh, as well as could be expected, I guess." Kathleen wondered idly why he was questioning her this way when she had undergone a very similar interview at the Weimer dinner table only four days ago. Not much could be expected to change in four days.

"Well, it just occurs to me," Frederick said, stopping in midstride, "that I should try to talk to Patrick this afternoon, see if he would like to go with me to Kutztown next week. It is so good to see him out of the house!" Without another word, Frederick turned around and strode purposefully back toward the blanket.

Kathleen turned to follow him. It was the strangest conversation she had had with Mr. Weimer in a long time. He used to do strange things like that: engage her in conversation and then simply walk away. Or call her out to the Weimer barn, when the Kellys visited, only to ask her one small question and then continue with his work as if she were invisible. But that had not happened in years, probably not since she had been Ben's age and still played kick the can with Daniel, Brian, and Abby.

Will reached out a hand toward her but stopped just short of actually touching her arm. "Miss Kathleen, will you still walk with me?" She paused, looked up at him. Brown curls hung in his face, his ears stuck out a bit too far, and his dimples were showing next to his hesitant smile. She nodded and kept pace with him easily as they made one more turn.

"I should cut your hair for you," she said unexpectedly. They walked in silence for half an hour as the two families packed up the picnic.

Meg sat in the tavern late Wednesday night, whistling while she washed glasses. She sent Will home when he finished mopping the floor. She enjoyed the peace and quiet late at night, even though her bones were tired and she could barely keep her eyes open. It was a good time to think, and if she began talking out loud to herself, as she was prone to do, there was no one around to hear it.

Things sure are different around here, she thought. *Ever since that picnic two weeks ago. Da walking around with a little less whiskey in his belly. Ma walked from the parlor almost to the kitchen. She fell, but she wouldn't let Kathleen put her back in the parlor or upstairs. She wanted to be in the kitchen.*

"That's a good sign, right?" Meg said aloud. She nodded to herself. *Yes, a very good sign. George and Will brought home eight dollars this week. Mr. Weimer paid them for all their work this summer.*

After the harvest is completed, probably three or four weeks of hard work, he will give them each another five. That is eighteen dollars total, and George handed it to Kathleen like he was the proudest little man around!

"I know she was proud of them. So was I. And it was so nice of Mr. Weimer to pay them."

Kathleen has been doing a lot of smiling. More than once, I've caught her dancing with the broom in the kitchen. She goes at least once a week to the Weimers she says just to visit. Then I watch Ma, which isn't quite so bad now that she is . . .

"What do I call it? It is almost like Ma is waking up. She has been asleep almost six months, and now she is starting to wake up." Meg wiped a tear away. Sometimes late at night, it all hit her like a runaway horse. And she missed Daniel more than she ever thought she would.

As she put away the last of the glasses, Meg decided to write a letter to her brother. He had been her best friend, even though she had not participated often in his adventures with Brian and Abby. It was mostly because she didn't like Abby. But Meg had especially enjoyed the hours of conversation with Daniel about the books he had read and the stories he had written. She missed the way he described a sunset or a flock of geese flying overhead.

There was much to tell him. First, she would admit that she now admired the very girl she had long despised. She and Abby were not that different after all. They were two young women who relished earning their own way in the world, doing what men often said they couldn't or shouldn't.

Meg also had to tell him the good news about Ma and Da that things were getting better. She would tell him about the boys working for the Weimers, about the tavern, about Will, and about Kathleen, and the way she seemed to be falling in love.

Meg stayed awake most of the night to write her letter. She finally sealed it, and set it on the kitchen table where Kathleen would see it to put it in the post. Then she curled up in her cold sheets and hoped her sister would let her sleep late, the thought fleeting across her mind even as it closed in sleep and the sun peaked over the horizon.

Chapter 7

THE SANITARY COMMISSION

Abby took a deep breath outside the thick oak door leading to the drawing room. She patted her dark chignon self-consciously, smoothed the secondhand deep-purple skirt and fichu, and knocked smartly on the door.

"In!"

Abby had not often had the privilege of entering the drawing room since she began working for the Rollinses ten months before. The ladies of the house spent most of the daylight hours in it reading, drawing, or entertaining guests. They took their places on the horsehair sofas after a delicate meal of four-minute eggs and tea in the breakfast room down the hall. They remained in the well-lit front room until dinner at half past noon, then returned to it afterward to continue their leisurely existence until getting dressed for supper or a party, at which time Abby's presence was required.

Abby didn't care whether or not she ever spoke with them, beyond the usual dialogue accompanying a dress fitting. The two Miss Rollinses, the young Mrs. Rolllins, and the old Mrs. Rollins never carried on a conversation that was worthy of her participation, as far as Abby was concerned: parties and money spent on hats and who had a new carriage and who was caught in a compromising position.

Now, however, she needed to speak to Mrs. Rollins about a very important topic. When Mrs. Rollins beckoned her with a voice that demanded obedience, Abby opened the door and, as demurely as possible, stepped into the women's sanctuary.

She bowed delicately, and Mrs. Rollins barked, "What is it, girl?"

"Pardon me for intruding, ma'am," Abby began. "I would like to speak to you regarding a very important matter, if I may."

"What is it?"

"Ma'am, I attended a meeting of the Philadelphia branch of the Sanitary Commission. Actually, I have attended three. The women of this city are striving to help our men at war by collecting quilts, pincushions, butter, eggs, cider, chickens, oh, just anything the men in the camps can use. Anything that will help them as they fight the damn rebels—"

The younger girls gasped. Mrs. Rollins glared. Abby was sure it was meant for her, but the old woman glanced at her daughters, and they dropped their eyes and embroidered furiously on their pillows.

Abby took a deep breath. "Forgive me, ma'am."

"Don't apologize, girl. They are damn rebels. Continue."

Abby hid a smile by biting her cheek. "Yes, ma'am. I heard Dr. Henry Bellows of New York City speak about the great need he has seen in the camps. It is just awful! I would like to help in any way I can, as I am sure you and your daughters would as well. Ma'am, I respectfully ask if I might have one morning a week to myself to go door-to-door to collect items for the commission to send to the Army." She waited.

Mrs. Rollins rang the bell for her maid. Young Sally quickly appeared, curtsied, and waited for instructions.

"Sally, bring my sewing basket and two of the quilts that need mending from the chest at the bottom of the bed," she said. The daughters glanced at Abby and their mother from time to time as they waited for the girl to return. Abby was not permitted to sit, and she tried not to tap her foot.

When Sally returned, Mrs. Rollins again turned to Abby. "I assume that you are not going to be walking around the city by yourself."

"No, ma'am! The ladies go in groups of four."

"What day of the week?"

"Most go on Tuesday, but I know there are at least two groups that go out on Friday, and one on Saturday."

"Well, then, is there a day you prefer?" Mrs. Rollins was unfolding a quilt, looking for the small tears that time had worn into the fabric.

"No, ma'am . . . Tuesday, I guess."

Mrs. Rollins looked squarely at Abby, and Abby felt like squirming but stood firm. "I think it is a wonderful idea, Abby. Allow us to mend these quilts, and you can take them with you next Tuesday."

Abby smiled and curtsied. "Thank you, Mrs. Rollins. Thank you!" This time when Mrs. Rollins's attention returned to the quilt, Abby knew she was dismissed.

Abby hurried out of the room, closing the door behind her. She almost skipped up to the room where she slept and sewed. The room was small and, at the moment, chaotic. Unlike most servants in the house, Abby had the room to herself to allow for the sewing, and for that reason, she loved it!

It was on the third floor, and the dormer window looked to the east over the small park on the Rollins's property. The morning light still shone in the window, which she washed herself every week. The pale winter sunlight was valuable to a seamstress and a girl who loved the outdoors. She refused to allow dust and dirt to stand in the way.

She made her bed hurriedly that morning, yanking the green-and-pink quilt so far up that three inches at the foot of the bed was uncovered. Her worktable was cluttered with pieces of white cotton, yellow cotton, purple silk, and magenta taffeta. Lace, scraps, and thread spilled out of the woven basket beneath the table. The chair in which she worked held her latest creation, a magenta silk dress for Miss Joy-Lynn Rollins.

Excited for the prospect of helping the commission, Abby sat down to work. Miss Joy-Lynn, aged fourteen, had been invited to a twelfth night ball, which would take place in two days on Sunday. Because a certain gentleman by the name of Mr. Thomas Oliver would be present, and as Miss Reena Patterson would not be, Miss Joy-Lynn had demanded an extraspecial gown.

Although she never said so, Abby thought the latest fashion was garish. A Mr. William Perkin had developed a synthetic dye from coal tar only a few years ago. The fabrics that were dyed using the new process were bold, at best, and appalling, at worst. Yet, many women were much impressed with the new magentas, purples, and brilliant blues. Of course, Abby wore the hand-me-downs that she obtained from her employers, but she still preferred a soft red cotton or wool. Next to naturally dyed fabrics, the new colors looked even worse.

The dress styles were pretty, though. Skirts were not as wide. Hoops were smaller these days. Shirtwaists were not attached to the skirts. Rather, the new style was to wear a white or light-colored blouse with a triangular-shaped fichu, which was usually made of the skirt fabric. Sleeves were fuller. Small ribbon ties were worn at the throat. Abby still enjoyed her work, and she looked forward to the refreshing changes that her profession encouraged. She hoped the next new trend would get rid of the flashy colors!

Abby sewed for hours, humming. Occasionally, she stood to walk around or simply to stretch. Jane came to get her when the servants' dinner was ready.

Because Abby's room was often a mess, Abby joined Jane in her room after their daily work was done. Jane's roommate, another housemaid, Helen, was also great fun, and the three girls too often stayed up talking until late. Today, as Abby took her place at the table, Helen and Jane looked exhausted, and Abby felt sorry about their late-night conversations.

"Well, Miss Abby, seems the news about you has already spread," Brona said. Brona was a fat middle-aged Irishwoman, dark hair pulled back in a bun, cheeks flushed and marked by pox scars. She was the cook, and therefore the head of all kitchen servants. Mrs. Frank, the housekeeper, presided over the maids. Officially, Edward, the steward, was in charge of all servants, but unofficially, even he deferred to be the woman who ran the kitchen. If Brona was unhappy, everyone was unhappy, and so she was the master of the house, whether the Rollinses knew it or not.

"What do you mean?" Abby asked, her fork stopping halfway to her mouth. The steaming potpie was tickling her nose, so she put it in her mouth, not caring about the rudeness of talking with her mouth full.

Brona sipped her tea. "The Sanitary Commission. Not twenty minutes after Sally came to the kitchen to tell me, Herself came to the kitchen." She meant Mrs. Rollins, of course; calling the mistress "Herself" was a holdover from her days working in a big house in Ireland as a young teenager. Brona always sat at the table and participated in the conversation but never ate. The servants kidded behind her back that she ate so much at the stew pot, her belly was full by the time it was done.

"What did the The Rollins say?" asked Harry, the twelve-year-old houseboy who was deathly afraid of his employers. The Rollins was what all the servants, except Brona, called her. His mother also worked for them as a laundress, and she just smiled at him across the table. He was a small boy for his age, sickly and homely in appearance, with washed-out blue eyes, blond hair, and a pale complexion that often looked flushed with fever.

"Herself told me to write out my grocery list. She wants to go through it to see what the household can cut out. Not to save money, mind ye. No, she wants to send the extra to the boys at the front, she does. And Miss Abby here will take it to the commission on Tuesday."

Abby found herself grinning as everyone turned to look at her. She told them the story of how she asked for permission to take one morning a week to herself, and Brona laughed heartily. "Not only do ye have the blarney of the Irish, ye have the moxy of the Deutch!" she said, knowing that Abby was both Irish and German.

"Moxy?" Harry asked.

Abby said, "Courage, daring, guts."

"Ah," Harry said. He looked at her with admiration. So often, he reminded her of Ben.

The meal was finished quickly, and Abby was grateful that she did not have to clean up. She had to admit this designated chore thing was marvelous! It had its downside, too, though. She sewed, and only sewed, which meant that she didn't work in the fields or garden. She missed being outside.

She was fearfully watching her body morph into a white flabby mess. She was no longer tan, no longer lean. She didn't work at anything! She ate as much as ever, but never worked it off. Her corset was not as small as it was six months ago, and she was afraid that the pattern would continue. Walking around Philadelphia at least once a week might help alleviate some of the problem.

The December wind was bitter cold as she and the other three women from the commission began their trek through the city. Abby had been introduced that morning to Mrs. Gwyn Johnson, Miss Teresa Johnson, and Miss Tabitha George. The Johnsons were good friends with the Rollinses, which put Abby in a class below them. But the necessity of the work seemed to override societal distinction. Miss George was Miss Johnson's lady's maid, which also put her above Abby. Miss George seemed less inclined to lower herself to Abby's position, which Abby found odd, considering the Johnsons were willing, and they had further to go to do it!

Mrs. Johnson kept up a steady flow of conversation as the foursome walked through the streets. Snow was standing in mushy gray piles of sludge. Before they had gone a block from the Johnson home, where Abby had met the others, all of their skirts were dirty and wet along the bottom edge. Their boots were slipping through the muck. Abby fervently hoped she would not fall.

It soon became evident that Mrs. Johnson would do the talking when they encountered possible donors. One of the young women knocked on a door, and when it was opened, Mrs. Johnson began a well-rehearsed speech.

"Good morning, ma'am. I am Mrs. Gwyn Johnson. It is so nice to make your acquaintance." Of course, the woman at the door, or in the parlor, offered her name and her hand, and this put Mrs. Johnson on an easier footing. Now they were acquaintances, and people were less likely to deny a request from an acquaintance than they were from a friend; an acquaintance might speak ill of you to others if you denied their request, but a friend never would.

"We are working with the newly formed Sanitary Commission. It has come to the attention of many physicians, including Dr. Henry Bellows and Mr. R. C. Wood, the surgeon of the Army, that conditions in our Army's camps are deplorable. Just deplorable! Men—our men"—not *Mrs. Johnson's* men, Abby was sure, but some of Abby's men—"are dying of disease before they see battle. There is not enough food, and what they have is inedible."

One woman on Lee Street actually stopped Mrs. Johnson at this moment to bring up a point. It was a very good point. "I thought every soldier was given meat, vegetables, and flour every day. And coffee and even some sugar," she stated. Abby immediately liked the woman because the only way she would know that information would be if her husband or son had written it to her in a letter. A letter similar to one Abby had received from Daniel.

Mrs. Johnson did not know what to say. Abby stepped into the silence.

"Excuse me for interrupting," she began, speaking around the dark cloak Mrs. Johnson wore. "It's true that last summer and fall, the men did have enough to eat. Beef and chicken, vegetables, bread, coffee, and sugar. Now, however, the fresh vegetables are gone. It's winter, and there's nothing for them to find as they march along the roads and fields. Cold fields, no doubt muddy and sloppy with snow," she added, recalling Daniel's latest letter. "The flour is full of bugs, and there is no sugar to be had. Please, ma'am, anything you can give would be greatly appreciated. We are collecting blankets, shoes, sewing necessities, butter, flour, sugar, coffee, canned vegetables. Anything you think your husband or son might need at the front. The Sanitary Commission will make sure the men get it."

"My son will get what I send?" the woman asked hopefully.

"I can't guarantee that, ma'am, but if every woman gives a little something, your donation might go to someone else's son, but her donation might go to yours."

The woman wiped a tear from her eye. The four women shivered on her front step. She quickly stepped aside and ushered them in, saying, "I'll just get some things together for you. Shall I put them in the basket?" Each woman carried a basket on her arm, and Mrs. Johnson nodded.

When they were back on the street, one quilt, two cans of beans, two pounds of flour, and one pair of boots heavier, Mrs. Johnson spoke to Abby, drawing her up to her side. Miss Johnson and her maid walked behind. "Miss Weimer, thank you," she said. After a pause, she asked, "You have someone you love in the war, don't you?"

"Yes, ma'am," Abby said. "My very good friend Daniel and my Uncle Brian. They are in the 69th Pennsylvania."

They continued with the task at hand, and the women were pleased with the contributions they were able to collect. For several weeks, Abby joined the Johnson contingent on their walks around the city. On one cold, drizzly day, Mrs. Johnson asked Abby about "her two men in the Army." Their conversation was interrupted many times by their frequent stops on doorsteps, and Mrs. Johnson often, though not always, deferred to Abby when speaking with the mistress of the house.

As the morning progressed, Abby described what she knew of Daniel and Brian's unit because Mrs. Johnson seemed to want to listen. "A senator from California started it. His name is Edwin Baker, I believe. He wanted Washington to know that California was for the Union and not for the Confederacy. So the unit started out as the 2nd California, but it was mustered into the 68th Pennsylvania in July."

Mrs. Johnson did not look at Abby as she spoke. "They are the Irish unit, aren't they? I thought it was the 69th unit?"

"Yes, they wanted to be part of the New York Irish Brigade, also the 69th, of New York. They asked Governor Curtin for permission to join them, but he said no and threatened to withhold their pay packets if they tried to go to New York."

"How awful!" came a cry from behind them. Abby didn't know if it was the daughter or her companion.

"Yes, but Governor Curtin did let them change their name to the 69th, instead of the 68th."

"My son, Richard, is in the Philadelphia Brigade as well." It was the only brigade in the nation to be called by the city in which it originated, but many also called it the Irish Brigade because most of the men in it were, indeed, Irish. Further conversation revealed Richard was not, however, in the same unit as Daniel. The designation of "the Philadelphia Brigade" was a source of pride to many, including Mrs. Johnson, and Abby was suddenly overcome as the stately older woman fought to keep her composure as they walked on South Street.

"Richard has not written in months," Miss Teresa Johnson said. Abby could see the worry in the lines around Mrs. Johnson's face.

"Did your son enlist in April?"

"No, July," Mrs. Johnson replied, her voice steady. The men who had enlisted in April had done so assuming, as so many did, that the war would be over by July. When it was not, a new call for volunteers went out. Many, though, Daniel and Brian included, had reenlisted and never left camp. They still believed in the cause for which they fought.

Since July, Abby had received numerous letters from Daniel. He always seemed to be in a new place marching around Virginia. Still, they had not seen much fighting; the commanding officers seemed reluctant to engage the Confederates. So, just as in Philadelphia, they marched and drilled, camped and drilled some more.

"Little Mac keeps us busy," Daniel had written. "He says we are unfit, and he works us until we are fit, and then he keeps us going until we can do it in our sleep. But we love him. Everyone loves General George McClellan." Local newspapers said differently, but Abby was glad the soldiers liked McClellan, even if the press did not.

Mrs. Johnson's voice was strong but far away. "The weather is cold now. They are in unfamiliar territory, and it's almost Christmas. They must be cold and wet and hungry and tired." She turned to Abby as they stood on a corner. "Has your friend said if it snows where they are?"

"He said it doesn't snow much," Abby said. "Spirits are low. I am sure all of this"—she lifted her basket—"will be a welcome relief."

Abby was pleasantly surprised with Mrs. Johnson, who was of the same social status as the Rollinses but was nothing like them. The older woman was kind and eager to talk about what she and Abby had in common. As they approached her grand home with heavy baskets, she invited Abby inside. Abby hesitated, but her feet were blocks of ice and her hands were numb, so she nodded and followed the group up the stone steps.

A maid met them in the front hall, a graceful, high-ceiling room that was paved with marble stones and decorated with gilt mirrors and woven baskets. The young woman took their wraps, bowing to Abby as if she were the same as the others. Abby followed the group into the drawing room.

"Alice," Mrs. Johnson called as the young woman retreated. "Bring us tea and sandwiches in the drawing room. I assume the fire is lit?"

"Yes, ma'am."

"Good." Mrs. Johnson closed the door behind her with a clunk and joined Abby on a pink sofa.

"Miss Weimer, tell me about your home. How did you come to be the most talked about seamstress in all of society?"

Abby started. She was talked about? Was that good or bad?

"Well, ma'am, I don't think you would find my upbringing all that interesting." Abby surreptitiously massaged her hands to get the blood circulating.

"I disagree," Mrs. Johnson said forcefully. Abby could see she was used to getting what she wanted.

Abby nodded slightly. She described Millerstown, the people, the farms, the new-fangled trains. She described her parents, seeing them in her mind's eye and suddenly missing them intensely. She expressed her enjoyment on the farm, her abhorrence for domestic chores, and her desire to live and work on her own.

"Yuck," Miss Teresa muttered.

The door opened, and Alice returned with a tray. The tea was piping hot. The cups were delicate white china with lilac roses and a gilt rim. Abby had expected sandwiches that would fill a soul: thick bread and sliced ham or beef and a wedge of cheese. What she saw was a plate of tiny squares and diamonds, bread, lettuce, and some form of meat—chicken? She watched as Miss Teresa nibbled one delicately while balancing her teacup on her lap, and she tried to follow suit.

As she resumed her discussion of Millerstown, her teacup tilted, and as she reached to grab it, it dumped entirely on her gown. Miss Teresa found this funny, and she actually neglected to cover her mouth with her hand when she laughed out loud. Her mother glared, but she cooed at Abby.

"Oh, dear, are you all right?"

With no less than four layers of fabric between her legs and the hot tea, Abby was just fine. Her pride was wounded. "Doppich!" she muttered.

"I beg your pardon?" Mrs. Johnson offered her a towel from the tray.

"Oh, nothing," Abby said with irritation as she dabbed at her lap. She glanced at her hostess. "Forgive me, Mrs. Johnson, I'm just clumsy."

Mrs. Johnson put her cup and Abby's on the tray and shifted slightly so as to see Abby fully. "Now, then, let's talk business."

"I don't understand," Abby said.

"How much is Mrs. Rollins paying you?"

Abby's eyes opened wide in surprise. Who was this woman? One didn't have such discussions with one's employer, let alone with a stranger. Abby felt like she had stepped off the hay loft and landed in another country. "Ma'am?" she said weakly.

"I want to steal you from her, that's all. But I want to make it worth your while," Mrs. Johnson said.

"I don't understand. Why do you want me to work for you?"

"Because I want to take a seamstress with me when I go to Washington, and the girl I have now would die of fright before the train left the station," the older woman said matter-of-factly. "You are just the kind of girl I need. I have been asked by the Sanitary Commission to travel to Washington to help the doctors there. You will be my companion as well as my seamstress. And I think you will like the work."

"May I ask a question?"

"Of course."

"You are married. Do you need a companion?"

"No, not for society's sake. For my sake. Teresa will remain here. My husband will as well. I will be staying with a relative. As I said, you will travel with me and help me with the commission's work. The fact that you are a seamstress is just another advantageous quality."

Abby was stunned. She felt herself rising in society. To be a companion was better than being a seamstress. Washington was better than Philadelphia. And to be working for the Sanitary Commission was the best of all. Compared to what the soldiers were doing, it wasn't much, but it was something for the cause, and she was ready.

"Yes, ma'am, I thank you for your consideration." She gave Mrs. Johnson a figure that she thought was exorbitant, and the woman threw back her head and laughed. Abby thought she had misstepped. She was about to retract it when Mrs. Johnson spoke. "Oh, yes, my dear, you are exactly right!" Mrs. Johnson said. "Give Mrs. Rollins notice at once and send a messenger when you are ready to move here. I will send a carriage for you. We leave next Friday."

"Will Mrs. Rollins release me that quickly?"

"I'll handle Mrs. Rollins. Don't you worry about it." So Abby didn't.

The carriage pulled up in front of the Johnson's home the following Wednesday. Abby had not walked with the commission ladies the day before. Mrs. Rollins, quite upset with Abby's defection, required her to stay at the house to do extra sewing. Abby felt dreadful in giving notice, but her replacement, an older widow named Mrs. Bennet, arrived Tuesday afternoon. She seemed quite capable.

The driver and the steward carried Abby's two trunks and three boxes upstairs. She was placed on the second floor, another improvement. Her room was connected with Mrs. Johnson's salon.

She was awed by the opulence of it. Her bed was dressed with linen sheets, lace-edged linen pillowcases, and gauzy draperies. It was larger than any bed she had ever seen. There was a green carpet on the floor, under the bed, and extending almost to the other wall. There was a tall chest of drawers with a lace runner and glass bottles on top. Abby recognized the delicate Irish lace she often saw at the market. Green gossamer curtains framed the tall windows, and when Abby looked behind them, she was surprised to see a balcony. One set of windows was actually a set of doors. It was too cold to be outside, but Abby stepped out anyway.

"My dear?"

Abby hurriedly stepped inside the room, closing the doors behind her. She felt guilty, but Mrs. Johnson was smiling at her.

"Come into the salon. I would like to speak with you." Abby glanced at her pile of luggage. "No need to unpack. We leave in two days," the older woman reminded her. Abby followed her employer into the sitting room.

This room was just as elegant, but Abby refrained from looking around. Mrs. Johnson poured tea. The older woman sat in an overstuffed brown chair with flowered cushions. Abby sat in a wing chair decorated with the matching fabric.

"Well, now, young lady. I wanted to tell you something about myself." Mrs. Johnson sipped her tea. "You remind me of me, you know. I was like you when I came to America. Fiery, ambitious, determined, and a little bit out of the ordinary. I was a companion for an old woman."

"Mrs. Johnson, may I ask what country you came from?"

"Wales, my dear. My name was Gwyneth Evans. I was a poor girl from the backwoods of Wales." She chuckled. "All of Wales is backwoods."

"I knew that there were many Irish who settled in this area. I did not realize there were also Welsh."

"Oh, yes. Bryn Mawr is a Welsh neighborhood. That is where I settled originally. When I began working for Mrs. Johnson, I moved here."

"Mrs. Johnson?" Abby asked in surprise. "Any relation?"

Mrs. Johnson nodded. "My mother-in-law." At Abby's surprised look, she added, "I told you I had ambition. I worked for Mother. In the evenings, she often sat in the parlor with her son Edmund. He was over thirty years old, a widower with no children. He was a lawyer. He took an interest in me. Before his mother passed away, she gave us her blessing, and we were married more than twenty-five years ago."

Abby was amazed. She never would have thought that a young immigrant girl could end up married to a lawyer with money and prestige. An idea came to her mind, and she smiled.

"What is amusing, my dear?"

Abby shook her head. "I was just wondering if you had hired me with the hopes that I would marry your son," she joked.

"His name is Owen," Mrs. Johnson said, "after my father. He is a surgeon, and he left his practice here to join the Army of the Potomac. It was he who first wrote to me about the Sanitary Commission. I will be working closely with him. It is with him that we will be staying. Owen is twenty-six," she added.

Abby quietly drank her tea. What had she gotten herself into?

Philadelphia was big, grand, immense. When Abby first stepped off the train nearly a year ago, she had been overwhelmed by the busyness, the noise, the people. She had stood nearly a full minute on the train platform ogling the people who passed. She had walked through the town in a dream for days.

She didn't know if she would have the words to describe to Daniel what she saw when she stepped off the Baltimore and Ohio Railroad car in Washington. There were more people than she had ever seen! There were men in tuxedos at two o'clock in the afternoon, top hats tipped to every lady the men passed. There were ladies in silken finery, dark in color to hide the soot that inevitably stained traveling costumers. There were servants, not dressed quite so fine but certainly well, white men and black men, white women, and even children. There were children holding onto the skirts of their mothers, children holding the hands of a nanny or older sister.

And everywhere, soldiers. The men in blue walked sedately through the masses. They carried their guns on their shoulders. Their steps were purposeful, and they did not meet the eyes of the people around them. Abby mentioned this to Mrs. Johnson, wondering if soldiers were no longer gentlemen who tipped their hats and helped women across the street.

A deep voice spoke from behind them. "They are under strict orders from McClellan: no funny business." The two women turned. A tall dark-haired gentleman in a gray suit and top hat, which he raised with a smile, stood before them. He leaned over to kiss Mrs. Johnson's cheek. "I am sorry I'm late, Mother. Traffic is terrible. I have a coach waiting, so let us go."

Mrs. Johnson pushed Abby forward ever so slightly with her white gloved hand. "Allow me to present Miss Abigail Weimer." Abby curtsied elegantly, dazzled by Owen Johnson's smile and good manners.

As he led them through the crowd, his manservant gathering their luggage from the baggage car, he continued to answer Abby's question. "General McClellan took over the Army last summer and did a complete overhaul. The men were undisciplined, rowdy, and often drunk. McClellan put his foot down. He demanded excellence and discipline, and he got it amazingly. And now, when you see the men in blue walking around Washington, they better be sober and polite and perfectly in line, or else. And no one asks 'or else what?'!"

Mrs. Johnson and her son talked amiably in the carriage as it drove through town. They allowed Abby to gaze out the window without interrupting her with questions and polite but inane conversation. For one brief moment, Abby wondered what Dr. Johnson must think of her, and then she didn't care.

The train platform had been huge and filled with people. The city was worse. But Abby knew she would get used to it; she had adjusted to Philadelphia, hadn't she? So she gazed with wonder at the buildings. They drove past the Capitol, with its pointed dome touching the gray winter sky. Men in long trench coats and tall top hats walked up and down the steps, and Abby wondered what went on within the governmental buildings.

Dr. Johnson's home was in a row of similar white stone structures along a wide, quiet street with naked trees grasping at blistering skies. The door was blue. The glass panes looked clean, and she saw a young face peering out of one of the upstairs windows.

Mrs. Johnson saw it too. "Owen, who is that child?" She indicated the second-story window with a nod of her chin as he handed her down from the coach. Owen looked, waved, and the child waved back and turned from the window. A moment later, as they walked up the few steps to the door, it opened, and the excited little girl was jumping into Owen's arms.

The blond girl was about six years old. She wore a yellow dress that, to Abby's perceptive eye, was well-made but probably extravagant for a little girl, with all its ruffles and lace. The girl had twinkling blue eyes and pale skin. Her smile was wide and genuinely happy as she giggled in Dr. Johnson's arms. He chuckled, too, and pulled gently on a bouncing curl. Then he turned to his mother and Abby.

"Mrs. Johnson, Miss Weimer, may I present my ward, Miss Sarah Cristoff?" He set her on her feet. She curtsied prettily. "Sadie, this is my mother, Mrs. Johnson, and her companion, Miss Weimer."

"How do you do?" Mrs. Johnson said. Abby repeated the phrase, as did the little girl. Then she took Dr. Johnson's hand, and the group entered the large front hall. It was not as large as Mrs. Johnson's Philadelphia home, and not as elegant, but it was stunning nonetheless.

Mrs. Johnson gazed around with disdain. "I love what you've done with the place."

"I apologize, Mother, that I don't have your exquisite taste," Mr. Johnson said. Miss Sadie was pulling him impatiently into the parlor.

Abby disagreed with her employer's assessment. The furniture was well-made and expensive-looking, although it was simple. Green sofa and two matching chairs, a brown carpet interlaced with red and rust-colored designs, deep green curtains, heavy crystal vases flanking a large painting over the mantel piece, and flowers everywhere. Before she sat down, Abby took a long drink of the fresh aroma from a vase on a side table. She didn't know the names of the flowers, but they were beautiful. Where did one find fresh flowers in winter?

"Go upstairs and play in the nursery, Sadie," Dr. Johnson said, giving the girl a kiss and pushing her gently toward the door.

"Will you eat supper with me?" she asked plaintively, holding his hand.

"You may join us for the special occasion of my mother's arrival." The words were like a jeweled crown to a pauper's daughter. Miss Sadie squealed delightedly and ran from the room.

"What a joyful child!" Mrs. Johnson said. "Who is she? Your ward, you said?"

"Yes, Mother, you remember Cousin Marared? She married Tom Cristoff when she came to America."

"Oh, yes, is that her daughter? I have not seen Marared and Tom in years. Are they out visiting?"

"No, Mother. Marared passed away two years ago in childbirth. The boy died the next day."

"Oh, how sad," Abby said softly, sipping the tea that had been brought by the maid.

"Tom is in the Army. He fought in the Mexican War and was given a commission in this one," Dr. Johnson continued. "He asked me to take Sadie until he should return . . . or if he does not."

"Have you heard from him lately?" Mrs. Johnson asked.

"No, not since before Thanksgiving," Dr. Johnson said evenly. "Last I heard, he was in Tennessee. I try to read the dispatches as they come in, and I have not seen his name on a list anywhere, but I haven't received a letter in many weeks."

"Do you have someone to care for the girl? Certainly *you* do not."

"Sometimes, Mother, you are such a snob," Dr. Johnson said lightly. "Have you been a Johnson for so long that you have forgotten you are also an Evans?"

"Tut-tut. Quite right!" Mrs. Johnson said. Abby smiled behind her cup. Mrs. Johnson was truly a woman who didn't fit with convention.

Abby set her cup on the table, not her lap. "Dr. Johnson, may I ask a question?" He nodded. "What exactly do you do with the Sanitary Commission? And what will we be doing?"

Dr. Johnson rubbed his hands together. "Ah, yes, your whole reason for coming. I am a runner, so to speak. I run from F Street to the Capitol. I meet with Dr. Clement Finley, the new surgeon general, and with different senators who always seem to be standing in our way. I go into the field and meet with generals help them make improvements in camps."

"And us? What will we be doing?"

"There are so many things for you to do! Mother, if you would take over the collection point here in Washington . . . all of the items the ladies of the North are collecting come to one collection point. They need to be inventoried and sent to the proper places, so it's management and paperwork duties that are needed there. We don't want to send blankets to men in South Carolina in June if what they need is flour." He shrugged. "You get the idea." He turned to Abby. "Miss Weimer, you can help Mother in whatever way she needs, but we also need help in the convalescent homes. Soldiers need to be fed sometimes, and we help them to keep in touch with their families." He coughed slightly. "Can you read, Miss Weimer?"

"Of course, I can."

Mrs. Johnson laughed. "Don't get all in a snit, my dear."

"Yes, ma'am." Abby dropped her head.

"Well, then, you must be tired, ladies. Please allow me to show you your rooms."

It was another room that was expansive and expensively arranged. The windows looked out over the backyard, which was shared with the stone house on the next street. With the gray light of early evening, dulled by immovable clouds, Abby was not sure which direction the room faced. If it was east, the sun would wake her—the large four-poster bed stood right next to the windows. She ran her hands along the carved posts, pineapples on top of cross-hatched stems. The coverlet, a black and deeply colored crazy quilt, was nearly covered by pillows. How would she ever sleep in this bed? The pillows would have to be put on the floor every night. Or on the sofa. Her room had a sofa! It was black with more elegant carvings on the armrests. The wooden floorboards were polished to a high shine, and small braided rugs, all with a black base, were strewn around the room. There were two dressers, a full-length mirror, and two rows of hooks, presumably for dresses. As she looked around the room from the vantage point of the window, she decided she didn't like it. It was dark, too dark; she would call it the "black room." She hoped it did not indicate how life would be in Washington.

The days passed quickly for Abby. There was little time for leisure in the Johnson household. They rose early to eat breakfast and were on the streets of the city before eight in the morning. For all of Mrs. Johnson's intent to keep Abby as a seamstress, if only a part-time one, there was never time for sewing. Dr. Johnson dropped Abby at her designated convalescent home (there were so many different ones) and then his mother at the warehouse by half past eight. He proceeded to the headquarters at F Street.

All day long, Abby wiped sweaty, feverish faces with a damp cloth or squeezed the hand of a frightened soldier. She read letters, wrote letters as the soldiers dictated them, and ran errands for the staff. Thankfully, she was not required to perform nursing duties; men assisted the physicians in surgery and treatments when necessary. As the brick house was a convalescent home rather than a hospital, it was almost never necessary.

Dr. Johnson fetched Mrs. Johnson at five-thirty in the evening, and the two of them arrived at the convalescent home at ten minutes to six if traffic was not too congested. Abby sank wearily into the cushioned carriage, and some days Mrs. Johnson gently shook her awake when they arrived at home. More often than not, Miss Sadie greeted them at the door. But only on rare occasions was she permitted to share supper with them. Dr. Johnson sat with her in the nursery and then joined his mother and her companion, all three elegantly dressed, for dinner at eight.

In the first eight weeks of her time in Washington, Abby barely had time to breathe. She wrote only one letter to Daniel and received none. As she and Dr. Johnson became better acquainted, during parties on Saturdays and at church on Sundays and through dinner conversations and short walks around the park afterward, Daniel almost never came to mind, except fleetingly, as she saw him in the eyes of a recovering soldier.

"What is your name, sir?" she asked one such soldier on another cold winter day. The tall glass panes behind the young man's bed clattered in the gusty wind. When she leaned over to adjust the man's pillow, she could feel the cold radiating from the glass.

"Nathan, ma'am." His voice was more like a boy's than a man's. But the dark bristles on his scarred face, the scared and tired brown eyes, and the horrible injuries from which he was recovering said he was no longer a boy, even if his age was less than twenty.

"Nice to meet you," she said softly. She carried a chair over to the bedside, picked the bowl of soup up from the tray on the bedside table. "Can you eat something, Nathan?"

"Yes, ma'am." As Abby leaned forward to spoon some of the hot liquid into the young man, he said, "What is your name?"

The woman in charge of the aides, Mrs. Albert Crosby, had given all of the new recruits specific instructions. Abby was unmarried, and that would throw a kink into the workings of the home.

"These men have been away from home for many months. They miss their wives and sweethearts. They miss all of the feminine contact they had at home, whether from lovers or not," the gray-haired woman added. She stood at attention, like any good soldier, with her hands in their lace gloves clasped in front of her dark dress. She dressed like a widow, but with a few whispered conversations, Abby soon learned that she was not. She was, however, very strict.

"You will not tell them your name. You will not spend more than ten minutes with each. You will not return to the same ward two days in a row."

"Why?" Abby whispered to the nearest non-new recruit, Mrs. Adam McMillan.

"Because we don't want the young men to become attached to us."

Abby wanted to again ask why but refrained, as she caught sight of Mrs. Crosby's flashing eyes on her.

So Abby did not tell Nathan her name. It was silly, but she obeyed the rules. Until she knew Mrs. Crosby had walked to the next ward. "My name is Abigail Weimer," she said softly, spooning more hot liquid into the young man. "I'm from Pennsylvania. Where are you from?"

"Indiana."

"Do you have a big family?"

"Naw. Just my pa and my two brothers. Kurt and John are both in the war too."

"Were you all in the same regiment?"

"Yes."

"And have you heard from them lately?"

Nathan shook his head, gently pushing the spoon away. After an agonizing moment, while he massaged the stump of the leg that was no longer there, he said, "Kurt was in the hospital with me. I don't know if he survived. John visited us before the unit moved on. But then they moved me here, and I don't know where Kurt is."

That afternoon, stealthily so Mrs. Crosby would not hear of it, Abby approached one of the nurses. She did not know his name, and she shook in her boots as she approached him. He was a big man, but he seemed like a good man, so she asked, "If I were looking for a specific patient, either here or somewhere else, how would I do that?"

It took several weeks of secret prying and sniffing like a hound, but Abby found Kurt Unger. He was in another Washington convalescent home. Of the two brothers, Nathan was the better healed. Abby squeezed the young man's hand as she watched him get loaded into an ambulance, a green wagon that buzzed with flies and looked like it had been through a war.

"Thank you, Abby," he whispered, kissing her hand quickly.

"Take care of yourself," she whispered back.

Later that afternoon, Mrs. Crosby cornered Abby. "Miss Weimer, that is not acceptable." The woman's voice was firm but low, frightening really. "We have rules here."

"I thought the whole point was to help these men get better," Abby said stiffly.

"Yes, but we have rules."

"I understand your rules just fine. But the *point* of the rules is to keep the men from forming attachments. He didn't, so what is the problem?"

It was a difficult conversation all around, one that continued long into the night.

"Abby, what were you thinking?" Mrs. Johnson demanded after dinner. A note had arrived during the meal telling Dr. Johnson of Miss Weimer's impropriety. Mrs. Johnson was distressed. Dr. Johnson was irate. After much kowtowing and many promises and submissions to his authority, Abby finally managed to placate him. He accepted her apology, but still, he stalked rather than walked from the parlor.

Dr. Johnson—she was now permitted to call him Owen—handed Abby into the coach as the manservant held the large umbrella over both of them. Mrs. Johnson was sitting in her usual spot in the center of the seat facing backward. Abby moved to the far side of the other seat, making room for Owen.

"I have heard good things about this play," he said as they began to move. He was dapper in his black tie and tails, his top hat on his lap. His dark hair was slicked back. Abby could smell the pomade. He had begun wearing a goatee, and he smoothed it constantly. He caught her looking and grinned. "Have I told you how lovely you look, Abby?"

"Yes, I believe you did," she said with a smile. It was her red wool dress, still her favorite by far, but she had recently added velvet ribbon at cuffs and hem and cascading lace at the throat, accented with a broach. She had changed the buttons from dull black to pretty pearls. She was quite pleased with it.

The coach let them off in front of Ford's Theater. The sidewalk was crowded with umbrellas and wide skirts. The hoops of the last few years had been replaced by layers of petticoats. In the cold February night, Abby was glad for three layers of cotton, flannel, and satin, but they made moving difficult. Owen pushed his way through the crowd waiting to purchase tickets; they had a reserved box.

It was not a large theater. It was lit by kerosene lanterns. The gallery was already filling up, and it was rather noisy. Owen led them up a flight of carpeted stairs to the boxes on the right. Owen pointed out several important people, and Abby was surprised that generals and their wives came to the theater.

"Shouldn't they be with the Army?" She sat between Owen and his mother, who was talking to another elegant lady on her left.

"They often come to town, especially if the army is close by."

It still seemed strange to Abby, but she let it go. She waited in silence for the play to start. When it was over and they were working their way toward the exit, she said, "I didn't particularly like it."

"Oh?" Mrs. Johnson asked, holding her son's arm. "Why not, dear?"

"I thought it was very sad. Everyone died at the end."

Owen laughed, causing others to turn their heads. Mrs. Johnson shushed him. He waited until they were in the carriage—it had stopped raining, Abby was glad to see—before he said, "Abby, it was a Shakespearean tragedy. Of course, everyone died!"

"What was the name of it, Owen?" Mrs. Johnson asked as the coach rumbled down the street toward the townhouse.

"*King Lear*, Mother."

Mrs. Johnson stepped down first. She was already up the steps when Owen turned to help Abby disembark.

"I truly enjoy your company, Abby," he said.

She looked up at him. A few street lamps burned, as did the lantern held by the servant at the door. She could not see his eyes, shadowed by his top hat, but his mouth was turned up in a smile. She smiled in return.

Letter from Abby to Mary

March 16, 1862

Dear Ma,

Life is still very busy in Washington. I spend each day sitting with convalescing soldiers. I read to them, help them write letters home, and feed them if they are too weak to feed themselves.

We have received word of a battle in Hampton Road, Virginia. We have received many soldiers that were in the various ships that were attacked by the *CSS Virginia*. Have you heard about the battle? It began on the eighth. There were several United States Navy vessels in the sea outside the town of Hampton Road. A ship came down the Elizabeth River. It was an unusual ship, to say the least: it was made of iron, first of all, and had sloping sides down to the waterline. It was apparently steam powered, which is not completely unusual. Some sailors have told us that the cannonballs and mortar shells with which they barraged the vessel were useless. They simply fell away without doing any damage. Unfortunately, the wooden vessels that these sailors were in could not withstand the onslaught of the *CSS Virginia*.

Many men have come to us recovering from burns and amputations as a result of that battle. The men that were injured on the eighth did not know about the second day of the battle, but it was in the papers. The *USS Monitor* arrived. It is also an ironclad vessel, and the two ships fired at each other all day with little effect. Neither side clearly won the battle, but the newspapers are all talking about a "new era in naval warfare." I guess because it is the first time two ironclad ships have fought.

I enjoy my job here. It is odd, Ma, that I am having such a good time, even though I have not sewed a stitch in nearly four months. I am planning on making myself a new spring gown, but I don't know when I'll find the time. But I really need one because Mrs. Johnson and her son and I and his ward often go to the park on Sundays. I feel like I should be better dressed than I am. I still have the hand-me-downs from Mrs. Rollins and her girls, but they are gaudy and idiotic dresses, and I don't think I will ever wear them.

Have I told you that Mrs. Johnson is trying to create a relationship between me and her son? He is a nice enough fellow, I guess, and very handsome, but I do not find myself interested in him. We talk, though, and I will be as nice to him as I can. But what if he proposes and I say no? Will I have to come home?

Say hello to the family for me.

Your loving daughter,
Abby

Letter from Daniel to Abby

April 12, 1862

Dear Abby,

I hope this letter finds you well. Our unit is still in Virginia. We have fought in light skirmishes, but no major battles, and I am fine.

We heard about several battles this spring, but we have not been in any of them. We heard about the battle at Forts Henry and Donelson in January. Those forts are in the western theater. Grant was leading our troops there. I hear good things about him: he is a strong, forceful, determined leader who is not afraid to do what soldiers are required to do. I must say, as much as we all liked Little Mac, he was one who was always afraid to move. Lee and Grant, however, seem like they are different, and I would be proud to serve under either. I know Lee is a Confederate, but from what I hear, he is a good man and an able commander. If those two ever meet in battle, I would be hard-pressed to say who would come out the victor.

The Confederates lost at Henry and Donelson. We heard about their defeat in February. When the news came through, we were in winter camp, cold and wet. But I had received a letter from you that day, and we all received some supplies from this new Sanitary Commission, so it was an all-around good day. Let me just thank you—and the other ladies too—who are working with the Sanitary Commission. The bugless flour and new candles are such a blessing. Pencils would be welcome, too, and not just for me. We are all running low on paper and pencils, and it pains us to think we will not be able to write home. I know when families don't hear from us for a while, they start to worry.

We also heard about a battle in Virginia, actually off the coast. A battle of two ships that are made of iron. I think it must be a mistake. Wouldn't they sink? How is it possible? I must say, though, that to have a ship, or any vehicle, covered in cannon-proof iron would be a great advantage on the battlefield. Have you heard details about this battle?

We also heard about the battle of Shiloh. It was bad. It was out in Tennessee, so I was not near it. Grant was again in charge of our men, just as at Henry and Donelson. He was waiting for Buell to arrive with more troops. I don't know how many he had, but it never hurts to have more. But I know that, unlike other generals we have had, Grant would not be afraid to strike with less if he was faced with the unhappiness of battle. Grant drilled his men instead of digging in. They were surprised by General Johnston on April 6. Shiloh is near the Tennessee River, which was Grant's goal—to control the river and the railroad that connects the west with Richmond. Do you ever find it odd that you are in our nation's capital and yet so close to the capital of another nation? I know I find it odd that I am in a leaky tent under dripping trees in a foreign nation. It looks like the United States. It feels like the United States. And yet it is not.

But Johnston attacked Grant, and many died. It is reported that many of our men sought shelter in the river. Our General Sherman distinguished himself by riding up and down the line, encouraging our men. I believe this man will continue to distinguish himself. Men are proud to follow such brave men as Sherman and Grant. And Lee.

The battle continued through the night and the next day. Grant led an attack at dawn. He surprised the Confederates, who eventually withdrew. I read the papers from the capital. They are saying unkind things about Grant. The men here are up in arms. They shouted when the paper was read out loud. We like Grant. We don't like the politicians and newspapermen and their contrary and unhelpful attitudes.

I have not seen or heard from Brian lately. I thought he might have been transferred, but then I saw him a few weeks ago. He said he has been on several missions. He is a sharpshooter. I know Brian is good at what he does. Every time I see him, even though he is tired and hungry, he looks happy and well.

You can pass that on to your family. And tell mine I am well. I don't know if I will be able to write to them soon, but I would be grateful if you would tell them for me.

Take care of yourself. What you are doing is amazing and wonderful, and I hope I never have to see you in a convalescent home!

Your well and wet friend,
Daniel

* * *

Brian walked through camp without responding to his comrades. He was just back from a mission. He was wet, dirty, tired, and hungry. He wanted a bath, food, and a bedroll.
"Father," he whispered, touching the priest on the arm. The young priest was sorting through a stack of letters, probably none of which were addressed to him. He looked up. "Father, can we talk?"
"Of course, my son." He led the way to the tent he used for confession, counsel, and his own sleeping quarters. He never fought in battles, but he followed the Irish Brigade from camp to camp, always ready to perform his own duty.
Brian had not been raised Catholic but rather Protestant. When he arrived in Philadelphia, he joined Michael and his family at the Catholic Church. He had not confessed. He had not partaken. He

knelt and sat and stood and sang and knelt and prayed. It hadn't really mattered.

But when the war started, and he joined the Irish Brigade, Michael and Katie had pressed upon him the need for absolution if war should bring death.

"You don't want to die unshriven," Katie had whispered, as if just saying the word was enough to bring it about.

After weeks of prodding, Brian gave in. He approached Father Flannigan, and from April to August, the priest had taught Brian his catechism, the prayers, the sacraments. In September, in a private ceremony, Brian had been converted and baptized into the Catholic faith.

Brian sat on a box in the priest's tent. "Father, I feel lost." Both the front and back flaps of the tent were tied open, but it was still dark within. Father Flannigan waited quietly. "I am a sharpshooter. You know that." A nod from the priest. "It's a lonely life. I sit alone in a tree or in a ditch. Or I ride my horse through forests for days. I wait for a gray or butternut uniform to come by. Sometimes I follow him to see where he will go, but if he's an officer, I shoot him on sight."

Brian put his head in his hands. How his chest hurt!

"You are doing your country a service."

"But what about my God?" Brian demanded. "What does God think of me? This is murder, Father! It feels like hunting. I am hunting for men. And I check their pockets, and I take what I find, and I leave them there. It is worse than murder!"

"No, my son. This is war. God is on our side."

Brian thought about that. Certainly, slavery was wrong. He did not argue that point. And perhaps war in itself wasn't wrong. But what he did was not war. He sat in silence for another man to walk past. Brian shook his head.

"I read my Bible, Father," he said. "When I'm sitting and waiting. My Bible says that vengeance is God's. He will punish evildoers."

"Yes, that is true. But sometimes God will use others to do it. Right now, He is using the United States Army to punish them."

"Doesn't the Bible also say we should share the Gospel with others? Bring them into the faith?"

"Yes, just as you were brought in to it."

"I can't tell them about God if they're dead!" He felt like screaming. The priest looked shocked, and for a moment, Brian wondered if he actually had screamed.

Brian fell to his knees before his priest. "Forgive me, Father, for I have sinned." The priest listened to his confession, gave him penance and absolution, and watched Brian leave.

As Brian rejoined the other men around the campfire, he cried in his heart, "Oh, God, save me! Save me from this hell!"

Chapter 8

MARY

Mary stood at the back door, looking southwest. Frederick, Ben, George, and little Will were approaching at a slow but steady pace. Frederick carried the heavy wooden-handled iron tools. The boys, growing in stature as quickly as they grew in character, led the team. Mary could hear their chatter and laughter from a distance, their youthful vitality not yet spent, even after a hard day in the fields. Frederick, on the other hand, walked with the tired and weary gait of a man used to a hard day's work and a good meal afterward.

Mary and Frederick did not have time to talk until after the dishes were washed and the evening farm chores done. As the sun sank in the west, Mary walked outside to find her husband. Frederick sat with his back against the house, his long legs stretched out before him. At first, she could not determine if he was watching the sunset or if he was sleeping.

He took her hand when she settled herself on the ground next to him, but he didn't speak. She, too, watched the sunset and closed her eyes at intervals. Finally, he spoke, "Where is Sarah?"

"In the kitchen, I presume. She was preparing to write a letter to Abby as I was coming outside."

"Is she a help to you?"

"Absolutely. If I were to go on a trip, I would not feel at all ill at ease to leave her alone with all of you. I know you would be well-fed and cared for."

"Good to know, good to know." Frederick paused then squeezed her hand. She could barely make out the smile on his face in the waning light. "You aren't planning on going anywhere, Mrs. Weimer, are you?"

"No, no, nothing like that. You asked, I answered. That's all."

They sat in the deepening dark and listened to the springtime evening unfold. The crickets were chirping, the leaves were rustling in a breeze that caused Mary to hold her shawl tightly around her shoulders, and a frog was serenading his lady in the distance. Mary could hear Frederick's breathing as it slowed and became the restfulness of full sleep.

But no, he wasn't asleep. "I had an interesting conversation in town yesterday," he said, his voice low, as if he didn't want to disturb the twilight.

"Oh?"

"I was waiting at the smithy for Walter to finish the shoes. He takes a long time, it seems, but I know I can trust the job. That new blacksmith in town now, he's quick about it, but the horses throw their shoes within three weeks. Anyway, we were talking about the fields and the war and whatever else, and young Mr. Gehman comes in." Frederick turned to look at Mary. "Do you know him, dear?"

"Yes, I know him. He was at the barn raising a few weeks ago, and I have seen him at church, but only from a distance."

"Yes, me too. Well, this young man starts talking to me as if we talk every week. Addressed me as Mr. Weimer, so I know he is a respectful sort. He goes on and on about his new piece of land and how he wants to grow apple trees and about selling the sauce and the cider and apples by the bushel. Walter was finally finished, and I walked the horses over to the wagon, and Mr. Gehman followed me. Odd, I thought. And then he says to me—he actually says to me—'Mr. Weimer, would you allow me to court your daughter, Sarah?'" Frederick turned with an incredulous look to his wife, who was smiling in the darkness. "Sarah! Can you believe it? Sarah is not old enough to be courted!"

"Frederick," Mary said. "Have you noticed the gray in my hair? Or in your own? Or the wrinkles around my eyes?"

"That doesn't matter, my dear, it doesn't change how I feel about you."

"Good, but that isn't my point, Frederick. *We* are getting older. That means our children are too. Look at Ben working with you day in and day out. He's just thirteen, but you've told me he works better than Brian ever did. Well, Sarah's almost sixteen, not too young at all really."

Frederick shifted uncomfortably. "If Sarah's almost sixteen, then Abby's almost eighteen," he said. "And I'm not even sure who she's walking home from church with or who asked to sit with her in the parlor . . . oh, Mary, what have we done? Abby should be here with us."

"Don't change the subject. We were talking about Sarah." Mary shivered. "Can we go inside to discuss this?"

They finished their conversation after all the clunks and shufflings of their children had stopped for the night. George and Will often stayed at the farm, easing Kathleen's burden and allowing them more time to sleep. After the first few nights of staying up until all hours talking and fooling around, the boys had learned that nights were meant for sleeping, or the days afterward would be miserable.

Mary lay with her head on Frederick's chest. The brown crazy quilt was pulled almost to their chins. The window was open a few inches to allow the sweet smell of springtime to air out the room, but the late April nights were still chilly. The sound of the crickets was loud, and the children slept soundly, so they did not bother to whisper as they talked. "So what did you tell Mr. Gehman?"

"I told him yes, but my heart wasn't in it. I figure I can get to know him in the next few weeks. We can invite him for dinner on Sunday if that's all right with you," he added.

"Mmm hmm."

"How old do you think he is?"

"Thirty, I guess. He's been on his own for many years now, even before his father passed away."

"Will he be good for Sarah?"

"That's what you need to find out, dear. You're the father." She laughed.

"Ha ha. Funny. And you'll get to sit back and do nothing so that Sarah can show off her cooking and cleaning abilities, Mother."

Frederick only called her *Mother* when he was exasperatedly amused. She laughed. "It will be all right, Father."

They lay in silence for a while, but neither was ready for sleep. Their conversation turned to the war, and their "other children." Frederick assured Mary that Abby was fine, only now he was as much trying to bolster himself as his wife. He assured her Brian was well, though they had not received a letter in months. He even comforted Mary's worried mind about Daniel; although not their son, they worried as much for him as for the others.

"Kathleen and Will are keeping company," Mary said suddenly.

"Yes, I know. Everyone in town knows."

"You know, Frederick, with Peggy and Patrick still . . . as they are, you should act as her father. Talk to Will. Make him declare his intentions."

"Already did."

After a moment's pause, "And?"

"Apparently, Peggy and Patrick are getting better every day. Patrick doesn't drink as much as he did, and he comes into the tavern occasionally, although only during the day when there are no customers. Will—well, Meg—still runs the place. Will says he and Kathleen will wait awhile just to see if her parents recover fully. If they do, he wants to ask her father properly."

"Good man, that Will," Mary said drowsily.

"Yes, a good man."

Letter from Sarah to Abby

April 30, 1862

Dear Abby,

Life is busy here. Planting is in full swing. Ma and I planted the garden already because it has been relatively dry and warm. We planted potatoes, cabbages, cauliflower, broccoli, radishes, carrots, beets, lettuce, onions, zucchini, butternut and pumpkin squash, pumpkins, and even two rows of flowers. There wasn't room for cucumbers because of the flowers. Pa said it was a waste, but I really wanted it so Ma talked him into it.

Ben is helping again this season. You should see how he has grown. He's only thirteen but almost as tall as Ma and taller than me. I think he'll be taller than all of us womenfolk before the year is out! I have made him two new sizes of trousers since October, and he'll need another pair by the end of June, I think. His shirt sleeves are too short as well, but with summer coming on, he can roll them up, and no one will know the difference. So I'll make him a new shirt for Sunday and leave it at that, although the shirts will start getting too tight in the chest pretty soon. He's not little Ben anymore! Boy, do I wish you were here to do the sewing!

George and Will Kelly are working on the farm too. Pa did not hire Joe this year. It seems so strange without Paul and Joe. I mean, last year we didn't have Paul because he married. Now this year, we don't have Joe. Pa pays the boys, I think, to help the family. Anyway, I don't worry about those things.

Ma and Pa are outside talking about me. Anyway, if they aren't now, they will be soon enough. When I went to town today, Claire Harris told me that her pa told her ma that when our pa was at her pa's blacksmith shop yesterday, Mr. Gehman asked if he could court me! I don't even know his first name. Henry I think, or Howard. Something with an H. Anyway, I don't really even know him, but he has sixty acres of grain, and I hear he has just bought twenty acres that he wants to put apples on. He has some big ideas about selling cider and sauce. I asked around when I was in town today, you know, just to find out what I could. Mrs. Timmerman says he has a nice big house with glass-paned windows. I asked how big the barn was because that always gives an idea of how prosperous a man is, although, knowing he has eighty acres shows he is prosperous enough! Mr. Timmerman overheard and said Mr. Gehman's barn is bigger than Pa's! This could work out very nicely, indeed. Too bad you aren't here. Maybe you could have a husband by now.

I always thought you would marry Daniel, to be quite honest. You were always walking and talking with him and Brian, although I don't think Brian wanted you around. He would just rather be there with the two of you than working.

Have you heard from Brian or Daniel lately? Kathleen received a letter from Daniel a few months ago. He told her about the recent campaign on the peninsula of Virginia. He said he is well but tired. We have not heard from Brian since before Christmas. I think Ma is beginning to worry. If you have heard anything, even just through Daniel, can you please send it to Ma? It would ease her mind a great deal, I think. And I thank you.

I hope you are enjoying the city. Ma said you are in Washington now working for the Sanitary

Commission. So the seamstress wasn't content to be a seamstress after all. I am sure the Sanitary Commission does important things, and you always wanted to do important things, so I guess you are where you belong. I wish you well. Take care, sister.

Praying God's blessings upon you,
Sarah

Letter from Bridget to Mary

April 18, 1862

Dearest Mary,

Oh, how I miss you! I hope you are well! If your children are anything like mine, they are growing faster than the weeds. I hope the children and Frederick are healthy and strong.

Peter has finished his seminary degree. The Gettysburg Seminary has taught him much, and we are both pleased. I am pleased because every night he comes home and plays with the boys while I put dinner on the table, and then after dinner, he allows me to sit with him as he studies. Have you noticed that my letters are more "educated" now? I read a commentary of the Book of John after he was finished with it, and I even read a book written by Harriet Beecher Stowe, *Uncle Tom's Cabin*. Have you read it? Three young boys in the house don't leave much time for reading, but it is nice to be able to, once in a while.

Peter will look for a pastorate after commencement. A trained graduate can go anywhere, it seems, but I am not sure I want to move. For now, he continues to work at the General Store as a clerk.

Peter Jr. is almost ten now. He is up to my shoulder in height. I am short, I know, but still, a mother should be taller than her son. He still has the bright red hair, like our brother Sean, and bright blue eyes. He is a smart boy, too, and he has been in the town school for three years now. He can read well, and cipher, and write. I shall have him write a letter to you.

Colum is eight. He started school just last year, and he can read almost as well as Peter Jr. Colum has trouble with mathematics, however. We struggle over simple problems each night, and if it were not for recess and a pretty teacher, I am not sure he would go to school at all. He gets so frustrated when he can't come up with the right answer. If he hands in the wrong answer, Miss Cabot makes him redo the problems until they are correct. Each week, the classes recite before the whole school. If they pass the oral examination, they proceed to the next lesson. If they do not perform sufficiently, they must redo that week's lessons. Many times, Colum comes home on Friday afternoon in tears because he must repeat the lessons. I don't know how to help him, Sister.

Robert is four, although he thinks he is as old as his brothers. He follows them everywhere. I am constantly reminding Peter and Colum to close the gate. We have a white fence around the front yard, and they always leave the gate unlatched. When I turn my back, even if the older ones have been gone half an hour, Robert is out the door and out the gate and down the street.

We had quite a scare last week. I could not find Robert. I searched the two blocks around the house. I walked the route to the schoolhouse. Sometimes, if he gets that far and school is in session, he'll play in the recess yard. But he wasn't there. I didn't know where else to look, and by that time, he must have been gone at least forty-five minutes because I'd been looking over twenty minutes by then. I ran downtown to the store, and Peter saw me and panicked. I love my husband, but sometimes he's worse than a woman. It's because he has such a good heart. Well, Peter and another clerk came and helped me look. We went back to the house and started over, and still we couldn't find him. Finally, we saw a young man carrying our Robert, and I ran down the street. Robert saw me and started calling for me.

He had fallen asleep in the man's wagon. Don't ask me how he climbed up in it. When the man was putting his feed sacks into the wagon bed, he saw Robert, but he didn't know who he was or where he belonged. Robert isn't talkative enough to say "I live on Grove Street." The poor man was walking around town as we were trying to find someone who knew Robert and could take him home.

I'm not sure, but I think Peter paid the man for his time. It is the least we could do. I for my part have begun tying my son to my apron strings, as they say.

The spring is wonderfully warm here. The crops are already growing in the fields. Sometimes after Sunday dinner, Peter takes us for a walk. Sometimes we go to Sean and Anna's, but sometimes we just walk. Well, the boys run, of course!

Sean and Anna are well. She is nearing confinement again. This makes six for them. Sean, Thomas, Ellen, Martha, and Grace, and now this one. Anna handles her pregnancies well. I wish I could do as well. I want a baby girl, but I fear another pregnancy.

Even though Sean and Anna live only three miles from town, we don't see them nearly enough. Ellen and Martha sometimes walk to town and stay with me for tea, and then Sean comes to get them after supper, but that's rare, and never in the winter, so I've not seen them in months.

I think that's what I miss most about Ireland. At home, all the family was nearby, and it was simply a walk across the brook and around the sidh to see everyone. Now, a few miles might as well be the ocean for all that we see each other. And you, dear Sister, are so far away that I have never seen your younger two children, and you have never seen any of mine. Dear Mary, don't let's wait until a wake before we meet again!

With all my love,

Your sister,
Bridget

IN THE SHADOW OF MR. LINCOLN

Letter from Mary to Abby

May 12, 1862

Dear Abby,

I received your letter. I want to speak a moment to the dilemma in which you find yourself, with Dr. Johnson. You are, indeed, in a bad spot.

However, you did say that he's handsome and a good man. If he's not giving you a specific reason to dislike him, then I think it's perfectly all right to continue as you are. You did not say if he is following his mother's lead, only that you are not agreeable to it. Has he made any advances of his own?

Abby, I know you don't want to hear this, but you must consider it. You are of marriageable age. Your sister is being courted as we speak. Marriage has always been a joy to me, and I think it would be for you as well. If you were able to find a man who would allow you to continue sewing, I think you would be very happy. This Owen Johnson has many good qualities: he is intelligent, well-off, kind, and a good man (your words). Would a marriage to this man be so horrible?

I suggest you simply keep doing what you're doing. If things don't work out in Washington, you're always welcome here. But I think you should give this man a chance.

Your loving mother,
Mary

Mary and Kathleen sat at the kitchen table. They each had a mug of tea, but Mary wasn't drinking hers. As they had for many months, they simply enjoyed each other's company. It had started out as a weekly teaching session. Now they were simply equals, comrades, contemporaries.

"How are things at home?" Mary asked.

"Oh, good. I thank you for keeping the boys some nights, but I do admit I miss them," the young woman said. "I don't miss the running and screaming, but I miss the happiness. Sometimes I feel so alone in the house."

"How is your ma?"

"Oh, much better! Better every day. She sits with me in the kitchen. She cannot talk, but I know she hears me now because she'll watch me everywhere I go. I talk out loud, even when I have nothing to say. I think she likes it."

"I'm sure she's proud of you, Kathleen. You're a fine young woman."

"Thank you, Mary." They sat quietly for a moment, a rarity in any farm household. "Da is getting better too. He sometimes sits in the kitchen just to be near Ma, I think. And sometimes he goes into the tavern. I think he even goes into town sometimes. He doesn't drink anymore, and that is the best of all!"

"Yes, I know it's been hard on your family for years. Men that drink are hard to bear. They cannot be controlled, or much influenced, and they refuse, by their very habit, to control themselves," Mary said, taking a sip of tea.

"Yes, that's true."

"Kathleen, does Will drink?"

"Once in a while, but I've never seen him drunk. He said he got drunk in New York City once, and he was so violently ill the next day that he hasn't done it since."

"Has he told you that Frederick has talked to him?"

"About our marriage?" Kathleen nodded. "Yes, he told me. I appreciate your concern, but you needn't worry. I can't abandon my family, so until Ma recovers or we find a way to help them pay for a maid, I cannot have a home of my own."

"Don't put aside your happiness on that account, dear. Your mother is getting better, and so is your father, and Meg is still at home—"

"Forgive me for interrupting, Mary, but why should I force my sister to give up what she enjoys so that I may be happy? That's selfish and unnecessary. Meg is much like Abby, you know. She does much better in business than she ever would in the home. I do much better in the home than I could ever do in business. Somehow, we'll make it work."

"Do you feel like Daniel has abandoned your family?" Mary asked softly.

"In some ways, yes, but he was following his dream too." She laughed lightly. "It seems like everyone else in the family dreams of leaving home. I dream of having a home."

"And you will, you will. Shall I get more tea for you?"

"No, thank you. Mary, do people talk about us? About me and Will, I mean?"

"Of course, people always talk, but no one is saying anything untoward as far as I know. You are both very modest, discreet, and proper. I'm not in town often, but everyone knows I am your close friend, and someone would have told me if things were not as I've said."

"He kissed me, you know."

Mary's eyes twinkled as she took a sip of tea. "Oh?"

Kathleen blushed, adding a pretty glow to pretty features. "And I enjoyed it."

Mary set her teacup down with a clunk. "Well, good! If you didn't, I would tell you not to marry him!"

Kathleen laughed. "Oh, Mary, I love you!"

"I love you, too, my dear. Will is a good man, a good man," she added.

* * *

Sarah slammed the lid onto the cast-iron Dutch oven. The biscuits smothered in chicken, and gravy were cooking nicely, and she covered the lid with ashes again. Then she sat back on her heels in front of the fireplace and cried.

Kathleen, Kathleen, Kathleen! Always Kathleen. Let's teach Kathleen how to make a mincemeat pie. Let's teach Kathleen how to make peach preserves. Let's teach Kathleen how to properly clean the copper bowls, none of which Kathleen even owned! Let's have tea with Kathleen. Let's invite Kathleen for dinner. Kathleen, Kathleen, Kathleen! Sarah had finally gotten rid of Abby, and after a very short time of her mother's undivided attention, now she had to share with someone who wasn't even in her family!

Oh, Sarah was sympathetic to Kathleen's situation. Who wouldn't be? A brother who skips town, a mother who has an accident and becomes an invalid, and a father who becomes a drunk, a sister who defiles herself by running a tavern, and a beau who won't ask her to marry him. Kathleen was eighteen, marriageable and pretty, but still she was single, and would be a spinster at this rate! Of course, Sarah was sympathetic.

But why couldn't Ma take notice of all that Sarah was doing? Did Sarah *need* to be taught all that Mary taught Kathleen? No, but was that any reason to punish her? Sarah's biscuits were fluffy and golden every time. Her strawberry jam won a prize last year at the Allentown Fair. She sewed a straight seam and used tiny stitches. Even with all the housework, she still had managed to accumulate a full hope chest: bed linens and quilts, towels, recipes, and necessary gadgets for homemaking.

All Sarah desired was a husband and a home of her own. She was tired of sharing the kitchen with her mother. Mary only wanted to share it with Kathleen anyway. Pa had given Mr. Gehman permission to call. When would he give permission for marriage? Tomorrow wouldn't be soon enough!

Kelly's Tavern was open and crowded and full of chatter and laughter. A musician had arrived in town on his way to wherever, and Meg had engaged him for a run of two weeks to start with. Business was booming, and the fiddle added to the atmosphere of the place. Most nights were busy, but since Ian O'Tara had arrived, the laughter was louder, and the drinks went faster. All in all, he was a good investment.

He was handsome too. Meg watched the young man furtively as she wiped the bar. He sat on a tall stool, one that was usually kept behind the bar for Meg to sit on as the evening turned into a late night. Ian O'Tara, just off the boat, had short curly black hair that danced as he played. His eyes were a deep blue, startlingly so, almost like a deep cold lake. He had chiseled features and a cleft in his chin, but it was the dimples in his cheeks that made Meg's heart flutter. And the deep voice that lilted and swayed like an un-Irishman with too much whiskey.

"Another one, Miss Meg!" a voice called from the center of the room. It was old man Hinderschlatt. He raised his empty mug.

"A beer, Mr. H.?" she called, filling one from the tap. She walked with it around the bar, handed it to him and took the empty one. "Is everything all right tonight, gentlemen?"

"Oh, we're fightin' the war here, miss," a stranger said. "No need to worry your pretty head. Tell your pa his beer is the best between Allentown and Kutztown!" A rowdy cheer went up.

"I'll be sure to tell him," Meg said. She smiled as she walked back to the bar. It was too much trouble to explain to strangers the truth, so she didn't bother anymore. At first, the locals had clarified the situation on her behalf, but even they got tired of the eternal questions and stunned looks. Someone had asked Meg how she would feel if they stopped explaining to people that it was she who ran the business and ordered the best beer between Allentown and Kutztown, and she had laughed and walked away. After that, no explanations were made, and Patrick had acquired an excellent reputation.

The music stopped with a crescendo and a squeal from the strings, and then the crowd howled. Ian O'Tara stood, bowed, and set his fiddle and bow on the stool. He walked over to the corner of the bar and motioned to Meg. He smiled as she moved his way.

"I still can't be getting over the prettiness of the barmaids on this side o' the pond." She blushed. He stroked her cheek and she moved away, but not immediately. "Can I have some refreshment, milady?"

She asked him his preference, and he chose a shot of whiskey. He downed it in one swift toss of the elbow, and set it neatly on the table, rather than noisily, as most men did. He winked at her. "Would your da be mindin' if the barmaid joined me?"

"I shouldn't," she said with a shake of her head, but she already knew she would. Although she worked around the drinks every day and night, she had never been tempted to try them. She often found it ironic that the two people running the tavern—herself and Will—never drank.

And she did join him for a drink every night for two weeks. First, it was one shot that burned its way down her throat. Then it was two, and then three in quick succession.

When Ian O'Tara left in the wee hours of Saturday morning, May 15, 1862, he left a tearful drunk Meg on the floor behind the bar, her skirts in a shambles and her heart broken. When the man known as Ian O'Tara arrived later that day in Kutztown, he introduced himself as the traveling fiddler Wilhelm Maeir, just off the boat from Heidelberg, Germany. He had lost his taste for whiskey—he preferred only the best German beer. He had also lost his Irish brogue. He sounded more German than the real Germans.

* * *

Kathleen cried against Mary's chest. As usual, Sarah was in the summer kitchen, and Kathleen felt no inhibition about sharing the disgrace of the Kelly family in Mary's kind arms. July 20, 1862, and Meg was pregnant. Every morning she was sick, and though she had tried to hide it, and had successfully done so for two months, that morning she had not made it to the privy. Kathleen came downstairs to find her sister tearfully cleaning the kitchen floor.

"I asked her what happened, and she said she was sick. And she looked sick," Kathleen said, wiping her face on a handkerchief. "I said I would help her back upstairs and tell Will to handle things today. But she insisted she would be fine." Kathleen burst into a fresh flood of tears. "I insisted, she insisted, then finally she told me. 'Kathleen,

I'll be fine in an hour. It happens every morning. I'm going to have a baby, I think.' Just like that, Mary. Without an ounce of regret."

"I don't know about that, Kathleen," Mary said softly. All of a sudden, Mary felt old. "If she's known for two months, then she's probably come to terms with what she has done . . ."

"You talk about it like she ruined an expensive piece of fabric!" Kathleen wailed. "It's not fabric, Mary, it's her good name. It's her soul!"

"God will forgive her," Mary said sternly. "He already has. Christ died on the cross for just such a need as this," she added. "You will forgive her, too, Kathleen because you are her sister, and she needs you."

"What will Da say? What will Will say? What will the town say?" Her voice was rising in volume and pitch, and Mary stopped her with a warm pressure on her arm.

"Your father will be angry or depressed, and either way, he'll start drinking again. Will will do everything he can to help you and Meg and the tavern. He loves you, and he adores your sister as if she were his sister. The town? They'll be like every town since the beginning of time. They will be harsh, unforgiving, rude, callous, and downright mean. So you must be kind and loving for Meg's sake, and for the sake of this child." Mary's voice was soft but unwavering, and she did not release Kathleen's arm until the girl composed herself.

"I'll go to town with you after dinner," Mary said. "Shall I go tell Frederick now, or shall I wait until you can tell him at dinner?"

The hysterics were close to the surface as Kathleen frantically shook her head. "Oh, please, Mary—"

"Kathleen, he's acted on your behalf all these months with the town, with Will, with your brothers. Your father is not well enough to handle this as it needs to be handled. Frederick will do what's right." Kathleen nodded, put her head in her arms, and cried.

Mary approached the field, the hot sun burning her unprotected head. She walked slowly, dreading the conversation almost as much as Kathleen but for Meg's sake rather than her own. Poor Meg, she had made the worst mistake she could possibly have made. She had managed, through Will and Frederick's timely and unobtrusive words and actions, to retain a proper reputation since taking over the tavern. Frederick had assured the town it was her duty to do so, and when Will arrived and men said she should step down, Frederick had reminded them of her excellent work so far and the disastrous theft in the spring of '61 and the way Meg carried herself as a lady, even as she did unladylike work. But, now, nothing he or Will could say would save her.

"Mary!" Frederick called, jogging over to her. The boys looked for a moment, then went back to work. They were farther than Frederick in their rows of corn, and Frederick and Mary's voices didn't carry. "Mary, what's wrong?"

"I don't know how to say this, except to just say it. Meg is pregnant," she said, hoping that she would see compassion on his face rather than disgust and anger.

He didn't let her down. "Oh, no. Did she tell you just now?"

"Kathleen is in the kitchen. I'll go to town with her after dinner and talk to Meg. What will you do?"

"There isn't much I can do now. Her reputation is ruined. I can't fix it. It is what it is. But we'll support them in any way we can."

"You know, Frederick, it's occurred to me that we might have this conversation about one of our own. Not that I distrust either of our girls, but I wouldn't have thought Meg would sin like this, either. How do we support without condoning what she's done? She has done a wrong thing, Frederick. She has to know that."

"I'm sure she does, Mary," he said. He, too, seemed so old, as he wiped his face and bald head with a handkerchief. "We'll say it once, so she knows we believe it's wrong, and then we'll just love her. And her child." He paused. "Do we know who the father is? I can arrange a marriage."

"I don't know. I'll ask her this afternoon." It was another conversation she dreaded.

When they arrived at the Kellys', Mary left Kathleen in the kitchen with Peggy. Kathleen almost appeared rather composed as she set to cleaning potatoes for supper. Mary knocked on the door between the house and tavern but didn't wait for an invitation. Will and Meg were in the storeroom, apparently counting their inventory of bottles and kegs.

"We've lost a few glasses," Meg was saying. "I dropped three last week. And somehow they just seem to disappear."

"If we were in Ireland, I'd say someone annoyed the Fair Folk, but fairies don't like America any more than they like England!" Will laughed.

"Ach. Da says the Fair Folk came over with the Famine just like we did. He'd say it is the Fair Folk, for sure!"

Meg smiled, then saw Mary standing at the end of the bar. "Hello," she managed, already knowing what this was about. Kathleen had been gone all morning.

"Will, is there something you can do elsewhere?" Mary said softly.

"Yes, ma'am." He put his paper and pencil on the bar and walked out.

"You know," Meg said without small talk. "Kathleen told you."

"Yes, Meg, she did. Shall we sit down?" They sat at a round table scarred and stained, and Meg absently picked at a rough gouge in the wood. "Do you want to tell me how this happened?" Mary asked.

"Not particularly, but I suppose I must." Meg sighed. She could feel the tears rising in her throat, but she was proud and wouldn't let them fall for anyone, not even Mary. Her voice was cold, almost harsh. "I was drunk, and I was stupid."

"Do you know who the father is, then?"

Meg glared at the older woman. "Of course, I know! Do you think I do this kind of thing on a regular basis?"

Mary shook her head. "I apologize, Meg. Of course you don't. But are you willing to say who it is? That's what I meant."

Meg wasn't sure she believed that. "It was Ian O'Tara."

"Who?" Faces flashed in Mary's mind, but none fit that name. She had heard the name before, however.

"Ian O'Tara. I hired him to play the fiddle in the tavern for two weeks." Meg swallowed the lump in her throat. "He actually stayed for three. The last night, I paid him his fee. He asked if I would like to join him for a round of drinks. Everyone had gone home, even Will, and we stayed in the bar and drank. I got drunk, Mary, and I don't know how it happened. He started kissing me, and I didn't tell him to stop. I didn't want him to. Da always said too much liquor in a woman makes her forget to do the right thing. Now I know he was right."

"And you had relations with this man and where is he now?"

"Don't know. Like I said, he was a traveling musician. He might be in Kutztown, but I doubt he stayed there long."

"Then Frederick probably won't be able to arrange a marriage," Mary said, reaching out a comforting hand. Meg pulled away. She stared at the other woman in angry silence for a moment.

"Who said anything about marriage?" she demanded. "I'm not marrying him, or anyone else, either, just because I'm having a baby. I don't care what everyone says. And why would Frederick do anything at all?"

"He's acted on your behalf before," Mary began, wondering how much Meg should know about the gossip that had circulated once already. "Since your parents have been ill—"

"Da's not ill. He's drunk. Or lost."

"Since your parents have been unable to take care of your family," Mary began again, "Frederick has acted as father in many instances with you and Kathleen and the boys too."

"How? What has he done?" Meg was beginning to have an inkling of what have happened already. This was going to be harder than she had at first anticipated. Moving to another state might be a necessity. Changing her name to Mrs. Something or other and calling herself a war widow might be the only real option. But she didn't want to leave.

Mary had not yet answered. Meg prodded again then looked away. "Let me guess. The town already thought I was ruined when I took over the tavern. He stood up for me."

"Yes, he did. He also spoke to Will about his intentions toward Kathleen—"

"How honorable."

"And he's taken George and little Will under wing on the farm. He enjoys having them around."

Meg's pride was splintering like a cracked rock in winter rain, frozen to the point of complete break. But it wasn't broken enough to let the tears out. She looked at Mary with dry but frightened eyes. "Now what do I do? What will *you* do?" She couldn't ask if Mary would abandon her to the wolves. She didn't want to believe that could happen.

Mary again reached out a hand, and Meg didn't move. "What you did was wrong, Meg, but I don't need to tell you that. Ask God to forgive you, and He will. You haven't sinned against me, and so I have no right to hold anything against you." Silent tears began to fall from Mary's eyes as she saw the painful future ahead for this girl. Meg finally broke under the sympathy. Mary held her while she cried.

"I'm so sorry," the girl whispered into Mary's shoulder. "I never meant for this to happen. Oh, Lord, please forgive me!" She cried for what seemed like an eternity. Since she and Kathleen shared a room, and because she spent all of her days with Will, she had not yet had the opportunity to cry over her sin. The tears flowed like rain, and Mary simply held her, her own tears falling on Meg's hair.

A chair scraped, and they both looked up. Kathleen was in a chair a few inches away, tears streaking her face. She anxiously reached out a hand toward her sister, and Meg took it. She began to speak, but Kathleen shook her head. Sometimes, sisters didn't need to speak in order to be understood.

The town was as harsh as Mary had predicted. Kathleen avoided town as much as possible, for she received the dirty looks on her sister's behalf. Will, too, received hostility, for as the man working for the Kelly family, didn't he have some unstated responsibilities for the character of the sisters? For several weeks, the family managed to hide the truth from Peggy and Patrick, and even the townspeople recognized where to draw the line. Though Patrick continued to walk around town on pretty days, no one mentioned his younger daughter's indiscretion to him.

On a warm Saturday evening in early August, George and Will joined the family for supper. The harvest would begin soon, but they still turned up at home on Saturday nights, and they didn't return to the farm until Monday morning. Kathleen often prepared a special meal for Saturday supper, and tonight was no exception. There was a beef roast with potatoes and carrots, sweet corn on the cob, a skillet of corn bread and a loaf of wheat bread, and a cake made with expensive white sugar and flour for dessert, iced and waiting on the pantry shelf. It was a rare treat, indeed, since the war had made white sugar even more scarce than usual.

The dinner was pleasant, with easy conversation between Will, Kathleen, and the boys. As was her usual lately, Meg remained mostly quiet. Peggy and Patrick watched as at a theater from one end of the table. Peggy was eating almost normally now, and Patrick ate heartily. He even contributed to the conversation once in a while, although his contributions were memories rather than news.

The girls rose to clear the table.

"Can we have the cake right away?" young Will asked excitedly. The eight-year-old had a sweet tooth, and he had spied the cake when he washed his hands for supper.

"I declare!" Kathleen laughed. "You can smell sugar a mile away!" Young Will grinned. He knew he would have his way.

Meg leaned over to take her mother's plate. "Are you finished, Ma?"

Peggy allowed Meg to take the plate, but she put a thin hand on the girl's belly. The bulge was barely noticeable when Meg stood before her mirror, and with her corset and dress, it was not noticeable at all. But Peggy put a hand on the belly, nonetheless. She looked at her daughter with worried, quizzical eyes, asking a question her mouth couldn't form.

Patrick's eyes went from wife to daughter and back and forth. Kathleen, stopping in the middle of the room as she returned for another load of dishes, looked at Will, sitting at the other end of the table. Sweat popped out on her forehead.

"Mr. Kelly, would you like to come and sit in the tavern tonight? I'm sure your neighbors would love to see you there," Will said, trying to divert attention from the hand still on Meg's belly. It was as if Meg was frozen. How easy it would be for her to simply walk away; neither parent had the ability to rise quickly and follow. But where would she go? She couldn't go for a walk now, could she? So she stood, three plates and forks still in her hands.

Patrick looked down the table at Will, and his brows narrowed. "You. Will. You and Kathleen," he said. Kathleen stopped breathing. What was happening?

"Yes, sir, what about me and Kathleen?"

"You love my daughter Kathleen?"

"Yes, sir, I do," Will said firmly but quietly.

Patrick started and stopped, opening and closing his mouth repeatedly. Finally, he said, "Walk with me, please?" He stood and did not wait for the young man to follow. Will joined him at the back door.

Patrick stared into the distance. "I want to thank you for all the work you've done."

"You're welcome, sir."

"I'm glad Meg has been able to keep the tavern open, and I'm glad you have been able to help." He shook his head sadly. "I've not been myself since Peggy has been ill."

"But she's getting better now, and so are you, sir," Will said. "I'm sure Meg would be glad to have you in the tavern again."

"You know a lot about my family, don't you?" It was not a question. "You are like a brother to my girls."

"Yes, sir."

"In the dining room just now. Peggy touched Meg's belly, and Meg looked frightened. Why?"

Will braced himself. "Meg is with child, sir," he said gently.

Patrick did not look at him. "She's pregnant, you mean."

"Yes, sir."

"But not yours. You're Kathleen's beau."

"Oh, sir, no, that baby is not mine! I wish to marry Kathleen as soon as we think you and Mrs. Kelly are well enough to . . . to take care of things. I . . . I told Mr. Weimer that I wanted to wait until I could talk to you about it. Kathleen doesn't want to leave you and Mrs. Kelly until she knows you're well—"

"Whose baby is it?" Patrick asked, finally looking at Will.

"Meg hired a man to sing and play the fiddle in the tavern," Will began.

"So no one I know? Is he gone?"

"Yes, sir."

"Then I can't kill him." He looked straight ahead.

Will was startled. "No, sir. I . . . I don't know how that would help."

"Help or not, it's what the father does to make himself feel better. This man defiled my daughter. He deserves no better. Are you sure I couldn't find him?"

"Mr. Weimer tried, sir. He was going to arrange a marriage."

Patrick nodded. "Frederick Weimer is a good friend. He has done much to help this family this past year." Patrick again looked at Will. "He hired my sons to work for him, you know, though I'm sure it causes more work than it relieves. Just so he could give money without hurting our pride."

Will was surprised. He hadn't realized Patrick had been that cognizant of what was happening around him. "You're wrong, sir. I've spoken with Mr. Weimer often, and he says your sons are a great help. He even let his other hired man go this season. He has his son and your two sons and himself, and that's all."

Patrick smiled, again looking into the distance. "I'm glad to hear that." He sighed. "So what about Meg? She's not married, will not be married and yet is having a baby." Will could not decide to whom Patrick was speaking. A tear fell from the man's eye, and he smiled sadly. "Two years ago, I would have been ranting and raving at her. Smacking people around. Drinking until I didn't have to think anymore. It's all different now. Where did that kind of living get me? My oldest son is gone and probably will never come home. My daughter is pregnant and unmarried. My other daughter is taking care of her mother and me."

"Mr. Kelly," Will began. He didn't know what to say next.

Patrick turned completely to look the younger man in the face. "But now. I almost killed my wife. I almost lost the one thing in my life that was worth anything at all to me. And I have realized I was wrong. She's not the one thing in my life worth anything. She's just one of many. I lost a son. I don't want to lose my daughters too." He broke down completely, the tears coming in great sobs. "Will, what can I do?"

Will awkwardly put his arms around the other man. This was not the man Kathleen had described so many times. But he hadn't been for the past year, and here was the evidence, the reason why. Ranting and raving would have been easier to handle, Will thought, but he did the best he could on the back step.

"Mr. and Mrs. Weimer have already done what they could, sir. The townspeople know and are unkind, but the Weimers are still friends."

Patrick shook. He raised his head and looked at Will. "What have *you* done?" It was not an accusation.

"I confess, sir, there isn't much I can do. Her reputation is ruined, and everyone thinks I should have done something to prevent it." He nodded. "I should have, but what could I have done except make Meg stay in the kitchen?"

All of a sudden, Patrick turned and walked into the house. Forcefully, his boots clomping on the hardwood floor, he stalked into the dining room. George and Will were silently eating their cake. The women were gathered at the other end of the table. Meg looked green, Kathleen sat silently, and Peggy was holding their hands. Peggy and Kathleen turned to see Patrick, and Meg lifted her head, then lowered it again. She began to cry.

Patrick paused in the doorway. The boys looked fearfully at him. Young Will left his half-eaten cake and hurried out of the room. George followed, trying to avoid his father's eyes.

But the boys were mistaken. There was to be no yelling or throwing things, no hitting or beating. Patrick was a new man. A broken man. He fell to his knees between Peggy and Meg, one tired hand on Peggy's lap, the other reaching for the clenched fist in Meg's.

"Meg, are you pregnant?" he whispered.

"Yes, sir," she said as strongly as she could, but it wasn't very strongly at all.

"Did he rape you, Meg?"

He was giving her an out, but she couldn't lie. "No, Da, he didn't."

"Are you sorry, Meg?"

"Yes, Da, very sorry." The tears fell onto their hands, still in her lap.

Patrick let go of her hand, reached up and wiped the tears from her face. "My darling Meg," he whispered.

Meg finally looked at her father, realizing that the expected blows, verbal and physical, were not going to come. "I want the baby, Da."

He nodded. "Have you talked to the priest, Meg?"

Meg nodded, the shame of the confession making her face hot, just like in the stuffy confessional closet. But as always, the priest had been kind, had absolved her of her sin, and she had taken Holy Communion that very day. The priest could absolve, the Lord could forgive, but the shame didn't automatically disappear.

"Meg," Patrick began. He paused. "I love you, my darling Meg." He stood abruptly, kissed her hair, and walked out of the room. They heard the door click gently behind him.

Patrick arrived at the farm as the sun was going down behind golden wheat fields. Mary and Sarah were chatting idly as they washed the supper dishes. They did not hear him come through the open door. As Mary turned to say something to her daughter, she caught sight of him out of the corner of her eye.

"Patrick," she said in surprise. "Is everything all right?" She quickly dried her hands on her apron and put a hand on his arm. "Is Peggy all right?"

He nodded. "Frederick. Where is Frederick?"

"In the barn. Sarah, run get your father. Quick now!" Carefully, Mary pushed Patrick toward a chair. Then she poured him some cool clear water from the jug. He immediately grabbed it, holding it so tightly that his knuckles turned white. They didn't speak until

Frederick hurried in, Ben and Sarah close behind. Mary waved the children back out the door.

"Patrick, is everything all right?" Frederick asked, sitting next to him, glancing from Patrick to Mary who simply shrugged.

"Thank you," Patrick whispered.

"Beg pardon?" Mary said, not quite sure what he had said, his head still down, his voice so low.

"I said 'thank you'. Thank you for all you have done for my family," he added.

"Don't mention it," Frederick said easily. "You would have done the same for my family."

"You know about Meg."

Mary and Frederick exchanged a glance. Patrick saw and simply nodded. There was nothing more to say, so they didn't say anything.

* * *

Mary sat down to write a letter to Abby, but she did not know how to explain all that had happened since spring. Of course, she had written to Abby since then, but she had not told her any of the disconcerting news. She had shared Sarah's excitement about Howard Gehman coming to call and his recent proposal. The wedding would be next June. She had described the farm in all its summer glory and the possibility of another addition of land next year if the harvest earned as much as expected. But Mary did not know how or exactly what to tell of Meg's healthy pregnancy, which was in its second trimester, or the change in the entire Kelly family. She finally rose from her chair, having not even begun.

Chapter 9

GOVERNOR CURTIN

Mr. Curtin stood behind his desk in the Capitol building in Harrisburg. Windows were flung wide to let in what little breeze there was on this hot July day. Harrisburg was bustling, and the roll of carriages and the clatter of feet echoed up to him.

Andrew Curtin, governor of Pennsylvania, was a man with a strong physical presence. He was young, not yet fifty years old. He had a high forehead, a tall frame, and a wide set to his shoulders—qualities that had attracted Catherine so many years ago. Once upon a time, he had rich chestnut-colored hair, but since the war began, both his brown hair and healthy body had gone gray. He felt old, not quite so filled with vitality as he once had, ill and weak of health.

A knock sounded on the outer door. It was his secretary who bustled in with a handful of papers. Since the president had issued a call for three hundred thousand more men on July 1, Curtin's office had been inundated with mail, from Pittsburgh, Philadelphia, and small towns, from senators and representatives in the assembly and farmers and farmers' wives. All of Pennsylvania was in uproar about the way the war was going.

Curtin couldn't blame them, really. As a devout Republican, he upheld what Lincoln demanded. Curtin believed in the Union, and it was for the sake of the Union rather than the freedom of the Negroes that he supported the War Between the States. He was elected the same year as Lincoln by an antislavery party, but Curtin had hoped to avoid secession. Yet, as governor, he also believed in his responsibilities to the people of Pennsylvania.

"What is happening today?" he asked wearily.

"We have news from Allentown," the secretary responded, putting a letter on the cluttered desk.

Curtin read it quickly, nodding. Allentown had filled its quota of soldiers, not with the draft that the United States Congress threatened, but rather with volunteers. The 128th PA Volunteer Infantry was on its way to Harrisburg to be trained and outfitted. The ranks were filled with men from Catasauqua and Allentown, tradesmen and shopkeepers, not farmers from the surrounding areas. The two companies, D and G, were the extent of the turnout from the call for more troops. It was the quota, but no more.

"Good, good," Curtin said. "They might be needed sooner than anticipated. What else?" He fidgeted with his silk cravat. The fact that Companies D and G were the full extent of the Lehigh County's contribution was not a good sign. In addition to that grim outlook, the heat was oppressive. Undoing the buttons on his long-tailed coat, he sat in his creaky chair.

"A letter from a wife, a Mrs. Thomas Yeager, of Allentown," the secretary answered, handing the letter to the older man.

"Allentown again." Not good that this part of the state was so much on his doorstep and in his mailbox these days. The letter was not a happy one.

Thomas Yeager, captain of the Allen Infantry, the so-called First Defenders, had been killed at Fair Oaks. He was a local hero, it seemed, and he was the first from Lehigh County to be killed. Mrs. Yeager was asking when she would receive his wages; there were children to feed.

"Find out how this Thomas Yeager was killed," Curtin said. "We'll give her some details of which she can be proud." He sighed. "I don't know when she'll receive his pay packet."

As the afternoon dragged on, Curtin recalled what had occurred since his election in November of 1860. He and his party had celebrated his election, and he recollected his wife's smile. She had stood with him at the inauguration figuratively and physically. It had been a mild March day, the fourth, as he stood on the platform. The rain had moved on, and the crowd waited expectantly for his speech. He had called for the Pennsylvania Assembly to repeal the laws that were offensive to slave holders or were in contradiction with national law. Pennsylvania had always been as belligerent against slavery as South Carolina had been for it, but the Union was paramount. Curtin hoped fervently that his speech had shown that.

Curtin remembered the day Fort Sumter fell. Yet, even then, everyone thought the war would end quickly with little loss of life. Curtin's people were fired up, and they met their quota for the allotted regiments within days. So many men enlisted that Curtin had organized one of his best ideas to date; at least, he thought so. All of the men who wanted to enlist but came after the quota was filled were put into militia regiments, trained, fed, outfitted, and paid by the state of Pennsylvania. Being so close to two slaveholding states, Maryland and Virginia, Curtin was keenly aware of the need that might arise.

Fourteen regiments had been formed, trained, and sent to join the Army of the Potomac. Eleven more regiments were trained and kept at home. Their commanding officer was a personal friend of Curtin, Major General George McCall, who had been born in Philadelphia and who had graduated from West Point. When the three-month enlistments were up, just a year ago, those eleven regiments were already trained and ready to join the Army of the Potomac. Lincoln had written and thanked Curtin for his foresight.

Curtin appreciated and admired Lincoln, but he did not envy the man. Curtin's job was not enviable, either. His idea to outfit the "extra" volunteers was a good one. But just as Lincoln did not control the money of the nation, neither did Curtin control the money of Pennsylvania. The Assembly did. The delay had caused the troops in Harrisburg during the first three months of the war to be without arms, ammunition, and equipment, even such equipment necessary for cooking purposes. But it had been spring and early summer, and new crops were brought to the city from around the state, farmers coming from all over to help the war effort by giving their produce. The men in waiting hadn't starved, at least!

News in July of 1862 was grim, however. McClellan, also a Pennsylvanian, had organized and led the Peninsula Campaign during the spring. He had moved his troops through Virginia from the coast near Norfolk up past Richmond. It had looked promising; everyone said so. But with the ever-able Robert E. Lee in command of the Confederate Army, things didn't look good for McClellan, or his men, so many of whom came from Pennsylvania. Curtin had read the dispatches as well as the correspondence published in *the New York Times*. From the Special Correspondents of *the New York Times*, dated July 3, 1862:

> ARMY OF THE POTOMAC, ON THE JAMES RIVER, MONDAY EVENING, JUNE 30, 1862
>
> Events of the gravest character have transpired within the last five days, touching the condition and prospects of the army on the Peninsula. Acting under the necessity which the Commanding General has long foreseen, the widely-extended lines of the army, with its miles of well-constructed defenses, stretching almost from the James River on the left, to, and beyond the Chickahominy on the right, have been abandoned, and the army before Richmond has fallen back to a more practicable line of defense and attack, upon the James River . . .
>
> Beginning with the fight at Mechanicsville on Thursday, our advance forces, while steadily falling back, have had a continuous running fight.
>
> On Friday one of the severest battles which was ever fought on this continent occurred on the right of the Chickahominy, near Gaines' Hill. On Saturday, after our forces had returned in good order across the creek and destroyed the bridges, we were attacked in front of our encampments,

> but General Smith repulsed the enemy, leaving
> the ground strewn with his dead . . .

Months later, Curtin listened warily as the men in his office derided McClellan and gave all sorts of advice that most of them would never have known how to carry out. The Seven Days Battles, as they were called, were a defeat for the Union. McClellan failed to take Richmond. He failed to drive out the Confederates. He failed to gain the decisive victory, which he professed was always within his grasp if he had but a few thousand men more.

Curtin sighed. McClellan was cautious and conservative; he always would be. Lincoln had tried time and again to light a fire under the man but had as yet also failed. Everyone wondered how long McClellan would still be in charge of the Army of the Potomac.

McClellan's failures were noticeable and many. Curtin's office discussed them all, berating a man who could not defend himself and only took a defensive position for the nation instead of taking the offensive one. The defeat at Ball's Bluff—a defeat for all, but a personal loss for Pennsylvania as Edmund Baker, senator from California and leader of the 69th Pennsylvania, was fatally wounded. McClellan's bout of typhoid; the men in the office cared not at all that the disease was a scourge of every soldier's existence, only that McClellan was investigated around the same time, December '61, by the Joint Committee in Washington. And then, the worst foible to date: Harper's Ferry, February 27, 1862. Curtin had hung his head in disbelief and sadness while men around him shouted and railed. A defeat that should never have happened—the pontoon boats meant to carry men and supplies had not fit in the canal. McClellan was a laughingstock.

But in Curtin's mind, things were getting serious.

On the first day of September, the crushing defeat of McClellan at the second battle of Bull Run was announced. The *New York Times* stated, "The battle of Bull Run substantially began the war – has been the common remark on the streets this morning – and the new battle of Bull Run is now ending it." But the correspondent was wrong in his assessment. Lee and his troops were still on the move.

Curtin feared Lee was on his way to Pennsylvania. Pennsylvania in September, after all, was bursting with produce ready for harvest: corn, wheat, buckwheat, potatoes, and various root and green vegetables. If Lee's army could grab the harvest, it would bolster their strength and morale, while having the exact opposite effect on the Union's troops.

And then came the news from Antietam Creek. Curtin obtained a copy of the dispatch from General Hooker made on Wednesday, September 17, 1862:

> A great battle has been fought, and we are victorious. I had the honor to open it yesterday afternoon, and it continued until 10 o'clock this morning, when I was wounded, and compelled to quit the field.
>
> The battle was fought with great violence on both sides.
>
> The carnage has been awful.
>
> I only regret that I was not permitted to take part in the operation until they were concluded, for I had counted on either capturing their army or driving them into the Potomac.
>
> My wound has been painful, but it is not one that will be likely to hold me up. I was shot through the foot.
>
> J. Hooker, Brig.-Gen.

After receiving the dispatch, Curtin also received another note regarding the battle in Maryland. The wounded would be brought to Pennsylvania to recover. Sharpsburg, Maryland, where the battle took place near Antietam Creek, was only miles from the Pennsylvania border.

"Mr. Oliver!" Curtin called as he straightened his cravat and grabbed his top hat.

"Yes, sir?" the secretary asked, standing in the doorway but moving deftly out of the way as Curtin strode past.

"I'm going to meet the wounded at the hospital."

They were in the hallway now, and Mr. Oliver put an arm on his shoulder. Others looked on in disbelief, one man even shaking his head in disapproval coming forward not to remove Mr. Oliver's hand but to second his opinion. "You shouldn't go, sir," Mr. Oliver stated forcefully, the other man nodding in agreement.

"I am going." Curtin shook off the restraining hand. "It's the very least I can do."

As much as his words established confidence, his walk down the hall was one of defeat and resignation.

Andrew Curtin delicately held a scented handkerchief to his nose as he walked through the wards of the makeshift hospitals. He was sorry he had come. But although the numbers were great, there were many bustling nurses dodging hither and thither through the dense heat of the place. Matrons in swishing skirts turned from one soldier to the next, holding cups of water to parched lips, wiping wet brows, and always cooing soothing words that could somehow be heard below the groaning, like the bass member of a quartet.

The dedicated doctors worked amid horrible screams and grotesque smells. Limbs were piling up because the new minié balls were more destructive. They exploded upon impact, and amputation was most often the only remedy. Flies buzzed around the patients, the doctors, and Curtin, as he walked slowly through the mess. Men were crying out for water as they waited their turn, for whiskey as they were under the knife, for mothers and sisters and lovers.

A young man, who seemed in better condition than most, reached out a hand. "Sir, might I have some water, please?" The young boy looked no older than eighteen, or maybe not even that old, with his blond hair and brown eyes, tanned face, and shaking hands.

Curtin got him a glass of water, a dirty glass, a glass he wouldn't have used to water his horse, but it was the only glass he could find.

"It's all right, my boy," he said softly. He held the young man up to drink, then eased him down again. "What is your name, son?"

"Harry Pines, sir, 128th."

"From Allentown, is that right?"

"Yes, sir, that's right." The blond head turned right and left to look around him. "Where are we?"

"Pennsylvania soil," Curtin said. He tried to smile for the boy's sake. It didn't work. "Can you tell me about the battle, son?"

"We moved out of Washington City a little over a week ago," the boy said. Curtin recalled that McClellan had moved the Army of the Potomac on September 7, heading west into Virginia. "I must say, sir, that morale was low. We were all glad to be under Little Mac's command again, but we didn't feel real good about moving out. So many of us, I think, have lost the will to fight, and sometimes we don't know what we're fighting for anymore."

The young boy's voice was low. Curtin had to lean closer to the bed to hear him. Perhaps, though, he thought, the boy was not talking to him at all, but only voicing aloud his own disheartened thoughts.

The boy's voice gained strength with his next words. "Our spirits lifted as we marched north, I think through Maryland. We all expected Maryland to support the Rebs, but the farmers we saw were pleasant and downright friendly to us. Farmer's daughters gave us dippers of cold spring water. Marylanders lined the streets of town to welcome us. We were all so surprised!"

Yes, that was an unexpected twist, Curtin knew. Everyone had expected Maryland to be for the South. Apparently, their American patriotism was stronger than their Confederate allegiance. Stories were filtering in with the soldiers that supported this boy's recollections: at Frederick, thousands of townsfolk greeted the army when they marched through late at night, and they spilled forth all the wrongs they had suffered as a result of the Confederates; at Boonsboro, during a skirmish between an Illinois regiment and the Rebels, the people stuck their heads out of upper story windows to cheer the Union soldiers to victory; at Jefferson, flags fluttered in the wind and ladies waved their handkerchiefs as soldiers marched through town.

"Word filtered down from Little Mac and the generals," the boy continued. "We were outnumbered at Harper's Ferry. Then we waited all day on September 16. How many days ago was that?"

"Five, son."

"Only five, seems like forever ago," he whispered to himself. "We had won, I guess, at South Mountain a few days before, but sometimes, when you look at the field after the battle, you can't tell who won and who lost. There's so many . . . so many." He let forth a sob. "I don't know what went wrong at Antietam Creek. We crossed the creek late on Tuesday. We skirmished with some of the Rebs, but it didn't last long. I guess it told them where we were, though, and maybe that is what went wrong on Wednesday. Only five days ago?

"We attacked at dawn." The boy seemed to be seeing the fields in his mind, and indeed, he described them to the governor. "Misty morning, cool. We were in a valley between South Mountain and the Potomac River. The Potomac was on our right. We were marching south on the Hagerstown Pike. When the fighting started, the air was filled with the sounds of cannon shell and musket fire. You couldn't see through the smoke to know if you were hitting anything, except that you could hear the screams . . . the screams." He shook his head as if to chase away nightmares that wouldn't flee. "We kept advancing, even though so many of us fell. We climbed a fence, and then we were in a cornfield. I don't know who we were fighting, but they got their second wind, or reinforcements, or something, and they pushed us back.

"They pushed us back, we pushed them back, on and on. I don't know how long we fired and reloaded and kept going. We couldn't even see the sun for all the smoke in the air. And I couldn't see the ground. There were so many men on the ground . . . then we were pushing them back again, and I thought we had won it. But no, our commanders told us we had to fall back because the Rebs were flanking us. I don't know how it was possible . . ."

Curtin didn't know how it was possible, either. Nor did he know how so many men ended up on his doorstep, wounded and dying, and so many others dead on the field. "When you retreated, did you fight again?"

The boy looked at him like he had two heads. "It didn't end then, sir. But I don't know what happened. I was shot in the shoulder, and I just lay there." He paused. "I couldn't believe the way the Rebels looked," the boy continued. "I was right up close to them there at the end." He choked, or sobbed, or gagged. Curtin couldn't tell which, but he squeezed the boy's hand. "I thought they would be . . . you know, the way the songs paint them. All dandified and pretty clothes, but they weren't like that at all . . . It was sad, really. The soldiers I saw were thin and looked like they wanted to eat the poor horses they rode. Their clothes were torn, not even patched, and they didn't have shoes, most of them." This time he did sob. "Sir, while I was waiting for the ambulance to come for me, I saw Rebels taking shoes off dead Union soldiers. I think they took mine when I passed out." He shook his head slowly. "I didn't even speak up to tell them not to."

"It's all right, son," Curtin managed to say. "We'll get you another pair of shoes."

Curtin returned to his office in Harrisburg. He received news, dispatches, and letters regarding the battle. The boy's account was accurate as far as it went. But there was so much more that happened after he was wounded. By midmorning, the Confederate troops were entrenched in the rutted road, cut deep by years of wagon traffic between two farms. They set up wooden rails from the fences to create bulwarks. They stayed behind the wooden stronghold as wave after wave of troops in neat blue rows walked toward them; it was child's play to mow them down like so much standing corn. People were already calling that stretch of road, only eight hundred yards long, Bloody Lane.

In the afternoon, another group of Union soldiers under General Burnside's command were decimated by sharpshooters near the bridge over Antietam Creek. Curtin couldn't make out what the numbers meant; it had to be a mistake. Burnside's troops totaled

12,000; only 450 Georgian sharpshooters seemed to be the cause of the devastation—12,000 against 450, strategically hidden.

But Burnside's men kept advancing on the town of Sharpsburg, Maryland, and they eventually pushed the Confederates back, back, back. The Rebels' retreat was almost cut off. The fight seemed over until another group of Confederate reinforcements attacked Burnside's flank and again pushed him and his men back to the bridge.

The heavy losses of the battle were not the heaviest thing on Curtin's mind as resumed work in the Capitol. He thought of the boy's description of the Rebels. Lee and his men were starving, and the best place to find food in September was the beautifully lush and full fields of southern Pennsylvania.

As news of the battle and the state of Lee's army spread through southern central Pennsylvania, the farmers and townsfolk were worried of invasion, even without Curtin voicing his own concerns. Lee was in need of food, and it was not beyond the realm of possibility that he would march into Pennsylvania to find it.

In the middle weeks of September, farmers began to panic. They harvested their crop. They packed up their families and, driving their cattle before them, marched their own small armies northward to the Susquehanna River. Harrisburg bulged at the seams like an old wineskin. Curtin added fifty thousand militia to the mix of city dwellers, displaced farmers, and fearful vagabonds. The city waited in terrified and tired expectation.

* * *

Later that autumn, Andrew stepped off the train onto the platform of the Logan House Hotel. As with many railroad-owned hotels, it was a grand landmark. He stood under the roof of the platform, barely watching as the multitudes brushed by him. His new secretary, Markus, stood at his left elbow, waiting impatiently to move on. Andrew turned as the porter approached with the luggage.

"Shall I have a boy follow you, sir?" the porter asked. Andrew noticed then the young black boy hovering behind the old man and the cart of luggage.

Andrew nodded absently, beginning to walk toward the hotel entrance. The hotel had been a train stop since 1852. The city had literally grown up around it. The Logan House was two stories in the center with twin squares of four stories on either side. It was a massive, grand edifice, with a total of 106 rooms that saw constant railroad and hotel traffic, as every train of the Pennsylvania Railroad on the east-west line stopped in Altoona.

Andrew entered the dining room just as many guests were leaving. The westbound train would be leaving within ten minutes. As Andrew stood at the entrance to the dining room, the maître'd moved from behind his podium with outstretched hand.

"Mr. Curtin, sir, it is a pleasure to serve you again," the young man gushed. He wore a fine black suit with shoestring tie. His black hair was slicked back with sweet-smelling pomade. His smile was genuine but too broad for his thin face, wrinkling in bunches at the corners. The young man led the way to a corner table, where Andrew and his secretary eased into pink fabric-covered chairs.

"When will the other governors be arriving?" Andrew asked. He relied on Markus to keep track of little details.

"Everyone will be arriving today."

At that moment, Governor John Andrew entered with his wife Eliza. Noticing Andrew Curtin in the corner, he raised a hand, spoke softly to Eliza, and led her forward with a gentle hand pressing on the small of her back. Andrew and Markus stood and bowed for the lady. She nodded politely as her husband pulled out a chair for her.

"How are you, Mr. Andrew?" Curtin asked. "How was your trip?"

The forty-seven-year-old governor of Massachusetts chuckled ruefully. Although steam travel had greatly improved over the years, the nearly five hundred miles of track from Massachusetts to Altoona would have proved a bumpy, sooty, tiring ride. In answer to the question, he merely nodded.

It seemed like only moments before Curtin, Andrew, and the other northern governors met in Curtin's suite. As servants offered coffee in delicate cups, the thirteen gentlemen settled themselves to discuss the war, the troops, and Lincoln. The morning began, though, with a casual rehashing of the Battle at Antietam.

"Over twenty thousand dead," said Augustus Bradford of Maryland. Although his state had provided the ground for the deadliest battle to date, all of them had provided the warriors, and there was an impromptu moment of silence.

"Mr. Curtin, I had heard that your own state took on some of the wounded," Samuel Kirkwood of Iowa said.

"Yes. I visited them after they arrived in Harrisburg. It's so hard to see these men, so young, and in such pain." Although each state received its veterans with open arms, never before had a battle been fought on northern soil. Never before had the wounded been transported to northern hospitals directly from the battlefield.

"Mr. Bradford, tell us the latest news of Antietam," one of the western governors said.

"General Lee was hidden behind Antietam Creek, near Sharpsburg," Bradford began. "The creek isn't very wide, maybe one hundred feet at the most. It does not provide a strong barrier to attack, but there are limestone fences. They *did* provide protection for Lee's troops when McClellan ordered Hooker to attack Lee's left flank at dawn on September 17."

"Even with Lee in a good defensive position, his force was so much smaller than McClellan's," Mr. Andrew of Massachusetts declared.

"Lee had what, thirteen thousand?" someone asked.

"Yes, and McClellan had at least three times that number," Bradford said.

"McClellan has been fearful in other battles lately. Too cautious," Kirkwood said. "Was he overly cautious at Antietam?"

Bradford nodded grimly. "Lee had less men, and his back was to the Potomac, with only one fording place nearby. How hard would it have been to circle round—"

Curtin interrupted. "We don't know exactly what McClellan was up against. We weren't there."

"How long will we defend him?" demanded David Todd of Ohio. "How many men will he sacrifice before this war is over?"

"Lincoln should replace him," suggested William Sprague of Rhode Island.

"I heard Lee had reinforcements," said Austin Blair of Michigan.

Bradford nodded. "Longstreet arrived from Hagerstown. McClellan did not fully attack until the afternoon and evening. Perhaps if he had attacked fully in the morning, the battle might have gone a different way."

"Mr. Lincoln agrees," said Curtin. He sighed. Since the 1860 election, Curtin and Lincoln had fostered a relationship more personal than Lincoln's relationship with his other governors. This was mostly due to the animosity between Curtin and Lincoln's first appointment to the War Department. Simon Cameron was another Pennsylvanian, but the two Pennsylvania politicians never got along, and Curtain routinely went over his head and spoke directly with Lincoln. Now that Cameron had been replaced by Edward Staunton, another Pennsylvanian, Curtain's communication with the War Department was less strained, but he still corresponded regularly with the president. "He asked General McClellan to pursue Lee's army across the Potomac River, but it seems the general simply refuses."

"He always has a reason." Mr. Andrew of Massachusetts continued to deride the general for several minutes.

"He needs to be replaced!" As Samuel Kirkwood spoke, others agreed vocally, but Todd of Ohio shouted his disagreement, and the debate continued for some time.

Curtin reminded the gathering of the reason for the meeting. "What we need to do is decide how far we will support the president."

Nathaniel Berry of New Hampshire shifted in his seat. "What exactly is Mr. Lincoln proposing?"

"He wants to free all the slaves," Bradford replied unhappily.

All of the men began talking at once. After a few minutes of uninterrupted clamor, Curtin raised his hand for silence. In a mild yet firm voice, he announced, "I do not necessarily support a complete emancipation of slaves. However, I back Mr. Lincoln 100 percent."

By the end of the meeting, twelve governors, all except Bradford of Maryland, journeyed to Washington, DC, to give their support for an Emancipation Proclamation. Bradford, as governor of a slave state, was still reluctant to sign such an agreement.

Letter from Patrick to Daniel

September 1, 1862

Dear Son,

I do not know where to start. There are so many things for which I must apologize. I am sorry for causing you to fear me, for the abuse suffered at my hand. I was wrong. Please believe me when I say I am a new man. Please forgive me.

I am sorry for trying to make you what you are not, what you never wanted to be. I want you to come home when this war is over. Not to take over the tavern but because I want to see you. If you want to write for a newspaper, please at least consider beginning one here in Millerstown. We need a good, solid, politically right newspaper written in English!

I am sorry I have not written. I am sorry I have not told you how proud I am of you. I pray God will keep you safe throughout this war so that you can come home, and I can say that in person. But until then, please accept this letter as a pitiful substitute.

Your proud father,
Patrick

IN THE SHADOW OF MR. LINCOLN

Letter from Daniel to Abby

September 21, 1862

Dear Abby,

There is so much to write, and I have immeasurable time to write it. I have been wounded; I am recovering in Maryland.

We were at Antietam Creek, near Sharpsburg in Maryland. Oh, Abby, it was a day straight out of the bowels of hell.

The wound is in my left leg above the knee, so my writing is not affected, but I still get so tired. I am lucky, though. So many men lose their limbs because of these minié balls. I'm sure in your work at the convalescent home, you've seen the effects. It simply tears through flesh and leaves such a hole. And the doctors, well, I'm sure they do their best, and I can tell you that at Antietam, there were too many casualties to count. I lay on a board, and I was covered with a dirty sheet for two days before anyone even came to me. A nurse had stopped the bleeding. I guess the bullet went right through. But the biggest problem is infection, and the doctor says I'm not out of the woods yet.

The hospital is some person's house. The daughter of the farmer is helping take care of us. She is very pretty. She has a nice smile. She's not afraid to see the horror of this place. To hear the horror of it. I cannot stand the sounds, the screams that I hear all day and all night. I hope I don't add to the noise. I have seen her simply squint her eyes and keep going.

The doctor just checked my wound. He asked me about the pain. I told him I'm fine, but I lied. I know that medicine is scarce, and I know I'm not as bad off as some, so they don't need to give any to me. But my young nurse saw my pain, and she brought me a spoonful of some bitter brown stuff. I must rest now.

Abby, I just got a letter from home. Da says he's sorry.

Letter from Abby to Mary

October 4, 1862

Dear Ma,

I just received a letter from Daniel. He didn't even sign it, but I know his handwriting. All it said was "Da says he's sorry." What in heaven's name is happening up there?

Abby

Mary again sat down to write to Abby, this time determined to tell her everything. She started at the beginning.

Chapter 10

MEG

Meg eased herself into a chair, placing the ledger on the table. With her progressing pregnancy, she no longer served in the tavern. She continued to oversee the inventory and finances, but even that was becoming more of Will's job. In the past seven months, she had been ill and in bed frequently, leaving a very able worker to care for things. Will still kept her informed, and she did her best to keep up the books. Even with the truth of her pregnancy well-disbursed around town, the tavern was bringing in enough cash money to support the family, but only as long as Meg was not overtly involved.

Meg worked through the stack of receipts on her right. She sipped a glass of water frequently but did not leave her post, except to visit the privy too often. The morning was almost gone before she looked up from her task. Da was approaching with more purpose and strength than she had seen in him in a long time.

"You must stop working in the tavern now," he said softly as he sat next to the pile of receipts that had moved from her right elbow to her left.

Meg shook her head. "No, Da, not yet."

"I will finish here." A pause. "You've done well for us, Meg, but I'm ready to work. Let me take care of you the way a father should."

Meg shook her head again. "No, Da, I can take care of myself." She was slightly unnerved, had been for five months, since Da's miraculous turnaround. His renewed interest in his family, walking to the Weimers's to walk home with the boys, reading to the family after dinner, even spending an hour or so in the tavern a few evenings a week. Things he had never done, things he had never said. Meg was still unsure how to respond to her father most of the time.

Da nodded. "Yes, you've proven that." A pause. "I want you to take care of your health, dear Meg. The baby will come soon. You should rest more."

Meg shook her head then smiled as she caught herself stretching her aching back. "Perhaps you're right. Just let me finish up the receipts." Da nodded and left her alone.

But giving it up was easier said than done. The tavern opened at four that afternoon with Meg behind the bar. The first hour or so, Kelly's was empty, as usual. Except it was completely empty, no Will, no Da, and Meg was forced to stay. Meg would have spent the hour trying to keep busy, but tonight, she simply sat on her stool. She took out a scratch piece of paper, started scribbling names. The decision had been made months ago—and now she could not remember who had made the decision—that the child would bear the name Kelly. Now all she had to do was choose a first and middle name.

Before long, the paper was filled with possibilities. Patrick William . . . Patrick Daniel . . . Daniel Steven, for Ma's father . . . Brendan Evan, for Da's dead brother . . . Erin Bridget, after Ma's sister . . . Kennedy Maureen, for Ma's maiden name . . . Nora Mary . . . and those were only the names Meg had thought of. The family kept her busy with their suggestions as well. Kathleen preferred names like William and Sean and Aidan for boys, and Bridget and Ellen for girls. Da had suggested Patrick and Margaret after the infant's esteemed grandparents. Even Will had suggested Bran and Brian after important Irish saints.

Meg had taken to talking to the baby. Not out loud, but alone in her head. She shared the possibilities with the baby. *What do you think, little one? Does anything jump out at you? I guess it would help to know if we were looking for a boy's name or a girl's name . . .*

The bell above the door jangled. Mr. Miller stood in the doorway, newspaper in hand. In a few hours, Kelly's would be filled with men, and they would hash out all the important and unimportant happenings of country, county, and town.

"Good afternoon, Mr. Miller."

He huffed, reluctant to speak to her. He dropped the paper on a table and walked out.

"Hey, you all right?"

Meg looked up. Will was watching her with deep concern written on his face. This was not the first time he had been late getting to the tavern. *Probably walking with your aunt Kathleen . . .*

Meg sighed. She looked up into Will's worried face.

"Meg, are you all right?" he asked again.

Suddenly, Meg felt tired, more tired than she had ever felt, too tired to move. One hand on her growing belly, she forced all of her energy into standing and then promptly sat again. Will was at her side, hand on her back, whispering in her ear, but her head was hurting so much she could barely understand him.

"I'll get Kathleen." And he was gone.

And then Kathleen was helping her to rise, guiding her out the side door into the kitchen. The kitchen was cold, wintry cold. Kathleen tried to direct her toward the hall, and the stairs, and bed, but they only made it as far as Ma's rocking chair by the cookstove. *Where's Ma?* she wondered but didn't have the energy to ask.

Kathleen was holding a cup of water to her lips. The ice-cold water—from the bucket outside—made the tin cup uncomfortably cold to her lips, but she drank. And shivered. Ma appeared and put a quilt over her legs.

"Ma," Meg whispered. Then she put her head back against the ornately carved headrest and slept. She was unaware, only half-awake, when they slowly walked her to bed.

She woke as dawn was pushing through gray December clouds. By the gray light coming through the east window, she could see and feel that Kathleen was not next to her in the bed. As Meg sat up, she saw her mother sitting in a straight-backed chair, leaning her head against the wall. The quilt that Ma had placed on Meg's lap the night before was on the floor, as if it had slipped off Ma's own lap.

Meg eased herself out of bed. She reveled in this time of the morning before the weighty skirts were pulled on. She had never liked her corset and had given it up since her belly had begun to grow. Every morning, after Kathleen dressed and went downstairs, Meg stood alone in the room, stroking her belly, talking to the baby, feeling at once silly and yet at peace.

Carefully, she squatted just far enough to reach the quilt. Ma stirred as the heaviness of it covered her lap. She smiled at her daughter.

"Ma, what are you doing in here? You should be in bed," Meg whispered.

Ma patted Meg's hand, gave it a strong squeeze. She still had not regained her speech, but she was so much improved that she had recovered her independence. Her looks and her gestures communicated her thoughts and feelings with her family. Apparently, she had reasserted some of that independence the night before and stayed up all night to watch her girl.

"I'm all right now, Ma, I guess I was just tired," Meg said, still whispering. "How about you lie down for a while. It's too early for you to be up and about."

Ma stood. She spun her daughter around, indicated she should take off the nightgown. Meg stood meekly as her mother helped her dress. First, the pantaloons, then boots. Meg sat on the bed, her foot in her mother's lap, as Ma used the button hook to close the shoes.

"Ma, who helped you when you were expecting?" Meg asked suddenly.

Ma smiled, pointed to herself. Then she lifted her unshod foot and indicated that she went barefoot. Ma helped Meg on with her skirt and bodice. The roundness of her belly made buttoning the top to the bottom impossible.

"Oh, the devil sweep it!" Meg muttered with a stomp of her foot.

Ma chuckled. It started softly, held back by a smile, then grew until Ma threw back her head and laughed out loud. The sound was so sweet, so missed, that Meg started to cry and laugh until they were holding each other on the bed.

Kathleen stood in the doorway, watching the silly women on the bed. "And what in the name of St. Brigid is going on here?" Her red hair was neatly coiled, her pale blue day dress neat and wrinkle-free.

Her mouth twitched, and her eyes twinkled. "Ma?" she began, and then she too was laughing just because!

Ma was the first to calm. A deep breath, a hand on Meg's arm, a raised finger telling her to "wait here," and she was gone. The sisters looked at each other, unsure what was happening. Oh, but it felt good to laugh! Meg started giggling again.

"Don't start!" Kathleen commanded with a grin.

"Peggy, my dear, what are you lookin' for?" Da's voice echoed down the hall. The girls could hear thumping and banging from their parents' room.

"Do you think she needs help?" Meg asked.

"I don't know what she's looking for, and I'm not sure she'd be able to tell me."

"What in the name of heaven is going on?" Da demanded as he stomped into Meg and Kathleen's room. The girls shrugged. When Ma returned a moment later, she was holding a soft white blouse with pearl buttons and an old-fashioned collar.

Ma pushed Da into the hall, closing the door behind him with a gentle click. Then she went to work, unbuttoning Meg's bodice from the back of the skirt, motioning for Meg to unbutton the line of buttons down the front. With Meg standing only in a skirt and a chemise, Ma shook out the white blouse, and a tear fell on her cheek, getting lost in the corners of her smile. She made a round belly with her hand.

"You wore this when you were pregnant with us?" Meg asked.

Ma pointed to her daughters and shook her head. With a hand at the level of her chest and then her waist, she indicated her sons. She held the blouse as Meg shrugged into it, and Meg allowed her mother to button her up. Meg allowed her mother to brush and bind her hair—and so quickly too—and then the three women were heading down the stairs to a kitchen already warming with the fire Da had started.

It was the beginning of the end for Meg. As her mother pushed her into the rocking chair, she realized she would not be back in the tavern until after the baby was born, perhaps never. It would depend on Da, and the town, she assumed. If she had her own way, she would work as soon as she was able. After 30 minutes in the kitchen, watching the preparations for breakfast, and then the eating of it, Meg was thoroughly tired of sitting.

"Meg, I want you to help me with the ledger," Da said as they ate.

"Sure, Da."

"I'll bring it in here. I'll take over from now on. I just want to check the ledger with you to see where we are."

Meg nodded. Her throat was tightening up. *Oh, stop this silliness! You just said to yourself that this would be the end of working. Why does Da saying it's so make you weepy? Oh, Baby, isn't your mama silly?*

But as they worked through the ledger's last few pages, the desire to cry grew. *This* was her baby, her pride and joy, her work, and she felt like it was being stolen from her. She had worked so hard! She was going to miss it. *Oh, my Lord, make it be enough.* She rubbed her belly. The baby kicked, not for the first time, and she felt like she had her answer.

"Do you have it now, Da?" Asking a statement masked in a question, she added, "I don't think you need my help anymore?"

Da nodded. "You did good, Meg, real good!"

Meg left him in the dining room. Kathleen was preparing water for washing. Ma was not in the kitchen.

"Where's Ma?"

"Upstairs, I think."

"Do you need help?" Meg silently prayed for a negative answer.

"No, I've got it."

"I'll go check on Ma then," Meg said as she walked toward the stairs. Ma met her at the top, her arms laden with cloth. She ushered Meg back downstairs, and the preparations for the baby hit the family like a gale force wind.

Christmas was a bittersweet time. George and young Will, unemployed since the end of the harvest, had whitewashed the stone house and tavern in the old Irish tradition. Ma put a candle in the window on Christmas Eve. The family attended Mass at midnight, and then gathered in the parlor the next morning, warm with the crackling glow in the fireplace. Kathleen's Will read from the gospel of Luke, Da prayed, and everyone enjoyed Kathleen's feast.

Ma clapped her hands like a little girl as they sat around the table. In the very center, flanked by mashed potatoes in one bowl and boiled potatoes in another, was a fat dressed goose.

"Where did that come from?" Da asked.

"Will," Kathleen said simply, smiling at him as she set carrots and soda bread on the table beside the gravy.

"Where did you get it?" Da demanded. "No one raises geese around here that I know of."

"No, sir, Mr. Gehman up the mountain shot three this fall, said they were flying real low near his place. I heard about it and asked if he'd be willing to sell one. It's been hanging in Mr. Gehman's smokehouse since." He looked at Kathleen across the table where she sat next to George. "Kathleen said Mrs. Kelly always talked about having a goose at Christmas, and my ma used to roast a goose for Christmas, too, back in Ireland so." He shrugged, and that was that.

The family enjoyed the meal and the conversation, and the boys loved their presents, especially the pocketknives from Will. But everyone keenly missed Daniel, and there hadn't been a letter for weeks.

"Kathleen, can we go play in the snow?" George asked as the family sat gathered in the parlor.

Kathleen looked out the window. "I suppose," she said.

The boys hurried out, clomping and chatting and slamming the back door behind them. The silence seemed magnified with the happy-go-lucky boys gone. Da closed his eyes. Ma picked up a piece of embroidery.

"Kathleen, will you join me in a walk?" Will asked. She smiled, and he helped her on with her cloak.

"Oh, how beautiful it is!" Kathleen said as they walked through the white world.

"Kathleen, may I hold your hand?"

Kathleen slid her gloved hand into his. "I can't wait until March. You won't have to ask anymore!"

"What shall we do about your parents?"

Kathleen sighed. She looked over her shoulder at her brothers, trying to buy some time. Although she and Will had this conversation regularly, they had made no definitive choices. She knew they needed to make a decision, but she was exhausted with the very idea of another discussion.

"Da has taken back the tavern. He won't need your help much anymore," she started.

"I already talked with him about it. He wants me to stay on. He said he wants me to take over the tavern as a son."

"What about his other sons?" Kathleen demanded, glancing at the boys far away now and thinking of Daniel even farther away.

Will hesitated. "I don't know what your father is thinking, exactly, but I can guess. Months ago, he said to me he was sorry he lost one of his sons, and he didn't want to lose his other children. I don't think he is expecting Daniel to come home—"

"He *will* come home!"

"And take over the tavern."

"Oh."

"If he is willing to let Daniel do what he wants for a living, why would he not do the same for George and Will? First of all, they are both very young. Secondly, they both seem to like farming."

"They are young and probably have no idea if they want to farm or run a business or do something else entirely." After a moment, she continued, "All right, let's say you work for Da. Where will we live?"

"That's what we need to decide."

Her look spoke volumes.

"Your ma is doing very well, and there is no reason to think she won't continue to improve. I think that means we can have a home of our own. Nearby, of course."

"I don't think Ma is able to take care of the house by herself."

"Well, she'll have Meg."

Kathleen shook her head. "Meg isn't a homebody. I can't see her being happy in the kitchen."

Very softly, confidentially, Will said, "She may not have a choice after the baby is born. She won't have many options. The town has shunned her, and I don't see that changing any time soon, if ever."

Kathleen nodded. She looked off into the white distance.

They walked in silence for a while. Will knew when not to push. Kathleen had observed that about him, and she appreciated it. He stated his reasons and waited for her—or whomever he was talking to—to make up her or his own mind. They walked up Main Street until they reached the middle of the hill, then they turned as one and headed back.

"We'll get our own place," Kathleen said.

"Great!" Will said, giving her a peck on the cheek. She blushed in embarrassment, hoping no one was looking out their parlor windows and simultaneously wishing for more. He continued, "Do you want to live in town or farther out? I don't mind either way. I mean, I don't mind town, but I would like to have a place to keep a horse and buggy. Not have to pay for a spot at the livery. Do you want a garden?"

"Yes! Oh yes!" And for the next half hour, they walked and talked, making plans and dreaming.

Kathleen shared their conversation with Meg as they lay in bed that night. The snow was still falling, covering the tracks the two had walked and adding to the snowmen the boys had built. The moon and stars were hidden by deep clouds, and the town and the house were dark. Will had left the family soon after he and Kathleen returned from their walk, so he would not be walking up the hill trail in the dark. The rest had gone to bed as the winter darkness set in. It was hours later, but neither woman slept.

"Are you asleep?" Kathleen whispered.

"No. I feel like I never sleep anymore."

"Are you very uncomfortable?"

Meg adjusted her body onto her left side, facing her sister in the dark. "Perpetually."

"Does it hurt?"

"No, not really. Not like if I'd burned myself or dropped a keg on my foot. But, certainly, it's not comfortable."

"We never really talk about the baby, Meg, we all just kind of . . . do for the baby. But are you excited, I mean, even a little bit?"

"Yes, I am," Meg replied. "I *want* the baby. I don't know if I'll ever be able to marry, so this may be the only child I'll ever have, and as much as you may not like the fact that I prefer business to home, I *am* a woman, and I want children. *A* child anyway."

"What do you want to do after the baby is born?"

"Don't have many choices, do I?"

"But if you had all the choices you had before the baby, what then?"

"I loved working in the tavern," Meg said in a voice so soft Kathleen almost didn't hear her. "But Da doesn't need me there anymore." Kathleen held her hand in the darkness. "But I prayed that God would keep me content with the baby, and I'll do my best to be so."

"Oh, Meg, I'm always in wonderment at you!"

"Wonderment?" Meg giggled.

"I don't think I could have such a good attitude if I were in your position."

"Kathleen," Meg began in a voice as voluminous as Kathleen's look, "you'd never be in this position."

No comment.

After a moment, Kathleen said, "I want a baby."

"You'll have one someday soon," Meg assured her older sister, "and you'll do it the right way—married. Speaking of which, are *you* excited?"

Kathleen's exhilaration tingled in the dark through the hands that were still clasped under the blanket. "We talked about it tonight when we went walking. We decided that we won't live here. Ma is getting better, so with you here to help her, you shouldn't need me."

No comment.

"And Da said he wants Will to continue with the tavern, so the only thing left to decide is where we'll live. A bit out of town, I think, but we don't know exactly where."

"He'll have to ask around, see what's out there that's for sale." *Spend more time away from the tavern for a while . . . What does that matter, girl, you can't work anymore.*

"Good night," Meg whispered, closing her eyes against the tears, glad for the darkness.

Time passed in an irksome sameness as the short days of January passed into February. Baby clothes were laid aside as they were completed. Kathleen's hope chest was filled by willing hands. Meg spent more time in the parlor sewing than she ever had in her young life. As she looked out the window at another soft snowfall in the beginning of February, she realized she had been sewing more diligently and sighing less, and she was pleased with the change in herself.

"Kathleen! Meg! Ma!"

Peggy jumped up from her end of the sofa as George and young Will stumbled in. Meg pricked her finger in irritation. The baby moved, and she felt nauseous.

"Do you two ever do anything quietly?" she demanded.

"I . . . we . . ." Will stammered.

"Leave them be," Kathleen said as she took the envelope George held out to her. "Oh, Ma, it's from Daniel! George, go get Da. He's chopping wood, I think."

The women and young Will waited in titillating silence until the entire family was assembled in the parlor. Kathleen read in a clear voice:

> Dear Ma,
>
> I have been working closely with my German friend. We've been keeping a journal of the unit. There have been a few skirmishes since Antietam in September, but nothing full scale until Fredericksburg. But I'll get to that in a minute.
>
> I am sure that you have read the news. After Antietam, because of the many mistakes, President Lincoln replaced McClellan. We all liked McClellan – Little Mac. He always has the morale of the men as his highest concern. We know that when we are fighting, he's thinking

about each one. It helps us fight better, knowing he cares about our well-being.

And he's a great leader. I think we'd follow him anywhere. He motivates and trains new soldiers quick as a wink. He is cautious in battle and weighs all his options.

I think this is why Lincoln replaced him, actually. McClellan has a hard time making a decision until he has all the facts and lays out all the possibilities and checks and rechecks them. I was near McClellan's tent when he received the notice that Lee was dividing his army in Maryland near Sharpsburg. We knew we had the advantage but still McClellan hesitated. Too long. By the time we reached Lee's army at Antietam Creek, Lee had reinforced his men and was ready for us. I won't go into details; I am sure you read about it. Just know I am perfectly fine. I did get a bullet in my left leg, but it went right through, and I healed completely and am back with my unit. Again, don't worry about me – I am fine!

Kathleen paused as Peggy moaned. As the others gathered around Peggy, worry wrinkling their brows, Peggy waved them away, motioned for Kathleen to continue reading. Kathleen silently cursed her brother for his stupidity in *telling* them he was injured, if he really was healed, and then cursed herself for such a thought.

And then Lincoln replaced McClellan with General Burnside. That happened on November 5, and being near the command tent, working with Fetterhoff, we heard about it almost the instant it happened! By now, McClellan is in

Trenton, New Jersey; I heard that he was ordered to go there and wait. For what, I'm not sure.

General Ambrose Burnside is in his thirties, I would guess. He attended the Academy, and he served in the Mexican War. Still, he has refused the position twice already, because he felt he was incapable of the task. That's what rumor says, anyway. I think he will be capable, but we'll have to wait and see.

Fredericksburg. The Rebels had the high ground. We suffered heavy losses, but again, God has protected me. And Brian – please pass that on to Mrs. Weimer. We are both fine.

My biggest complaint, still, is that I am away from all of you. I have not witnessed a Pennsylvania snowfall for nearly three years. Snowfalls, yes. But not the snow as it rests on the edges of Swabia Creek or in the boughs of the trees on the hill. I miss walking leisurely through deafening snow. Standing in deafening snow on the corner of a camp in the middle of the night is not nearly as restful! Quite the opposite, in fact. Christmas is coming, and we have snow in these mountains of Virginia, but it isn't the same. It should be about time to whitewash the house, put up the holly and the candle in the window. I wish I were home with you all!

I have never been good with numbers . . . letters are my thing! But if I do my math correctly, it has been seven months or so since Kathleen's letter telling me I will be an uncle. Am I an uncle yet? How is dear Meg?

Kisses to all! And Merry Christmas!

Your Son,
Daniel

Again, the family sat in silence after Kathleen finished. "I'm glad he is well," Da finally said.

"Yes, good news!" Kathleen said. She turned to her brothers. "Is it still snowing?"

"No," George said.

"I think I'll walk to the Weimer farm and give them the good news," Kathleen said. As the menfolk disbursed, Kathleen asked Meg if she would be all right for a while and prepared to head out into the cold. Ma stood, again communicated with her hands. "You want to go, Ma?"

A nod. Ma was walking quite well now. She lifted her feet instead of shuffling, walked a straight line instead of swaying. Still, though, Kathleen worried that the walk—two miles through snow—would be too long and difficult. Before Kathleen or Meg could argue, their mother had wrapped her tartan shawl around her head and shoulders and had put her arm through Kathleen's.

"Ma, if you go with me, you must wear a heavier coat," Kathleen said.

Moments later, the two women were walking beside the train tracks, heading east. Kathleen kept up a steady battery of one-sided conversation.

"What a beautiful day! If Daniel were here, how would he describe it? Clouds breaking up to show the bright blue of a winter sky. Clear and crisp, like a fresh apple. The snow squeaks underneath our boots. Our breath floats away like a cloud." Her voice faded away. Ma patted her hand.

Sarah answered the door. She smiled as brightly as the winter sunshine, hugged Peggy, and ushered Kathleen into the kitchen. "Ma, look who came to visit!"

"Oh, Peggy! So good to see you out of the house!" Before they even had their coats off, the water was on for tea, and slices of bread and butter were set on the table.

"How are you?" Mary asked. Peggy nodded, smiled, and patted Mary's hand. Then she reached into her apron pocket and handed the letter to her friend. "Oh! Well, I know it must be good news because you're too happy for it to be bad." She hurriedly opened and read the letter.

"Ma?" Sarah asked after a moment. "What does he say?"

"He's fine, and he asked Peggy to tell us Brian is fine too," Mary said simply. There was nothing more to say—Daniel had not supplied any information about Brian—so the conversation quickly moved toward the realm of wedding plans. "How are the plans coming, Kathleen?"

"Oh, fine!" Kathleen said. "You know, if Abby were here, I'd ask her to make my wedding dress, but I guess we'll have to do it ourselves!"

"I wish she could be here for both of the weddings," Sarah said. "I'd like her to stand with me."

"And are you almost ready?" Kathleen asked.

"I have been working toward it for months, and I have longer to plan than you! I'll be ready." She sighed. Frederick had given Howard permission to marry Sarah last fall, and her hope chest was almost full. "But it would be nice if Abby were here to help with the dresses."

The three women talked until the teapot was empty. They included Peggy in the conversation, and she smiled and nodded and seemed to enjoy the company. When Sarah moved toward the stove to stoke it for the evening meal, Kathleen helped her mother with her coat. They said their goodbyes and headed home.

"Meg, we're home!" Kathleen called as they entered the kitchen some time later. No answer. "Meg!" Still no answer. Leaving her mother in the kitchen, Kathleen hurried into the tavern. It was still hours until the tavern opened. Will was counting bottles. Da was washing windows.

"Hello, my darlin' Kathleen," Will said, coming from behind the counter. He wrapped his arms around Kathleen's waist, stole a furtive glance at his future father-in-law, whose back was turned, and then took the kiss that was eagerly offered. "Your father told me about the letter. I'm very glad that your brother is well!"

"Where's Meg?"

Will was taken aback by the non sequitur. "I . . . don't know. I haven't seen her all day. I've been in here." He released Kathleen and turned toward Patrick. "Patrick, do you know where Meg is?"

"No, haven't seen her since you and your mother left," Patrick told Kathleen. "She probably went upstairs to rest."

And that is where Kathleen found her. But her younger sister was not resting.

"Kathleen, I'm glad you're back," Meg said as Kathleen opened the door. Her face was strained, sweat pricked her brow. Kathleen could actually see Meg's belly contracting beneath her shift.

"Is it time?"

"I don't know. It shouldn't be time yet. But it hurts so much!"

"I'll get Ma." Meg watched Kathleen leave.

Time. It's time . . . O Lord, help me! I'm so afraid. I don't know if I can do this.

Kathleen and Ma were back in the room before the prayer was complete. "It hurts, Ma," Meg whispered. Her mother nodded, putting a basin of water on the dresser. She wrung out a cloth and put it on Meg's forehead. It was cool, and Meg breathed a bit easier.

The calm did not last long. "Ma, what's happening?" Ma sat on the edge of the bed. Kathleen stood at the foot, looking uncomfortable. There was nothing Ma could say. Still, though, Meg was grateful her mother and sister were with her.

Meg stared at the ceiling as her mother examined her. She was already uncomfortable, and this wasn't helping. But Kathleen held her hand, and that was a help.

Ma made motions with her hands.

It isn't time yet, my little one. Be patient. We'll do this together, you and me.

Two hours passed, and then two more. Mary joined the watch. Kathleen took a break from the birthing room to make supper for the men waiting downstairs. Every so often, Ma sent Kathleen to check on them, usually when Da's parlor pacing made it halfway up the stairs.

Late in the night, when Meg felt her strength draining, Mary examined her yet again. "All right, now, Meg, time to push," Mary declared. The early winter evening had arrived with the third examination. Da was still pacing downstairs. Snow was again falling outside the window. *I just want it to be over.* Kathleen left to start water to boiling, and instead of the end, Meg found the beginning.

Meg's world became very small. For the next quarter hour, she heard no voices, felt nothing but pain, and wanted nothing but death to release her. Over and over, she wailed for mercy. She was barely aware of her mother's reassuring hands, barely aware of Mary's firm commands, barely aware of Kathleen speaking, encouraging, helping.

"I can't, Ma, I can't," she said, over and over. *Will it never end?*

"Yes, you can, Meg. Almost done. Give me one good push," Mary said.

How many times has she said that? But she pushed anyway, chin to chest, gripping Ma's hands, aware of nothing but the pain.

"Keep going, Meg," Mary urged, her voice rising half an octave. *Please, God.*

"I see the head, Meg. Push, now."

Please, please, please.

"Head's out!" Kathleen whispered from her waiting position, hands outstretched with a towel to receive the baby. "You're doing it, Meg!"

Almost, almost. You can do it, girl. Come on . . .

"There we go, Meg." Mary's voice was no longer firm but rather soft, almost tender. As Ma wiped Meg's brow, Meg saw a slimy little body pass from Mary's hands to Kathleen's.

"Is it a boy? Is it a girl?" she whispered, straining now in a different way.

"A boy," Kathleen said excitedly. Meg was waiting for a sound, but none came from the corner where Kathleen was cleaning the baby.

My baby boy, I have a baby boy. She wiped the tears from her eyes. "Is he alive?" she managed.

"He's perfect," Kathleen whispered. Mary took the baby, gave a swift slap on the rump, and the baby wailed. Kathleen took him back from Mary, swaddled him in the blanket his mother had made for him. The tiny wrapped bundle stared up at his mother, and Meg's world was once again small. It revolved only around the child in her arms.

"He *is* perfect," Meg whispered. She looked up at the Mary, watching from a short distance away, wiping her hands on a towel.

The other woman smiled. "I won't argue. Does he have a name, Meg?"

Meg looked into the deep blue eyes staring up at her. He had dark hair, and lots of it. She touched his soft cheek with her finger, traced the little red lips, the cute little ears. She thought through all of the names she had weighed and tried over the past weeks. "Daniel," she whispered. "For his brave uncle."

Peggy kissed the tiny head and then her daughter's. Meg saw the happy tears falling without apology.

"But I don't know about a middle name," Meg continued. *Patrick . . . William . . . no, too many Wills in this house already . . . Steven . . .* "Boru. Brian Boru." *You and I are going to have many battles to fight, my little one.* "Daniel Boru Kelly."

"Welcome to the world, Daniel," Mary whispered.

Chapter 11

OWEN

Abby walked briskly down the nearly deserted street. She had given Mrs. Johnson the excuse of needing some air, but that had been a lie. She needed time and space to get over her anger.

Life in the nation's capital was everything she had hoped it would be. She was confident in her role with the Sanitary Commission. She enjoyed the work, knew she was doing something important. She loved the city. The capitol dome was going up right before their eyes. She often walked past at lunchtime just to watch the scurry and bustle of the construction crew. Soldiers still roamed the streets, and she was becoming used to them. Their apparent rudeness no longer bothered her.

Abby sighed. Owen's rudeness, however, was another story.

They had been keeping company under Mrs. Johnson's watchful eye. Every evening, the three housemates shared a leisurely dinner. The dining room was always immaculately set with gold-rimmed china, Waterford crystal imported from Ireland, and sweetly scented candles. Servants placed dishes of potatoes, greens, soup, plates of roast beef or lamb, baskets of rolls on the lace-draped sideboard. The conversation was usually pleasant and continued long after the dishes were removed.

Abby found herself intrigued by Owen's stories, found herself falling in love with his gentlemanly ways despite her earlier reservations. Strolls in the parks, theater shows, carriage rides in the country.

She especially enjoyed the rides in the country. The flat openness reminded her of home.

"Perhaps you can come to Pennsylvania," Abby had said this afternoon. They were spending the Saturday driving east toward the bay. It was a crisp winter day, wind blowing wisps of hair from beneath her new hat. Owen always hired a driver; in a conspiratorial voice, he told Abby he liked to hold her hand. And hold it, he did all afternoon.

Owen pointed his wide smile in her general direction. "If you want."

"My father will want to talk to you."

"I need to ask his permission, you mean."

Abby frowned. His voice made it sound as if he thought it was an unnecessary and archaic idea. But further conversation revealed that he had rather traditional ideas of his own.

"When we're married," he continued, "you'll take over Sadie's education. Hire a governess if you wish. You'll oversee the household as well. It will be a load off my mind to have you serving me that way."

"I don't understand," she said. "Serving you?"

He chuckled. "Just a figure of speech."

"But you expect me to stay home."

"You can continue with the Sanitary Commission until the war is over," he said.

"As if I need your permission," she muttered, turning her eyes toward the marshy flats through which they passed.

The pressure on her hand was anything but tender. His voice was anything but loving when he said, "You do need my permission."

She took her hand back. "I have never asked nor needed permission from anyone," she said. A brief image of her mother's face was replaced by the red behind her eyes. "I am a seamstress." She was vaguely aware of the petulant tone of her voice.

"I can afford to provide you with the very best. You can buy any garment you wish. There will be no need for you to make your own." He reached into her lap and took her hand. She tried to pull back, but he wouldn't give his tacit permission for even that.

"I don't sew because I have to. I could have stayed in Millerstown, sewn only what my family needed. I made the choice to become a seamstress. I want to be independent, earn my own way in the world."

"No wife of mine—"

"Then perhaps I shan't be your wife," she seethed.

His eyes burned through her. The muscle under his jaw worked silently, but she understood the message clearly.

"Driver, take us back to town."

It was nearly an hour before the carriage pulled to a stop in front of the townhouse. Sadie was watching at the window, then greeted them on the step, and Owen greeted her as he always did, swinging her in a happy arc. He did not offer Abby a hand down, but the liveried driver did, and she mumbled a thank you. By the time her dainty boots touched the stone steps, Owen and Sadie had entered the house, closing the door behind them.

Abby was surprised a few short hours later because dinner seemed to be as it always was. China, crystal, candles, dishes of luxuriant food, chipper conversation. Mrs. Johnson had been resting when they arrived home, so Abby had not remarked on the horrible ride, and Owen probably had not revealed anything when they convened in the parlor. Mother and son were chatting amiably as Abby entered.

"Abby, how was the ride?" Mrs. Johnson asked.

Owen handed Abby her customary glass of sherry. His mouth smiled, but his eyes didn't.

A servant girl entered the parlor with a knock and a curtsy. "Dinner is served," she said in her soft voice.

Owen ushered the ladies into the dining room. He pulled out his mother's chair, then moved to help Abby. He placed a firm hand on her shoulder as he pushed her in. She took another sip of sherry.

"Owen, dear, you've been so busy this week. Abby and I feel we haven't seen you at all!" Mrs. Johnson said as the girls began serving the small family. "At least Abby had her time with you this afternoon"—a smile in her direction—"but what about your mother? When do I get my turn?"

"Whenever you wish, Mother," he replied with a smile. "You could even come with us if you wish."

"Oh, no, dear! You young people need your time alone." She laughed. "You need time to make your plans, get to know each other."

"No, really, Mrs. Johnson, you should come with us next time. Give us something pleasant to talk about."

Abby did not need to look at Owen or hear the angry clatter of silver on china to know she had overstepped. She wondered idly if he had intended to tell his mother anything. Perhaps he simply assumed he would bring Abby around to his way of thinking.

Mrs. Johnson waited until the servants had withdrawn. "Whatever happened out there today?" She looked from one to the other, and for some reason, Abby could not meet her eyes. "Abby? Owen?"

"Abby seems to feel that marriage to me would be a step down from what she could do for herself," Owen said through gritted teeth. And still the clatter of silver on china, as he avoided eating the delectable things on his plate.

"I never said any such thing," Abby answered in the same clipped tone. "I simply said I want to keep working."

"Married women don't work."

"Why not?" she demanded.

"Because they don't!"

"That is the stupidest argument I've ever heard. That's not a reason. It's what you say when you know your reason is illogical."

"Abby, I realize that where you come from, some women must work," Mrs. Johnson began softly. "I come from that place, too, back in Wales. But Owen can take care of you. There is no need for—"

"No need, I agree," Abby interrupted as politely as she could. "But I *want* to. I *like* it."

"But—" Mrs. Johnson began.

"Mother, just leave it," Owen said. "Shall we talk of something else? Ford's Theater is putting on a new play next week. Shall we all go see it?"

Abby allowed the talk to swirl around her. She sipped her sherry and ate her food, but she tasted none of it. She marveled at that—she had heard that expression before that one could eat food without tasting it. At the time, she had wondered how it could be possible. Now she knew: her mind was so preoccupied that the fork transferred food from the plate to her mouth, and she mechanically chewed and swallowed, but she did not notice what she was doing. She vaguely wondered if she would notice if a piece of potato got lodged in her throat. And would the good doctor across the table do anything to help?

"Excuse me, please," she muttered as the dessert was served. She folded her napkin, pushed back her chair, glared at Owen as he stood in his gentlemanly fashion, and left the room. She hurried up the stairs, grabbed her coat, and headed for the street.

"Where are you going, dear?" Mrs. Johnson asked, striding down the hall.

"Just out for a walk. I need some air."

And so Abby was on the street, her angry steps becoming less so with each block. As the sun set and darkness drew in, she fought the urge to be sensible and turn back. She needed space, time, more than she could get here. When had it become such a joyless existence? How had it happened? She loved the city, absolutely *loved* it! So how had she ended up at the edge of the park, shivering and staring into darkness, tears burning her eyelids, ready to give it all up and go home?

"Abby! Abby!"

"Miss Weimer!"

"Miss Weimer!"

Abby turned toward the voices. She recognized them: Owen, Drake, and Collin. There were three men looking for her in the dark. Two of them were there for her every beck and call to do whatever she asked. And one wanted that servitude from her.

With a swirl of skirts, she turned toward the voices in the dark. She could see the gaslights on the street. The leaf-less trees allowed her to see the three men walking quickly down the block, looking this way and that as they called. She could call out to them and relieve their anxiety; she had no doubt that Owen was anxious just as the other two were concerned for her safety. But he didn't love her. And she didn't love him.

She could have called out, but she didn't. She walked quickly and quietly toward them.

"Oh, Abby, there you are!" Owen said with a sigh and a half smile. He stopped a few yards from her. "We were worried when you weren't back by dark."

She passed him without a word or a glance. Her back straight, steps steady, she continued the three blocks to the townhouse. At some point, Owen caught up with her, took her elbow. She did not bother to shrug him off. She could hear the two servants behind them.

Mrs. Johnson greeted them in the parlor. Abby was suddenly very sorry for the worry she had caused. It was clear on Mrs. Johnson's face, and in the idle hands in her lap, no needlepoint in sight.

"I'm very sorry, Mrs. Johnson. Please forgive me."

The older woman took Abby's chin in her two wrinkled hands, kissed her on the lips, and then sat her on the settee next to her. Mrs. Johnson delicately wiped a tear off her cheek. With a deep breath, she was again in command. A word to the maid to bring tea, a command to Owen to go see Sadie in the nursery, and the two of them were alone in the parlor.

"I'm sorry—" Abby began again.

Mrs. Johnson took her hands. "Please don't speak, Abby. I've thought of you as a daughter these many months. I guess I forgot, somehow, that you are still an employee, no more obligated to stay with me than I am to pay you fairly. I have enjoyed your company, but it is time for you to go, I think, and I will certainly miss you!"

"You're firing me?" She was stunned. This was not what she had expected at all!

"No, dear," Mrs. Johnson said as Kate returned with the tea tray. As always, Mrs. Johnson refrained from speaking in front of the servants. She continued after Kate had retreated and closed the door. "I am releasing you."

"I don't understand." Abby sipped her tea. This time, she was aware of the warmth it brought, the sweet smell of chamomile.

"You and I are very much the same. That is what I like about you!" A cheerful laugh. "But we want different things, and I made the mistake of assuming that because we are alike in so many ways, we would be alike in that also." Abby waited patiently because she still did not understand. "We are both independent women, very strong women. We can think for ourselves and fend for ourselves. But whereas I always knew I wanted to marry—and well—I did not realize you did not want the same. You would prefer to remain single and a seamstress instead of marry and be of society?"

"I would not mind being married," Abby admitted, perhaps for the very first time. "But I don't want to sit at home and do nothing."

Mrs. Johnson nodded. "Owen loves you, you know."

"No, he doesn't," Abby said, spilling tea as she clunked the cup and saucer on the table. "He wants to marry me, but he doesn't love me. If he loved me, he would understand why I'm so angry at him."

"Don't assume that, dear. Men can be incredibly dense sometimes." She, too, put down her cup. "He does love you, and therefore, it would be wrong for you to stay here. If you want to continue your work with the Sanitary Commission, I can find another place for you. As a seamstress or as a companion—"

"No, I want to go home."

"Philadelphia?"

"No, home. Millerstown." *I want to see my mother, and my sister is to be married,* she thought. *I should be there. I want to be there.*

Mrs. Johnson nodded. "I will send Owen to buy you a ticket first thing in the morning."

"I shall buy my own ticket."

Mrs. Johnson smiled. "Yes, of course." They both stood. "Oh, dear, I will miss you!"

Owen rode with Abby to the station. They did not speak. He instructed the driver to load her trunks—she had arrived with one and was leaving with three—while she bought her ticket at the window. Most of her money was hidden in her trunks, sewn into dress linings, just in case the locks were smashed and her belongings ransacked. She was carrying fifty dollars in her reticule, however, not knowing if she would need to stay in Philadelphia overnight. The ticket from Washington to Philadelphia was $6.25.

"Do you know what time the train will arrive in Philadelphia?"

"Before noon," the ticket man said.

"Oh, then could I get a ticket to Reading?"

"Pennsylvania?"

"Yes, sir."

"$9.50. And that train will arrive around three in the afternoon."

"Is there a telegraph office around here? I'll need to wire ahead for someone to meet me."

The ticket man pointed in a vague direction, handed her the ticket, and looked past her to the next customer.

"All set, then?" Owen asked. He had moved infinitesimally nearer as she waited in line.

"Not quite. I could get a ticket to Reading, but that means I need to wire ahead to my father, so he can meet me." She looked at the large clock on the wall above the platform. "I have time to get to the telegraph, I think."

"No, please, let me do that for you."

His manners had changed dramatically in the past two days. He was almost apologetic when he offered, as if he was sorry he was taking even that small bit of independence from her. She nodded.

"Reading, three o'clock." She reached into the reticule and pulled out a piece of paper and a pencil. She wrote her father's name, the name of the town, and a message.

> Coming home. Monday, Three o'clock, reading.
> If you can't come, will stay the night in a Hotel. Abby

She handed it to the man standing across from her. Tall, dark, and handsome, like every image of the prince in the fairy tales, comes to rescue the damsel in distress. But she was no damsel in distress, and he was no prince. She sighed. But perhaps he was close enough.

"Thank you, Owen. I am sorry things didn't work out for us. I wish you well," she offered.

"I'm sorry too." He kissed her cheek, cleared his throat. "You should get on the train. I'll take care of the wire."

"Thank you. Again."

She was on the train in a moment. He waved. She returned the goodbye. And then he turned and walked away. She saw him speak to the driver, probably telling him to go to the telegraph office, and then he was gone. And soon she would be gone, too, away from the busyness and bustle, home again in the open fields of corn and wheat, probably still covered with snow. She sighed and smiled at her seatmate as the train pulled out of the station.

Chapter 12

BRIAN

Brian sat among the circle of soldiers at the campfire, listening to the chatter. They discussed guns and fighting and women back home, and just home, and the new general, Hooker. It was always the same, really. If Brian had once thought farming was boring, he had quickly realized that army life, between battles, was just as repetitive and dull. Their unit had not fought since Fredericksburg in the late fall. They sat in winter camp and waited.

"I got a letter from me Bridie."

"I did na' know Bridie could write."

"She canna'. The Father writes for her."

"Ah, and what does Bridie Cavanagh say?"

"Her sister and brother-in-law have come to Philadelphia."

"Ach. By choice, have they come?"

"No, seems they were evicted."

Brian looked up from his boot polishing as the tone of the conversation went from kindly to angry. Everyone was shouting at the news. Finally, Connor Cavanagh was given the opportunity to tell the gathered group what his wife had asked the priest to write. Bridie's sister Mary and Mary's husband, Michael, had worked the landlord's farm for nearly fifteen years. Since 1860, Ireland had suffered exceptionally bad weather. Michael had been unable to pay the rent for two years running.

"And Lord what's-his-name evicted them. They spent a few weeks with Michael's sister's family, but fifteen people in a cottage is too close for comfort!"

"Can't be any worse than sleeping with Sean O'Leary's feet!"

"Ach." The offended soldier threw a stick at the offender, another Sean.

"I can't say I agree, O'Daire," said Billy Bradigan. "Me and Katie spent three months with my brother in their cottage. Me and Katie had five little'uns then, and Patrick and his Katie had seven. I love me family, but I wouldn't wish that on me worst enemy."

"I would," O'Leary said. "My worst enemy is English!" General laughter filled the warmth of the circle.

"And we all know that the cottage wouldna' be the worst of it," Cavanagh said. "The farm only has eight acres."

"Eight acres for fifteen people?" Brian asked, finally entering the conversation. He thought of Frederick's sixty acres in Lower Macungie Township. How could a farm of eight acres support fifteen people? Eight acres might be easier to farm, but it certainly could not grow much.

The eyes turned toward him. Very often, those eyes looked at him with pity. *Poor American*, they seemed to say, *never been to the sweet Eire.*

"Those eight acres dona' belong to Michael's sister and her husband, dear Brian," Cavanagh said. "They belong to the landlord. Except the landlord doesna' live there. He lives in England. He doesna' visit often, just demands the rent. The farmer must pay, even if the crop is bad."

Well, sure, Brian thought, but he knew better than to say so. *If Frederick doesn't pay the mortgage, the bank comes after him, whether there was a bad crop or not.*

"But with even four children on a farm, eight acres is na' enough to give them enough to eat *and* pay rent. But the landlords do na' care," Billy Bradigan continued.

"And they do na' care when the people are starving," another man added. As Brian looked at the faces in the fire's warm glow, he shivered in the cold. Their faces still bore the pain of that starvation;

most of these men had lived through the Great Blight and come to America for some hope to hang onto.

"And eviction does na' mean that the family must simply move," Billy continued. "The father is arrested until he can pay."

"How can he pay if he's in jail?" Brian asked.

"Exactly my point," Billy continued. "He canna', can he? So the wife is left with the children. If the sons are old enough, they might find a job right quick, but not usually because who would hire them? And so the father is in jail, and the mother and the children are put out." Tears began to fall from his painfully blue eyes. "And they stand and watch while the landlord's agents burn the house to the ground. Sometimes, the agent will throw the possessions into the street before burning, but na' always. And then they have . . . nothing." The man's voice broke, and all eyes stared into the orange flames.

"Did these landlords buy the land from the farmers? Or how do they become landlords?" Brian asked after a moment.

"Landlords inherit it," O'Leary said.

"Oh, so, like from the beginning of time," Brian said angrily. He brushed his boots just for something to do.

"Ach, bite yer tongue!" said one man.

"No!" said another.

"Do ye know nothing of yer history, boy?" Billy demanded. "William of bloody Orange won at the Boyne, and Ireland was overrun by bloody English. The year was 1690. Parliament was trying to put William on the throne—"

"Taking James off," Cavanagh interrupted.

"And somehow Ireland became the battleground," Billy continued. "And William won at the Boyne, and James lost. A treaty was signed in 1691. It was supposed to protect Catholics, but then they passed more laws that did anything but protect. We've been rebelling ever since."

"And that is when the Irish Catholics who owned land lost it," O'Leary said. "And the English took it."

"The treaty said Catholics could hold office and jobs and have land, but it never happened that way," Cavanagh said.

"The Irish parliament forgot they were Irish," Billy muttered. "The penal laws were passed in 1695. A Catholic could no longer receive education, or bear arms, or own a horse worth more than five pounds."

"That's insane!" Brian said. Living with Frederick, he could have owned a horse as a boy, let alone as a man.

"That's na' all, boy," Billy continued. "They added more laws with Queen Anne. Catholics could na' hold office, or be in a profession, like doctoring or lawyering—"

"Or purchase or lease land—"

"Or live in a town—"

"Or vote—"

"Or attend Mass," Billy finished. "How can a Catholic *not* attend Mass, I ask you?"

"So you didn't attend Mass until you came to America?" Brian asked.

Laughter. "The bloody English may make the laws does na' mean we follow them," O'Leary said. "In secret, of course!"

"But let's na' give the boy a wrong impression," Sean O'Daire said. "The men that fled Ireland, the ones who the laws tried to stop from owning land and such, they were noblemen, not like us. I do na' think any of our ancestors owned land, ever! The noblemen fled to Europe and left us to fend for ourselves."

"And we did. Just fine, for the most part, until the famine," Billy said.

"Except for the landlords." Someone laughed.

Sometime later, Brian lay in the dark, listening to someone snore. His feet were cold, even in two layers of socks. His nose was cold, too, and he wiggled it every few minutes to make sure it didn't fall off.

The men around the campfire had talked about the abominations of tenant farming in Ireland. Brian could not deny it was a bad situation. But he remembered again the freed slave, Benjamin

Hagerty, who had given a speech near Southwark the year before. Benjamin had talked about his childhood:

"I's the third chil'. My ma went back to work the day after I's born. She died when I's four, birthin' her fifth chil'. Of the five chil'n, I's the only one to reach full age."

Benjamin had talked about life on a cotton plantation: "Up afore dawn. We did not eat until we been workin' for nearly four hours. Cotton farming's very predic'able work, and certain things must be done at just the righ' time. There's ne'er time to rest. Worked all day until dark. Then we 'ould take care of our'n vegetables, eat a little somethin', and sleep for a few hours."

Benjamin had talked about his father: "My papa's killed when I's a young man. The overseer did not like him and said he did not do his share of the work. He whipped my papa almost ever' day. One day, my papa stood up to 'im and said, 'No!' For that, he's strapped to a wagon wheel, arms and legs spread, stripped of his clothes, and lashed until he died."

Brian could not help but see the image in his head. It was wrong, so wrong! No human being should be treated that way. To die because of a word. To be enslaved because of a color. He did not care what Daniel said. He, Brian, was not fighting for the Union. He was fighting for freedom.

"Have you heard about Hooker's new furlough system?" Tommy Kennedy asked Brian as they sat in their tent a few days later. The gray of early morning hung in the air like a wet blanket; it would probably snow later.

Brian stuck a cold foot into a cold boot. He had heard of it, but he didn't offer his opinion. He wasn't sure yet if the idea would work. It was supposed to be that one man in each company, one at a time, would be on furlough for ten days. He would return, and the next would go. But how turns were determined was not clear, nor was how the policy would be enforced. There had been a lot of desertions in the last six months.

"Sean O'Leary is going today, I heard," Tommy continued, stomping around in the mud outside the tent. "I hope I get to go next." His voice dropped considerably when he added, "I don't know how much more of this I can take."

Brian had no use for Tommy or others like him. He was a string-bean thin, gangly wimp of a soldier. He complained about everything, from the weather to the camp conditions, to the food, to homesickness. Tommy did not seem to care that he was certainly not alone in his complaints. Brian's attempts to win him to the side of the glorious fight had gone unheeded. Tommy was simply content to complain.

Brian joined Tommy outside the tent, breathed in the crisp coldness of the March morning. He could hear the sizzle of fat in pans, the chatter of soldiers as they woke up and ate a meager meal of biscuits and bacon and coffee. Or what passed for coffee. Morale was low, had been for months, but it had been improving steadily since Fighting Joe had taken command. Brian and Tommy joined a circle, surprised to see his old friend.

"Daniel!" Brian exclaimed. "How have you been? Mary wrote that you wrote to your ma and said we were both fine. But I haven't seen you in months!"

The eyes that looked up at him from the log at the edge of the campfire circle were full of suffering and pain. The hand and arm that held the plate of food was half-hidden inside his sack coat, the right sleeve hanging empty at his side. He was gaunt and unusually pale. "I lied. About me, and about seeing you. I thought it would make them feel better."

Brian sat down on the log, and someone handed him a plate of food. "What happened, man?"

"Fredericksburg happened."

The circle immediately quieted. Everyone still remembered the bungled job Burnside had orchestrated in November and December.

It had started in the beginning of November when Lincoln replaced McClellan with General Ambrose Burnside. The men knew they would miss Little Mac, but Burnside promised to move when McClellan would have waited. Burnside created a plan, which would be acted upon with due speed. The plan included crossing the Rappahannock River, with the intention of attacking Richmond.

Unfortunately, Burnside's army hit a snag. The pontoon bridges did not arrive as planned.

The men began marching on November 15, but the bridges did not arrive until November 25. Burnside was counting on that all-important strategy of surprise, but with the administrative blunder, Burnside and his army lost the advantage; Lee was waiting. Burnside decided his best course of action was to avoid crossing east of Fredericksburg, as originally intended, and cross directly in front of the town. He had more men. Lee had the advantage of hills.

"Did you catch a bullet from sniper fire?" Brian asked. Before the battle began, as Burnside sent his men across on pontoons, Confederate snipers exacted a fierce toll, but it was the only opposition they encountered at first.

"No. I wasn't with the first crossing."

"Me neither," Brian said, finally digging into the soggy breakfast. "I heard the first ones across the river looted. You hear that?"

Daniel was trying to hold the plate steady with an arm that was obviously still hurting. "Yeah."

After a moment, he added, "It was the third day."

Brian nodded. He remembered well. They faced the heights. Brian had been situated only a few hundred paces from the telegraph road. The line of men stretched from that road, far off to his left.

Longstreet's men—and heavy artillery—fired down from the heights and from the sunken telegraph road. The scream of artillery went right through him, just as a bullet would. It made a man shrink into himself. The sound of screaming artillery shells was far different from the whistle and thunk of rifle fire.

For hours, wave after wave of blue coats marched through white smoke amid the scream of cannon and the crack of gunfire. Wave after wave of blue coats fell on the road below Marye's Heights. It was a steep face, but less so than the surrounding hills.

"We made it halfway up the heights," Daniel said. "People were falling on either side of me. They say you don't hear the bullet that gets you." Tired eyes looked at his old friend. "I don't know if I heard it or not. There was so much gunfire. Whistles and thumps and cracks. Ten yards into it, my ears were ringing, and my eyes were watering, and I tripped over . . . something. I kept walking. Why run? I couldn't see where I was going. All of a sudden, I was pushed up against other soldiers. It was like we were trying to put a horse through a mouse hole. We were getting stuck. And that was going to be the death of us. I was with the group that crossed the canal ditch, but I didn't make it much farther." He looked again at Brian. "I was shot as I came up out of the ditch. I just lay there."

Brian stopped eating. How lucky he had been! He, too, had stormed the heights. He, too, had walked through a bog of cannonballs, white smoke, prone bodies, and bloody mud. Daniel must have been ahead of Brian in the line; it sounded like he was with the group of Irish Brigade soldiers that made it halfway up the hill. They were the only unit that day to do so. The cannon eradicated most of the advancing blue coats. It wasn't until the final assault that the actual gunfire had come out of the sunken road. Brian had advanced against it only a few steps before the retreat sounded. He had seen the line of fire, red fire like someone was flinging a burning whip, coming at them. He had been glad to retreat.

"I don't know how long I waited to be found," Daniel's voice was small and weary.

"We had to wait for the truce."

"Yeah, I know. When did the battle start?"

"Start? I don't know. It was after noon when my group started."

"It was twilight when the nurse came for me," Daniel said. Brian shook his head at Daniel's word choice. "Twilight" was the time of fireflies in the corn, pink ribbons along the horizon. It was definitely not a word used to describe a battlefield after the gunfire stopped. Except, except, perhaps Daniel was describing the state of his soul, somewhere between living and dying, when the nurse found him.

"He was a strong man, big," Daniel continued. "Picked me up as if I were no bigger than George. He put me on a stretcher, and two of them carried me. It was such a strange feeling, almost like being in a tree branch when the wind blows. I think I faded in and out. I wasn't thinking much. I woke up in the surgery tent."

Brian fervently yet silently hoped Daniel would not describe the tent. Others had, and even at the memory of it, the little bit of breakfast Brian had eaten threatened to come up again. Brian knew that the surgeons' tent was the one place he never wanted to be. If Daniel ended up in that place and still had all of his limbs, then he, too, had been very lucky, and Brian said so.

Daniel looked down at the shaking arm. It hurt, burned. A minié ball had penetrated from front to back, all the way through, taking an inch of flesh with it. Now he had two scars, the two-inch-long white one on his upper thigh and the red burning one on his right arm near the shoulder. The surgeon stitched him up and told him to hope for the best. Amputation was not out of the question yet. Daniel said, "Very lucky. What happened after the battle?"

"We retreated to Stafford Heights. Waited. Then we started marching. It was the end of January the twentieth, I think. It rained and rained. I remember wondering why it wasn't colder, and then I stopped caring because it was cold enough. We slopped through ankle-deep mud. Remember that really rainy spring we had a few years back? Rained for a month straight, and we wondered if we'd ever be able to plant the fields." Daniel nodded. "Yeah, it was worse than that. The caissons kept getting stuck. Every few feet, we had to dig them out. And the wind kept blowing. It was cold as hell. I heard they got a few caissons through to Falmouth. It took us all night to go a few miles. We camped somewhere. Some place on the backside of nowhere. And then it snowed. Oh, how it snowed. Three inches if it was one! We ended up turning around and camping back near Fredericksburg."

"What was the point?"

Brian shook his head. "Who knows? I don't know if Burnside knew! Maybe that's why Lincoln pulled him out and gave us Fighting Joe."

"I hear Hooker has a plan."

"Yeah, well, we'll see. They've all said that, haven't they? McClellan, Burnside, and now Hooker. They all have their good points, and they all failed."

"Hooker hasn't. Yet," Daniel said. The two men looked up as the command came for formation and drill. "Tell me why we're doing this again?"

Brian laughed without humor. "If *you've* forgotten, then we're all in trouble." But even as he said it, he thought of Billy Bradigan's family, and Cavanagh's Bridie's sister and brother-in-law, and Benjamin Hagerty.

As the two friends grabbed their rifles and headed toward the line, Brian said, "You know, Daniel, glory is looking duller and duller every day. If it weren't such a worthy cause, I think I'd quit. I really just want to go home."

"Me too."

Chapter 13

MILLERSTOWN

Sarah stood at the door impatiently waiting for Pa and Abby to return. It had snowed earlier in the week and then warmed up. The roads were muddy. The trip to Allentown would take longer than usual.

"Sarah, they'll be here soon enough," Ma said from the stove, stirring whatever she was preparing for dinner. Sarah didn't pay much attention to that anymore. Ma had bestowed upon her the task of keeping up with bread and desserts. Ma did the regular meal cooking. Abby was too busy to help.

But it didn't bother Sarah as much as it once had. "Maybe they didn't have it. Maybe it didn't come yet," Sarah said.

"Well, standing at the door won't bring them back any sooner."

"I know, I know." And still, she waited. As she watched the light fade from the gray March sky, she saw the wagon coming down the muddy road. Two figures sat on the seat. It was too far away to see any features, but she knew it was them. "Ma, here they come!" As Sarah ran out the door without her coat, or even a shawl, her mother took her place at the door.

"Did you get it?" Sarah was calling out before they could even hear her. But Abby understood the excitement that was so obvious in her sister, and she held up the package that was in the wagon bed. "You got it! You got it!"

Soon enough, the two sisters and their mother were spreading the maroon fabric on the table. Mary stood behind them, hands on hips, wooden spoon in hand looking over their shoulders. As Sarah delicately fingered the fabric, Abby produced her newest *Godey's* and flipped through the pages.

"Don't start cutting anything just yet," Ma said. "You'll just have to pack it all up so we can eat. Wait until tomorrow."

Sarah groaned. She was tired of waiting.

"I know," Ma said, rubbing her shoulders. "But one more evening won't make a difference. I promise."

Sarah smiled. "I know. At least Abby's home! And she'll make the dress!"

Abby's arrival had been a surprise and an answer to a secretly whispered prayer. The wire had been delivered to the farmhouse around ten in the morning. Pa had left immediately for Reading, nearly thirty miles away. Because winter days were so short, Pa and Abby had stayed the night in a hotel. The next day, midmorning, Pa and Abby had arrived.

"Oh, look at you!" Ma had said, almost spinning Abby in her excitement. Abby hugged her and laughed.

"Sarah," Abby said then. "I am so happy for you." Mentioning the wedding went a long way toward solidifying a newfound friendship. Later, as Abby was settling herself in their shared room, Sarah had bubbled about her betrothed, the farm he owned, the June wedding.

"Have you made your dress yet?" Abby asked.

"No. I was . . . well, now that you are home, would you be willing to make it?"

Abby bounced onto the bed, wrapped her arms around Sarah. "I would be glad to!"

Sarah stood as still as a dressmaker's dummy as Abby pinned the dress pieces. The deep maroon cotton was smooth on her skin. When Abby finished pinning, Sarah would move and bend to see that the dress would fit properly. It was a tedious process.

"So tell me about Washington."

Abby sighed past the pins in her mouth. She answered without removing them. "I enjoyed it. I liked working for the Sanitary Commission."

"I don't think I could have done that. Working with wounded soldiers, I mean. Wasn't it horrible?"

"Yes, it was hard to see them like that. Infection stinks, and it attracts flies. And it hurts. So the convalescent home was always filled with crying, stinking sad soldiers. But holding their hands or writing letters for them or feeding them . . . well, it's a gratifying experience. Hard, I won't lie. But I felt useful and important."

"That means a lot to you," Sarah said softly. "Feeling like what you do is important."

"Yes."

After a moment, Sarah said, "You know, Abby, what you did for those men is not that different than what Ma does for us. When Ben had pneumonia when he was little, she kept cool cloths on his head and spoon-fed him broth and read to him when he was feeling better."

Abby made a sound of assent, but did not reply.

Sarah continued. "Do you really think less of me for choosing to be a wife?"

Abby took the pins from her mouth. She looked up at her sister, half pinned into her wedding gown. "No, Sarah, I don't think less of you." She shrugged. "Maybe I did once. Now, though, I just want to be allowed to do my own thing. I just don't want to be forced into anything."

"No one is forcing me."

"I know." A moment passed, and then the pins found their place back between pursed lips. Still looking up at her sister, she said, "Do you think less of me for *not* choosing motherhood?"

Sarah vehemently shook her head. "No. I don't think less of you."

Abby again turned to her pinning. "Do you think Ma is very disappointed with me?"

"No. She's proud of you. Pa is too." She laughed. "And if you ask me how Ben feels, I'll have to admit I don't know what he thinks about anything!"

Abby laughed, too, and it felt good. She breathed a bit easier, and the dress was pinned in no time at all.

"Mama, do you need anything in town?" Sarah asked her mother as she entered the kitchen. Ma was sweating over a laundry tub. She turned around without ceasing the up-and-down motion of shirt on board.

"Are you going to town?"

"Kathleen wanted me to stop by sometime this week. She's nervous! I guess she's hoping I can help, but I think before long I'll be in worse shape than she is!"

Ma wiped her forehead and paused in her work. "Check the flour and sugar jars. We promised Kathleen three cakes for Saturday."

Twenty minutes later, Sarah was walking toward town, swinging her basket like a schoolgirl on summer vacation. She didn't skip, but occasionally, her feet hopped over a mud puddle or cheerfully kicked a stone. She passed no wagons, saw no people. She enjoyed the solitude as she walked beneath a clear blue sky and a bright, yet cold, sun. No trees were budding this early in the season, but it wouldn't be long now. The frequent rain had rejuvenated the grass—winter brown just last week, vibrant green today.

Sarah heard a wagon approaching from behind. She stepped to the right, waited along the ditch for the wagon to pass. She looked up to greet the driver and squealed with delight.

"Daniel!"

The driver, Mr. Lichtenwalner, tipped his hat. Daniel grinned, and as the older man pulled on the reins, he jumped down. He hugged Sarah with one arm and a hearty laugh.

"How are you, Sarah? You look wonderful!"

"I am well, Daniel, how are you? What are you doing here?"

"Furlough. I have eight days before I have to leave again. You heading to town? Can we give you a ride?" As Sarah hesitated, he changed his mind. "Can I walk with you?"

"Absolutely!"

Mr. Lichtenwalner called down from the wagon seat. "I'll drop your bag at the tavern."

"Mr. Lichtenwalner, could you wait until you're ready to leave town? If you drop off the bag before I get there, it will ruin the surprise!" Daniel said.

"No problem! Welcome home, son!" And he was off again.

Sarah and Daniel fell into step behind the wagon, avoiding puddles and sloppy mud wherever possible. They walked in silence for a while.

"You picked a great week to come home!"

"Has Meg had the baby?"

"Yes, a boy. But what I mean is Saturday is Kathleen's wedding."

Daniel stopped walking. "Saturday?"

"Yes. You knew about that, right? I'm not telling a secret."

"Oh, I knew she and this Will person were getting married, but I didn't know when." He set off at a quicker pace. "Well, now, that does make me happy for the randomness of furloughs! I've been waiting over a month for my turn. I guess God knew what He was doing!"

As the two young people entered the small crowd on Main Street, they parted ways. Sarah headed for the post office. "Tell Kathleen I'll stop by in a little while." Daniel nodded and turned toward Kelly's tavern.

Daniel walked around the tavern. He gently ran his hand along the stucco, looking in the just-washed windows. There was a man behind the bar. His curly dark head was bent over a book on the bar, and he was writing. Daniel watched him work for a minute before opening the door.

The man looked up. "I'm sorry, sir, but we don't open until four."

"You don't need to serve me. I'll just sit for a minute." This must be Kathleen's Will. Daniel decided to simply sit and observe him for a moment.

"Are you new in the area or just passing through?" Will asked, offering a mug of beer despite his opening statement. One point for Will: taking care of people, customers. A kind man.

Daniel took a sip. "I've been in the war. On my way home."

"Oh, well, welcome home, then, sir," Will said, returning to the ledger.

"You're not a Kelly."

"No, sir. Will O'Neill, originally from County Meath. I've been here for nearly a year now. How long have you been gone?"

"Three and a half years. I left home before the war even started. I went to Philadelphia to seek my fortune." He paused, took another sip of beer. "The Kellys had sons last I heard. Business must be booming if they hired someone."

"Oh, well, I don't want to be tellin' tales, sir, you'd best talk to them about that."

"This is a small town, sir. It isn't gossip, it's called being neighborly." Another point for Will: protecting the family.

"Their oldest son went off to war too. And Mr. and Mrs. Kelly were ill for a while. The daughters hired me to help."

"Are Patrick and Peggy doing better?"

"Oh, yes, much. Mr. Kelly actually helps in the tavern now. And Mrs. Kelly is helping around the house again."

"And Kathleen and Meg? How are they?"

Will's face lit up as Daniel mentioned Kathleen. Another point. "Miss Kathleen is very well. We're to be married this Saturday."

"Congratulations!"

"Thank you. And Meg is doing well."

"Remembering Meg as I do, I would have expected her to be helping out in here." Will suddenly looked uncomfortable, and for a split-second, Daniel felt guilty for his little charade. "Listen," Daniel began.

"Will." Both men turned to see Meg entering from the kitchen. Daniel stood, smiling. Meg's face lit up. "Daniel," she breathed.

"Meg." He crossed the room with four strides and swung her around. "Oh, it is good to see you!"

Daniel turned and stuck out his hand. "I'm her brother. I apologize, Will, I should have told you who I was. I guess I . . . well, I should have told you. I'm sorry."

Will shook his hand. Their eyes locked. Daniel could see the measuring rod in Will's eyes. Finally, Will said, "Understandable. That's what brothers do, I guess. It's a pleasure to finally meet you."

"Thank you." Daniel turned back to Meg. She was still clinging to his arm. "How are you, Meg? You had the baby."

253

"Oh, come and see him!" Meg pulled Daniel toward the kitchen. At the door, she turned around. "Will, Da said to get a list ready. He'll go to Allentown tomorrow."

Kathleen was in the kitchen. She was looking out the window with a wistful expression. She turned as the door opened. With a squeal, she dropped the pie plate in the sink and ran toward her brother. She cried on his shoulder as he swung her around. He put her back on the floor and wiped away the tears falling from her eyes.

"Daniel, are you all right?" Kathleen asked. "Why are you here? How long can you stay?"

"Definitely long enough for a wedding," Daniel said, "and to see this baby."

Meg was still standing close by, as if she didn't want to be too far from Daniel. "He's with Ma in the parlor."

As the three turned, they saw Peggy standing in the doorway. She, too, was crying silently. With one arm, she held a bundled baby, and with the other, she reached out to Daniel.

"Ma, oh, Ma," he said. With great strength and gentleness, he crushed her in his arms. The baby began to cry, and still he didn't let go. Finally, he did, looking down at her from his greater height, and his heart was breaking, knowing her silence was at least partly his fault. "Ma, I'm sorry. For leaving the way I did. I shouldn't have done it—"

Peggy cut him off, putting her shaking fingers on his lips. She smiled. She pulled his head toward her own, kissed his forehead.

Baby Daniel finally made his needs unavoidable, waving arms and kicking feet, and lungs expanding and reexpanding with every wail. Daniel looked at him. He looked to his mother, to the baby's mother, and they assented with a smile as he took the baby in his own arms. Kathleen pulled out a chair for him, and he sat. Ma and Meg joined him at the small kitchen table.

"I'll go find Da," Kathleen said.

"His name is Daniel Boru," Meg said. "For his very brave uncle and the Irish warrior of old."

"Thank you, Meg," he whispered. "When was he born?"

"February 6."

"I'm sorry, I missed it."

For several minutes, the three adults enjoyed each other's silent company and the sweetness of the child. Peggy reached out and touched Daniel's face. When he looked at her, she smiled, touched her heart.

"She's happy you're home," Meg whispered.

"Yes, I can see that."

"Daniel!"

Daniel's heart skipped a beat. He gingerly handed the baby to Meg as he stood up to face his father. The old man was standing just inside the doorway, still wearing his coat, boots covered with mud. His face was more wrinkled than Daniel remembered, his hair more white. But the eyes were the same piercing blue.

"Daniel," Patrick said again. He crossed the small space with open arms, and he gripped Daniel as if his life depended on it. "Welcome home, son."

"Da."

Sarah hurried the last few hundred yards to the back door. Darkness was coming, but that wasn't the reason. After stopping at the post office, she had finished her errands in record time, stopping at the tavern only long enough to tell Kathleen she'd stop by in another day or two, wanting to get home and share the good news. Mary and Abby were in the kitchen as she stomped her boots in the mudroom; Sarah took a moment to catch her breath before opening the door.

"Potatoes are almost done," Abby was telling her mother.

"Roast is done. Just needs to rest," Mary said as she placed the roasting pan on the counter. She turned slightly to glance at Sarah. "You look winded."

"Yes, Ma, I ran the last little bit."

"Why?" Abby demanded, an incredulous look on her face.

"You'll never guess!"

"You saw Harold."

"Howard," Sarah corrected. "And no." Abby did it on purpose every time. She had come up with at least half a dozen names for her future brother-in-law, all beginning with the letter H. Sarah returned the smile.

"Was there any mail?" Mary asked.

"Oh, yes, from Aunt Bridget. But that's not why I ran." She pulled the envelope from her basket and handed it to her mother, who glanced at it and put it in her apron pocket.

"Well, what then?" Abby demanded impatiently, forking potatoes out of the water and onto a plate. "Hand me the butter, Ma?"

"I saw Daniel." Sarah laughed as Abby dropped a potato into the water with a scalding plop, and the butter dish fell from Mary's hand onto the floor between them. "I knew you'd be surprised!"

"Of course, we're surprised!" Mary said, grabbing a towel to pick up the buttery mess. "Is he all right?"

"Fine. Home on furlough, he said. For the wedding."

Abby removed the last few potatoes from the water. "Sarah, supper's ready. Pa and Ben are in the barn. Can you go get them, please?" Abby felt her hands shaking, and she didn't know why. Yes, she did—it would be so wonderful to see Daniel again, so many things to say that couldn't be written in letters.

The table was filled with happy chatter only moments later. Sarah repeated her news. Then Mary read the letter from Bridget. Bridget shared the news of her latest pregnancy, how hard the first few months had been, how her husband had joined the army as a chaplain, how much she and the children missed him. As always, she voiced her hope of someday seeing Mary and her children.

"Perhaps you should go see her," Pa suggested when Ma finished reading.

"I don't think it would be very practical," Mary replied, spooning more vegetables onto Ben's plate.

"Must everything be practical, Mary? You have not seen your sister for over twenty years. She wants to see you. You should go."

Sarah looked from one end of the table to the other. Mary was still shaking her head. "Ma, you should go."

"Sarah, I don't need you to tell me what to do," Mary said uncharacteristically short.

"Ma, I didn't mean—"

"Someone needs to take care of *this* family," Mary said.

"I can do that," Sarah whispered. "It will be good practice. You can even take Abby with you."

"Absolutely, Mary. Sarah can certainly take care of things here for a few weeks. And take Ben, let him see his cousins. We won't start planting for a few weeks yet."

"Fine, fine," Mary said as if she was giving in against all her better judgment, but the smile on her face revealed otherwise. "We'll send a wire and leave next week."

Abby took another helping of potatoes. "I won't be able to go."

Frederick sipped his water. "Why not?"

"I need to work on the wedding dress, and I want to make a new dress for Ma—"

"Not necessary," Mary interrupted.

"And I want to put out an advertisement, let people know I'm back in town and ready for business," Abby finished.

"Will you be staying in town then?" Frederick asked simply, looking across the table at Mary. He could see the hidden joy in Mary's eyes, hoping that Abby really would stay nearby.

Abby looked around the table at each face, the faces she had missed for three years while running after a dream. After three years of working for the Rollinses and the Johnsons, she had been able to save a rather large sum of money, which now sat in the bank. She hoped that before next year's planting season, she would have a piece of land of her own. Sewing work would keep the ready cash coming until her first crop. "I hope so, Pa. The valley is filling up. I think I should do very well for myself."

Frederick stretched to hold Abby's hand. His fingers barely touched her outstretched hand, for she sat in the middle of the long side of the table, while her siblings sat on the other side. Frederick pushed back his chair and walked around to stand behind Abby. She tilted her head to look up at him, and he kissed one cheek and then the other. "You will always have a home here, my dear," he said needlessly.

Saturday began before the sun. By the time Sarah and Abby opened the kitchen door, Mary had the lamps lit and the icing ingredients spread out on the table. She barely looked up as the sisters put on their aprons.

"One of you needs to start the filling." Mary separated an egg.

"I will," Sarah said.

"The jam is in the pantry," Mary said.

The women worked by lantern light until the sun came up, and then they blew out the lamps and kept on. The three cakes, two white and one chocolate, needed to be iced with a layer of raspberry filling in between the layers. Sarah mixed a few spoonfuls of last summer's jam with a batch of her mother's white icing, spreading the mixture between the three layers of each cake. Abby iced each round as Mary started another batch of icing with more egg whites and sugar. The family had been doing without eggs for weeks to prepare for these cakes. Mary used nearly three dozen egg whites, putting the yolks aside to make omelets for breakfast.

"No coffee?" Frederick said, walking through the war zone on his way to the barn. He looked around the kitchen, uncomfortable like a pig in a desert.

Mary looked up, continuing to whip the egg whites. They were starting to stiffen, starting to reach the point where her arm throbbed.

"I'll get it, Ma," Sarah said. Her job was finished; Abby could fill the chocolate cake while Mary finished the last batch of icing. "I'll make breakfast."

Frederick disappeared, closing the door gently behind him. By the time he returned, after feeding the stock and milking the cows, Mary was finishing her task, and Sarah was setting fragrant omelets on the dining table. The coffee pot was already next to Frederick's spot. Ben arrived just as Sarah returned with a plate of bacon.

"That smells good!" he exclaimed.

"Don't sit down," Frederick commanded gently. "You haven't done your chores yet."

"Yes, sir." Ben left the room to gather eggs and feed the chickens.

"Mary!" Frederick called.

"Yes, dear!" Her voice drifted from the kitchen through the closed door. He knew she would not leave a task half done, even to come to answer him.

"Come and sit with me!" he called.

"In a minute!"

Frederick started on the omelet on his plate. Mary soon joined him. She kissed his cheek before walking to the far end of the table.

"Come sit by me," Frederick said softly. Mary looked at him for a moment then pulled out Ben's chair. She began eating without a word. "How long have you been at it already this morning?"

"Since four."

"Mary!"

She smiled at him with tired eyes. "I had a lot to do this morning. We have to get those cakes to the tavern before the wedding. I hope they'll be okay until we come back from the ceremony."

"I'm sure they'll be wonderful!" Frederick assured her.

The next few hours passed in a whirl. Sarah pressed Frederick and Ben's Sunday shirts while the men did Sunday chores; Ben brushed his shoes while Frederick studied the family finances, making plans for the spring planting. Mary and Abby finished cleaning the kitchen. Soon the family all began preparing for the wedding and party in town.

"You look lovely," Sarah said as Abby finished buttoning the white and blue toile dress she had inherited from Mrs. Johnson. Sarah sat at the dressing table, still in her pantaloons and stays, brushing and curling her hair. She was muttering in consternation as she attempted to pin the curls up on top of her head.

"Darn it!" Sarah slammed the brush onto the tabletop.

Abby smiled as she took up the brush. Humming slightly to herself, she finished the job. Sarah patted and tilted her head and smiled. The soft brown curls cascaded at the back of her head. Everything in front was slicked along the sides, and she liked the way the tips of her ears peaked prettily from the style.

"Is this a new style with the ears showing?" Sarah asked.

"Yes, very new. I don't have a snood for you to borrow, but this is very pretty."

Sarah looked at her sister's reflection. She pointed to the red crocheted hairnet, a red velvet bow at the crown for even more decoration. "Is that what you call a snood?"

Abby nodded. "I'm sure we can find one for you in Allentown next time we go."

Sarah reached into the middle drawer and pulled out a delicately carved wooden box about five inches long and four inches wide. "Howard gave this to me last week." She smiled at her sister in the mirror. "He likes to give me presents." She opened the hinged top, revealing a plush black cushion. Sitting on the cushion was a silver-and-pearl hair comb. The curved top was carved to look like a rope, wound round on itself, with a medium-sized pearl at each intersection. The tines—four of them—were three inches long.

"Oh, it's lovely," Abby breathed. She carefully picked it up. She slid the ornament easily into the style, just above the cascade of curls. "Beautiful." After using the hand mirror to look at it, Sarah agreed. "Now to get you dressed," Abby added, patting her sister's bare shoulder.

Sarah was soon dressed in her Sunday best. It was a green and purple plaid with green velvet trim. It fit nicely over the hoops, gracefully brushing the tops of her boots. The white linen collar and cuffs were edged with crocheted lace. The buttons down the front of the bodice were white pearls. With a final swish of skirts and stomp of boots, she was ready to follow Abby downstairs.

"Ah, my lovely ladies," Frederick said, watching from the parlor's doorway. He looked dashing in his three-piece gray flannel suit. It was the same suit he had worn to his own wedding; it still fit, and he refused to wear another, so Mary never bothered to make one. The shirt was relatively new: a white lawn with blue stripes. The collar was decorated with a dark brown bow tie. He wore clean boots, a pair saved for Sundays and special occasions. Ben stood next to him, looking very uncomfortable in similar attire; his suit, brown rather than gray, and his polished boots, the ones he wore every day. The boy pulled at the collar of his shirt, already tired of the tie that choked him.

As each lady kissed their father, he smiled at them. Then his gaze traveled back up the staircase. It was empty. After a moment, Frederick walked to the base of the stairs staring into the dimness at the top. "Mary!" he bellowed. "Mary, we must go!"

The muffled answer flowed down the stairs. "A few minutes! I'll be ready soon!"

"Pa, should I go hitch the team?" Ben asked.

"Already done," Frederick said. He sighed. "We just wait." He turned into the parlor.

"The cakes, Pa," Abby asked, "are they out in the wagon?"

"Oh, no, they're not. Do you girls want me to carry them out?"

"No, we can do it," Sarah said. "Ben, you can help if you promise not to drop them." The three siblings walked toward the kitchen.

Frederick tapped one booted foot and then the other. He heard the swish of fabric and turned to watch Mary walk down the stairs. He smiled. She was even lovelier than their daughters. Her brown hair was pulled away from her face, the gray strands almost acting as silver decoration along with the ruby hairpins he had bought for their tenth anniversary over ten years ago. Her dress was steel blue, with a dark plaid trim at the collar, cuffs, and hem of bodice and skirt. She wore hoops, just as her daughters were doing, and she seemed to float down the stairs.

"My dear," Frederick said simply, offering his arm and a smile as she reached the first floor. "Shall we go?"

"Of course," Mary said, smiling up at him as they walked down the hall.

Frederick helped Mary onto the seat of the wagon. The horses had been brushed, their manes and tails combed, as if they, too, would attend the wedding. Abby, Sarah, and Ben sat in the back of the wagon, each in charge of a cake. Each cake was draped loosely with cheese cloth, sitting on a board covered with a white towel. The siblings sat on a wide board which Frederick had rigged a few days ago, specifically to accommodate his daughters' hoopskirts, while the cakes sat at their feet. It was only eleven o'clock, but Frederick would drive slowly to preserve cakes and hairstyles and dust-free clothing. The wedding was scheduled for two o'clock in Bally.

"You ladies stay put," Frederick said when they reached the tavern. "Ben and I will handle the cakes. Ben, go knock on the door. Make sure we can get in."

Daniel followed Ben back out to the wagon. "Hello!"

"Daniel, so good to see you!" Mary called down.

"Hello," Sarah and Abby said together. Abby unconsciously smoothed her unwrinkled skirt with one hand as she gripped the seat with the other.

"The rest of the family is at the church," Daniel said after the third cake was safely in the tavern. "I was only here to help with the cakes. May I ride with you?"

"Of course," Mary said. "Climb in."

Daniel climbed easily into the wagon, sitting on the floor of it and immediately striking up a conversation with Ben. Daniel was wearing his dress uniform, and Ben asked him about the war. As they talked, Abby was uncomfortably aware of Daniel's frequent glances. When they arrived at the Catholic Church in Bally, Daniel hopped down, straightened his jacket, and reached around to help the ladies. Ben had spotted George and young Will and had already walked away.

"You look nice," Daniel said softly to Abby. She smiled. He turned toward Sarah, reached up to hold her around the waist, wincing slightly as she hopped down. She, too, smiled, and then her smile widened as she saw Howard approaching.

"Daniel, may I present my fiancé, Howard Gehman. Howard, this is our dear friend, Daniel Kelly," Sarah said, easily moving to Howard's side. As he shook Daniel's hand, she gazed up at him. He was over thirty years old but still handsome with a full head of auburn hair and brown eyes. He was clean-shaven, except for the thick, wide mustache that he had slicked upward for the occasion. He had a slight paunch, very slight, and in his handsome stylish suit, it was barely noticeable.

"Sarah, shall we go inside?" Howard asked after the obligatory small talk with Daniel. He nodded to Daniel and turned his future wife toward the church.

"Just think," Sarah said softly, "only four months, and it will be us in front of the church." She felt his arm stiffen, but he smiled down at her, so she didn't worry about it.

Howard led Sarah down the aisle. He ushered her into the pew behind her family. He chatted easily with Frederick. Sarah sat comfortably next to him, waiting for the service to start.

The Weimers had always attended church. Every Sunday morning, they walked or, in bad weather, drove to the Baptist church at the top of Church Street in Millerstown. The Kellys, she knew, were Roman Catholic. There were not many in the Lehigh Valley who followed the pope. The Kellys drove the eight-or-so miles down Kings Highway to Bally, the nearest Catholic church, every week. It was a small congregation, by what Sarah could ascertain from the size of the building, and part of the Philadelphia parish. Sarah enjoyed looking at the stained-glass windows, the sun shining through from the west, as they all waited for the service to begin.

Sarah watched with barely concealed joy as the service began. Kathleen was darling in a crisp brown wool dress, her red hair piled up and decorated with brown velvet ribbons. She wore a cameo at the throat. She did not carry flowers—none were in bloom yet—and she did not seem to know what to do with her hands, but she fairly glowed with happiness as she stood next to Will.

Sarah's mind wandered as the priest said the words that were so strange to Sarah's ears. She thought about June: the dress that Abby worked on so diligently, the tablecloths and napkins and towels that Sarah was putting in the hope chest, the plans for her own home that went with it. Sarah had only been to Howard's home once, with Frederick, and she had trouble recalling the layout and size of the rooms. She did, however, remember that it was well-furnished. She had been impressed with the outfitting of the kitchen.

Soon the ceremony was over, and the congregation began moving outside.

A chill wind had picked up by the time the wedding guests gathered on the front steps of the church. Gray clouds were rolling in from the west. Everyone glanced nervously upward waiting for the bride and groom to appear. Peggy and Patrick appeared first, leaning on each other, smiling as they hadn't in so long! Meg followed, baby Daniel in her arms, and she in Daniel's protective hold. Then George and Will, looking uncomfortable and nervous in new suits but grinning just the same.

And then the newlyweds. The crowd cheered. Men clapped, women waved lacy handkerchiefs. Will guided Kathleen through the crowd to the waiting carriage. He had reportedly bought the stylish rig, along with the horse, only the week before. He handed her up, squeezed himself in beside her hoops, kissed her again as the crowd hollered, and then they drove away.

"Mr. Weimer, sir," Howard said. Sarah looked around, saw her parents approaching. Her father held out his hand, Howard shook it. "Sir, might Sarah ride back to town with me?" he asked.

"Of course, if she wants to." Frederick smiled at Sarah, and she hooked her arm once again through Howard's. Frederick nodded. "We'll see you in town then."

Sarah nodded and smiled at friends as she walked beside Howard to his rig. It was not a covered buggy, like Will's new rig, but it was a sturdy wooden box wagon. He helped her onto the seat; it had plenty of spring and made treks over rough farm roads bearable. Howard had groomed his team of black horses, just as Frederick had done. Howard's team was not a matched pair, but they were obviously good animals: solid, strong, and pretty. As Howard climbed up, pulled the brake, and "hupped" to the horses, they pulled out in an easy gait, another fine characteristic.

"They really are lovely," Sarah said after a moment. Howard rarely spoke first; she was getting used to starting the conversation.

"Will and Kathleen?"

Sarah giggled. "No, the horses," she said, pointing to the trotting pair.

Howard shifted on the seat, obviously pleased. "They are a good pair."

"What are their names?"

He looked at her with wrinkled brow. "They don't have names, Sarah. They're horses, not dogs."

She did not speak at once. "Did you buy them in Fogelsville?"

"No, Kutztown. At auction. They were a good price. One-hundred sixty dollars apiece."

"That seems like a lot."

"No, it's not. The price of everything has gone up since the start of the war. But I'll breed them this year. We'll do well with them, you'll see."

"I'm sure we will."

"I'll be hiring help this season."

"The farm is doing that well?" Sarah asked excitedly. Very few men in the township hired help.

"Yes," he replied with a firm nod. He looked at her, more than a glance. "I promised your father you would be very comfortable, and you will be." She smiled at him, and he smiled back.

They followed a long line of wagons and carriages down the hill into Millerstown. Howard pulled the wagon into an open space in the grassy lot behind the tavern. People were milling about, chatting, laughing, and waiting for their hosts.

"Mr. Gehman, Miss Weimer," a voice said. The couple turned to see another young couple from the township. Hannah Kristof and Anselm Bachman were also engaged and planning to marry the week after Sarah and Howard. Anselm greeted Howard with a handshake, tipped his hat to Sarah. The two couples chatted easily as they waited for the tavern to open.

Anselm was a farmer, though not as prosperous as Howard. He owned a small piece of land on the southern edge of town. He certainly would not be hiring any help. Anselm was only a second-generation American. He was short, balding, and hardly handsome, but Hannah seemed satisfied. Hannah was older than Sarah; she was lucky to get Anselm. She was pretty enough: blond hair, brown eyes, freckles that were not unbecoming, and a thick waist. She was taller than her fiancé, but it did not seem to bother her. Her father owned a small farm as well, not nearly as large as Frederick's, so Anselm was probably a very good catch. Sarah looked up at Howard very pleased.

A cheer went up from the crowd. Sarah craned her neck to see over the heads in front of her.

"Daniel has opened the door," Howard told her. "Shall we go in?" It was not a question, and she did not resist as he led her forward.

"Oh, Kathleen, you're beautiful," Sarah gushed, embracing her friend. Kathleen glowed, standing beside her new husband. Will shook hands, never stopped grinning, and stole glances at his bride as often as he could. Will shook Sarah's hand and then Howard's, and the two moved on, greeting Peggy and Patrick and Kathleen's siblings.

"Sarah, over here!" Sarah turned toward Abby, walked through the crowd with Howard's hand on her elbow. Abby stood with Frederick and Mary. The small family cluster greeted friends and waited.

Soon, Will climbed up on the bar. "Friends! We thank you so much for joining us today! We Irish always love a good party, and a wedding is as good an excuse as any. So eat, drink, and be merry!" He jumped down amidst cheers and applause. The party was soon in full swing.

"Wasn't it beautiful?" Sarah gushed to Abby as Howard moved off to fill two plates. Frederick guided his wife and daughters to a table.

Sarah glowed almost as brightly as Kathleen. Abby said, "Yes, it was beautiful."

Hours passed as the neighborhood celebrated. As the food was consumed, the conversation got louder. As it neared crescendo, someone pulled out a fiddle. Conversation dropped as tables and chairs were pushed out of the way, dropped even more as partners were chosen. Boots on boards soon made any conversation difficult, though the spectators tried.

"Sarah, shall we dance?" Sarah placed her hand in Howard's, and off they went.

Abby watched them spin and sway, laugh and clap. Abby listened to the fast-paced music. Soon her feet were tapping inside the bell of her skirts.

"Abby, do you mind if I take your mother?" Frederick asked, holding Mary's hand and indicating the dance floor with the other. Abby smiled and watched them spin away.

"Hello."

Abby turned. Daniel was sitting at the table, close enough that his voice could be heard within the commotion. She smiled at him. "It's so good that you could be here for the wedding."

"Yes, God worked it out, didn't He?" A pause. And then, "I'm sorry I didn't get out to the farm this week. It's been so busy." He grinned. "I've spent quite a lot of time with my namesake! But how are you?"

"I am well. How about you?"

Daniel touched his right arm. But he smiled when he answered. "I'm just glad to be here."

"What happened?"

"What do you mean?"

"Don't lie to me, Daniel. We've been friends a long time. Are you hurt? I thought it was your leg."

He nodded, not meeting her eyes but watching the swirling dancers. "Another injury in my arm. I'm better, though. I'll be just fine."

"Tell me."

Daniel stared into the distance. She could barely hear him when he answered. "I got shot, Abby. That's it. I don't want to talk about it."

"You can tell me, Daniel, it won't bother me. I worked for the Sanitary Commission, remember?"

Daniel's eyes pierced through her. Was it anger or pain or fear that she saw? "It bothers *me*." The chair scraped. He walked away without another word or a glance back.

Daniel's strange attitude dimmed some of the day's joy. Watching Meg sitting in a corner caused the light to fade almost completely. Abby walked over to her, her skirts swirling as she made her way across the dance floor.

Meg looked up from her son. He had grown since his birth, of course, but he was still so small. He waved tiny fists, made tiny gurgles, and kicked tiny feet. He lay on Meg's lap, lightly wrapped in a white blanket fringed with plaid. When Meg met Abby's eyes, her smile could not hide her sadness.

"Meg, how are you?" Abby sat on one of the many empty chairs near Meg.

"I'm fine. You?"

"Are you sure?"

Meg looked at the stomping, laughing, joyful crowd. "I'm as happy as I have any right to be, I guess."

Abby sat with Meg in the corner, cooing over the baby, even taking a turn at holding him. Not a single person, except Kathleen, came over to speak to Meg. In the hour that Abby spent with Meg, not a single person came over to speak to her, either.

As April flowed past on waves of rain, Sarah continued to work on the hope chest. Abby finished the wedding gown and began working on Mary's new dress. The sisters took care of their father after Mary and Ben left for Gettysburg, sharing chores in a way they never had before.

"Kathleen said Daniel is back with his unit. They're sitting somewhere in Virginia. Not much has happened lately," Sarah said as she rubbed dirty laundry against the board. "He's doing well."

"That's good to hear." Abby was putting the wet clothes through the wringer.

"Has he written to you lately?"

"No, why would he?"

"Abby." Sarah paused in her movements, looking pointedly at her sister.

"Sarah," Abby replied in the same tone.

"Why hasn't he written?"

"I have no idea," Abby said truthfully.

The kitchen door blew open with wind and rain and Frederick. Before either sister could even get out a word, he tossed an envelope to Abby, who was closer, and left again.

"He didn't even get mud on the floor," Sarah commented, continuing her task.

"Water, though." Abby looked at the soggy paper in her hand, an envelope that was already open. "It's from Mother." Sarah wiped her hands on her apron and moved toward Abby as she began to read.

IN THE SHADOW OF MR. LINCOLN

April 1, 1863

Dear Family,

I'm very glad I allowed myself to be talked into taking this trip! Ben is enjoying his cousins, and it is wonderful to see Bridget after so many years.

Bridget has three boys, very energetic and into everything! The oldest, Peter, helps his mother as best he can since his father is gone to war. Ben is helping Peter plant the corn and wheat on the small plot behind the house.

Bridget is not well. I asked the doctor to come because I could see from the first that she is not well. She is too tired, and she has had pains. Well, the doctor came and is gone again. He has ordered that she stay in bed until the baby is born, sometime in late July. He told me that he does not like her color or the sound of her heart.

I can certainly take care of the house while I'm here. One house is the same as another. The boys are wearing me out after only four days, but I can manage them too. My concern is what happens when I return home. Frederick, we had planned for me to stay until the first of May. That would allow plenty of time to finish preparations for the wedding. I could certainly return after the wedding to stay with Bridget until the baby is born. Anna, Sean's wife, said she could help until I returned, but that would be nearly two months, and Anna has her own home and little ones to care for. I would feel badly, knowing she was neglecting her own family, but there is nothing else to be done.

I will write more next week. Be well.

Mary

Sarah pulled out a chair and sat at the table. She leaned her head in her hands, scrunched up her face in thought.

"Ma is asking our opinion, I think," Abby said, sitting down next to her sister.

"I agree."

"The problem is the wedding."

"I beg your pardon," Sarah said, irritated with the implication.

Abby shook her head. "I don't mean you shouldn't get married. Not at all! But look"—she handed the paper to Sarah, as if there was a picture to clarify her thought—"if Ma leaves Gettysburg on May 1, arrives here the third, and the wedding is June 20. That is nearly two months."

"Yes, the letter says that."

"Sarcasm is not becoming in you," Abby said with her own sarcasm. Sarah snorted with laughter. "We have two possibilities, as I see it. Either Ma can stay in Gettysburg until just before the wedding—and we finish all the work ourselves, which shouldn't be too hard—or Ma comes back in May, as planned, and we move the wedding up to maybe May 20, or whatever Saturday falls in that time frame, and then Ma goes back to Gettysburg right after."

Sarah pondered the two options. It was true that she and Abby could successfully finish the wedding preparations. The dress was done; Abby would complete Mary's as she could. Kathleen was doing the cakes, and the rest of the food could not be made until the days before. Whether May or June, that would have to wait. And either way, Sarah and Abby could do it without Mary.

But the truth remained: Sarah wanted Mary's help. She had been anticipating the day of her wedding for years—years! She had thought of the dress, and the food, and the home she would make for herself and her husband. And always in her imaginings, Mary had been with her every step of the way, teaching and guiding and helping. They would laugh and share, and Mary would tell her how it had been when she was a young woman. Sarah and Abby *could* do it, but Sarah wanted Mary.

Sarah stood, moved back to the wash bucket. "Let's get this finished."

The sun had finally come out of hiding as Sarah walked toward Howard's farm. It was nearly two miles from Frederick's. She was walking east, and the sun blinded her as it came out from its cloud cover. The road was muddy, so Sarah was walking in last year's weeds along the side, getting her hem dirty and wet. Oh, well, Howard wouldn't terminate the engagement on something so frivolous.

Sarah bypassed the house. At ten-thirty in the morning, the two-story stone house would be empty. She took a moment to look at it, though. Only a few weeks, and she would be cooking in its kitchen and beating its rugs. It was lovely from the outside; tall and sound glass windows with shutters, two trees shading the front door. Or they would when the budding leaves finally unfurled in the warm May sunshine.

Howard was in a wide field, walking behind the team, holding onto the handles of the plow. He would plant corn here. In another field, green winter wheat had already sprouted; it would ripen in the summer and be harvested in mid-July. A third field would be planted with various vegetables, some for sale but mostly for their own consumption.

"Howard!" she called when she reached the edge of the field. She hoped he would come to her because the field was a sloshy mess.

Howard wiped his forehead with a red handkerchief as he walked toward her. "Sarah. What a surprise! Is everything all right?"

"Yes and no." She took a deep breath. "My Aunt Bridget is very sick. Ma is with her now. In Gettysburg. Somebody needs to stay with Bridget until the baby is born. Abby had a suggestion, and I wanted to ask your opinion."

"All right, I'm listening."

"Ma is going to come home in the beginning of May. If we move the wedding up to May 23, then Ma can help me with the final preparations for the wedding and yet only be away from Bridget for a few weeks." She waited for his reply, leaning forward as if that would help.

"I suppose it can be done. Can your father do that?"

"I don't see why not."

Howard smiled. "Sarah, I'll work until the day before the wedding. Other preparations need to be made but by your father. He's hosting the party, after all. Can he afford to leave the fields in May to do all of that? That's why weddings are in June, dear. The farmwork can wait."

He was laughing at her. She didn't mind. He thought of things she never did.

"I'll ask Pa," she said. "Can I tell him you said yes?"

"Yes, dear." He had also started calling her "dear" on a regular basis. She did not mind that either. She smiled, he smiled, then he returned to his horses, and she walked away.

Sarah came upon her father by chance. As she crossed the northeastern field, she saw him plowing in the distance. In a few days, when the mud dried, he would plant potatoes in this field. She hulloed to him—he was facing away from her—but he did not turn until she was closer and called again. Her feet were completely covered with mud by the time she reached him.

"Sarah. What a surprise!"

She laughed. "Everyone keeps saying that!" He looked at her quizzically, but she continued. "I have talked to Howard, and he agrees."

"About what?"

"Moving the wedding to May 23."

Frederick blinked at her for a minute, as if he was unsure about what she had said. "Why would we do that, Sarah? June is soon enough."

Sarah explained everything to her father. Again, he blinked for a full minute before he answered. Finally, he nodded and agreed.

"Write to your mother and tell her the change of plans. Don't wait until she gets home to tell her."

"Thank you, Pa."

"You're welcome." He kissed her forehead.

As Sarah walked back to the house, she muttered to herself about the state of her shoes. She removed them on the back step. She would need to let the mud dry before she tried to scrape it off.

"It's settled," Sarah said as she walked into the bedroom she and Abby shared. Abby was replacing the rug she had been banging on the back wash line when Sarah had left. Abby straightened.

"What's settled?"

"The wedding will be May 23. Howard agreed, and Pa said it was fine, so that's that." She shrugged. "Can you have Ma's dress finished by then?"

Abby sat on the bed, seemed to ponder the question. "It's all basted. I don't want to do the final sewing until Ma tries it on. That obviously has to wait until she gets back. I should be able to finish it. I don't anticipate any problems."

"Will you have time to make a new dress for yourself? You never mentioned it, but you should have a new dress too." Sarah grinned. "I'm sure that with your earnings from the past two years, you've saved enough for the yard goods."

Abby shook her head. "I don't need another dress. Did you see how many trunks I brought home?"

Sarah laughed as she headed for the stairs. "Good, then you have time to work on the gift you will give me!" she called over her shoulder.

Abby immediately dismissed the comment. They all knew that the family was doing everything they could for Sarah. Additional gifts were not expected. But as she replaced the rugs in the other bedrooms, Abby gave the thought further consideration. She walked back to the bedroom, stood for a moment just looking at the three trunks lined up against the wall.

The original trunk was the one her parents had given her two years ago. It had been new in 1861. It was sturdy but unadorned. And after the travel between cities and different places of employment, the corners were banged, and one end had a gouge in it. The other two trunks, however, were newer. Either of them would make an exceptional gift.

Abby knelt, opened all three lids. Now to choose the dresses.

"Abby!" Kathleen called, waving from her new front door. The April rains had stopped, even if only for a few days, and Kathleen was obviously taking advantage of the beautiful sunshine to wash the windows. Will had purchased a small clapboard house on the east edge of town; the Weimers would pass it every time they went to town.

"Kathleen! How are you?" Abby left the road and walked up the grassy knoll to the house.

"Oh, wonderful! Come in, come in!"

Abby followed Kathleen into the kitchen. It was bright and airy, though chilly with the windows open wide. Kathleen closed one completely and left the other open only a few inches. Still, it smelled slightly musty. The house had been empty for almost a year.

"It's a nice place," Abby said truthfully. She sat at the table. It was covered with a white cloth, a low, wide bowl of river rocks in the center. "What's with the rocks?"

Kathleen smiled as she put the kettle on to boil. "George and little Will gave those to us for a present. They said they broke through the ice in Swabia Creek and picked the prettiest ones they could find. And they asked Pa for some of *their* money from last summer to buy the bowl. I'm not supposed to know that, though. Aren't they pretty?" she finished.

Abby picked up a light-brown one. It was smooth, cool to the touch. A line of white ran through it, like pulled cotton.

"Have you heard from Daniel?" She tried to sound casual. Kathleen would probably assume—rightly so—that Sarah had shared the news.

"He's bored, which in my opinion is good news. I'd let you see the letter, but Ma has it," Kathleen said, preparing the silver tea service, another gift. She poured cream into the little pitcher, placed a few cups on the tray, and brought it to the table.

"Why three cups? Is Will coming home?"

"Oh, no, I'm expecting Meg." Kathleen went back to the new Majestic, a shiny stove that was the envy of nearly every woman in town, waiting for the water to boil. "She hates being kept in the house. She tries to visit at least once a week." Finally, the water was ready, and Kathleen poured it into a ceramic teapot, which she brought to the table. "It will be ready in just a minute. So what brings you here?"

Abby shrugged. "Nothing important." She had really wanted to see the letter. "I get tired of being cramped in the house too."

"Yes, you and Meg are two of a kind. I couldn't do what you do. Work, live in a big city all by myself." She shrugged, pouring the dark tea into the cups. "I guess, really, I wouldn't want to."

"It's been a long time since the two of us have been friends, hasn't it? I'm sorry about that," Abby said sincerely.

"Why? Did you do something wrong?" Kathleen shook her head, put some sugar in her tea and sipped. "You and Meg are very similar, but you and I are very different. That doesn't make you wrong, any more than wanting to be married and raise children is wrong."

"I think I'm beginning to see that."

There was silence as the two women sipped their tea. Finally, Abby spoke again. "There was a man in Washington with whom I was keeping company. His mother was my employer. I think she really hoped we would marry."

"What was his name?"

"Owen Johnson. He's a doctor."

"Did things not work out? Is that why you came home?"

"Yes, I guess so. He wanted a submissive wife. He wanted me to take care of his ward, her education, and run the house. And he would *allow* me to work with the Sanitary Commission as long as the war lasted."

"Ah, I see. And no one *allows* Abby to do anything, is that right?" There was a slight smile on Kathleen's face. "I'm not saying this Owen was the right man for you. He sounds a bit weak if you ask me. Weak people like to control things. But I think you have marriage all wrong." She laughed then a hearty laugh filled with pure joy and contentment. "Listen to me! As if I know the first thing about marriage!"

"No, go on. What were you going to say?"

"You seem to think that taking care of a home and a husband is beneath you. You have talent, and you don't want to waste it. But taking care of a husband is not a step down." Owen's angry words came back to Abby. A lump formed in her throat. "Marriage is teamwork. Like four-in-hand horses."

"That sounds great," Meg said. The other two women turned to see Meg, baby Daniel in her arms, standing in the opening to the hall. She sat down, handing Daniel to Kathleen, and poured herself a cup of tea. "Oh, please, continue. Don't stop your conversation on my account."

"Well, think about a team. Any team. They work together to accomplish the task. In a four-in-hand, you have two teams. One team is the lead team. That team feels the full of the reins, but it doesn't mean the other team is less important. If the second team suddenly stopped walking, the lead team would have to stop too. The same thing with us. God made the husband to be the lead, but that doesn't mean the wife is any less important. We simply make it easier for the husband to do what he needs to do."

"I still think your analogy is stupid," Meg said.

"But I think I understand what you're trying to say," Abby said. She finished her tea, stared idly in the cup while the two sisters fussed over baby Daniel. Daniel. What did he need to do? What did he *want* to do? And how could she help him do it?

"It was good to see Daniel," Meg said. Abby's head snapped up. She hadn't spoken out loud, had she? No, Meg was looking at Kathleen. She turned to Abby. "Daniel and Da talked while he was here. It was good for them to see each other."

Kathleen smiled at baby Daniel, spoke in a baby voice. "And your grandpa forgave your Uncle Daniel, and your Uncle Daniel forgave your grandpa. And everything is going to be okay."

"Your pa is going to let Daniel stay in the city? Write for a newspaper?"

Kathleen looked at Meg. "No, I don't think so. Daniel said something about coming home for good, didn't he? When he left?"

"Yes," Meg answered. To Abby, she explained, "Da and Daniel talked about Daniel starting his own paper, right here in Millerstown. Daniel was willing to come home and take over the tavern, but Da said no. With Will here now, and me to help too . . . well, anyway, Da decided he'd rather have a son who writes than no son at all."

Abby stared out the window. Thoughtfully, she said, "It amazes me how much things have changed in the past two years. Mr. Kelly is a completely different man, Daniel was willing to give everything up for family. Meg is a mother, Kathleen and Sarah are married, will be, anyway, and I'm willing to be . . . War really changes people."

"Do you think we would have been as changed if the war hadn't happened?" Meg asked.

Neither woman answered, but Meg hadn't really expected them to. Abby shrugged, still looking out the window.

"Back to what Abby said," Kathleen said softly. After a moment, "You'd be willing?"

"To be married," Abby clarified, turning back to the conversation.

"Yes, I figured that was what you meant. I was just making sure that was really what you meant."

"Kathleen, that doesn't make sense," Meg said.

"It doesn't make sense," Abby said, but she meant something completely different. "If someone would only ask me."

"He will," Kathleen said encouragingly. "When the war is over."

"Who will?"

"He's loved you for a long time," Kathleen continued, ignoring her sister.

"But he walked out on me at your wedding. I upset him. I didn't mean to, but I did, and I don't even know what I said, so I can't promise it wouldn't happen again. And he didn't say goodbye to me, and he hasn't written. He used to write all the time."

"Daniel," Meg said with some surprise.

"Of course, Daniel," Kathleen said. "Who did you think we were talking about?"

"Daniel and Abby? That can't be."

"And why not?" Kathleen demanded as if she were the one who had been insulted.

"We all grew up together. We're like family. That would be like me marrying Brian."

"Not the same thing at all," Kathleen countered.

"I have to go. I have to go to town to mail a letter to Ma." Abby headed toward the door. "Oh, I almost forgot! Sarah and Howard's wedding is being moved to May 23." She hurried down the hall and out the door before her host was off the chair.

"Margaret Rose Kelly! How could you?"

"What? I don't think they should get married."

"Just because you think it would be strange to marry Brian does not mean they would find it strange to be married to each other. Daniel has loved her for a long time."

"How do you know?"

"Have you ever listened to him talk? It's quite obvious! And if Abby is willing, I say God bless them!"

"They'll need it. He'll have his hands full."

Kathleen smiled. "But that still doesn't mean they won't be a good team."

Meg groaned. "Back to that again!"

Brian sat on the wagon seat, gazing at all the open fields around him. The man with whom he had hitched a ride was a stranger, but he was traveling toward Millerstown, so he was willing to give a soldier a ride.

"Virginia is nothing like this," Brian said to himself. "I've missed this."

"You been fighting in Virginia?" the man asked.

"Yes, sir."

"And you're all in one piece. Lucky son of a gun."

Brian did not respond, but his heart beat a bit faster. He was sure it was *not* luck, but rather God's grace. But one piece or not, he wasn't sure he was unscathed. Images bombarded his sleep every night. Screams exploded like shells in his dreams, sometimes screams without faces. Soldiers without faces riding through mist, shot down by his own gun.

Brian shook his head to clear the cobwebs. It was a beautiful April day in Pennsylvania. They must have had rain recently because the road was muddy, but there was not a cloud in the sky now. The sun shone so brightly it made him forget there was a thing called darkness. He tipped his face to its warmth.

"Well, son, I'm turning left here. I think you want to go right." The stranger stopped his wagon at a crossroads. The crossroads was familiar, but there was a new barn in the field and an addition on the house across the way.

"Farmers are doing well these days," Brian said as he climbed down.

"Yes, sir! I added ten acres myself this year," the man said proudly, indicating the seed in the back of the wagon. "War's good for farmers."

Brian winced. "Thank you again for the ride," Brian called as the man drove away.

Brian looked at the sky. The sun was on its descent, and from this crossroads, he still had three miles to go. He'd arrive just before supper, unless another farmer gave him a ride.

Brian enjoyed the walk. In late April, the fields were mostly planted but still brown dirt rather than green life. Even the winter wheat was barely up. Fields were bordered by trees not yet in full leaf but getting there. The trees acted as windbreaks and helped deter erosion, but they served another purpose too—the oaks and maples made for great hiding places when a boy didn't want to work. He smiled at fond memories like at an old friend.

Brian cut across the edge of a field. The field bordered Frederick's, and he cut across that one as well. In the distance, he could see three figures, backs bent, probably hoeing, but they were too far away for Brian to see them clearly. Too far away to yell for their attention as well, so he trudged through the moist dirt, staying in the valleys between rows of planted seeds. This had been a cornfield for several years in a row, so it was time to rotate and put something else in the ground. Potatoes, maybe.

"Hello!" he yelled when he thought he was close enough. He still could not see faces, or even forms, really, but he knew one was Frederick. The other two looked very short, like children, and he wondered who they were.

Frederick looked up, took a few steps. He dropped his hoe and ran.

"Brian! You're home!"

One of the two boys dropped his hoe and ran for the house. Probably to find Mary. The other boy hung back.

"Frederick," he said as his brother-in-law wrapped him in a bear-hug. Brian did his best to return it.

"Brian, my boy," Frederick said, pulling back to look at him. "Oh, my, you look well. I think you've grown. Army life agrees with you."

"Yes, sir."

"Brian!" The call was faint, but they both heard it. Abby and Sarah were running toward him. Abby was faster, holding her skirts well above her knees. It was she who called and kept calling. "Brian! Brian!"

"Abby!" he said, twirling her around. She laughed.

"You've grown! But you're thin, too thin. Sarah, don't you think he's thin?"

Brian hugged Sarah, lifting her off the ground. When he put her down, she stepped back, giving her appraisal. She nodded. Brian grinned, and he could already smell the overabundance of food that they would force him to eat.

"Where's Mary?" he asked then, turning back to Frederick.

"She's with her sister in Gettysburg," he said.

Brian frowned. "For how long? I only have a few days."

"How long is a few?" Sarah asked. "I'm getting married on May 23. Will you still be here?"

He shook his head, still looking at Frederick. "I only have a week."

Frederick motioned toward the house. "George and Will, can you take the hoes back to the barn, please? We'll talk at the house, Brian."

Brian turned to the two boys picking up the tools. One was about chest height and one only a bit shorter. They both had dark hair and brown eyes shaded by worn felt hats. They were thin but looked strong.

"Is this—are you George and Will *Kelly?*" Brian demanded, walking backward next to Frederick. He grinned. "Heavens! I didn't even recognize you!" The boys grinned and trotted to catch up.

"They've been working for me. This is the second summer now," Frederick said. "Good strong workers." His large hands reached out to grab each one by the neck. Brian suddenly felt sad.

"Frederick," he said.

"No, son." Frederick looked him in the eye, shook his head. Brian even thought he saw a tear.

When they reached the house, Frederick took the boys aside. "I'm going to write a note, and I need you or Kathleen's Will to get it to the telegraph. I need to tell Mary to come home. Wait here."

Brian was going to wait with the boys in the yard; they seemed eager to pepper him with questions. But the ladies had other ideas. Sarah took him by the hand and pulled him into the kitchen. The aromas engulfed him, and he willingly sat at the table.

"Dinner isn't ready, but how about a muffin?" Sarah said. "We made muffins for breakfast, with dried blueberries, and there are a few left, I think."

"Do you want water or tea?" Abby asked, placing the plate of three muffins and the butter jar in front of him.

"Is there any milk?" he asked softly.

"Listen to him," Abby teased. "Talking as if he has no right to what we have on hand. Of course, there's milk!" A large glass of cold milk was placed in front of him, and the sisters sat, one on either side of him.

"How are you, Brian?" Sarah asked. "When Daniel tells us about you, it's never much."

"We don't see each other, really." Brian looked Abby in the face. He was slightly surprised to see the strength and joy in her, things that had replaced the haughtiness and defiance of her youth. Then, again, maybe his eyes were different. But he knew one thing hadn't changed, so he said to her, ignoring Sarah for a moment, "Daniel lies, sometimes, when he writes to his folks. About me, and about other things."

Her nod and the sadness that came into her eyes said she understood. "But you, are *you* all right?"

Brian grinned, first at one sister then the other. "I'm a whole lot better now! A bath and a soft bed, and I'll be right as rain!"

Mary and Ben took the first train to Reading, and Frederick went to get them. It was early afternoon when Mary jumped down from the wagon and hugged Brian until he thought he'd suffocate. She cried on his head, and he cried on her shoulder. It had been her he had wanted so badly to see, and he hadn't really been home until this moment.

"Oh, Brian, you're too thin, too thin!" Mary scolded as she pulled back. "Girls, let's feed this boy!"

Brian looked at her as she walked with him to the house. "You don't look well, Mary. Are you feeling all right?" She was haggard, pale, and whiter and more wrinkled than he remembered. It seemed to him that she, too, had lost some weight.

"I'm fine. Just tired," she said with a smile. Her smile was genuine but not quite as wide as it might have been. She certainly did look tired.

Mary spent the next few hours bustling around the kitchen as if she didn't have two capable daughters to do the cooking. She was quite proud of herself when she presented Brian with a meal fit for a king, despite the fact that it was still so early in the season.

Over the potatoes and gravy, roast chicken and dried peas, Abby said, "So, Brian, if you don't see Daniel much, then you probably don't know what's going on around here."

"No, not really. Tell me!"

"I'm getting married!" Sarah declared from across the table.

Brian grinned. "Yes, I believe you said that yesterday. Who's the lucky fella?"

"Howard Gehman."

"Don't know him."

"You've seen him around," Frederick said. "He's always lived here to the east a few miles. You've seen him in church."

Church, Brian thought. *What will they think of me when I tell them I converted?*

"We're going to have apple trees and sell the cider and sauce."

Abby said dryly, "She doesn't realize how much work that will make for *her*." She did not allow her sister to respond with more than a look before she added, "Meg Kelly had a baby."

"Yes, I think I did hear that. Or, at least, that she was going to have one. Do I know her husband?"

The table fell silent. Brian looked from one to another.

"Is he in the war? Did he die?" he asked.

"She never married," Mary said carefully. "The child is called Kelly. Daniel Kelly."

"Meg?" Brian said in disbelief. Mary nodded once. The meal continued in silence for a time. "Is she still living with her folks?"

"Where else would she go?" Ben said.

Brian looked at the young boy, then to Frederick and Mary at either end of the table. "She might have gone away. Some people might have sent her away." He meant a girl's parents might have sent her away.

"Many things have changed since you and Daniel have been gone," Frederick said. "I won't say that Meg is having an easy time of it because I don't think she is, or ever will, but her family is still her family. They're taking care of her."

"You mean everyone else isn't," Brian said, decidedly setting his fork on his plate.

"Can you really blame them?" Sarah asked. "I mean, look at what she's done."

"What has she done, Sarah?" he asked softly. She flinched at the fire in his eyes. "Go ahead, say it." He challenged.

"Brian," Frederick said.

Brian pushed his chair back. "We all make mistakes. Is that any reason to be shunned?"

"She *sinned*," Sarah said.

"She had a baby out of wedlock," Brian said.

"She *sinned*," Sarah repeated.

"So have I." Brian left them in silence.

The barn was warm. The cows and horses were placid in their chewing and barely looked at him as he climbed into the hay. It wasn't long before the door slid open and heavy boots crossed the floor. Brian didn't need to sit up to know it was Frederick.

Frederick leaned on the wall. "I always hated when womenfolk would ask me, 'Are you all right?' as if anyone fighting a war could ever again be all right."

"I beg your pardon?"

Frederick climbed over the wall with some difficulty, then dropped down beside Brian. "I was in the Army when I was a young man in the '30s. I didn't see any fighting. We weren't at war then. But I was on the march to Oklahoma, taking the Cherokee out of Georgia."

Brian turned his head in surprise. "I never knew that."

"No, because I've never talked about it. I'm not sure I've ever talked about it with Mary." Frederick shifted uncomfortably. "It still isn't easy to talk about. If you weren't there, you can never understand what I saw." He looked at Brian in the gloom. "I expect it's the same way with you. What you've seen has changed you forever. And I honestly wish it wasn't so."

"I kill men," he whispered.

"Yes."

"No, I . . . I'm a sharpshooter. I sit and wait for officers, and I shoot them in cold blood."

Frederick was silent for a moment. "Are you told to do it?"

"Yes."

"Then I'm not sure it is wrong. We could sit here and argue what is moral and what isn't, what is godly and what isn't. But war is ugly. Can't get around that. And I believe God gives special blessings to soldiers serving their country. But I'll tell you this, son. Walking with those people all those months, watching them die off and be left on the side of the trail changed me completely. Most people now, most people didn't see them as human beings. They were Indians. But I saw mothers cry for their children, and wives wail for their husbands. I saw bleeding feet. I saw broken spirits. I'm telling you they were people. And it has always made me look at people differently since them."

Brian wasn't sure he had ever heard Frederick say so much. "I saw you with a runaway slave once," he whispered. Frederick turned in surprise. Brian met his eyes in the gloom that had become almost dark. "I would never have said anything except when this war is over, it probably won't matter. You'll be a hero, if anything. And I've seen freed blacks in Philadelphia, and I heard their stories, and it changed me . . . They are people too."

Frederick nodded, turned again to stare at the roof they couldn't see. "I came back home in '40. I felt lost and inhuman. Yes, that's how I'd put it. I felt inhuman because of what I had helped to do. I traveled around the country, not wanting to stop anywhere for too long . . . I can see the demons in your eyes. They chased me too . . . But I heard a preacher in Boston talking about sin and forgiveness. I thought, if anybody needs forgiveness, I do. And I prayed, not really expecting God to do anything. I fully expected He would turn away. But He didn't. And that changed my life too."

"I'm Catholic," Brian said bluntly. "I converted."

"Have you asked God to save you? That's the main thing."

"Yes."

"Then be the best Catholic man you can be, son."

"You keep calling me 'son'."

No answer.

"Frederick, I'm sorry. I'm sorry for everything—"

"Brian, you *are* my son. When the Kellys brought you to me, I had a daughter, and I rejoiced that God gave me a son. When Sarah was born, I had two daughters and a son. Now I have two sons and two daughters. That's all."

Frederick and Mary talked later, their usual evening conversation, but it soon turned to other topics.

"How is Bridget?"

"Not well," Mary replied.

"And you, Mary?"

"I'm fine, Frederick."

"No, you're not. It's quite clear that you're not, and Ben said that he has been worried about you."

Mary sighed. "Please don't worry. I'm fine." She began sifting through the clothes in the trunk. "I was taking care of the house, my sister, and three children and Ben. I know he's only thirteen, almost fourteen, but he works like a man and eats like a man, and quite frankly, I don't think he fits into the category of children anymore."

"No, he doesn't. Don't change the subject."

"I'm tired, Frederick. I admit that I'm not used to little children running around under foot. It seems like so long ago that Ben was that age. He's been so helpful to you the past few years that I had forgotten how much energy it takes. And I hadn't realized how much the girls have helped me around the house. It was like when we were first married. I was doing everything myself. But, let's face it, Frederick. I am not as young as I once was."

Frederick sighed. "I want you to rest as much as possible between now and the wedding. I'll call in the doctor if I have to."

Mary patted his hand. "As if that would do any good."

"Mary, I mean it."

"I'm sure you do, my dear."

Ben and the women did not hide their surprise when Brian was up with the sun on Sunday morning, ready to walk out the door before breakfast was made.

"Where are you off to so early?" Abby demanded, tying an apron around her waist as he sliced some bread and slathered it with honey.

"Mass. I'm going to ask the Kellys if I can ride with them."

"Mass? Since when do you attend Mass?" Sarah asked incredulously, scrambling eggs with a fork.

Brian kissed Mary's cheek. "I'll see you after church."

Sunlight twinkled on dewdrops, creating rainbow crystals on the weeds along the road. Brian wanted to stop and gaze at them, but he was in a hurry. He wasn't sure what time the Kellys left for Bally. He had been busy with Frederick and the boys for the past few days and hadn't been able to see them as he had wished. He passed

Kathleen and Will, climbing into their rig, and he trotted over to them.

"Hello, Mrs. O'Neill!" he called with a grin.

"Ahhhh! Brian O'Bern! How are you?" She spoke and grinned in exclamation points, climbing back down.

Will came around the rig, holding out his hand and smiling. Kathleen introduced them, and then Will looked sheepish. "I'm sorry to be rude, but we don't have time to chat. We're on our way to church."

"Oh, yes!" Brian said. "You go to Bally."

"Yes," Kathleen said, again climbing up and arranging her skirts.

"I'm going to Mass. May I ride with you? At least to town. Your folks probably have more room than you do."

If either Will or Kathleen was surprised, they hid it as Will indicated the back seat. Brian climbed over the wheel, getting his boot caught between Kathleen's seat and the bars that held the cover up. When he was finally settled, they headed out. They chatted a bit on the way to town and stopped at the tavern.

"Well, well, look who's here! We heard you were home," Patrick said, shaking his hand. Brian was about to climb down, but Patrick told him to stay. "We'll talk later."

"Da," Meg said, walking over with a bundle, which she handed to Kathleen. "Help me up?"

When Meg was settled next to Brian, Kathleen handed baby Daniel to his mother, and Meg smiled at Brian. "Welcome home. Are you on furlough, or are you home for good?"

"Furlough. I leave Tuesday." He moved the white blanket to peek at the child. Daniel was sleeping, but his nose wiggled, and Brian laughed softly. "His name is Daniel?"

"Yes, after his brave uncle," Meg gave her characteristic response.

"I'm sure he likes that," Brian said. He looked at Meg, a pretty young woman in a dark blue dress with her brown hair pinned in a neat bun. She had pretty eyes. "Last time I saw you, you were a kid, and now you are a beautiful young lady," he said.

Kathleen turned around, then quickly back to look at the road. Meg blushed. Brian became distinctly uncomfortable.

"I didn't mean anything by that," he whispered.

Meg nodded. She didn't meet his eyes, neither on the trip nor in the church nor afterward. When they arrived back at the Kellys', he jumped down and held up his hand to help her down. She handed him the baby instead. Meg thanked Will, waved to Kathleen, and the two newlyweds drove off.

"I guess I'm not getting a ride." He laughed, looking again at the baby whose eyes were now open.

"Did you want one?"

"No, a walk is nice too," he said. "Will you walk with me a ways?"

Meg hesitated. "Everyone else is still in church," she said.

"No, your folks were right behind us," he said in confusion. "Should we wait for them so they can watch the baby?"

Meg shook her head. "Not the family. Everyone else. The Baptist and the Lutheran and the Reformed churches won't let out for another forty-five minutes. So if you wanted to walk with me, now would be the time to do it."

"I don't understand," he lied.

Meg didn't reply but started walking. He fell into step beside her, still carrying baby Daniel.

"You noticed how they treated me in church, I know you did," she said accusingly as they walked west along the tracks, instead of east toward the O'Neill's and the Weimers.

Brian nodded but did not speak. There had been two empty pews in front and two empty pews behind the family, although the rest of the church was full. No one had spoken to them, except the priest and one old woman who had walked over to speak with Peggy, although Peggy could only smile and nod. Plenty of people, though, had watched them and whispered to each other as the family and Brian walked to the rigs. Meg had looked straight ahead, chin up, teeth clenched, tears barely held back. Kathleen had kept up a steady stream of conversation until they were well down the road. When Brian had looked over his shoulder, he noticed others coming to speak with Patrick and Peggy, now that Meg was gone.

"I'm assuming the town is no better," he said softly.

"No, worse. They won't come into the tavern if they see me there. Once or twice someone has come in, seen me, and turned right around and walked out. I love working in the tavern, but we can't afford for me to be in there. There's no business when I am." Her voice cracked.

"I'm sorry, Meg."

"Why, what did you do?" she asked bitterly. A sigh. "I'm sorry. I'm trying very hard to change my attitude toward people. They aren't the ones who sinned. I am."

"That doesn't mean they can treat you that way."

"Of course, they can!"

The baby started to fuss, and Brian quickly handed him to his mother. "But they shouldn't. Have you gone to confession? Have you been forgiven?"

"Yes." Meg bounced Daniel up and down lightly, making soft clicking noises with her tongue, her eyes on Brian. He watched her for a moment.

"Then they have no right to treat you like this," he repeated.

"I've talked to Ma and Mary about it," Meg said after a moment. She looked off into the distance where the tracks curved out of sight. "Women like me have been treated this way since the beginning of time, and Millerstown isn't going to do things differently. The only way things would change is if I moved away or got married. But no one will marry me now." Again, the bitter tone. She shook her head sadly.

"I am sorry, Meg," he said again.

Frederick made three trips to the Reading railroad station within four weeks, more than he would for the rest of the year. The first time, he picked up Mary and Ben, loading them and their one trunk into the wagon. Six days later, he returned with a wagon full of people, women crying, men shaking hands, as they set Brian and his haversack on the platform. Then, on May 25, a Monday, Frederick drove Abby to the train station.

She was leaving with one trunk; she was quite sure that this time she would return with one as well. She was not going to the city to be a seamstress, or a companion, or a Sanitary Commission worker. She was on her way to Gettysburg to stay with Bridget.

"Frederick, this is ridiculous!" Mary had said. Abby had heard them arguing several nights in a row. Mary insisted her health was not an issue, even allowed the doctor to examine her. Dr. Krommer had agreed with Frederick, but Mary had not acquiesced gracefully nor any other way. Even with Abby and Sarah doing most of the housework, Mary's energy and vitality had not returned.

"I need to take care of Bridget," Mary had insisted. Bridget was very ill; she was having pains with this baby. Standing up caused her to faint. She slept much, ate little. Women had been caring for other pregnant women for generations, but Mary had immediately called in the doctor, and he was very worried. He had whispered to Mary that the baby might be lost, and he could only hope to save the mother. "If that happens, Frederick, if she loses the baby, I need to be there!"

"I won't let you go, Mary. You're not well, either."

"I'll go," Abby said. "I'll take care of Aunt Bridget."

And so the arguing had continued into the night. Mary wanted to go. Frederick would not allow it. Abby was determined. Poor Mary, she did not have the energy to fight them both.

"Take care of yourself," Frederick said as he handed her trunk to the porter. "Write to us often."

"Of course."

"Make sure you come back to visit."

Abby stared at him. "I'm not leaving forever."

Frederick hugged her, oblivious to the churning crowd. "That's what you said last time. I can't assume my luck will hold out twice."

As Abby sat on the train, she relived the conversation. She certainly had not made the conscious decision that she was leaving for good and all. However, after giving Sarah a trunk full of dresses, perhaps it looked to her parents as if she was taking everything with her. Illogical assumption, considering there was still a trunk full of dresses in her room.

But what if she never came back? She had already proven to herself that she could do just fine on her own. She could earn her way. She had the means to buy a piece of land and the ability to work it, but . . .

Maybe Gettysburg would provide another Owen. Maybe Daniel would choose to not stay in Millerstown. Maybe she would give in and be part of that team that Kathleen had talked about. Maybe.

* * *

Sarah finished the dishes, drying the last plates and putting them in the cabinet. She dumped the basin of dirty water out the back door. The sun was gone, but the sky was still purple pink. The barn and privy were deep shadows in the growing dark. The trees were funny-shaped phantoms against a dark blue sky. Howard was walking back from the barn, carrying the milk can. Tomorrow she would begin the process to make her first cheeses.

They had been married nearly three weeks. Unlike Sarah's family, Howard's family lived in the area within a day's drive in any direction. For that reason, they had taken the traditional wedding trip. First, they had stayed with his sister's family for four days, then his brother's family for four days, then his two maiden aunts for one day, and his cousin's family for two days, and finally his parents for three days. They had arrived back at their own home the day before yesterday. Howard had thanked Frederick and Ben for looking after the farm, and while he was visiting them, Sarah had roamed the house, getting acquainted with her new home.

Now, the daily routine was established. As she accepted the milk can from her husband, she looked forward to continuing the weekly routine. Howard kissed her cheek and walked past her into the hall and up the stairs. She finished setting the milk can in the pantry and gave the table one last swipe with the rag. She banked the fire in the stove, blew out the lamp, and headed upstairs.

It was a good ending to a fine day. Sarah found herself smiling as she climbed the stairs. "This is my life," she said to herself. She paused at the top of the stairs. Her stairs. Her home: a kitchen, dining room, and parlor downstairs, four bedrooms upstairs, a root cellar, summer kitchen, and attic. It was her responsibility, her domain. It was all she had now. It was all she needed.

Chapter 14

GETTYSBURG

"In!" Andrew Curtin called gruffly as a sharp knock sounded on the office door. His new assistant, John Unger, stepped through it, his perfectly buffed shoes barely making a sound. He was a soft-spoken middle-aged man. Curtin's previous assistant had joined the army; this man had been highly recommended by a senator.

"I have the daily dispatches, sir," the soft voice said. John was tall and gangly, clean-shaven, and his hands shook almost constantly. It was unfortunate that the man's mannerisms were getting on Curtin's nerves. Unfortunate but not surprising: Curtin's nerves were so frayed that he was only recently back from a leave of absence.

"Yes, go ahead."

John sat in a leather chair on the far side of the desk. Curtin got up to pace. He listened as closely as he could to the news, but his mind wandered. The mention of General Hooker brought his mind back to the tasks at hand.

"Say that again, Mr. Unger."

"Major General Darius Couch has been transferred to the Department of the Susquehanna. He has arrived in Harrisburg. Apparently, he was so upset with General Hooker's lack of leadership at the battle of Chancellorsville that he said he could no longer serve under the general." John paused. "Shall we have a reception for General Couch?"

"No."

After John left, Curtin sank into his desk chair, stared out the window at the buildings of Harrisburg. Hooker was making a mess of things, just like every general before him. Would President Lincoln ever find a general who could successfully end this war? He leaned his head against the chair and closed his eyes.

Abby walked quickly down the street. Her shopping basket was filled with groceries. Her feet kicked the hem of her skirt. She held tightly to Robert's hand. A driver yelled as they crossed the street, but she barely noticed.

Abby rushed through her morning chores. The parlor was dusted. The bread was punched—she had set it to rise before going to town—and put in the oven. She scrubbed the kitchen floor, working up a sweat and wishing she had a summer kitchen in which to do the baking. She pulled out the bread and put the two loaves on the bread board to cool. If it would in this unbearable heat. She checked on the boy playing in the dirt outside the back door. She'd have to bathe him later.

Finally, she sat at the kitchen table with the newspaper. The door was open so she could watch Robert. But when her eyes found the story, he was all but forgotten. The local newspaper reprinted what *Harper's Weekly* had reported in its edition two days ago.

As reported in *Harper's Weekly*, June 27, 1863:

THE INVASION OF THE NORTH

> General Lee has verified the predictions we published in our last number with startling exactness. A part of his army has invaded Pennsylvania, now occupies one or two of the southern towns in that state and menaces Harrisburg. A wild panic pervades the state, and the military organization which should have preceded the invasion by several weeks is now being hurriedly completed . . .

They were coming.

Abby had the care of three children and an invalid. Maybe she should send the boys to Sean and Anna's. But the farm was only four miles out of town on the road to Harrisburg. If predictions were correct, their home might not be any safer. But Bridget couldn't be moved. And she had to stay with Bridget.

Andrew Curtin summoned yet another assistant. Mr. Unger was at the telegraph office with messages for the mayor of Philadelphia, the governor of New Jersey, and President Lincoln. Mr. Hampton was on the way to find couriers to ride a message to each volunteer regiment captain within the state. Mr. McFinney was gathering every high-ranking official in Harrisburg and the southern counties for a meeting to lay out the plan of action.

"Who are you?" Andrew demanded, not unkindly, to the young man standing in front of him.

"Lionel Crumb, sir. I work with Mr. Gregory."

"Fine, fine. Take this proclamation to the newspapers." Andrew paced as he dictated. The man scrambled to keep up. Within six minutes, the young man was running down the hall, bumping into people. Andrew could hear their cries of dismay from his office.

The proclamation ran in that evening's Harrisburg newspapers. It would run the next morning as a special bulletin in all Pennsylvania counties by every press, and it would be distributed as fast and as far as possible.

> A proclamation from Governor Mr. Andrew Curtin:
>
> The state of Pennsylvania is again threatened with invasion, and an army of rebels is approaching the borders. The President of the United States has issued his proclamation, calling upon the state for fifty thousand men. I now appeal to all the citizens of Pennsylvania, who love liberty and are mindful of the history and traditions of their Revolutionary fathers, and who feel that it

is a sacred duty to guard and maintain the free institutions of our country, who hate treason and its abettors, and who are willing to defend their homes and firesides, and do invoke them to rise in their might and rush to the rescue in this hour of imminent peril . . . That it is the purpose of the enemy to invade our borders with all the strength he can command, is now apparent.

I therefore call on the people of Pennsylvania who are capable of bearing arms, to enroll themselves in military organizations, and to encourage all others to give aid and assistance to the efforts which will be put forth for the protection of the state and the salvation of our common country.

Andrew G. Curtin, Governor

"He's done it again!" Daniel hollered with dismay. He angrily flung himself onto a log next to Brian.
"What?"
"Lincoln pulled Hooker. Now Meade is in command."
"I heard Lee is set to invade Pennsylvania."
"He already has. We'll try to catch him."
"North, always north. I wish it was north to home."
"We'll get home, Brian. One way or another."
"Anybody know where exactly we are?" Brian asked the crowd at large.
"Maryland, I think," someone called from the next fire circle.
Meade's army was in Frederick, Maryland, only a few dozen miles from where scouts said Lee's army was located. Some people speculated that Lee was looking for food. Some said he was looking to rob the shoe factory. Some people said Lee was trying to disrupt the railroad. It didn't matter. This was the second time Lee had invaded Pennsylvania, and he had to be stopped. The order came down from General Meade: be ready to march at dawn.

They started marching, wool uniforms and fifty-pound rucksacks weighing them down. The late June heat was oppressive. The soldiers talked little, simply marched. It was a procession like any other, although unbroken by skirmishing, as it had been so often in the month of June. By the end of the day on June 29, the soldiers had covered twenty-five long, hard miles.

Meg leaned on the bar. A special rider had come into town around noon, bringing notices that were posted on storefronts. Before midafternoon, townsmen and farmers were pouring in for news, company, and drinks. Kelly's was overflowing; some men had taken mugs outside into the long June twilight. Patrick and Will were unable to handle the crowd, so Meg had been called in for reinforcements. No one came to her to be served; they waited for Patrick and Will, so she simply washed glasses. But at least no one had walked out.

She put clean mugs on the shelf, listening to the conversation.

"The governor is calling for more troops."

"That's what I've heard."

"And Lee is headed this way."

They don't really think Lee could get this far?

"You don't think he could get this far north, do you?" asked a farmer. He was on his third mug. His eyes were red, and he was sweating. Whether from the oppressive heat of the room packed with bodies or the drink or fear, Meg couldn't tell.

"He might," the first talker said. "We haven't had a good general yet. How many generals have passed since '61? And yet, Lee is still in charge of the Confederates and doing quite well!"

"That's treason!" someone shouted. Meg watched warily for the possibility of flying fists, but she stayed behind the bar.

"No, it's truth. Every general we've had has been namby-pamby and left the job half done."

The man who had cried treason started to shout, but a third speaker cut him off. "He's right, gentlemen. As much as I like President Lincoln—and I'll vote for him again if given the chance—

he hasn't chosen good leaders for our army. How many needless deaths have there been because of these weaklings?"

"Meg!" Patrick called from the end of the bar.

She hurried over with the full mugs to replace the three empties in his hands. "Sorry, Da—"

"Don't worry about them, Meg. Men need someone to blame. Everyone thinks he knows best."

"If the new general can't lead well, if he is weak like the others, then more men will die—"

"Meg," Patrick said sternly. He leaned across the bar, gripped her hand, still holding an empty mug. "Don't. Don't worry about Daniel. He'll be fine."

Meg wasn't convinced. "Do you think this general will be different?" she asked.

"We'll see."

"How are you feeling, Aunt Bridget?"

"Tired, Abby, always tired."

Abby set the tray on the bed next to her aunt. The other woman, who could not be much past her thirtieth birthday, seemed old and feeble. She had lost weight in the weeks since Abby's arrival. Her facial features were drawn, and wrinkles had appeared around her mouth and eyes. Her red hair was smudged with gray, and it needed to be washed. Abby put it on her mental list of things to do.

As Abby fed Bridget the soup, she steadily discussed the news of the day. If she needed to send the boys away to safety, she wanted Bridget to know about it. At the same time, though, she needed to try as hard as possible to keep Bridget calm and resting easily.

"President Lincoln has put General Meade in charge of the army."

"Oh?"

"I read a piece about him in the paper yesterday. Meade went to West Point. His men think he's tough and reliable. Those are good qualities in a leader, don't you think?"

"Uh-huh."

"They say he's rather quiet. I'll take that to mean he isn't the boastful sort. He won't make promises he can't keep. If he says he'll chase Lee out of Pennsylvania, then he will."

"Wait." Bridget put a hand on Abby's wrist. "Lee is in Pennsylvania?"

Abby lowered the spoon to the bowl, the bowl to her lap. She sighed. "Yes, but Meade will get here soon and chase him out."

"Here. Here as in *here* or here as in Philadelphia?" Bridget's voice was rising. Abby put a reassuring hand on her arm. The skin was cool. The arm was rigid.

"Reports say he's west of here. Near Chambersburg." Bridget was becoming agitated. Chambersburg was only twenty miles away. Abby leaned forward, lowered her voice. "We're perfectly safe," she said. She fervently hoped it was the truth.

Abby sat at the small writing desk in the parlor to begin a letter to her mother. She doubted she would finish it; she was so tired. But she needed to communicate with someone what had happened earlier in the day. She suddenly realized why writing was so appealing to Daniel.

June 30, 1863

Dear Mother,

Lee's Confederate army arrived in town today. They marched in from the west.

We had heard they were near Chambersburg. They have taken what ripened crops they could find. We have heard such horrible stories that I was quite frightened.

Mother, they are surely a ragtag bunch! These men look weary and tired and hungry. Some of them don't have shoes. Many of them are no longer wearing the gray uniforms we have heard about. They are wearing homespun and flannel. Many seemed to be wounded, or recovering from wounds. And yet this army has beaten ours at battle after battle. Does that speak of the strength of their army or the bad leadership of our own?

The Confederates approached. Then they left as suddenly as they had come.

Only moments later, we saw the Union troops approaching from the south. We could see the dust cloud they raised. It has been hot and dry here.

Abby heard a crash and a cry. Little Robert had fallen out of bed again. She put the letter aside until another time.
"I am so very tired," Thomas groaned, sinking onto his bedroll. Darkness had fallen. They had marched all day at double quick, and the entire company was sinking wearily into sleep.
"We won't meet up with Lee tomorrow," O'Leary muttered from somewhere in the dark on the other side of the canvas tent wall.
"What makes you think so?" Billy Bradigan mumbled, already on the road to sleep.
"Didn't you hear? They were in town this morning, and they saw us coming and ran away."
"They could be just over the next ridge, waiting for reinforcements," Brian said. He was weary but doubted he would sleep. His feet burned from walking.
"You sound like McClellan," someone said with disdain. Brian couldn't tell who it was. Before he realized it, the entire row of tents was asleep, and he was left with his thoughts.

Dawn pushed at the fog. Three miles west of Gettysburg proper, the trees were not dense enough to scratch away the soft whiteness. It was open space, fields, rolling hills. Lieutenant Jones walked up and down the picket line to ensure his men were alert.

"Five-thirty, and all is well," the Illinois cavalryman told his commander.

Jones was not listening. He turned to the west, his back to the sun. He couldn't be sure, with the fog and the shadows, but there appeared to be a line moving toward them. A line of shadows.

"Sir, do you see that?" he whispered to the soldier. He did not point, only indicated with his chin.

The young man beside him looked. He barely nodded. There certainly was a line of men marching silently toward them coming down the Chambersburg Pike. As the two watched, the mounted officer that led them moved to the side of the road, letting them pass.

Jones barely turned toward the other man. "Sir, give me your rifle."

With the borrowed gun in his hands and the officer in his sights, Jones fired. The crack shattered the dawn like a pitcher dropped on a stone. The nearest horse neighed in confusion, unprepared for the sound. Jones and the soldier watched the approaching line. The shot had not found its mark. Instead, the officer called to the column, and they dispersed in a line nearly half a mile wide, ready for a skirmish.

Jones was not ready for that. Handing the rifle back to its owner, Jones hurried away. His men, the pickets deployed specifically to watch for the enemy, responded to the Confederates in kind.

Abby woke as the sun peaked through her window. The heat was already climbing. She didn't lag in bed, therefore, but hurriedly dressed and headed downstairs. As she finished tying her shoes, she heard gunshots.

With laces of her left foot dragging, she ran out the front door. The gunshots sounded so close! The house was near the Lutheran Seminary where Bridget's husband Peter had studied, on the eastern side of Seminary Ridge, half a mile from town. Chambersburg Pike was one block in front of her running east to west. As she searched the horizon, she saw it.

As the fog dissipated, the smoke rose above the ridge in deceptively benign drifts. The wispy clouds of smoke were accompanied by more cracks, like hammers striking nails.

Abby was shaking as she served up the pancakes for the boys. They were innocently oblivious. The gunfire had stopped, maybe even before the boys had wakened. Perhaps Bridget had not heard it either.

"Boys, I want you to stay near the house today. Don't leave the yard."

"Why?"

As calmly as she could, painfully aware of the fear rising in her throat and voice, she replied, "Just do as I say. Don't go anywhere that I can't see you."

The boys glanced at each other and shrugged. Adults very seldom explained themselves.

General John Buford had known they were coming. Last night, against the optimism of tired soldiers who desperately wanted to believe the Confederates had retreated, Buford's voice of reason had spoiled their hopefulness. "You'll see them in the morning. They'll wake up fighting."

And now he knew it was true. As early morning merged into midmorning, about nine o'clock on Wednesday, July 1, Buford sat on Seminary Ridge. He used his spyglass to watch the advancing line of Confederates. He estimated the enemy had about seven thousand, and he knew he only had two thousand.

"Runner!" he shouted.

A messenger appeared out of the air at his elbow. Buford didn't take his eyes off the advancing enemy. "Message to Major General Reynolds on the left wing. Send reinforcements. We are outnumbered. Go!" He did not watch as the young soldier made haste down the ridge, mounting his horse on the run.

Buford continued to watch the skirmish unfold. As the enemy descended the low rise called Herr Ridge, the Federal troops in the valley along the sluggish stream opened fire. Buford watched as the hour passed. How long would it take for Reynolds to respond? How long could his two thousand men hold them off?

Buford put the glass up to his eye yet again. The fog was being replaced by acrid gun smoke. Through the man-made fog, he could see his commander, Gamble. He was leading the Federals in retreat back across the stream, coming closer to Seminary Ridge, closer to his own post, closer to the sleepy town at his back.

The boys came running into the house. They had been in the yard only minutes when the crack of gunfire sent them scurrying for safety. They all clung to Abby, even twelve-year-old Peter.

"What's happening, Cousin Abby?" little Robert wailed.

"There's fighting," she replied. She pushed the boys away just far enough to close the damper on the stove. She was doing no work today.

Her mind raced. Where was it safest? In the root cellar? But Bridget was upstairs.

"Boys, don't be concerned, but the armies are fighting. Somewhere close, so you must listen to me carefully." She watched the three pairs of blue eyes turn toward her, fear and trust on their young faces. "We're going to go upstairs and sit with your mother. She's ill, and you must be quiet, but she would love to spend some time with you. But, and this is important, if I tell you to run to the cellar, you *run*, do you understand?" They nodded, still afraid, even more so now, but still trusting.

"Good morning, boys," Bridget said with a forced smile. She was tense; it was apparent in the lines around her eyes, the stiffness of her body. But she would do everything she could to keep it from her voice.

"Aunt Bridget, we're going to sit with you for a while if you're feeling up to it." Abby was pleased with the calmness in her own voice. She smiled for the boys' benefit. They quietly climbed into the bed next to Bridget. Abby moved to the window. It faced the west.

Sometimes commanders were replaced because of ineptitude. Not this time. The messenger arrived to tell Major General Oliver Howard the news: Howard was given Reynolds's command because Reynolds was dead.

Howard was in one of the town's taller buildings. He was watching the not-so-distant ridges. Reynolds had sent for him, needing reinforcements, and Howard had ridden hard from Emmetsburg, ahead of his men. What he had seen when he arrived at ten-thirty made his stomach lurch.

Bluecoats were retreating.

"A message to General Meade," he called to the nearest courier. He sent the ominous news to Taneytown.

"General Howard, sir," a breathless rider said.

Howard turned from the window. "Yes."

"Message from General Doubleday."

"Yes." Howard waited impatiently for the young soldier to catch his breath well enough to speak.

"Reynolds is dead, sir. You have command."

Damn.

"Any news on the retreat?"

"No retreat, sir," the young man said, confused.

Howard pointed out the window. The Federals he had seen had turned were standing their ground.

"No retreat, sir," the man repeated. "Just a new position." He waited. "Do you have any further orders, sir?"

"I'm hungry," Colum whispered.

Abby turned from the window. Her back and neck were stiff; she had not moved in nearly two hours. "I'll go make us something to eat." The guns had not been heard for at least an hour. It was afternoon. Perhaps the boys should play outside for a few minutes while she made lunch.

"Boys, come downstairs with me. You can play outside for a few minutes."

As she ushered the boys ahead of her, she turned to Bridget.

"Abby, do you think it is over?"

Abby glanced toward the window. From this angle, all she could see were the trees on McPherson's farm. No smoke, no soldiers, although that was the direction of the fighting. She hoped the McPhersons were safe.

"No, Aunt Bridget, I don't think it's over yet."

Howard watched with relief as his own eleventh corps came running into town. He left his position, running with as much speed as they exhibited. He looked at the troops standing before him. They were tired, sweaty, and dusty. They held only their rifles. Their rucksacks would be back along the road somewhere. But above all else, they were good men. If he asked them to go farther, they would, without complaint.

"Steinwehr," he called. The brigadier general stood before him as out of breath as the troops under his command. "Steinwehr," he began again, "I want you to keep your men here on this ridge. The town square is half a mile that way." Howard swung his arm to the north. He turned to the troops. "Men!" he boomed, "I want you to hold this position at all hazards!"

Howard turned away. He needed to find Major General Schurz, who would take official command of the eleventh corps now that Howard was in command of the whole scene. Schurz would take two-thirds of the corps to reinforce the Federal troops to the north. One-third, under Brigadier General Adolf von Steinwehr, would remain on Cemetery Ridge, south of town.

Howard hurried back to the position he had chosen for himself. He watched as the column of the eleventh corps headed north.

The boys didn't play. They huddled together on the back steps. They didn't speak, they didn't tease. Peter sat between his two younger brothers, an arm around each. Robert rested his head on Peter's shoulder. Colum sat with shoulders hunched. Their spirits were as heavy as the hot July air, as heavy as the dust coating thick green leaves on oaks and sycamores.

"Boys, come and eat!"

As the three youngsters sat at the table, Abby placed cold chicken, thick slices of bread, wedges of cheese, and the last of last year's apples on the table. She served the two younger boys; Peter served himself. She kissed each sweaty head.

"I'm going to take some up to your mother."

"Will you come back?" Colum asked quietly.

"Yes, I'll come right back down. Eat, please." She didn't expect that they would.

"I'm worried, Abby," Bridget said as soon as Abby appeared in the doorway.

"We'll be fine," Abby assured her. "I brought you some bread and cheese. Please eat it."

"I want you to take care of my boys," Bridget said with more determination than she had ever shown Abby. "If the armies get close and it's not safe here anymore, you leave me behind. *Leave me behind.* You save my boys." Tears streamed unheeded down her weary face.

"It won't come to that, Bridget. Don't worry. You need to rest." Abby adjusted the sheet. As hot as it was, the quilt was at the foot of the bed. "I have to go down to the boys."

"You'll bring them back upstairs?"

"Yes, of course."

They spent the afternoon in Bridget's room. The hot room grew hotter as the sun sank in the west, hitting the window with the force of a cannon. The boys roused a bit; Abby was pleased that Bridget and Peter took turns reading to the younger boys. Abby remained at her post in the rocking chair by the window. She watched the smoke, listened to the shots, both cannon and muskets now. She tried very hard not to think.

Daniel waited for his next assignment. He was still the unofficial record keeper, but today the generals were keeping him busy running messages.

His last message had been from the general in charge of the troops by a farm called McPherson's. The general had been watching the unfolding scene from the heights around the seminary. As Daniel waited, the older man watched the hill across the narrow valley. Suddenly, he drew breath.

"Sir?" Daniel said tentatively.

"It's Lee. Here, look."

Daniel cautiously took the spyglass. The man next to him was excited, nervous. He seemed to be anticipating something wonderful along with the bad.

Daniel looked through the glass. A bearded man was sitting on a horse. Both were as still as a statue. The western sun caused the broad hat to shade the face, but he was definitely a high-ranking officer.

Lee had arrived on the field. As Daniel watched, the man on the horse nodded to another officer, who gave a command. A line of butternut-wearing soldiers moved down the hill.

That had been earlier in the afternoon. The fighting had continued worse and worse as the sun sank lower in the sky.

"Sir!" a tired voice said.

Daniel turned. He was at Meade's command post, south of Cemetery Hill. Another messenger had just arrived. Meade looked up from the map he was perusing. He did not speak, only waited.

"The first corps have fled from Seminary Ridge, sir. Lieutenant James Stewart used cannon to fend off the rebels."

"Were you there, sir?" Meade demanded.

Daniel had come to know that generals always wanted to know if the message was carried by an eyewitness. Many times they were, but today he had been everywhere and nowhere and had barely been anywhere long enough to draw breath, let alone watch a battle. Somewhere during the afternoon, the messengers had ceased to call them skirmishes. Now they were battles. The entire Army of the Potomac would be embroiled at the Battle of Gettysburg before the fight was won, Daniel was sure.

"Yes, sir, I was behind the line. The Confederates came on, sir. Stewart's cannons sliced them down. Like a scythe through wheat, sir. The sounds were deafening, with canister screaming and booming and guns cracking. But we could still hear that infernal rebel yell."

"And the outcome of the engagement?" Meade asked.

Daniel marveled. The man never seemed to be the least bit weary. "The line broke, sir." And the young messenger *did* sound weary. Daniel hung his head. "The entire first corps broke, retreated down Seminary Ridge. They've met up with the eleventh corps in the town."

Daniel was still waiting for an assignment when, by looking at the sun, he knew it was nearly five o'clock. Another rider came in, and Daniel inched his way closer to the gathered generals.

"General Meade, sir!" Meade waited, as always, silently. "A message from General Hancock, sir!"

Meade turned to another officer, one who had ridden into the command post only half an hour ago. "I called Hancock up from Taneytown to take command."

"Sir, I thought Howard was in command since Reynolds has fallen?" the officer asked cautiously.

"He was. I admire Hancock. He breathes out confidence for others to breathe in. He'll take command."

"Sir," the officer wavered again. "Sir, doesn't Howard outrank him?"

"No matter."

"Sir?" It was the messenger. Meade turned toward him. "Sir, there was indeed a minor problem when General Hancock took command. Howard refused to give over."

"Dear God, must we fight each other now?" the officer muttered to himself.

"Howard was trying to keep the eleventh corps from running completely away. They finally worked out the problem, sir. General Hancock says to tell you they have chosen Cemetery Hill as the battlefield."

Without another word, Meade and his associates returned to their map.

"Look here, gentlemen," Meade said with soft confidence. "Cemetery Hill meets with Cemetery Ridge to the southeast. It is a low ridge. Over here, on the east, is Culp's Hill about one hundred feet higher than where Hancock and Howard are now."

"He'll be strung out," another officer said.

"He'll need reinforcements, but he'll hold," Meade said with finality. Meade turned this way and that looking for something.

No, not some*thing*, Daniel realized, some*one*. Daniel stood up from where he had been crouching.

"You, soldier."

"Sir, yes, sir!" Daniel snapped to attention, waited for the assignment.

"Take a message to Hancock. Generals Sickles and Slocum are on the way."

"Yes, sir." Daniel headed out. He did not hear Meade turn to the other officers.

"Let's hope they arrive in time, gentlemen."

"Boys, let's get ready for bed," Abby said softly. She stretched, stood, stretched again. The three boys were huddled on their mother's bed, had been for hours. After another cold meal in the late afternoon, they had rushed upstairs finding solace in simply being close to Bridget.

Peter looked at her. As he moved to get up, Abby realized the other three bedmates were already asleep.

"How can they sleep, Abby?" he asked. "With all that banging going on?"

The fighting had changed in the afternoon. No longer did they hear the simple crack of guns, like an ax into wood. It was deeper now and thundered in her chest. A thundering boom followed by a thump. Over and over and over.

"I don't know. Just worn out, I guess," she muttered. She looked at the sleeping figures. "Do you want to stay in here with the rest of them?"

"Oh, yes," Peter said, revealing as much enthusiasm as the fear and fatigue would allow.

Abby nodded. Bridget and her boys were resting comfortably, it seemed. Abby went to her own room, grabbed the pink quilt and the pillow. Returning to the other room, seeing Peter was already asleep, she made a nest on the floor by the window. But she didn't lie down. As the last light of the first day of July faded, so did the booms and cracks of battle. Suddenly, she realized it would soon be Independence Day, and she wondered what would be done. *We will celebrate, don't you worry,* she told herself. *If we're still here.*

Abby stared into the growing darkness, hoping sleep would come soon.

Brian sighed as the eastern sky lightened. How long had they been walking? It seemed like days. Certainly, he hadn't slept in over twenty-four hours.

As if reading Brian's thoughts, Thomas said, "Do you think they'll let us sleep for a few hours?"

"I doubt it," Brian replied without turning his head. "We haven't been marching for a day and a night so that we could sleep. They'll need us to fight."

Billy Bradigan looked around at the younger men behind him. "Lovely country, isn't it?" he said with a smile.

"What are you so happy about?" Brian muttered. He forced his tired legs to lift his heavy feet. He had been shuffling again. *Soldiers don't shuffle.*

"We're nearly home." Billy grinned. He pointed to the golden ball coming up over green fields. "Fifty miles or so that way is Philadelphia. What do you say? Should we go steal a kiss from our girls?"

Brian stole a look around. The sun sparkled on the wheat field to the east, nearly golden, nearly ripe for harvest, and the rows of corn on the left side of the road seemed to jump out at him. He seemed more aware of them than he usually was. Strangely, he realized, while the fields were passing in a green blur, he could see every vein in every leaf. He could somehow sense the ripening kernels inside the small husks; it would be two months before the corn would be ready for harvest. The tassels were still yellow, not yet brown sticky knots. The stalks were not yet up to his shoulders. They would grow at least another twelve inches before all was said and done.

"How much farther do you think?"

Thomas's mature word choice did not mask the immature statement. Brian wrinkled his brow at him. "I have no idea."

But soon enough the column was pulling up to stop. The information worked its way down the line. They were south of Gettysburg. Brian looked back toward the south. A column of dust still followed them. More troops were coming. Another two or three hours—by nine or so—the entire Army of the Potomac would be assembled.

In Gettysburg

Daniel sat with other messengers, waiting. He held a mug of coffee, not real coffee though, and he winced with every sip. Still, it gave a body something to do to hold a mug in his hands.

"Where are you from?" a blond soldier asked from across the circle.

Daniel looked up. The man was talking to him. Daniel had not realized they were the only two left at the circle, all the others having been summoned away. He must have been daydreaming.

"I'm from Millerstown, Pennsylvania," he said.

"Is that anywhere near here?" the man asked.

"No, not really. A few hours by train. Have you ever heard of Reading?" A shake of the head. "Allentown?"

"I'm from Illinois," the man said.

"Oh, really?" A nod. The conversation faded into the sunshine.

Another messenger pulled up a log, took a mug of coffee, and plopped down halfway between Daniel and the blond soldier. "Hey, boys," the newcomer said cheerfully.

"Good morning," the blond said kindly.

"Just come from Sickles," the newcomer said without preamble. "He wants Meade to go out and inspect some little hill he's found." Neither man said anything. "They call it the Peach Orchard. Sickles was told to hold Little Round Top—"

"I thought Geary was on Little Round Top," the blond said.

"Meade moved him. Sickles was supposed to go take his place. But he found a better spot, I guess."

Daniel did not appreciate the enjoyment with which this man was telling his story. He winced, drank, held his tongue.

"But here is the greatest part," the man continued. "Meade isn't sending a return message."

The three men exchanged glances, wondering what it might mean.

Abby encouraged the boys to go out to play. The day had dawned hot and quiet. Perhaps the armies had moved on. Perhaps small groups were waiting for reinforcements. Whatever the case, it seemed safe enough for the boys to play in the yard while she did the washing. She could not spend another day in painful idleness.

Abby was exhausted. Her arms moved rhythmically, automatically on the washboard. The water was hot, her hands red. The smell of the homemade soap always tickled her nose. The metal always scraped her knuckles.

"Kick the can! Let's play kick the can!" Colum suggested.

Abby looked over to the shade of the tree where they played. Peter shook his head. "No, we need more people."

"Let's go see if Carl and Nan can play."

"No, Abby told us to stay in the yard."

Colum ran over. Abby smiled at him but didn't stop grating her knuckles and the trousers on the metal board. "Carl and Nan live just down the street, don't they?" He nodded. "Go ahead. If their mother says it's all right, come back and play here. But if she does not want them to leave their yard, then you come back here without them, understand?"

Abby watched little Robert follow the other two. "Keep an eye on your brother!" she called after them. Today was not a day she wanted to scour the town looking for a lost little boy. Peter turned and took his brother's hand.

As tired as she was, Abby found herself smiling and humming as she worked. Yesterday, she was as close to the fighting as she had ever been. She had been scared. It was completely different than helping the Sanitary Commission. Knowing the wounded soldiers had been in battle was only intellectually scary, like knowing there was a monster under the bed. But hearing the guns and smelling acrid smoke invoked a fear that wrenched her gut. She did not sleep at all but kept waiting for the booms to start again. She was so afraid the battle would come closer. She had almost expected the sun not to rise. It had been easy to believe the world would end.

Abby paused, staring at the graying water. Thinking about the end of the world made her think of Bridget. Bridget had been so clear, so determined that if the battle got too close, Abby should take the boys and leave her behind. Abby fervently hoped it would not come to that. She didn't know if she could defy her aunt, but she was certain she could not abandon her. Abby started humming and scrubbing again. So much to do today because she hadn't done anything yesterday. One thing she definitely needed to finish, though, was that letter to Ma. Would the mails be delivered if there were armies outside town? The letter might have to wait a few days to be posted, but she still wanted to finish it.

By midafternoon, Daniel had been on several assignments and was back at the command post yet again. He was told by an officer to sit down and eat, and he complied, but he also took the opportunity to write in his journal.

July 2, 1863

> The world is topsy-turvy. The days are bright and sunny but filled with horrors unspeakable. I thank God today that I have not been in the battle itself. I have ridden back and forth for the generals. I have seen our position, many of our positions. We have nearly one hundred thousand soldiers. I have no idea how many are the enemy. There has not been any fighting yet today, but the armies are massing. We are on the outskirts of Gettysburg, Pennsylvania. I know we are in the same state where my family live, but I do not consider myself close to them, neither in physical proximity nor emotional intimacy. I feel so different than the boy I was a few years ago. I do not consider myself a boy any longer. I have seen too much, experienced too much, loved and hated and feared too much, to be considered a boy any longer. And yet, sometimes, when the guns are cleaned and put away, when the cannons stop, when the fires are burning, and the soldiers are laughing, I feel as free and childlike as I ever

have. When the war is over, perhaps I can get some of that back.

"Hey, come look!" someone called.

Daniel gingerly closed his notebook, pencil caught in the spine, and joined the three messengers standing at the edge of the command post. They were just south of Cemetery Ridge. He looked to the west where the soldier was pointing.

From where they stood, they could see ten thousand blue-coated men marching across the open expanse toward the Emmetsburg Road. It must be Sickles.

"They look like they're on parade!"

Indeed, they did. Daniel watched as the men marched in perfect formation, flags waving, guns gleaming. Drums beat before them. Artillery followed behind. They certainly looked impressive.

But his eye was drawn to the line they were leaving behind. Sickles had moved nearly half a mile ahead of Hancock's line, which was on his right, closer to the command post. The space left Hancock's left exposed to attack.

"Very impressive," Daniel said sarcastically.

"Hey! You!" The shout caused all four messengers to turn. An aide was summoning.

"Who?" one man asked.

"All of you. Now!"

Daniel jogged off. All four men were summoned to deliver messages: Meade wanted a council with all of his generals.

"Get ready to move!" someone shouted.

Brian jumped up, grabbed his gun. He had actually slept some. There had been no fighting all day. He stumbled over Thomas.

"Wake up, it's time to move," Brian told him.

"What time is it?" the sleepy young man asked, grabbing his gun automatically.

Brian looked at the sky. The sun had passed its zenith a few hours before. "Three or three-thirty."

As he spoke, they heard the booms of cannon. In his mind, although he couldn't hear it, he knew the ear-splitting whistles preceded the thump. If the whistle didn't come, it was because the canister had met its target. He thanked God that he had always heard the whistle.

"Where are we going?"

"Don't know yet," Brian said. They were falling into line, waiting for instructions.

Finally, the word came back. They would be in reserve to cover Sykes. Sykes had to move in to cover Sickles.

"Oh, Abby, it's starting again!"

Abby hugged her youngest cousin. It certainly had. They could hear the cannons, but they were much farther away.

"Listen," she whispered. "Do you remember how it sounded yesterday?" Robert nodded. "Does it sound the same?"

He paused, listened to the next rumble. "I don't hear it here," he said and touched his chest.

She smiled. It was an apt description. "I know what you mean. They're farther away. I would say they're south of town."

"Will they come back over here?"

"I don't know, but we're safe. Go see if your mama wants anything to eat."

Abby sent him off with a pat on the rump. She glanced out the kitchen window. The other two boys, along with three or four friends, were still playing a rowdy game of fox and geese in the dirt, the yard being mostly dried up from lack of rain.

She listened. Yes, definitely south of town.

Daniel again sat with the other messengers. They listened. They waited.

"I wish I had a spyglass," Daniel said.

Amazingly, someone produced one from a pocket. Daniel had never before seen the man, but he didn't look like an officer. He was young, thin, with scraggly brown hair and beard. When he smiled, his teeth were shockingly white in a face that had not been washed recently.

"Where did you get that?" someone asked.

"I found it." He shrugged. "The poor man was dead."

Daniel cringed at the thought, but when the spyglass was handed to him, he took it. He looked to the south, shocked by what he saw.

"There are Confederates on that little hill over there," he said.

"We'll move them, don't worry."

Daniel wasn't so sure. As he watched, the commander of the enemy was also looking through a spyglass in his direction. Whether the man saw him or not was irrelevant, but he shuddered anyway. Daniel examined the man's position, as the man himself seemed to be doing. The group of butternut soldiers were doubled over, as if they had run a race, as if they had just worked very hard for their achievement.

Daniel swung the glass to look at the hill on which they stood. It was a scrabbling of rocks and bushes. The men certainly had worked hard. Daniel groaned.

"What's wrong?" the owner of the glass demanded. He took the glass and looked. "What is it?" he demanded again.

"That's the tallest piece of land around. If the Rebs have it, we might be at a great disadvantage," Daniel said.

Someone laughed. "You always talk like such a professor."

Daniel shook his head, not amused. He watched the round hill in the distance. As he watched, the Confederates, looking like toys whittled from dancing wood, moved down off the hill on which they stood. They crossed a distance of lower ground and made their way up the next hill. That hill was not quite so tall, and Daniel wondered why they were moving.

Suddenly, those men weren't moving anymore. A group of bluecoats fired furiously at them from an outcropping of rock.

"They'll retreat," the spyglass owner said.

But the young soldiers watching from a distance were surprised. The Confederate soldiers, though falling like cord wood against the volley of heavy fire, kept coming. And again. And again.

"Are they insane?" another messenger muttered softly.

Daniel heard the word and thought of his own insanity. He turned away, grabbing his arm. It didn't hurt anymore—Marye's Heights was more than six months ago—but the thought of it still pained him. Soldiers often were insane. Maybe the whole damn thing was insane. As much as he didn't want to, he turned back around, and, still gripping his arm, he watched the repeated attack of that little hill.

Daniel wasn't aware of the passing time. It might have been ten minutes or forty. Suddenly, the Federal troops holding the hill rushed out in a crazy charge of bayonets. One man left the safety of the rocks, then a few, then twenty, and thirty. It was almost comical the way the Confederates stopped in their tracks, but Daniel didn't laugh anymore.

"Oh, dear Lord," someone whispered with painful awe.

The Confederates were caught in a crossfire. They had bayonets coming at them from the front and bullets from their rear and left. The butternut soldiers were falling in every direction. From this distance, Daniel and the others could not see any more than the smoke and the fallen, but he imagined it was horrible. All of the gathered messengers had seen and experienced battle; this far away or farther, it was something they would see in their minds and feel in their guts for the rest of time. Daniel actually sighed with relief when the Confederates retreated.

Again, as they watched, men in blue had reached the top of the lower hill, dragging and carrying their artillery with them. They started firing to the west. From where they were standing, the messengers could not see that part of the battle.

Abby folded the clothes as she took them off the line. A hot wind had sprung up, dried the clothes quickly. They snapped vigorously in the wind. The boys were hidden somewhere in the pirate ship in the green leaves of the trees, but she could hear them, and she smiled.

Abby bent to lift the basket. It overflowed with clean laundry. Hadn't she just *done* the laundry? She wondered idly, humming as she walked, why a basket full of wet clothes was heavier, but a basket full of clean clothes was fuller? *The heavy water replaced with light, space-taking air.* It was a silly thought, but with the distant boom of big guns, it was a comforting one.

It had been a few hours since she had checked on Bridget, so after she put the clean trousers and shirts in the boys' room, she headed across the hall.

"Abby," she gasped. Abby rushed to the bed. Bridget was sweaty, gasping for air, clutching the bedclothes with white knuckles.

"Oh, no," Abby groaned. It was time. Too soon, but it was time. "I'll go get the doctor."

Abby ran down the stairs, taking the last three on a jump. Out through the kitchen into the yard. "Peter!" she called. The boy jumped out of the tree.

Abby took a deep breath. She crouched down in front of him, fought to keep her voice calm and low. "Peter, I need to go get the doctor for your mother. I need you to stay out here with your brothers. I'll be back as fast as I can."

Abby ran next door first. Mrs. Landon was in her kitchen garden, dragging a hoe along a line of beans. She wiped her face on her apron and leaned on her hoe.

"Bridget is in labor," Abby said. "I'm going to get Dr. Wilson. Will you stay with her?"

"Nan!" Mrs. Landon hollered. The young girl appeared from nowhere. "Finish the hoeing. I'll be at Mrs. Pummer's. Take care of your brother."

"Yes, ma'am."

Abby headed toward town at a run. She was sweating before she reached the first of the houses on the Chambersburg Pike. Where the Chambersburg Pike met the Hagerstown Pike, Abby took a left. Dr. Wilson's house and office was on the block behind the main road, third from the end. Abby pounded on the door with a staccato that matched her heart.

The afternoon heat was unbearable. Abby glanced at the sky—cloudless, blue, hazy. It would be a hot night, rough on Bridget. Abby turned back to the brick house. Curtains fluttered in the upstairs windows. Abby pounded again.

"Dr. Wilson!"

"He's not there, dear," an old woman said from across the street. Abby turned around. "He went to the front to see if they need help."

"I need a doctor," Abby fairly wailed.

"Dr. Oswald is on Main Street," the old woman said. "I always prefer him myself," she went on, but Abby was no longer listening.

Abby burst through the door of the practice, jangling the bell and banging the door into the wall. The man who must be Dr. Oswald came through a door, looking irritated.

"Can I help you?" The doctor was older than Dr. Wilson by about a hundred years. He was tall, with flowing white hair, clear green eyes that pierced the distance between them. He wore shirtsleeves and trousers with suspenders, looking more like her father than a doctor.

"I need a doctor. My aunt, Bridget, she's having a baby—"

Dr. Oswald turned away, went back into the other room without a word. Abby waited for him to return with his bag, but he didn't. Finally, when the seconds stretched to an everlasting minute, she forced her way into the inner office. Dr. Oswald was listening to the chest of a young boy, who was obviously having trouble breathing. The boy's mother was sitting anxiously in a chair. They all turned to see who was rudely interrupting the exam.

"How dare you." The doctor's voice was hard and unforgiving.

"I'm sorry, sir, but we need a doctor."

"Delivering babies is woman's work," he said, once again turning his back on her.

"But Dr. Wilson said she would need a doctor when her time came—"

"Then get Wilson."

"He's at the battle. Please, we need help." She begged.

"I'll be there when I can." He was dismissing her. She told him how to find the house, but as she ran out, she knew he would not come.

Dr. Tobias Wilson examined another soldier at the edge of the battlefield. The man was groaning, only semiconscious. His left arm was completely gone, and he was bleeding from a neck wound.

"We need to amputate," he grimly told the steward on the other side of the board.

"Excuse me?" The man was shocked. Without delicacy, he added, "His arm is already gone."

"Yes, but not cleanly. Look here." Wilson shook his head. "Never mind. No time to explain. Just get me the saw." He started to cut through the flesh four inches from the shoulder. A few minutes later, he was tying off the bleeding veins and arteries and moved to the next patient.

Ambulance drivers were delivering the wounded from the Peach Orchard and the Wheat Field as the oppressive late afternoon heat pressed down on Wilson's body, mind, and spirit. He had been at the tent most of the afternoon. He never looked up, never stopped moving.

Sickles was holding the Orchard; that was the report. Last year, Wilson had picked peaches with a group of young people, supposedly acting as a chaperon. But he and Amy Jansen had taken a walk on the Emmetsburg Pike and left the group to themselves for quite a while. That late summer day was a lifetime ago. And it would be another lifetime before such an outing took place again.

Wilson moved to another patient, and another, and another. He heard snippets of conversation. The battle had moved into the Wheat Field, another quarter mile in from the Emmetsburg Pike. And the wheat would be gone now too.

"They made us move back," the boy on the table whispered. He was bleeding from a leg wound. Wilson probed carefully as the chloroform kicked in, but the boy pushed the rag from his face. "We could have held the field, but they made us move back."

"Son, keep the rag on," Wilson ordered, trying not to think of how young the man was, hoping he could save the leg. They didn't save many.

"I was with Trobiand, you know, the Frenchie. Barnes was supposed to cover the right. They had the wall for protection. But Barnes pulled back—" the last was muffled in a scream as Wilson pulled a sliver of metal from the man's shin. He began wrapping, and after a few gasping breaths, the boy continued. "We had to fall back because our right was open. Barnes was supposed to hold the right. Hold the right." His voice faded as Wilson moved on.

"I don't like this, not at all," Mrs. Landon said softly when Abby joined her in the hallway. The room was hot. The air felt damp, and Abby welcomed the relative coolness of the hall.

"I know," Abby replied, but she didn't. Not really. She had witnessed one birth in her lifetime several years ago. It had been the woman's sixth, and she might have been able to do it all on her own, but her husband had sent for Mary, and Abby had gone too. This was different.

Abby glanced at her aunt on the bed. The graying red hair was matted to Bridget's face and scalp. Sweat trickled down her cheeks, glistened on her collarbones as she arched her neck in pain. Another contraction.

"How long has it been?" Mrs. Landon asked.

"Four hours." The sun would set in another hour.

"No, since the last time you went for the doctor."

"Two, I think." Abby had known Dr. Oswald would not come, not if she went a hundred times.

"You need to go again. I don't like this. Not at all." Without waiting, the older woman returned to the bedroom, tried to soothe the pain-wracked body on the bed.

"He won't come," Abby whispered, wishing she could cry.

"You there," Sickles said calmly, summoning a young boy to his side. The boy was pale, sweaty with exhaustion and nerves. He was a drummer boy, couldn't be more than fifteen, but he was a big, broad boy and was acting as a litter bearer.

"Boy, tie a tourniquet." Sickles watched as the boy shakily tied a tourniquet around his dangling leg.

"What happened, sir?" Sickles looked up to see one of his aides watching from a safe distance.

"The damn Rebels broke down the fences along the Emmetsburg Pike," he said. "They took the Orchard. I ordered the troops back."

"But how did you—" the other man vaguely indicated the leg.

"I was near the farm, half a mile from the Wheat Field. My command post," he added unnecessarily.

"Yes, sir," the man replied just as unnecessarily.

"Hit by a solid shot off the horse, and the leg nearly off." He lay weakly back on the stretcher. "Tell Birney he has command." As the drummer boy and another litter-bearer began moving him to the back, he added, "Someone get me a cigar!"

Daniel rushed up Culp's Hill. He had been summoned from his inactivity to deliver a message for Meade. The Federals were losing lots of troops between the Emmetsburg Pike and Cemetery Ridge, where Daniel could see everything. But Meade needed someone to take a command to the twelfth corps to help cover Little Round Top. As Humphreys was leading tired but still fighting troops up to Cemetery Ridge, Daniel was on his way down. "General!" he called, standing at attention.

"Speak!"

"Message from Meade. Leave your position on Culp's Hill and take position on Little Round Top."

The officer put his spyglass to his eye. Little Round Top, the shorter of the two round hills Daniel had been watching earlier in the day, was nearly two miles to the southwest. Most of the fighting was farther west than the general's march would take them; they might get there in reasonable order. Putting the glass in its case and handing it to an aide, he gave the order.

The twelfth corps moved out. Doubleday led his first corps to the fight in double quick time. As Daniel stood to the side, thousands of troops jogged off toward the sound of guns.

Rest, just rest, the young soldier cried in his heart. He leaned wearily against the wheel of his twelve-pounder. He and three others had pulled and maneuvered the heavy artillery piece for hundreds of yards. As the unit had retreated from the Orchard, they had fought valiantly, but the horses that pull the cannons can't carry guns. They had lost so many to the flying Confederate bullets, that Billy and his comrades had pulled their cannon with their own hands the last dozen yards.

Now they rested near a two-story white farmhouse. It was owned by a man named Trostle who had wisely retreated. Sickles had been shot nearby, was on his way to the surgery tent. Some said he might die. Billy chuckled, not amused. The same could be said for any of them.

"Here they come, boys!" an officer shouted, riding past on his dirty white horse.

Billy and the others turned the gun, grunting and swearing. They could see the Confederates approaching. Billy reached for shot on the caisson.

"Hold the line here, boys!" The officer was shouting and pointing to six teams. "The rest fall back! Set up a defensive line—"

For the next minutes, Billy loaded and doubled to hide from the impact, stood, did it again. Six cannons against the onslaught. The blue line somewhere to their rear.

"Keep at it, boys," Captain Bigelow hollered.

Billy and his buddies were keeping at it. The damn Rebels were nearly in their faces, but they kept on, hours flying past in minutes. Billy saw the blood on Bigelow's uniform but didn't stop to ask why he wasn't on his way to the rear. He wanted to ask if reinforcements were coming, but there wasn't time to ask, let alone hold them off.

Pain. Red spreading across his chest. *Damn.*

Billy sank to the ground and saw his nearest buddy watch him fall. Nothing to say, nothing to do. Billy heard Bigelow command the retreat, saw the boots running by. In seconds, he couldn't tell the difference between the blue's boots and the butternut's.

Dr. Wilson didn't even blink when he came to the Confederate officer. On the surgeon's table, all soldiers were equal: dying or dead and worthy of every skill he possessed.

The man before him was riddled with the shot from inside the cannon shells. His chest heaved with every red bubbly breath.

"Your name, sir?" Wilson asked. There was nothing he could do.

"William Barksdale, Twenty-First Mississippi. Tell my wife I am shot, but we fought like hell."

Wilson patted the man's hand, wishing he could do more, wishing he could do even that.

Daniel was back in the fray. It had been months since he had fired at another human being. But he had been summoned not to deliver a message but to fill a hole. There was a hole on Cemetery Ridge. He was able, fit, and apparently idle, so they pulled him in.

Confederates were trying to breech the hill. The butternuts stood behind a wall, firing at the cannons. Daniel stood with the cannons but fired his rifle. Cannons were inadequate for the task, an ax where a scalpel was needed. But such was the army.

The infamous Rebel yell pierced the thick smoke. Daniel could see them coming over the wall, bayonets bared, dull and ugly in the smoke, unable to grab light from the veiled sun. The Confederates dealt hideous blows with their sharp instruments and the dull butt ends of guns. Daniel fought them off as best he could, slamming his own bayonet into a soft belly, turning without thinking to the next. *Call retreat, dammit! Call retreat!* Another went down. "Call retreat," he begged.

"Charge!" commanded the new brigadier, Webb.

Brian did not like the man, and he liked the order even less. Still, he was a soldier, and it was his job. With the rest of the Philadelphia Brigade, Brian swarmed forward. They had been shielded on the eastern side of Cemetery Ridge, the Federal guns above them on the crest. As butternut uniforms and rebel yells came over the summit, the Irish surged.

The Confederates turned and ran. No, Brian realized, they weren't running. They were fighting. Bluecoats had them from the back and the flank. Brian kept at it, for no one had called retreat.

Abby sat wearily in the rocker by the window. Mrs. Landon had fed the boys, then taken them home with her. She would put them to bed with her own children. Tomorrow she would care for them, leaving Abby to do what needed to be done.

The doctor had come. Abby had literally dragged him with her, not releasing his hand until he started following on his own accord. He grumbled and complained the whole way, but she didn't care.

"Bad, very bad," he had muttered as the sun set outside the window. "Get lamps. Lots of them. You should have come for me sooner."

Abby had held back the scream until she was downstairs, and still she muffled it in a towel. The man was infuriating. Her head was pounding along with her heart and the cannons in the distance. But she had done everything he asked, and now they waited.

"There is nothing else I can do," he said, towering above her.

"You're not leaving?" Abby demanded in a strangled voice, rising with difficulty.

Dr. Oswald looked toward the weak form on the bed. He shook his head sadly. "I'll stay until the baby is born." He placed a firm hand on Abby's shoulder. "But I must tell you the truth. I don't think we can save either of them."

Brian sank wearily into a fitful sleep. The guns had stopped, both the large and the personal. It was nearing midnight. The smoke was dissipating, but it still obscured the stars. There were no tents tonight, so he stared up at the dispersing smoke.

With the guns quiet, and no campfires around which to blarney, he heard everything with painful clarity. The wounded and dying.

"Mr. Lincoln," a soft voice said, entering the office carefully. It was late.

But the president was not sleeping. Nor was he working. He was standing at the window, looking out at the city. He had a perfect view of the unfinished monument to the nation's first president. Ironic, he sometimes thought, that the monument was being constructed at the exact same time that the nation was torn in two.

Mr. Lincoln turned, hands clasped behind his back, looking weary but still completely dressed. He waited for the secretary to continue.

"We have a message from Meade at Gettysburg." The man handed a folded paper to the president, waited quietly for further instructions.

"Meade has held position. He will remain there tomorrow." It was neither a happy message nor a hopeful one. The fight would continue tomorrow. And the day after tomorrow was Independence Day. There was much to be done.

"Have we heard from Grant at Vicksburg?"

"No, sir, the siege is still under way."

"Fine. It's late, go home."

"Yes, sir." The man left his commander-in-chief still standing at the window. Brian jumped. Other soldiers were rousing and moving.

Boom! Brian jumped out of his bedroll. He tied his shoes, grabbed his gun. "Where's it coming from?"

"It started!"

"Men, get a move on!" That was an officer, rousing those who were not yet mobile.

"Where is it, sir?" someone asked the mounted officer.

He wheeled his horse to face the question. Then he waved an arm. "Culp's Hill. We'll be in reserve for now."

"It's barely dawn," someone groaned.

Brian didn't respond. The adrenaline was already pumping. This was day three of this battle. Hopefully, it would be the last.

The second the thought skittered across his mind, he wished he could take it back.

Abby barely moved when the guns started. On the western side of the house, the rising sun still had everything in shadows. It was cool. It was misty. But there clearly would be no relief for any of them.

"She's resting," Dr. Oswald said softly from the far side of the room. He had carried another chair up, sat stiffly in the corner.

Abby stood as heavy and weary as she had ever been. She barely glanced at Bridget. She had ceased to hear the moaning at some point during the night, but now that she was awake, it was still there. As persistent as the guns off to the south.

"I'll make more coffee," she said, walking past the doctor.

"Eat something. I need you well."

She barely acknowledged him. She wasn't hungry, not in the least. She didn't care to eat or sleep or not eat or not sleep or even breathe. Everything she did was automatic. It had to be because she couldn't hold a thought in her head.

As she waited for the coffee to boil, Abby sank to the kitchen floor. She buried her face in her dress. It smelled. She had not changed her clothes for days. Not even to put on a nightgown. Not even to wash.

Abby cried. It was too hard. She'd rather be in Philadelphia. With hot tears streaming down her dirty face, she recalled with sorrowful pleasure those months in the attic room, the gaudy colors of the rich ladies' dresses. With some surprise, she realized she could not even remember their names. But she remembered Mrs. Johnson. And Owen. And Daniel.

She tossed her head back, leaning against the wall. Abby took deep breaths, trying to chase away the fear. Dr. Oswald had said Bridget would die. It was too much. Being a woman was too much, too hard, impossible to bear.

Abby finally swallowed the tears. If she could live on her own in the city, she could do this. Strength was strength, wasn't it?

The good doctor needed coffee. And she needed to eat.

Daniel was back with his unit. After his brief hand-to-hand skirmish yesterday, the officer had asked him his name and unit. Then he had been sent back to the fighting Irish. He managed to find Brian.

"Hey," Daniel said softly. He walked up to Brian, waiting patiently under a tree. While other men sat or paced or talked or whittled, waiting for the command to move, Brian simply stood. For two years, it had been his habit. Daniel often wondered what he was thinking. These days, though, he tried not to delve too deeply into anyone's thoughts, not even—especially not—his own.

"Hi." Brian's eyes stared into the pounding distance. After a moment, his blue eyes met Daniel's. "Do you know what's happening?"

"Not really. The twelfth corps are holding Culp's Hill. Meade sent twenty guns to the Baltimore Pike to fire at the Confederates. I wonder how long they can hold it."

Brian shrugged. He recalled the layout of the hill. Infantry were entrenched at the top. The guns were no doubt being used to open up the line, allow the infantry a chance to charge.

"How's Mama?" Peter asked carefully.

"What are you doing here?" Abby was eating a thick wedge of cheese on an equally thick slice of bread. She had taken the doctor his coffee, and he had reiterated his command for breakfast. He had actually hinted that she should do women's work, and he'd call her when he needed her. So she was sitting in the kitchen, eating, but otherwise doing nothing, intending to do nothing.

"Why aren't you with Mrs. Landon?" she demanded.

"I told her I needed the privy," he said. "And I did," he added hastily, so that she wouldn't think he was a liar. "I just wanted to know if Mama had the baby yet."

"No, not yet. The doctor is still with her."

"Did he say how long?"

"No, Peter, he didn't. We just have to wait." Abby finished the last bite of cheese. "Peter, go tell Mrs. Landon that I need your help today. We'll work the garden. You go tell her, and I'm going to change my clothes, and I'll meet you outside."

It was an impulsive decision. Ma always kept busy, no matter what. Abby had always assumed that she did it because there was always something to do. But Abby was realizing that a woman's life was not always what it seemed. Perhaps activity would be good for both her and Peter.

A few minutes later, as the clock on the mantle read half past eight, Abby headed for the back door. She felt much better, fresher in a clean dress. She had run a brush through her hair, rebraided it, and pinned it up. She had splashed some water on her face, and the coolness felt good, even though the sun and the dust stole the feeling almost the instant she stepped into the yard.

"Where should we start?" she asked the boy.

They were moving. Not far. Only from Cemetery Ridge to a flat place just west. The 69th was ordered to dig in. There was no stone wall, those farm walls so prevalent due to the rocky soil, only a split rail fence. There was no breastwork of any kind. So the soldiers built up their own, only about a foot of earth which they could lie behind, resting their rifles.

And then they waited.

"It's hot," Brian whispered.

It wasn't a complaint, and Daniel didn't take it as such. The man was simply stating a fact. It must be pushing ninety degrees, and it was not even noon. If they were simply waiting in a camp—the army's infernal waiting!—Daniel would have unbuttoned his coat. But the thick wool offered some protection from projectiles. At least, he told himself it did. Otherwise, what was the use?

"That's a wide-open space," Daniel commented.

Indeed, it was. Webb had strung out their brigade, just over five thousand men, over half a mile. Men were dozing in the heat. Since eleven o'clock, the shots had ceased. It was eerily quiet. In front of the half-mile of bluecoats was a field. To their back was a row of trees. In the distance was the Emmetsburg Road, and in the farther distance, Daniel imagined he could see the congregating butternuts.

Abby had grown accustomed to the banging of cannons. They were in the distance, obviously not a threat, and she and Peter worked in the field without noticing them.

But then they stopped.

"Do you hear that?" Peter asked suddenly. He was a few rows away in the green pumpkins. Abby was in the beans, bent over, and she straightened.

"Yes," she said very softly. She heard nothing. It was eerie. It was bizarre. It was unnerving. She looked toward the south. She wondered where the armies were and where they were going. "I don't see any dust. I don't think they're moving," she said.

"Will they start fighting again?"

Abby sighed and returned to her work. "I don't know, Peter."

Dr. Oswald felt the weak pulse in Bridget's wrist. He replaced the hot cloth on her head with a cool one. Twice since breakfast, he had asked Abby to bring cool water from the well. The heat of the day warmed the water until it was useless as a cooling agent.

The contractions were constant now, but Bridget was no closer to delivering than she had been six hours ago. She gripped the bed in agony. She writhed in the dirty sweat-soaked sheets. She groaned and cried until the tears dried up, and there was no strength left in her body.

Oswald hated this. He was a doctor, not a midwife. There were certainly other people he could be doctoring. Especially since Wilson was in the army hospital. All the same, he was reluctant to leave. Abby could probably do just as much as he could at this point, but he had promised he'd stay.

He walked to the window. He could just barely see Abby and the boy in the garden. He had heard her crying when he came down for coffee in the early morning. He had walked back up the stairs without it, thinking to himself that women were so lucky, so blessed to have the release of tears. Not that he would cry over Bridget. Or her baby. Or her children. But he felt so damn useless! He was a doctor, and he knew he couldn't save her.

"I'm hungry," Brian whispered.

"I don't know when I ate last," Daniel admitted. Hell, he didn't even know what day it was. "Hey, do you know what day it is?"

"Um, Friday, I think. The fourth, no, the third, of July," Brian said after a moment.

Boom! Boom! Boom! Boom!

"Here we go," Brian whispered. He glanced at the sky. After noon, maybe one o'clock.

"It's not us," Daniel said, glancing over his shoulder at the artillery.

Brian was watching the trees on the other side of the Emmetsburg Road. "I know. It's them."

The shells exploded, sending metal and dirt and rocks high into the air. Brian had to turn his head to the left to see where. There was a clump of trees a few hundred yards down. That seemed to be the target, although artillery was notoriously inaccurate.

"Holy hannah!" Daniel breathed. "It's Hancock."

The men around them muttered back and forth as they watched their general. He sat his horse with a ramrod-straight back and easy manner. His aide followed on another horse, carrying the flag of the first corps. The general and his aide pranced up and down the line between the soldiers and the enemy artillery.

"He's going to get himself killed," someone said with more derision than awe.

"Sometimes it's what a general has to do," Brian said. Daniel turned quickly to see his friend's face. Brian's voice was pure awe.

"Here we go again," Abby muttered to herself. She glanced over at Peter, who had again stopped hoeing, this time in the beets.

"We're safe here, Abby," he said stiffly.

"Yes, thank you." She didn't know why she said it, but it felt right.

"Abby!"

They turned toward the house. Dr. Oswald was hanging halfway out the bedroom window. He silently beckoned.

"What's wrong?" The doctor had scared Peter more than the cannons.

"I'm sure it is nothing," Abby lied. "Perhaps it's time." Abby ran inside. She did not see the boy run with joy toward the neighbor's house.

"When will they fire?" Billy Bradigan demanded from Brian's right. He was a few men away, addressing no one in particular. Everyone kept looking over their shoulders at the silent cannons.

The dirt in front of them was now being churned up by the enemy's shells. Most were going over their heads. Some fell short. Some had torn through the line, although everyone Brian could see and identify was still in position.

Finally, they heard the booming of their own guns begin. Through the smoke, Brian watched the sky. Minutes passed, then more, then an hour, and then another quarter and a half. The men far to their right were hammered with shot.

Daniel and Brian exchanged glances. Lucky for an hour and half didn't mean lucky.

Another eerie silence fell on their ears, and Brian looked at the sky. An hour and a half, the Federals had bombarded the enemy. It must be two-thirty, and the cannons were silent.

"Our cannons have stopped," Daniel whispered.

Brian could barely hear him because the whistling and booming of the Confederate guns had not abated.

"What do we do now?" Abby asked.

The baby was, indeed, coming. Bridget, only half-conscious, was screaming in torment. Abby cringed with each wail.

"Just hold her up. She's weak. She'll need us to help as much as possible."

"What can I do?" Mrs. Landon asked, suddenly appearing in the doorway. Without being asked, she said, "I've sent the children to Willoughby Run to play in the water."

"Will they be safe there?" Abby asked anxiously.

"Focus, Abby," Oswald said through gritted teeth. Then, glancing quickly at Mrs. Landon and back to his task, he said, "There's nothing you can do. The mother will die, and most likely the babe too."

"Doctor!" the woman cried out, taking up a supportive position at Bridget's left shoulder. She and Abby bore the weight of the pregnant woman together.

"It's true," Abby said softly.

Of course, it was true! Mrs. Landon had known that yesterday. But the doctor's bluntness shocked her.

"I know," she whispered, "but to say so out loud!"

"It's all right," Abby said. "We'll help her through this, and then we'll manage, somehow."

Oh, hell. It was the most fearsome sight Brian had ever seen. The Confederates were coming. But they were silent.

The butternut soldiers were not wailing that horrible yell. Somehow, in the heat of midafternoon, with the guns on both sides now silent, the silently running soldiers invoked more fear than they ever had before. It was as if the demons of hell were coming for them across a hazy mile.

Daniel's eyes scanned the distance. The sun coming down the sky; it would blind their vision in another hour or so. But in the light, he could see the approaching men, carrying quiet guns, waving a blue flag and two reds. What craziness was this?

"Hold, men!" O'Kane called out.

Daniel looked over his shoulder at his commander.

"Wait for them! Wait until the last possible minute." After a moment, the colonel added, "Let your work this day be for glory or death!"

Daniel looked at Brian. He was nodding as if he firmly agreed with the colonel's statements.

They really are demons, Brian thought as he watched. One Federal battery was still scything them down. As he watched, the Confederates were turning slightly to their left, his right, joining up with another group. Their holes disappeared, were swallowed up by the butternut uniforms. As if Satan himself were filling in the ranks with an unconquerable enemy.

Time slowed to a crawl as the damned Rebels crawled over the distance. Still falling, ever coming.

Suddenly, the Federal line, somewhere to their right, opened fire. Muskets and cannon downed hundreds of the approaching butternuts. The noisy onslaught caused a wail and fury to erupt from them. Brian's breath caught in his throat.

Here we go.

But not yet. Time was immeasurable as Federal cannons started firing from both ends across the butternuts. The damage was devastating. Brian didn't know where to look.

"Push, Bridget," Oswald said calmly, softly.

"Push," Abby and Mrs. Landon whispered in her ears.

Eventually, all in an instant, the blue line was firing. Daniel was vaguely aware of blues climbing out over a wall, nearer to the trees. But he couldn't think. Everything was automatic: fire, load, fire, load. He barely paused to breathe.

The cannon behind their line were firing again. After one such volley, as Daniel was aiming at the mass of butternut uniforms in front of him, there was no one in front of them.

"Holy hannah," he breathed. Not a single Confederate in front of him was standing.

Brian, too, paused beside him. "Damn." Again, the awe in his voice.

But it didn't last long. Angry, yelling, sword-wielding Confederates were closing the gap, only a few yards away from their faces now.

"All right, ladies," the doctor said. His voice was low, hoarse with fatigue.

In his hands, he held a tiny form. A perfect creation. A silent, lifeless being.

Abby didn't let herself cry, but how sad it was! Bridget had tried so hard!

"Let her down, Abby," Mrs. Landon whispered.

They laid Bridget's head and shoulders back onto the pillows. Abby stroked her face, listened to the raspy breathing, turned to watch the doctor with the baby.

Daniel and Brian's guns exploded at the same instant. The two men directly in front of them fell, one of them screaming in pain. But they were quickly replaced with four more.

Abby stood near Dr. Oswald. She watched him wrap the tiny baby in a blanket. The baby was perfectly formed with tiny hands and feet. But her eyes were closed, and her skin was blue. Abby reached out a tentative finger.

"You were very much loved," she whispered, a tear escaping as the adrenaline subsided.

"Doctor," Mrs. Landon said softly from the bed. He handed the baby to Abby, hurried the short distance to Bridget's side.

"Charge!"

They heard the command, but it wasn't for them. It was for the 72nd. Only, the 72nd refused to move.

"Charge!" The order came again a moment, a year later. This time, it was for the 69th.

With a yell, the mass of blue surged forward to meet the enemy. Within half a dozen steps, Daniel was face-to-face with a Confederate. Another yell met by a return yell. A slash of metal met by another.

Daniel felt his eyes popping out of his head. The pain was intense. He looked down to see the sword being drawn from his side, and he sank to the ground, aware of nothing but the burning sensation and the wetness on his hands.

Dr. Oswald pulled the sheet up to cover Bridget. He realized suddenly that it was thick with grime, and he tossed it aside. He left the room, returned a moment later with a quilt. He gently covered the form on the bed.

Abby sank to the floor.

A form. Aunt Bridget was a form. No longer a person. No longer a mother or a wife or simply a woman. She was a form, a lifeless thing under a blanket.

As darkness fell on the battlefield, Brian pushed his way through the bodies at his feet. When the firing had stopped, Daniel was no longer next to him. Hours had passed, but he had not joined the rest of the group, as they waited for whatever was next.

Brian searched near the group of trees. They had managed to hold against the Confederates. The enemy was decimated. Rumors were running hot and fast that Meade would have them on the road soon following the retreating army of Virginia. Brian couldn't worry about that now.

For the second time that day, time was standing still. The sun hung only inches above the horizon. The air hung, too, heavy and thick with cries and groans of men.

"Daniel," he cried out, dropping into a squat. He couldn't kneel. There was barely enough room for his feet between Daniel and the man next to him. Daniel's eyes were open, and as Brian wept, the eyes blinked.

"Oh my Lord," Brian breathed. He lifted Daniel into his arms. The blood had soaked the ground, but Brian sat in the empty space left when he lifted his friend. Daniel didn't make a sound. He was alive but wouldn't be for long.

"Nurse!" Brian hollered, looking around for the crew of litter-bearers who would carry the wounded to the field hospital. "Hold on, Daniel. Nurse!"

Chapter 15

NOVEMBER 19

Abby watched the boys walk over to Mrs. Landon's waiting warm kitchen. Abby was going to the dedication of the cemetery, but she thought it would be too much for the boys. Firstly, it was raining, though slightly, and secondly, the pain of their mother's death was still very raw, and she did not want to surround them with more sorrow.

The crowd was large. It was early. The procession scheduled to wind its way through town would begin at nine-thirty. President Lincoln had arrived the night before by train. Abby had heard that, strangely, he was not the keynote speaker. The vice-presidential candidate, Edward Everett, would provide that speech.

Abby was cold and wet by the time the parade arrived at the cemetery. The president sat on a chestnut horse, calm and proud and somber in his black suit and hat. He was tall, very tall, even taller on the horse. He was not a man to gain much attention, but Abby felt her heart skip a beat. She had admired this man for years, appreciated his willingness to make the hard decisions. He was here out of respect for the dead, and it earned even more of her respect for him.

Abby stood with the crowd—thousands of people had come—for hours. There was some music and prayer, and then Mr. Everett spoke. He spoke for two hours. She shifted her position at least a dozen times, as did many others, and barely knew what he said. She clapped delicately with the rest but waited eagerly for the president.

"Four score and seven years ago, our fathers brought forth on this continent a new nation, conceived in liberty, and dedicated to the proposition that all men are created equal. Now we are engaged in a great civil war, testing whether that nation, or any nation, so conceived and so dedicated, can long endure. We are met on a great battlefield of that war. We have come to dedicate part of that field, as a final resting place for those who gave their lives that that nation might live . . ."

Tears formed in Abby's eyes. Daniel was one of those soldiers, one of the men who gave their lives. Despite the fact that Brian had carried him to the surgery tent. Mary had written that when Brian laid Daniel on the ground, the doctor had thought it was Brian who was wounded because he immediately fell to the ground with fatigue and covered with blood.

"It is altogether fitting and proper that we should do this. But, in a larger sense, we cannot dedicate—we cannot consecrate, we cannot hallow—this ground. Brave men, living and dead, who have struggled here have consecrated it far above our poor power to add or detract."

Someone brushed against Abby's arm. She moved a few inches to the right, feeling very squashed.

"The world will little note, nor long remember what we say here, but it can never forget what they did here. It is for us the living, rather, to be dedicated here to the unfinished work which they who have fought here have thus far so nobly advanced. It is rather for us to be here dedicated to the great task remaining before us—that from these honored dead, we take increased devotion to that cause for which they gave the last full measure of devotion—that we here highly resolve that these dead shall not have died in vain—that this nation under God shall have a new birth of freedom—and that government of the people, by the people, and for the people, shall not perish from the earth."

"I think Daniel would like that. I'm not sure he could have written anything better."

Abby turned, looked at the tall man standing next to her. "Brian," she breathed.

They shared the silence through the last song and the benediction. Then she turned as the crowd began to disperse and hugged him.

Abby looped her arm through his. They began walking. Many people were going to wander through the cemetery, giving more respect, talking quietly. But she needed to head back to the boys. Since their mother's death, they had clung to Abby.

"I've been staying with Aunt Bridget. I was actually here during the battle. I had no idea you and Daniel were so close by."

"How is Bridget? She had the baby?"

Abby looked up at him, then rested her head on his shoulder, still walking. "She died. So did the baby. It was a girl."

"Oh."

He seemed unmoved. She had been his sister, but he did not remember her. If he had seen her in July, she would have been as much a stranger to him as she had been to Abby in May. They walked for a while. She was leading him back toward the house.

"What now?" she finally asked.

"I think I'll go back to Millerstown. I've served my time. Going home."

"I'm so glad. But what will you do?" She still could not see him as a farmer.

"I don't know. I've thought about going into politics."

She didn't know what to say.

Brian said after a moment, "What about you? How long will you be staying down here?"

"Only a few more days, actually. I'm taking the boys with me. They'll stay with us for as long as necessary."

"That's good. But what will you do back home?"

"Buy my own farm," she whispered.

"What?"

"I've been saving my money. I want to have my own place. Grow wheat and corn and maybe raise horses and pigs."

"I thought you wanted to sew."

She looked up at him. "That was only a means to an end."

"I must say I never would have guessed, but somehow, I'm not surprised."

"That's a little contradictory."

"Perhaps."

"Are you sorry?" she asked then, stepping away from him and tilting her face up to the rain.

"About what?"

"About everything. Running away. Joining the war. All of it."

Brian shook his head. "No, I'm not. We do what we have to do. We have to make the hard choices sometimes and live with the consequences." He paused, not looking at her.

They stopped. They were in front of the house. It was already packed up for the most part. Someone would help get the trunks to the station. The furniture was covered with sheets. The shutters would be closed, the doors locked, and hopefully, one day, the boys would be back to meet their father and continue living.

"This is it," she said, turning toward him and the gate, but not looking at him.

"Abby," he began and paused.

"I'll see you at home," she said.

"Yes, at home."

Letter from Daniel to Peggy
(Not dated)

>Dear Ma,
>
>This is the letter you have been dreading. There is no way for me to make it easier on you. A soldier's life is filled with doubt and danger, but I must say I don't want you to receive this letter any more than you want to receive it.
>
>There are few things that sustain a soldier at war. Very few things. Food is not one of them. Not army food, anyway. But thoughts of home, and

family, and your soda bread and jam, and whitewashed Christmases and loud tavern rooms. I miss those things every day. I think of those things every day.

I don't think this will surprise you: I am in love with Abigail Weimer. If you are reading this letter, then she is reading a similar one. I ask of you a favor, Ma. Please give Abby my journals. All of them. The one that I have carried in my pocket throughout this war, and all of the journals in the box under my bed. You may read them if you wish, but I want her to have them.

I must go. I love you.

Forever,
Daniel

Letter from Daniel to Abby
(Undated)

Abby,

Miss Abigail Weimer, I love you. I have always loved you. From the time you wore short skirts and pigtails. I love your fiery eyes and the way you tackle life like a horse that needs to be tamed. I love your willingness to go against convention, ankles and all. But I love watching you grow too. Once upon a time, you were a headstrong girl who showed her ankles when she shouldn't, but now you are a refined young lady, and one I would be proud to walk down the street with.

I hope I can someday tell you all this face-to-face. But if you are reading this letter, it is not to be, and I wanted you to know.

This damn war ruins everything, doesn't it? Sometimes, I wish it had never started. But then I think what we're fighting for—to save the United States of America—and I know it is right. Sometimes I think of Mr. Lincoln, and I think I would not want his job! I would not want to be the one making these decisions. But we all make decisions, and we all must live with the consequences. Leaving home the way I did. Joining the army. Never having kissed you. I surely hope you never get this letter because that means I'll come home, and I surely will kiss you then!

I want you to have my journals. All of them. I am telling my mother too. She may want to read them, and as far as I am concerned, she may. But I want you to have them. It is as close as I can get to giving you my heart.

I will always love you.
Daniel

Epilogue

1866, CHOICES MADE

Abby walked slowly toward the house. The wheat was growing nicely; a few more weeks, and it would be ready for harvest. She would have to make sure her scythe was sharp; she put it on her mental list.

The sun was still hot as it lazily fell toward the western horizon. The windows of her house glowed, as if someone had lighted the lamps inside. But there was no one inside. Peter and Colum and Robert had left for Gettysburg with their father in the spring. She had to admit the place seemed empty without them. And Peter had been a great help when she was first getting the place started.

"I say, Abby!" Meg called as she turned the corner, coming from behind Abby's one tree, waiting for Abby to join her and little Daniel by the porch steps. "I can hear your place from ours!"

Abby laughed, and the two women climbed the steps and sat facing west. On this side of the house, away from the animals, the noise was only slightly less. Abby had enough land to grow wheat and corn but only enough to feed her livestock. Her cash crop was pigs and chickens. She had a lucrative if informal contract with several Allentown butcher shops, and in the two years since she had started her farm, she had done quite well for herself.

"Isn't the tavern open tonight?" Abby asked after a few leisurely minutes of rocking.

"Brian has his cronies over. He handles things on nights like this. I don't particularly like his political friends."

"I thought he gave that up."

"He won't run for office again, probably, but he still likes to be involved."

Abby glanced at Meg who gently rubbed her slightly rounded belly. "Are you happy, Meg?"

Meg smiled. "I am very happy." She paused. "I didn't expect to be."

"You've never really talked about it. I mean marrying Brian and all." Abby gently prodded.

"You have to admit it was all rather unexpected." Meg laughed. "He came home from the war, when was that? November of '63. We were married in January."

"How did he ask you though?"

"It was a purely mercenary decision," Meg said without bitterness. "He knew I couldn't live on my own, and living with my parents for the rest of my life would not have been ideal. I would have done it, I suppose because that was my only real option. But he said he could help me buy my own tavern, and I could keep house for him, and he'd give Daniel his name." Meg shrugged. "He got something, I got something. We were both willing to try to be content with that." Meg smiled again, looking down at her belly. "Happiness came later."

"But why? I mean, why would he even think of it?"

"I don't know." But she did know; she just would not tell Abby or anyone. The reasons went deep, so deep that Brian still woke up in the middle of the night, sweating and breathing hard and jumping if she said his name. He never talked of the war, and she never asked. But it was there between them, and somehow it hurt his heart to see her treated badly. That was all she knew. Somehow, her predicament was connected to the war in his mind, anyway. Perhaps saving her from shame eased some hurt within his soul.

"You look happy. And healthy. Was Daniel this easy?"

"Hardly!" Meg said, looking at her son, who had moved down the porch to watch some bugs. "We want a girl this time," she added. "We decided if it is a girl, she'll be Bridget Mary."

"And if it's a boy?"

"Abraham Frederick."

"Lots of people are naming their children after Lincoln since the assassination."

"Hard to believe that was a year ago."

"Hard to believe the war has been over that long. I wonder what Gettysburg looks like now?" Abby thought of the cemetery, the churned-up mud of the Peach Orchard, Seminary Ridge. She wondered if it was all back to normal, or at least back to the way it was. She rested her hand on her pocket, tapping it idly.

"How is Kathleen?" Abby asked next. Living four miles south on the King's Highway on a side road, she did not see everyone as often as she wished.

"Up and around. The doctor says she'll be just fine. And little Patrick is feeling better too. But Sean is still sick."

"Oh, I thought both boys were doing better!"

"They were, but Sean had a setback. The fever went back up is all. The doctor says a few more days. And how is Sarah? And the baby?"

Abby laughed joyfully. "Twins! Who would have thought! No wonder she was so big!"

Meg laughed, too, and little Daniel came to investigate. She pulled him onto her lap. "And their names?"

"Thomas and Nathaniel. And Ruth is so happy to be a big sister!"

"Very nice."

They were quiet for a while. As the sun began to sink, the air felt a little cooler. Both women sat up when they heard a wagon approaching.

As it approached the house, Meg whistled. It was not a wagon at all but rather a coach. It was black with gold trim painted on it, and Jenkins & Sons in gold and red on the door. A man in red and tan livery drove. Meg had never seen anything like it. But Abby had in the city. Abby looked over at Meg and Daniel, whose mouth hung open in awe.

The coach stopped; the driver hopped down. Before he could open the door, Owen Johnson was standing in Abby's front yard.

It was Abby's turn to stare. He was much as she had left him: goatee, brown hair, top hat in his hand, and the rest of his outfit exquisite although slightly dusty. He was as fit as she remembered, if a bit older. How long had it been? March 1863 to July 1866—nearly three and a half years. She patted her hair, smoothed her skirt as she walked out to meet him, and her hand stayed unconsciously on her pocket.

"Owen," she said stupidly. "What are you doing here?"

"Abby, how are you?"

"I am well. And you?" Her mind finally engaged.

"I am well."

"And your mother?"

"Oh, fine, fine. But fit to be tied."

"Why?" They were standing in the dust of the yard. The open coach door still behind him, Meg and Daniel somewhere off to Abby's right. The sun was almost set.

"Because I'm here. She thinks you should come to me. That you should come to Philadelphia." Before she could respond (but her mind still was not *that* engaged) he rushed on. "But I don't want to be in Philadelphia. Richard died in the war, and Father died last year of a sudden and complete heart attack—"

"Oh, I'm sorry!"

"And Teresa is married, so it's just me and Mother in that townhouse, and she's driving me crazy!"

"Sadie?"

"Her father came for her last year."

"Oh, I am glad!"

"Abby, I can be a doctor anywhere. If you want to be in Millerstown, I'll stay in Millerstown." A very significant pause. "If you want me to, that is."

Abby's hand clutched her pocket. She didn't have an answer, and at the moment, she was too stunned to even think of a temporary one. But it was too late for him to go back to Philadelphia tonight. Meg!

"Oh, I beg your pardon!" Abby cried out, turning to Meg and motioning her forward. "Owen, may I present Mrs. Meg O'Bern and her little boy Daniel. Meg, this is Dr. Owen Johnson."

"How do you do?"

"A pleasure." They shook hands.

"Meg, you have room?"

"Oh, I'm sure we can come up with something."

"Mr. and Mrs. O'Bern own the tavern and inn down the road. Perhaps you passed it," Abby said. O'Bern's was slightly less than a mile farther south right on the King's Highway that led to Philadelphia.

"Yes, I believe we did. That would be wonderful. May I offer you a ride, madam?"

"Yes, thank you." Meg and Daniel climbed up. The little boy's mouth was again hanging open, stunned at the opulence of the coach.

Owen turned to Abby as the driver climbed up to his seat. "How long am I staying, Abby?"

"I don't know, Owen."

She stood in the yard long after the coach and the sun disappeared.

Author's Note

ACKNOWLEDGEMENTS

Rome was not built in a day, and *In the Shadow of Mr. Lincoln* was not written in a year. It's the culmination of several years of research, one summer of writing, and ten years of shelf-sitting. I hope my readers will learn something about the Civil War by reading it, but more than that I want you to learn that it's never too late to follow through on a dream.

This is a work of fiction. Abby, Daniel, Brian, and Meg did not exist, but they might have. What I mean is this: the world I created for them is real, and someone, somewhere might have experienced the Civil War in the way they did. There are several real people in the story, and I would like to introduce them to you.

The first person I want to introduce doesn't have a name, but rather a title. Brian tells his new Philadelphia friends that his father was a shenachai. A shenachai (SHAWN-a-key) is a traditional Irish or Scottish storyteller. You may find other ways to spell it, but the function is the same. A sheanchai originally served the ancient kings of Ireland. He told the stories, legends, and exploits of the Irish people, passing these down in oral tradition. By the time of the mass exodus of Irish people to America, which is how Brian arrived in Pennsylvania, a sheanchai was a revered member of society. He traveled from town to town, earning his meals and lodging by regaling the audience with a story or two. The listener often thought he was getting the better end of the deal.

Andrew Curtain served two terms as Pennsylvania's governor, from 1861 (elected the same year as Lincoln) until 1867. He supported Lincoln's war policies and valued the Union. As described in the book, he formed Camp Curtain to train soldiers instead of sending them home once the quota was met in the first days of the war, and these men were vital to the defense of Washington, D.C. He also called the northern governors together in Altoona to discuss how they might enhance the war effort. It's likely that Governor Curtain visited soldiers in the hospital, but all conversations are fictitious. He also served in the U. S. House of Representatives.

The Confederate Army was led by Robert E. Lee, who served as commander from beginning to end. Daniel and Brian served in the Eastern Theater of the war, the Army of the Potomac. Unfortunately, this division of the Union Army did not have consistent leadership. McClellan, Burnside, Hooker, Meade. Primary sources are invaluable when writing a novel such as this, but the *Time-Life* book series on the Civil War was instrumental as well, and most libraries will have a copy if you'd like to read more. Conversations in the Gettysburg chapter were taken from such sources. Any mistakes are my own.

Dr. Henry Bellows and Miss Dorothea Dix played an important role in the Civil War, even though they only make a quick run through our story. Dr. Bellows was trained as a clergyman, but as the Civil War began, he organized the US Sanitary Commission to improve the unhealthy atmosphere ubiquitous in army camps. Women in northern cities gathered blankets, boots, butter, vegetables, and other items to be distributed to the soldiers. Miss Dix organized the nurses. She was a social reformer before the war, but she won the job of Superintendent of Nurses, beating out Dr. Elizabeth Blackwell for the job. Miss Dix trained women to serve in hospitals, but she was ever at odds with the male doctors, who did not want to allow women in the wards. Clara Barton is more well-known for her work with nurses during the war, but Miss Dix's contribution was priceless.

Mr. Lincoln, of course, needs no introduction.

Millerstown is a real place, although it's now called Macungie. It sits halfway between Allentown and Kutztown. It's also equidistant from both NYC and Philadelphia. For this reason, there has been a population boom in recent years, but in the mid-nineteenth century it was rolling farmland. Abby describes it as a town with a few churches, a few taverns, and a few mills, and that's exactly right. In 1860, there were three taverns. The Buckeye Tavern still stands, as of 2019. Grace Lutheran Church still stands on Main Street, and both Solomon's UCC and Macungie Christian Community (the Weimer family's Baptist church) are on Church Street. The train tracks run east to west, curving out of sight toward Alburtis; freight trains pulled by diesel engines run many times a day. You can still see remnants of all three grist mills working during the Civil War.

Abby lived on a fictitious farm, but I can see it in my mind. If you follow Brookside Road north past the Buckeye Tavern (not the model for the Kellys'), you'll pass a white school house on the left just before the underpass where the train tracks run. This school house is now a private home. Keep going. You'll pass a whitewashed farmhouse on the right and Swabia Creek on your left, where Brian avoided work and Abby showed her ankles. Swabia Creek now runs through a golf course. Farther up the road is a traffic light, with the Fairways housing development on the left. Turn left on that road, and eventually you'll see a school. The gristmill is in the distance to your right. Between Brookside Road and the school is where I imagine Abby's farm might have been.

As long as it took to research, write, and edit this book, so is the list of people to thank. The librarians at Emmaus Public Library and Lower Macungie Library were invaluable. If you ever want to know something, don't bother with the Internet; make friends with a librarian! Thank you to Donna Miller and Claudia Shulman, for encouragement and support, even before any of us knew what this would be. Thank you to my family and friends, who believe in me when I don't. Thank you to Ashley Matthews at Covenant Books for her infinite patience, and to all of her team for a job well done. To my former students, I loved being your teacher, and if nothing else, you learned American History! I wish you only the best, and the best is a relationship with God through the sacrifice of Jesus Christ.

And to Andrea Santiago and Adrienne Bodisch. We all know I do not know how to be brief. There's so much to say it's best I don't say anything at all. But thank you.

About the Author

Melissa Zabower is a former middle-school teacher who has always enjoyed writing. *In the Shadow of Mr. Lincoln* is her first novel, and she hopes it will make the Civil War come alive for middle school and high school students. Many of her works reflect her love of history. In fact, *In the Shadow of Mr. Lincoln* is set in the town where she grew up. Lehigh County in Pennsylvania is perfectly situated for history buffs to visit Gettysburg, Valley Forge, and Brandywine, and historic Philadelphia. She is currently working on a YA novel set in western Pennsylvania before the French and Indian War. Follow Melissa on Instagram, Twitter, her Melissa Zabower Facebook page, and her blog, http://mzabower.wix.com/lifeandthought.